continued . . .

"The indomitable Charlie is, as always, irresistible." *—Kirkus Reviews*

"Timely and topical. . . . T. Jefferson Parker is considered one of the finest crime writers working today. In the past decade, he has garnered three Edgar Awards . . . two of them for best novel of the year. In *Iron River*, Parker once more delivers the goods . . . rich, satisfying." *—North County Times* (CA)

The Renegades

"Deft characterization and hard-boiled action played out against smartly detailed Southern California landscapes." *—Los Angeles Times*

"Take[s] us in unexpected new directions. An interesting and inventive writer." *—The Washington Post*

"In *The Renegades*, Parker surpasses himself in . . . a book that ranks among his most original." *—The Toronto Star*

"Superb. . . . Two-time Edgar winner Parker vividly evokes the spirit of the Wild West. . . . He delivers steady suspense and a cast of damaged characters. . . . Readers will likely find themselves rattled—and riveted." *—Booklist* (starred review)

"A typically streamlined T. Jefferson Parker thriller. . . . Think of Parker's work as sunshine noir. It's akin to that of Don Winslow, another specialist in the soft white underbelly of Southern California, and that of Louisiana crime poet James Lee Burke. The writing is so lean . . . and the dialogue can ricochet." *—St. Petersburg Times*

"It's quite a showdown, done the Edgar Award–winning Parker way, in this engrossing tale of justice and redemption. Highly recommended." *—Library Journal*

"Another stylish, cleverly plotted yarn by one of the most consistent performers in the crime novel genre." *—The Associated Press*

"A beautifully crafted thriller." *—Mysterious Reviews*

"[A] wild ride . . . turns and tensions and brilliant dialog . . . a testament to Parker's abilities as a master storyteller and a true craftsman. Parker's fans will love *The Renegades*, and it will certainly draw in some new readers." *—CrimeCritics*

"Parker is one of my favorite authors. He writes smart, challenging plots. . . . If you're not reading T. Jefferson Parker, you should be." *—Fresh Fiction*

L.A. Outlaws

"Vivid writing, strong characters, clockwork plotting, agonizing suspense . . . *L.A. Outlaws* is popular entertainment at its most delicious." —*The Washington Post*

"Think of Elmore Leonard's *Out of Sight* with a gender twist . . . totally compulsive reading." —*The Seattle Times*

"Hard, fast, and etched with characters so sharp they'll leave you bleeding." —Robert Crais

"*Out of Sight* meets *Gone in 60 Seconds.*" —*Entertainment Weekly*

"The best book of its kind since *No Country for Old Men*. . . . Simply stated, once again Parker has penned the best mystery of the year." —*The Providence Journal-Bulletin*

"At once a noir thriller and a Western ballad of desperadoes and doomed lovers. The book is both hard-boiled and heartbreaking, Ross Macdonald as sung by Marty Robbins. . . . Casting Parker as a mere mystery writer is a little like writing off Graham Greene's work as espionage fiction." —*Los Angeles Times*

"[A] marvelous love story wrapped around a rip-roaring plot." —*The Cleveland Plain Dealer*

"A suspenseful and original story, *L.A. Outlaws* . . . is a fun one to read." —*Chicago Sun-Times*

"One of the genre's most original authors." —*The South Florida Sun-Sentinel*

"No one does tough like T. Jefferson Parker." —Elizabeth George

"Brilliant. . . . Parker takes a seat at the head of the class next to Michael Connelly." —*The Sunday Oregonian*

"Compulsively readable." —*The Toronto Star*

"[An] irresistable antihero . . . [an] outstanding thriller." —*Publishers Weekly*

ALSO BY T. JEFFERSON PARKER

Laguna Heat

Little Saigon

Pacific Beat

Summer of Fear

The Triggerman's Dance

Where Serpents Lie

The Blue Hour

Red Light

Silent Joe

Black Water

Cold Pursuit

California Girl

The Fallen

Storm Runners

L.A. Outlaws

The Renegades

IRON RIVER

A CHARLIE HOOD NOVEL

T. JEFFERSON PARKER

NEW AMERICAN LIBRARY

NEW AMERICAN LIBRARY
Published by New American Library, a division of Penguin Group (USA) Inc.,
375 Hudson Street, New York, New York 10014, USA
Penguin Group (Canada), 90 Eglinton Avenue East, Suite 700, Toronto,
Ontario M4P 2Y3, Canada (a division of Pearson Penguin Canada Inc.);
Penguin Books Ltd., 80 Strand, London WC2R 0RL, England; Penguin Ireland;
25 St. Stephen's Green, Dublin 2, Ireland (a division of Penguin Books Ltd.);
Penguin Group (Australia), 250 Camberwell Road, Camberwell, Victoria 3124, Australia
(a division of Pearson Australia Group Pty. Ltd.); Penguin Books India Pvt. Ltd.,
11 Community Centre, Panchsheel Park, New Delhi - 110 017, India;
Penguin Group (NZ), 67 Apollo Drive, Rosedale, North Shore 0632, New Zealand
(a division of Pearson New Zealand Ltd.); Penguin Books (South Africa) (Pty.) Ltd.,
24 Sturdee Avenue, Rosebank, Johannesburg 2196, South Africa

Penguin Books Ltd., Registered Offices: 80 Strand, London WC2R 0RL, England

Published by New American Library, a division of Penguin Group (USA) Inc.
Previously published in a Dutton edition.

First New American Library Printing, January 2011
1   3   5   7   9   10   8   6   4   2

 REGISTERED TRADEMARK — MARCA REGISTRADA

New American Library Trade Paperback ISBN: 978-0-451-23242-7

The Library of Congress has catalogued the hardcover edition of this title as follows:

Parker, T. Jefferson.
Iron River: a novel/by T. Jefferson Parker.
p.   cm.
ISBN 978-0-525-95149-0
1. Police—California—Los Angeles County—Fiction.
2. Firearms industry and trade—Fiction. I. Title.
PS3566.A6863I76 2010
813'.54—dc22   2009029307
[B]

Printed in the United States of America

PUBLISHER'S NOTE
This is a work of fiction. Names, characters, places, and incidents either are the
product of the author's imagination or are used fictitiously, and any resemblance to actual
persons, living or dead, business establishments, events, or locales is entirely coincidental.
The publisher does not have any control over and does not assume any responsibility for
author or third-party Web sites or their content.

For Robert Ford Parker

IRON RIVER

There, then, he sat, holding that imbecile candle in the heart of that almighty forlornness.

—Herman Melville, *Moby-Dick*

I

The car hurtled west towing a swirl of black exhaust into the first light of day. It was old and low, with Baja plates and a loose muffler that dangled and sparked on the dips. The woman drove. She was silver-haired and flat-faced and though her eyes were open wide to gather the light, her face was still slack from sleep. Her husband sat heavily beside her, boots spread and hat low, nodding slowly through the rises and falls of the highway, a coffee cup riding on his thigh.

"*Cansada*," she said. Tired. Then told him about a dream she had had the night before: an enormous wave made of white lilies, a blue sun, and a nice talk with Benito, thirty years dead, who told her to say hello to his father.

Cansado, he thought.

He looked out. It was desert as far as he could see or remember seeing. He worked on cars at the gas station in Bond's Corner. She had motel rooms to clean in Buenavista.

She told him about another dream she had had, and her husband lifted the cup and sipped and set it back on his thigh and closed his eyes.

The sun rose behind them. The woman checked its progress in the rearview mirror. Something registered ahead and she dropped her gaze back through the windshield to a young coyote sitting just off the shoulder next to a paloverde. She had never seen a coyote sitting down. She wondered if all her maids would show up today or she would have to clean a block of rooms herself. The sore neck. The weak arm. She steered the car down a steep dip and lifted her eyes to the mirror again. What did a wave of white lilies mean? In her dream, Benito looked young and sweet, exactly as he had in life. Benito the Beautiful. She was crossing herself as she neared the rise and still looking back at the sun while thinking of him and when she looked ahead again, she saw that she had drifted far into the oncoming lane. When she topped the rise, the truck was barreling down on her, the grille shiny and looming and the windshield a sun-forged plate of armor. Her husband cursed and reached for the wheel, but she was still in her genuflection and his hand closed not on the wheel but on her wrist so that she could use only her half-crippled left hand to correct the course of the big heavy Mercury.

She swung the wheel to the right with all her strength. She felt the back end come around and the front end slide away and she clutched the wheel with both hands now, and her husband was thrown against her, and orbs of his coffee wobbled in space but he held the wheel, too, and the truck thundered by with a sucking howl. The sedan broke loose from the pull and spun twice quickly and she was so utterly dazed by the force that when she saw the man crouching on the right shoulder by his pickup, she had no idea which way to turn the wheel in order to miss him. Then it was too late anyway. She saw the long hood of the car sweep across him and she felt the sharp impact, but the Mercury kept spinning and when it finally ground sideways through the gravel to a stop, she had no idea how she had missed the pickup, or where the dead man had landed.

She threw the shift into park. They sat for a moment, breathing hard, hearts pounding, dust rising around them in the sudden silence. She looked west down the highway and saw nothing but road, and when she looked behind them she saw the pickup truck and the rise far behind it.

"*Dios*," she whispered.

The man looked hard at his wife then pulled the keys from the ignition and tried to brush the coffee from his new jeans. He pushed open the door and stepped into the morning.

It took them a few minutes to find the dead man sprawled back in the desert on the white sand between clumps of yucca. He was a gringo. He was small. His face was covered in blood and his body was misshapen. He wore the same kind of clothes she saw at Wal Mart. He had a watch but no rings.

"Don't touch him, he's alive," said her husband.

The man's breath whistled in and out, and a tooth moved in his broken mouth. Then for a long time nothing. Then he breathed again.

She crossed herself and knelt beside him. Her husband looked around them, then back at the sun just above the horizon now.

She asked God and Ignacio what to do with such a broken body. She said there was the hospital in Buenavista, famous doctors who treated important people.

"Go away," whispered the dead man. He opened his eyes. They were blue beneath the blood. "Please."

"You will die," she said.

The man was silent for a long moment during which he did not breathe. Then another breath, this one deeper, followed by another. The tooth moved and the air whistled in and out.

The husband said they would be arrested and deported, so if this man wanted them to go away, then they would.

She looked up at him. "No. We drive to the hospital. We tell them where he is."

"Tell them. Nothing," whispered the gringo. His eyes looked malevolent, but the woman thought that any eyes would look that way in a face so ruined and bloody.

"We have a duty to God," she said.

The gringo drew a long breath, then he raised his hand very slightly from the sand, and he pointed his index finger at her, then curled it toward himself.

She shuddered.

He curled the finger again, then lowered his hand back to the ground. He was watching her.

Maria Consalvo Reina Villalobos stared into the blue eyes. She looked at the broken, doll-like body. And she knew that if they were to leave the gringo here and drive away and not say one thing, then he would die and his blood would be on her hands twice—once for thinking of waves of lilies and her beloved son Benito, and once for not telling anyone that there was a man dying in the desert not ten miles from town.

She leaned in closer. She saw him watching her through the blood. His broken tooth whistled again. She sensed Ignacio hovering behind her. The little man said something that she couldn't hear, so she leaned even closer.

"*Señora y señor,*" the gringo whispered. "In the name of Benito the Beautiful, tell them nothing."

Maria Consalvo scrambled to her feet, hitting at herself as if she were being attacked by hornets. Ignacio stood tall and glared down at the gringo who called his dead son by name. He saw a boulder of quartz lying just beyond the yucca, a single boulder, as if dropped there for a purpose.

He took his wife by the arm and led her away. Ignacio knew that the man would probably be dead before the heat of afternoon, and certainly dead after it. He brought his wife to the passenger side of the Mercury and he opened the door for her and steadied her as she spilled into the cracked vinyl seat.

They were silent until Buenavista. As they entered the little border town, they agreed to say nothing to the authorities. They passed the zocalo and St. Cecilia's church and the Rite Aid and the Denny's. At the Ocotillo Lodge, Ignacio left the Mercury idling while he opened his wife's door and kissed her formally before he drove off for Bond's Corner. He had not opened her door or kissed her before work in twenty-four years.

Within five minutes Maria's conscience prevailed and she called the Buenavista police station and told them about the man in the desert. She gave a good location based on the gringo's pickup truck. She hung up when the deep-voiced policeman asked her name. She knew that voice: Gabriel Reyes, chief of Buenavista's police force. Reyes ate breakfast alone at the Ocotillo on Thursdays, his uniform crisp, his face sad.

Ignacio called no one. When he got to work, his gringo boss walked him to the far part of the lot and lifted the tarp from a GM Yukon peppered with bullet holes. He told Ignacio it was *muy importante, número uno*. Fine, thought Ignacio. He preferred *narcotraficantes* to tiny devils any day.

Not long after Maria and Ignacio had left the man, the tractor-trailer that had nearly obliterated them arrived back on the scene of the near disaster. It had taken the driver two miles to still his nerves and face down his fears and make the laborious two-lane turnaround. He pulled off the road just behind the pickup truck. From his elevated position in the cab, he could see the big skid marks. He surveyed the desert around him and saw nothing unusual. There had been a man working on a flat tire. Then the Mercury coming at him in his own lane.

He got out and walked over to the pickup and saw the blown tire and the jack resting in the sand. The keys were still in the ignition and the driver's window was down. He reached in and honked the horn and waited. A moment later he walked out into the desert beyond the pickup, but not far. Rattlesnakes liked the cool mornings this time of year. He'd run over one last spring not far from here that reached almost all the way across his lane, then he'd taken the time to turn around on the narrow highway and run over it again. He called out, and a jackrabbit bolted and his heart raced. A minute later he climbed back into the Freightliner and continued on toward Yuma. No good came in this desert.

Reyes looked at the skid marks, then up at the sun, then he followed the footprints that led into the desert. There were two sets. One was made by cowboy boots that left deep heel marks in the sand. The other was smaller and lighter and could have been pretty much any kind of shoe. The woman, he thought.

The tracks ended and Reyes found blood and a slight indentation where someone had rested. Apparently rested. The two tracks turned back toward the highway. But a third set of footprints, smaller than the boots but heavier than the shoes, continued away from this bloody lie into the desert beyond.

Reyes had no trouble following them. Half a mile to the north in the foothills that would later offer shade, he found a bloody little man half dug into an old den beneath a honey mesquite, legs protruding. Reyes knelt and saw the glint of an eye back in the darkness, and he reached down and lightly touched the man's leg and told him he would be okay. Then he stood and on his third try was able to place a cell call to Imperial Mercy for an ambulance. Procedure was to call county first, but Reyes figured this guy would be dead if he had to wait for paramedics out of El Centro.

"They're on the way," he said.

The man groaned.

2

Charlie Hood lay on the roof of Guns a Million and aimed the video recorder down into the back parking lot. Behind him the bright yellow letters of the store sign flashed on and off in the close desert night. Hood could hear the lights buzzing and the electrical switches clicking and see the air around him pulsing yellow. He figured the roof would be hot so he had bought a bright Mexican blanket with the shape of an Aztec warrior woven into it and folded it twice for padding against the infernally hot gravel.

Sean Ozburn drove up right on time and pulled his white panel van into a space in the back lot. There were other cars but most of the Guns a Million customers had parked out front, a shorter walk in the heat. Hours were ten A.M. to midnight, six days a week, and Hood, in his two days so far here in Buenavista, had never seen fewer than six cars out front.

The van lights went off and Ozburn stepped out. Hood zoomed in. Ozburn was a big ATFE buck with blond hair to his shoulders and blue, hateful eyes. He wore jeans and a plaid flannel shirt with the sleeves cut off to show his arms and tatts. His supremacist's air was a solid act, Hood thought. Hood was on loan to Operation

Blowdown from the L.A. Sheriff's Department, and he'd been immediately impressed by the ATFE's courage and black humor in the face of bad odds. The border here was awash in guns, the Iron River, they called it, and ATFE and their task force brethren like Hood were just rafts bobbing upon the great current of firearms headed south. Hood saw that the ATFE agents worked their muscles strong and got good with their weapons. They lived on adrenaline and heat, and they prayed for luck. Hood was glad to be a part of them.

Ozburn leaned against the van and lit a cheroot. He was wired for sound and set to buy six weapons from an unlicensed dealer named Joe Tilley. Tilley was a part-time employee of Guns a Million and he said guns and money were two things not unusual in the back parking lot of his store. Ozburn had complained about the public setting, but Tilley prevailed. Tilley said the Buenavista PD was nothing and the feds were concentrating on Arizona and besides, Guns a Million was on a quiet outskirt of town. Tilley had promised two Mossberg combat 12-gauges, two Smith .357 Magnum autoloaders, a Phoenix Arms .22, and a Raven Arms .25. All were used and in good condition.

Hood had learned that six weapons weren't enough to justify the arrest of a low-level crook like Tilley, even though most guns entered Mexico just a few at a time, *contrabando hormigas*, the Mexicans called it: contraband of the ants. For now, the task force team would focus on the video and audio evidence. Ozburn and his superiors had set a magic number, and Tilley's was twenty. If the six went down right, they'd contract for twenty, then pinch him and try to trade him upline to his suppliers. Hopefully, his suppliers were his employers at the store. The big prize was the licensed dealers who bought and sold legally, then got greedy or made a mistake. These guys were capable of quantity: thirty, fifty, even a hundred guns at a time.

Hood rested on his elbows and felt the gravel trying to get him through the blanket. Ozburn had told him that gun buys could go from boring to violent in the blink of an eye, so Hood wanted an edge but not too much of one. Weapons freebooters like Tilley were generally considered higher risk than drug runners—unpredictable, amply armed, often skilled in the use of their products. This was their first buy from him.

Hood panned the camcorder from the peak of the Guns a Million roof. He saw the tow truck with the blackout windows that housed Agent Bly, parked on a diagonal across three spaces in the far corner of the back lot, closer to a Dairy Queen than to the gun store. It had the look of an operator on a dinner run.

Then he saw the Dumpster that was temporary home to the unlucky Jimmy Holdstock. It stood behind the store near the two real trash bins. Known as Hell on Wheels, it was clean and outfitted with holes for ventilation, vision, and taping, and with padding to dampen sound. But the holes were no match for the border heat. Young Holdstock had gotten the Hell on Wheels gig by losing a game of butts 'n barrels to Janet Bly. The game was like spin the bottle but played with a handgun. A small parabolic mike fed into a recorder that sat on the padded floor, and the concave receiver dish just barely cleared the top through a cutaway. The plastic lid had been drilled with a three-quarter-inch bit and had padding at the contact points to muffle the exit if Holdstock threw open the lid and charged. These modifications had been done over beers and a boom box in Holdstock's El Centro garage while Jimmy's daughters splashed in the yard pool and his wife, Jenny, kept an eye on both activities. For transport, the Dumpster fit nicely onto Bly's tow truck.

Tilley came in ten minutes later, cruised the lot in his blue Trooper, stopped beside the tow truck and hit it with a mounted hand-held searchlight. Hood tracked the bright circle as it moved across the cab window, then stopped on the windshield. Then the beam raked the back end of the DQ, turned to the Guns a Million, and came up the roof at Hood. He flattened and wriggled down a couple of feet, almost dropping the camcorder. His sidearm dug into his ribs, but the blanket saved his cheek from the gravel. When he crept to the peak again, the Trooper was pulling in slowly beside Sean Ozburn's van and he zoomed in to get a good shot of Tilley as he stepped out.

Tilley was squat and muscular, with a black T-shirt and an Orioles baseball cap. Hood guessed late thirties. He had a wallet chain and a knife on his belt, and biker's boots with brass rings on the sides.

Hood could hear his voice as he approached Ozburn, but the words weren't clear. Tilley looked pissed off. Ozburn was looking around like a hunted man. His eyes looked weirdly blue and murderous. Hood admired the acting.

The two men made their way to the back of the Trooper, and Tilley swung open the back doors. The back of the vehicle had been outfitted with sliding wooden drawers. Tilley pulled one out and Hood saw the shotguns gleaming dully in the lot lights.

Hood's heart caught when a second man hopped out of the Trooper. He was slender and young and he wore a trim black suit, a white shirt, and a tie. Hood guessed the guy's age at twenty-five. *A damned suit in this heat,* he thought. *Buttoned.*

Ozburn got loud, lumbered over and gave him a shove. The young man backed up lightly and his suit coat fell open and his hand went inside. Hood heard Ozburn's curses. Tilley stepped between them with his hands placating, and Ozburn pushed him, too. Then he turned and went back to the drawers of shotguns. He looked down at the guns, then up at the men, and he shook his head. Hood tried to read his lips through the camcorder. It looked like: *Let's do business, assholes.*

Enough, thought Hood. *Close the deal. We've got audio and video, and Tilley is good for a bigger payday.*

Tilley slid the sawed-offs into an old duffel bag and carried them to the van. Ozburn stood by the open back door with the cigar in his mouth, watching the guns go in. While they worked, Tilley seemed to be telling Ozburn something long and detailed, a joke or a story maybe. Ozburn handed him a wad of money. Black Suit stood a few feet away, scanning the lot.

Tilley went back to the Trooper and bagged up more product. Hood couldn't make them out, but they were handguns. Tilley was still jabbering away, like the deal had suddenly become minor and what was really important was what he had to say. Hood guessed he was talking about the next deal. Good.

Ozburn gave Tilley another wad of bills, then slammed the van doors shut. Tilley worked the money into his jeans pocket and walked back to the Trooper. The young man in the black suit closed the doors, and the three men stood facing each other in the poor light of the parking lot.

Hood saw that all three men were more relaxed now. There was a postgame feel in their postures, and Ozburn seemed to be telling some tale of his own. He reached out and straightened the young man's necktie.

Then Black Suit stepped forward and pulled at something on the chest of Ozburn's flannel shirt. *Tit for tat,* thought Hood. It looked like a button string unraveling.

Then it caught the light and Hood realized what it was.

Black Suit gave it a yank and the wire lengthened.

Hood knew that this was where they either killed Ozburn or ran for it. They ran for it: Tilley barging through the hedge of spindly oleander and off into the darkness, and Black Suit right past the tow truck and into the DQ lot. Ozburn spat out his cigar and went after Tilley, and Hood slid down the back side of the Guns a Million rooftop, dangled from the service ladder, and dropped hard to the pavement.

He followed Ozburn and Tilley. From the corner of his eye he saw Bly jump from the tow truck with her weapon drawn and Holdstock pinwheel over the top of the bin like a gymnast and run toward Bly.

Hood left his weapon holstered, tucked his elbows in tight and made time. Past the oleander was one of the large vacant lots common to desert towns, vast, for sale, lumped with sage and cholla in the slight moonlight. Beyond the lot was a stout adobe wall and within the wall was old Buenavista—the town square, the bars and restaurants and the hotel. And beyond the heart of the city was the border fence.

Big Ozburn plodded along a hundred yards ahead of Hood. Hood couldn't see Tilley. When he pulled up even, Ozburn pointed and Hood saw Tilley another hundred yards ahead, coming up on the wall.

A few seconds later Hood scrambled gracelessly over the rough adobe and plopped down into the town square. There were lanterns in the trees and a fountain gurgling and lovers walking and sitting on the benches, the women sleek and the white shirts of the men faintly luminescent. Through them barged Tilley, then he rounded the statue of Buenavista's founder and turned up the street toward the restaurants.

Hood gained. The street was narrow and steep and the desert cobblestones were uneven. He heard Ozburn huffing along behind him and he felt the sweat burning into his eyes. He saw the crowd breaking up ahead of him, parted by stout Tilley. Hood ran past an ice cream shop and a festively lit bar and a leather shop and a jewelry store, though he was barely aware of them.

At the first intersection, Black Suit appeared from a side street and fell in next to Tilley. Both men looked back at Hood, and when he saw Black Suit reach inside his coat, Hood dove behind a decorative clay planter filled with succulents and yelled back at Ozburn to get down. A little bullet grazed the planter and ricocheted, buzzing like a fat hornet. A twenty-two, thought Hood. He heard a sharp crack, and another bullet took a chip off a paver and whined off into the darkness.

Then there was silence, and Hood looked through the succulents and saw the empty street ahead. He drew his sidearm and came up running.

Bly and Holdstock merged from the side street. Ozburn caught up with the other three, muttering curses, a big automatic in his hand. They followed the gunrunners through an outdoor marketplace that was shutting down, dodging stalls of Coachella Valley dates and Imperial Valley grapefruit. The shoppers were gone by now, but the vendors ducked quickly and efficiently because they had seen this kind of thing before. Up ahead, one of the bad guys upturned a table of cantaloupe, which rolled toward Hood, but he long-jumped them and saw that he was catching up. The gunrunners took to the sidewalk that ran behind a colonnade of rounded arches facing the street. Hood heard music. Near the top of the gentle hill that Buenavista was built upon, the road ended in a large open square ringed by restaurants and bars. There were tables with white linen set up in the patios of the restaurants and there were horses tethered to hitching posts amidst the gleaming sports cars and SUVs and luxury sedans.

As Hood entered the square the music was louder, a disco tune throbbing from Club Fandango at the far end. Ahead of him he watched Tilley and Black Suit shove through the small crowd waiting to get into the club. The revelers hustled away under the protective archway columns of the colonnade and the gunrunners disappeared inside.

Hood figured they were headed out the back into an alley, so he ran left around the building. He saw Ozburn split off the other way, and Bly and Holdstock heading straight in.

Behind the building was another dining patio, quieter here, tables lit by candlelight, and a fountain gurgling. Hood leaped the short adobe wall and waved his hand for the young couple to get up and out. They scrambled over the wall and headed off into the darkness.

Then Hood was aware of two new things at once: Black Suit and Tilley heaving toward him through the open back doors of the building, and a young teenaged couple rising from their table in the private far corner of the patio. The boy held the girl's hand in an elevated, courtly way. The girl looked frightened, but the boy looked cool. Hood waved them to his left and the boy nodded to him, steadying his date toward the short wall.

Ozburn rounded the building just as Black Suit and Tilley burst onto the patio from inside, and Ozburn yelled, *Drop the guns!* Tilley dropped his weapon. Hood set Black Suit's chest atop his front sight and waited for him to drop his pistol. Black Suit was deciding when three shots roared from inside and the young dealer collapsed in a dark heap.

Tilley was jumping up and down, hands up: *Don't shoot, don't shoot!*

Bly and Holdstock stumbled through the open doors and fell into shooter stances.

In the abrupt silence, a girl screamed from the darkness beyond the wall.

3

So I'm sitting at my desk on the third floor of Pace Arms and studying the guy across from me. He says his name is Bradley Smith. He's even younger than me, which pleases me because I think the young should grab what's left of this world before the old piss away every last bit of it.

"Your company is French?" I ask.

"The management is French. I already told your secretary that."

"With how many armed employees?"

"Two thousand."

"That's a lot of armed guards."

"We're international. I told your secretary that, too."

"Sharon relayed everything to me with perfect accuracy, Mr. Smith."

"She has nice paint, as the Mexicans like to say."

I smile at this. "No kidding. And she composes letters, figures out my calendar, and keeps the assholes out of here."

"Quite a woman."

"She's engaged," I say, wishing it were to me.

"I am, too."

"Really? I wouldn't mind that someday."

"What kind of thing is that to say? You get what you take, my man."

I nod and silently cede the point. I look out the window to the mild Orange County morning. The blinds and the glass are dirty because we quit paying the custodial contract ten months ago, not long after Pace Arms was sued into bankruptcy. But to the east I can still see the swirl of concrete where the 405 meets the 55, and the malls stretching into the distance, the mirrored corporate buildings, the Performing Arts Center and the evangelical Christian broadcasting compound. Uncle Chester showed me pictures of that land when it was still bean fields, and gave me a stern warning that laziness never turned a bean field into a shopping mall. I was six. And Chester said if I wanted my piece of the American dream someday, it was going to take energy, vision, balls. It would take *Pace*. He usually smiled after saying that, not a pleasant thing. He's huge but his teeth are small and even, like infant teeth. Back then, Pace Arms was making 145,000 handguns a year, right here in Orange County, right here in this building. Hardly anybody knew what we did. The guns were semiautomatic, semidependable, and dirt cheap. *The workingman's equalizer* was what Chet called them. Most everybody else called them Saturday Night Specials. Uncle Chester is a lecher and a bore, but he knew how to make a buck on cheap guns.

"Okay, Bradley Smith," I say. "*Director* of North American operations for Favier and Winling Security of Paris, France. You made this appointment. You were late. You tell me my secretary is stupid but hot. You tell me I'll get what I take, my man. Maybe you should tell me something that might be worth my time, like, for instance, what do you want?"

"Time? You've got *time*. You're bankrupt. But maybe I can help you with something else."

"Help away."

Bradley gets up and goes to the dirty window and looks out. He's wearing the five-hundred-dollar Jimmy Choo boots I tried on a few months ago but had to get less expensive ones. And pricey jeans and a white shirt that's cleaned and pressed, and a leather vest. He's got long dark hair and a goatee and something about him besides his attitude bothers me but I don't know what.

"You ought to get these windows cleaned."

"We fired the custodians."

"They fired you, actually, because you failed to pay them. Look, Ron, I did my due diligence on Pace Arms. I always liked your products. The twenty-five Hawk was decent, and the twenty-two LR was better. The nines weren't bad, either. If you'd have gotten the design on the forty caliber right, your gun wouldn't have killed the little boy, and Pace Arms would still be cranking out guns, money, and happiness. But . . . well, no need to rehash all that."

"No."

"So. In the course of my research, I reviewed the court transcripts and the financial declarations and the terms of the corporate dissolution. And I got out my trusty calculator and pushed a few keys, and guess what I saw."

"Numbers?"

"Inventory still unsold."

I figured this was where Bradley Smith was going. "And you're going to help me by taking it off my hands."

"Maybe I should know what it is."

"Maybe I should know what you want it to be."

"We've got two thousand men on the business end of things, all over the world. Some are in the most vile places on earth, some are in the most beautiful. Some in cities, some in mud. They go where they are needed. And what they all need is short-range stopping power, concealability, and one-hundred-percent reliability."

"That would be the Hawk nine. We have a few. Thirty or so."

"I need a thousand."

My heart does a quick little somersault. "That's quite an order for a bankrupt company, Mr. Smith."

"And if the Hawk nines do what they're supposed to do, we'd like to have all our people carrying them by the end of next year. So, a thousand more."

Now, I attended church this last Sunday. I'll admit it was to meet available women in the singles ministry, but it was church nonetheless. *Thank you, God in heaven* is all I can think.

I nod and push back in my rolling chair and glide across the carpet protector. "Come with me."

I raise my eyebrows at Sharon on the way to the elevator. She smiles at Bradley Smith in a way that she has never smiled at me. But I knew she would smile at Smith that way because Smith has the thing that most women can't resist. *The thing.* I've been trying to develop it for my entire adult life but I can't even define it, so there's no place to start. I once reverse-engineered an Egyptian submachine gun, and it was easy compared to developing *the thing.* You can't reverse-engineer what you can't define. Maybe it's his goatee. I don't know.

The elevator takes us down to the basement. The door opens and it's dark. The basement is almost wholly below ground level, so the only natural light slips in through the long narrow windowpanes up top. I step out and key on the lights. I light only the lobby and part of the third floor these days. No use wasting money. My secretary, Sharon of my heart—Sharon Rose Novak is her full name—is my last pretense at solvency. Last week she actually braced me for a raise to help her pay for her wedding, which is set for next month. I haven't met the groom, though I dislike the way he talks to her on the phone. She's normally talkative but during their calls there are long silences on her part, then short, quiet replies. He takes something out of her. They registered at Bloomingdale's and I bought them all twelve of the requested service settings, a Wedgwood design that was not cheap. Maybe they'll have me over for dinner someday. She's a blue-eyed blonde and has the prettiest face I've ever seen.

Anyway, I've spent almost all of what little money I had on keeping the doors open here at Pace Arms. Eighteen months ago when we correctly foresaw the courtroom mud bath, Chester got some building department friends to fast-track a city permit for a small penthouse up on the third floor, making the building a residence, which is outside the terms of the settlement. So I sold my home and bought the penthouse from Chet and I live here now. Chet holds the deed on the office footage. He left the country before the judgment and there have been only three postcards from him since—Thailand, Berlin, and Tahiti. They were addressed to "All" at Pace Arms. He took the last of the company cash with him, thirty grand. I pay his property taxes. Before leaving, he told me that any dreams of saving Pace would be foolish pride, but I still think there's a way to salvage the business.

And I think the way to salvage it is now standing right next to me.

We pause in the basement vestibule for a moment. It used to be a waiting area for customers about to test-fire one product or another. Gone are the genuine 1878 walnut bar from a saloon in Bodie, the King Ranch furniture and the Remington bronzes and the framed Catlin lithos and the big-screen hi-def and the bear and bison mounts. Uncle Chet also made off with the proceeds from the sale of these beauties, approximately eighteen paltry grand. Now all we have here in the vestibule are cobwebs and daddy longlegs. The air is stale and warm.

"The first floor was manufacturing," I say. "Second was R and D. Third was management, sales, and marketing. Uncle Chester had the big corner suite on the third even though I was running the shop at age seventeen. I was the one bringing the runs in under budget and making rain. Down here in the basement, we did all the testing. The square footage of this building is much more than you'd think from the outside, which is one reason Chester bought it back in 1980. I wasn't even born then."

"Looks a little neglected."

"I think of it as a bear in hibernation."

"I think I smell him."

"But check out the range."

I lead Bradley through a set of swinging insulated doors that close behind us silently. The range acoustics eat sound. It takes a few seconds for the banks of fluorescent tubes to flicker to life, then the firing range spreads before us. It has carpeted floors stained by decades of gun smoke and gun oil and foot traffic and spilled cups of coffee. It has a low ceiling and the same foam-lined walls you would find in a recording studio. Back when business was good, ten of us could test-fire arms side by side at the firing line, with plenty of room between their benches. The targets were set out and retrieved by motor-driven pulleys. You could put the targets anywhere from five feet away to two hundred. I still remember the first time Dad and Mom brought me here. I remember how each time a gun went off, you could feel it right in the middle of your chest, like someone had tapped you there. I look at station two and think of my father, Tony. He died when I was ten.

I look at the dusty benches and the cobwebs drooping from the light fixtures. There are still old silhouette targets, corners curling, hanging in some of the firing lanes. Everywhere are stacks of un-used silhouettes. A year ago, when we ceased manufacture after the judgment, the former night crew had a last-night party here and of course they got drunk and brought out their favorite weapons and blasted one of the silhouettes so the figure was pretty much gone, then they brought the target in on the pulley and signed their names out in the white paper, around the bullet holes. They just left it where it was.

Bradley Smith nods and looks around. He looks at the auto-graphed target. He has a thoughtful face for a wiseass. "Looks like somewhere the Addams Family would play."

"I liked Morticia when I was a kid."

"I still smell gunpowder," he says.

"The smell of money, the guys used to say."

"So, do you have a thousand nines or not?"

"Before I answer that, I'd like to show you something."

I sit at station four, and Bradley takes station three. I unlock the station four gun case and remove a heavily lacquered wooden box with the stainless steel Pace Arms insignia on the lid. The box was a gift from Mom, tenth birthday. Beautiful, really. I set the box on the bench and use the key I still carry on my chain to unlock it, and then I pull out the gun. It's a handgun, not large, not light. It is well balanced and feels good in my hand.

"This is the Love 32," I say. "It's engraved on the right side of the slide."

"Love 32? What kind of a name is that for a gun?"

"Thirty-two is the caliber. The Love is for the California lawman Harry Love. He shot down the bandit Joaquin Murrieta and cut off his head and brought it back in a jar of alcohol. It toured the state back in the early 1850s. Cost a dollar to see it. Joaquin was California's first rock star. Harry Love was his promoter. It's myth and legend and a little history. I like history. It was the only class in high school I stayed awake through. I dropped out junior year."

The look on Bradley Smith's face isn't something I can readily ID. He looks like he's been kicked in the balls but trying not to show it. For just a second he looks like he's going to come up off the bench, but in order to do what, I couldn't tell you.

"Most of what people believe about Murrieta is pure bullshit," he says.

"The part about Harry Love isn't."

"You don't know anything."

More of that look of his. He could be deranged. "Okay."

"So who do you like, Ron," he says. "The outlaws or the lawmen?"

"Both. The Joaquin 32 didn't sound right."

"What about the Murrieta 32?"

"Too wordy. It's my gun. I designed it, so I get to name it. I built this thing by hand."

He nods and looks over at the autographed target, takes a deep breath and lets it out. He stands and pulls one of the spotter's stools over and sits down next to me. "How many rounds in the magazine of the Love 32?"

"There are two ways to answer that. As you see it now, the magazine holds eight thirty-two-caliber ACP rounds, and one in the chamber if you want. It weighs twenty-nine ounces, it's seven and three-sixteenths inches long, blowback operated, with an alloy frame, sixteen grooves of right-hand rifling, and a trigger pull of four and a half pounds."

I drop the magazine to the bench top, rack the Love to make sure the chamber is empty, then close the slide and lower the hammer and hand the gun to Smith.

"It's heavy."

"There's a reason for that."

Smith hefts the gun, then aims it one-handed at the station four target fifty feet away. "But the balance is good."

"Thanks."

"I don't love the thirty-two ACP load," says Bradley. "It's slow and it doesn't hit hard."

"There's a reason for that, too," I say. "The load, I mean. Why I chose the thirty-two ACP."

"Sounds like you've got all sorts of reasons, Mr. Pace."

"Just Ron is fine."

"Ron. The Ron of Reason."

"Just a few reasons, actually. Want to fire it?"

"I don't want my people carrying thirty-twos, I can tell you that right now. I don't care how good a deal you'll make me."

"Fine. Just fire it. Glasses on the bench there."

I get some ammo from the gun safe and thumb the shells into the magazine. Bradley slaps the magazine home, stands and plants eight bullets in the black at fifty feet.

What a sound. Just like the old days. Even fancy acoustics can't keep a handgun from sounding like a handgun. I inhale the wonderful smell of exploded gunpowder and watch the brass bounce and roll around the carpet.

"Dope trigger," he says. "Those four and a half pounds are smooth as butter."

"Here." I reload the gun and hand it back to him. I listen to the sound of music as eight more circles of light appear in the black body of the enemy.

He pops the magazine, checks the chamber, safes the gun, and tosses it to me. "I still can't arm my men and women with it, Ron. Try stopping a drunk, three-hundred-pound Tutsi warlord with this thing. Or some cranked-up Detroit carjacker."

I nod and look at the target, then back at Bradley. "Appearances are deceiving."

"Stopping-power isn't."

"Watch this." I give him a wry look and glance at my fake Rolex. Then I set the gun on the bench and use a punch from my pocketknife to push the frame pins through. Then I pry the frame apart, exposing the inner firing and reloading and eject mechanisms.

"You can use an eight-penny nail for that matter," I say. "Toss me those needle-nose from off the box there, will you?"

I catch the pliers midair and swoop them down into the body of the Love 32. I invert the trigger bar pin, remove the catch spring, reposition the detent notch of the extractor, and reverse the block plate and line up the witness marks. It takes twenty seconds, and another fifteen to position the frame and drive the pins back in with the punch.

"Less than a minute," says Bradley.

"It was exactly fifty seconds. My personal best is thirty-six, but that was after two beers. After three beers, my time went up fast."

"Really? Will it really fire full auto?"

"Behold." I remove the extra-capacity magazine from the lacquered box and push in fifty rounds. This takes a little time, but we say nothing. I slam it home and now the Love 32 has eight inches of gracefully curving clip extending below the grip.

Then, holding the gun in my right hand, I cup my left hand over the back of the frame near the magazine release, and I simultaneously depress two inset buttons. This releases the telescoping graphite butt. It's like the retractable handle on a piece of rolling luggage, but of narrower gauge and shorter. Fully extended at fifteen inches, the rubber-backed butt can then be braced against the crook of the shooter's elbow, rib cage, or even hip. It collapses in one-inch increments to fit smaller people.

I snug the butt against the inside of my elbow and look at Bradley Smith.

"Stallone should play you," he says.

"It'll burn through those fifty rounds in five seconds. Or you can use short bursts. Do you notice anything else different about this little genius?"

"The raised comb along the barrel top. It's like on a trap gun, but wider. It has nothing to do with the sights."

"Correct." I turn and aim the machine gun downrange, with telescoping butt still braced against my elbow. Then I place my free left hand over the comb and push down.

"For the muzzle rise," says Bradley.

I nod. Machine guns are notorious for rising as they burn through the rounds. The barrel wants to shoot the sky. Many an inexperienced submachine gunner has pulled the trigger, let the barrel jump up, and pretty much invited the bullets into his head. So long. But not if you brace down on the barrel with your free hand. The brace comb on the Love 32 is raised for cooling because the barrel itself gets hot.

"Allow me," I say. I set the Love 32 on the bench and bring in the old target, put on a fresh one, and send it back fifty feet. Then I take up the Love and stand just in front of the bench, feet spread, retractable butt snug in my elbow, left palm firm on the comb. I look downrange at the target, glance once at the barrel of the gun, then I let it rip. There's a five-second Armageddon of noise and smoke, then silence, and the black silhouette has a ragged hole in the middle about the size of a grapefruit.

"Wicked cool," says Bradley.

"Your turn."

I reload and Bradley puts up a fresh target. He's practically beaming as he steps up and gets ready. He's slow and meticulous about it, savoring the prep and the moment, not a trigger-ditzy moron like half the people I've sold weapons to. I hear the safety click off.

Five seconds later he's standing in a cloud of fragrant gun smoke, and the bottom half of the target is almost detached.

"Unreal."

"It's real," I say. "And there's *more*."

I take the noise suppressor from the lacquered box and screw it on. The barrel threads are recessed into the frame, such that a casual observer won't see that the gun is fitted for a silencer.

"That's your reason for the thirty-two ACP," says Bradley.

"Right. Nine hundred and five feet per second. Subsonic, no boom, easily quieted."

"I'm starting to like you, Ron."

"You're going to love this. Put up some fresh paper, please."

I reload and step up and fire. You can hear the muffled tap of the rounds going off and the cartridges chattering through and the ejector spitting out the brass, and you can hear the empties pinging on the carpet and you can even hear the ringing in your ears from the prior shooting, but what you mainly hear is the paper silhouette being torn to shreds and the bullets spitting into the sandbags at the distant far end of the range.

"I'll remain briefly speechless," says Bradley.

"There's more," I say. "These guns are untraceable to me. Untraceable to Favier and Winling. No serial numbers. Nothing that says Pace. Just Love 32, etched with subtle beauty on the forward slide. I can see legions of law enforcement officers worldwide mystified by these guns. Where did *these* come from? Did they simply spring from the earth, like the skeleton men in *Jason and the Argonauts?* Or drop from the sky, like manna? Something tells me that you would like to bedazzle law enforcement, Bradley. I think you like the outlaws more than the lawmen."

"How much per gun?"

"There's just one small catch. They don't exist. This is the prototype. Do you like martinis?"

4

Hood got up early to move the last of his possessions into his Buenavista rental home. The dawn was pink, and a vapor light on the carport burned white over the driveway. He carried the boxes into the house. His old Camaro wouldn't hold much so he'd rented a trailer. He would soon receive an ATFE take-home vehicle. Hood was thirty and never married and he had few things. As he wrestled another box from the trailer, he was thinking it would be nice to have a dog.

The house was a 1920s adobe, one of ten tucked amidst the hills on the northwest side of town, a development that never quite caught on. The place came furnished and had a new swamp cooler. The road in was graded dirt with ruts for gutters, but the hillside views were good: south to old town in which the bell tower of the church was still the highest point, east to infinite desert, and west to more desert and black-orange sunsets that covered miles.

Hood had arrived in Buenavista forty-eight hours ago, just enough time to meet the local chief of police, shake hands with the three members of the ATFE task force he was assigned to, then participate in the gun buy that had resulted in the killing of two men. One of the dead was a teenaged boy named Gustavo Armenta, who was on a date that night, and as Hood carried another box into the house, he pictured the way Gustavo had led his girlfriend by the hand from the restaurant patio and how a few moments later an errant bullet had found his heart in the darkness fifty yards away, stopping eighteen years of past and sixty years of future dead and forever. The other dead man was a gun dealer with a revoked license.

Hood heard a distant noise and through a window saw a vehicle coming slowly up the road. The headlights raked and bounced, and a while later the police cruiser came to a stop just outside the carport light.

Gabriel Reyes got out and let the door close quietly, bumping it shut with his hip.

"I'm glad I didn't have to wake you up," he said.

"Coffee?"

"Please."

In the kitchen Hood poured a cup and Reyes looked around the old home. His uniform was clean and pressed. His expression was that of a man expecting the worst.

"I guess you don't come out this early with good news," said Hood.

"Benjamin Armenta ring a bell?"

"Gulf Cartel."

"The boy who was killed last night is Gustavo, his son. He lived in Buenavista, on the Mexican side. Engaged to the girl. It's a shame and a mess."

"Was he mixed up in his dad's business?"

"Who knows? He was on his way to UCLA."

Hood sighed and looked out at the lightening day.

"So be extra careful, Deputy. [...] vengeance for Gustavo. It's a po[...] that, even though I probably don[...] don't you?"

Hood knew they were the lates[...] ing in Mexico, paramilitary killer[...] of them, across the nation. "The [...]

"They've been busy. Thirty-fou[...] dren in eight days. All of the vict[...] Cartel. Of course, Benjamin Armenta has lost ninety-seven of his own. That's one hundred and thirty-seven killings in a week and a day."

"Have you talked to my task force people?"

"I called them."

"Thanks for coming out."

"Gustavo and the Zetas aren't why I came out."

"So there's even more good news."

"Let's sit outside and watch the sun rise."

They sat on the low courtyard wall because there were no chairs. Hood saw that Reyes walked with a slight limp. The chief looked sixty, gray-haired, thick.

"Be careful at dusk and dawn this time of year," said Reyes. "If you step on a western diamondback, it can ruin your whole day. I still limp."

Hood nodded and looked down at Buenavista.

"I got an anonymous call two mornings ago," said Reyes. "It was the same day you got here. It was a woman, and she told me there was an injured man in the desert outside of town. She told me to drive east on 98 until I saw a pickup off to the side. I did that. Big skid marks at the truck. A rear flat and a jack ready to use. I fol-

tracks to a bloody patch in the sand about fifty
ghway. Then those two sets doubled back, then I
hird set into the desert. He'd walked half a mile or so.
m dug in underneath a bush, just about dead. Half an hour
the med center ambulance got there and they carried him out
a stretcher."

"Did she hit him while he was getting the jack ready?"

"That's a reasonable explanation, but she didn't say anything about it. I called for a tow and did a DMV check on the truck. Registered owner is Mike Finnegan of Los Angeles. Later in the impound yard, I went through the truck. He had a big tool chest in the bed and ninety thousand cash dollars inside it. Wasn't even locked. So I went to the hospital. He was in surgery to set two broken legs and a broken arm. His jaw and both cheeks were broken also. And four ribs. Serious internal injuries. The ER doctor told me the X-rays showed two skull fractures. The doctor said there would certainly be damage to the brain—the question was just how much. I examined the guy's wallet. Valid CDL, same address as DMV had. No credit or debit cards, no phone or insurance cards. No pictures of the wife and kids. He had a chain video store membership card, a key, and a punch card for a car wash up in Los Angeles. He had four hundred and sixty-four dollars. And a folded piece of plain white paper with your name and your new Buenavista P.O. box number on it."

"Mike Finnegan?"

"So you know him."

"No. I don't."

Reyes looked frankly at Hood in the morning's new light. "I went by the hospital about half an hour ago. He's still in the ICU but he's conscious and talking. He said: Tell Charlie Hood to come by and say hello."

• • •

Hood stood over bed 11 in the ICU. Finnegan's legs were fully engulfed in thick plaster casts, and one arm bore a cast from shoulder to hand. His entire head was wrapped in gauze with small openings for his eyes, nose, and mouth and was pinned upright for stability by skull clamps affixed to stainless steel rods that rested on a rigid collar.

"What are *you* looking at?" asked the man. His voice was soft and strained and it sounded as if it came from a mouth that could barely open. Hood thought he heard a humorous edge to it but knew he must be mistaken.

"I don't know you," said Hood.

"Maybe, under all this, I'm your long. Lost. Brother."

"My brothers aren't lost. And they don't have a voice like yours."

"Well, don't be disappointed. Because I don't know you. Either."

"Charlie Hood. You had my name and address in your wallet. You told the police chief you wanted me to come and say hello."

"Oh, Charlie. I don't know how that piece of paper got there. I'm Mike. Finnegan. I'm sorry I can't shake your hand."

Hood looked down on the man. Hood guessed that he was short and slender underneath all the plaster and gauze. All Hood could see of his actual body was a pink spot of mouth, two twinkles far back in the head wrap, and part of his right arm and hand, bruised and bandaged and spiked with an IV drip and a finger cuff for the monitor.

"Who would have thought you could get top-drawer medical care here in this desert?" asked Finnegan. "Of course I'm sure it helps to be a cash customer."

"What happened?"

"A flat tire, a speeding Mercury, and a heaping helping of bad luck. I wish I could have a cigarette now, but I've never smoked one in my life. No telling what zany ideas are getting through the new cracks in my brainpan."

"The doctors say you're lucky to be alive."

"*Really.*"

"Another couple of hours out there would have done you in."

"I'm nodding in agreement."

Hood located the twin glimmers deep in the gauze. "What are you doing in Buenavista?"

"Trying to pass through Buenavista."

"What's your business?"

"I'm self-employed."

"What business?"

"Business is all the same, Charlie. Buy low, sell high. Wait for the bailout."

Hood watched a thin stream of bubbles rise up through the saline bag. A woman in scrubs appeared from behind him and she glanced at the vitals monitor, then back at Hood. She was young and pretty and when she took up the chart, Hood checked her ring finger but before he could look away she caught him.

"Who are you?" she asked.

"Charlie Hood. I think I'm here on the basis of some misunderstanding."

Finnegan laughed tightly. "Is this a cosmic misunderstanding? Or a comic misunderstanding?"

"Mike, you talk too much," she said. "You talk to me about the effects of steroids on cranial pressure. You talk to Chief Reyes about the boy who was killed last night. You talk to the nurses about party boats on the Colorado River and you talk to the janitor about floor cleaners and his brother in prison. Now you're yapping away to Mr. Hood about selling high and cosmic versus comic."

"That's *Deputy* Hood, Doctor," whispered Finnegan.

"Oh?"

Hood said he was "on loan" from the Los Angeles Sheriff's Department. She offered her hand and he shook it.

"Beth Petty."

"She's a female doctor," whispered Finnegan.

Beth Petty smiled and shook her head. "Careful, Mike, or I'll sedate you."

"Use something pleasant. Please."

Dr. Petty held Hood's look. "Los Angeles? I studied medicine at USC."

"I studied psychology at Bakersfield State."

"There's a conversation killer," said Finnegan.

There was in fact a brief silence as Petty made notations on the chart and hung it back on the wall next to the sharps collector. "I hope you like Buenavista, Deputy."

She smiled at him and walked out and Hood heard her footsteps no longer.

"Is she beautiful?" whispered Finnegan.

"Yes," Hood whispered back.

"She's not in focus and neither are you. The ocular swelling is horrendous. Oh, Deputy, I just remembered how that piece of paper got into my wallet. It was pressed upon me by a reserve deputy you once worked with. Well, who you once shot and killed, actually. Coleman Draper."

Hood studied the small, plastered man. "For what purpose?"

"He said you were a good man and you might be able to help me."

"Do what?"

There was a longer silence and Hood saw that the twinkling lights of the man's eyes were gone. His first thought was that Finnegan had died. Then he heard the deep, slow breathing.

"Find my daughter."

"I already have a job."

"As we all do. Consider it pro bono or even charity. Deputy Hood, I'm a crushed and tired man. If it's okay with you, we'll. Talk. Later."

"Where did you get the ninety grand?"

"I earned it, of course."

Hood waited a moment. Then he heard the yawn enclosed within the bandage and he walked out.

5

Jimmy Holdstock was bright and affable and still built like the Wisconsin tight end he once was, but this morning his brain was sleepless and his heart was heavy.

He kissed Jenny and told her he loved her before he even cracked the front door of their El Centro home, to keep the heat out and the cool in as long as possible. The girls were still asleep, and Jimmy touched his wife's cheek and walked outside to the new day. He was twenty-six.

He had rented the house two months ago for his assignment to ATFE Operation Blowdown. It was a fifties home—pink stucco and squat—smack in the middle of five hundred acres of cotton a few miles from town. Holdstock liked the desert, which surprised him, because until two months ago he had never seen one except from the sky. This desert was full of unexpected beauties. Like now: a trio of doves cutting toward him low in the gray sky, squeaking softly as they sped over the miles of green plants tufted with white. Jimmy glanced up at them, but all he could think about was Gustavo Armenta.

He slung his war bag over his shoulder—vest, holster, his standby gun and ammo, a Bible in case he got a minute to himself, lunch, a plastic liter bottle of frozen water that would melt during the day and always have an ice-cold swallow for him when he needed it. He was wearing a suit and tie and he already had beads of sweat trickling from his armpits despite the extra antiperspirant. Holdstock's regular sidearm, the one he had discharged during the Buenavista sting, had been taken from him by a senior ATFE agent early the next morning.

Four short years ago Jimmy had graduated from Madison and was headed for the priesthood through a Minnesota seminary. But his desires were powerful and he fell in love with a St. Paul coffee shop waitress, Jenny Reuvers. He dropped out, and six months later he was married and happy. Not long after that, Jenny had shown him the positive drugstore pregnancy test, the same week that Holdstock was accepted into the ATFE training program in Washington, D.C. ATFE was a good fit for Jimmy because he was smart and could think on his feet and always knew what the rules were. He was afraid of nothing. There was Miami and New Orleans and Chicago. When Blowdown came along, Jimmy and Jenny went for it. ATFE needed some fresh faces for the battles on the Iron River. Southern California!

He unlocked the side door of the garage, stepped in and found the switch for the motorized door. When the door had clanged up into place, Jimmy slung the duffel onto the front seat of his Five Hundred, tossed his jacket in the back, and climbed behind the wheel.

He arrived at the Federal Building in San Diego just over an hour later, having noticed almost nothing during the drive, having heard hardly a word of the Christian radio show. He parked and took a swig of ice water.

Mars came to the ATFE lobby and took Holdstock upstairs to the regional director's office. Mars was pale and unforthright and he said nothing on the elevator ride up. The SAC was Frank Soriana, a large and often jolly man who this morning looked at Holdstock with no jolliness at all.

"Jimmy, the bureau got the Armenta bullet from the sheriffs down in Imperial and did a hurry-up on the toolmarks. You killed him *and* the gun dealer. So, good shooting on the one, and bad luck on the other. Armenta was almost fifty yards away when you fired. Incredible bad luck, Jimmy. I'm sorry it happened."

Holdstock had known that the toolmarks testing was pointless. His first two shots had hit the gun dealer—he could hear the smack of the bullets hitting the body—and the third had missed to the left. And just a moment later, he had heard the screams.

Jimmy nodded and looked down at his hands. He had been a half step ahead of Janet Bly, and he could see the young gunrunner in the black suit standing there like Death himself in the patio light, his gun out and ready. He could see Tilley with his hands up. He was aware of Ozburn and Hood in the periphery of things. He was aware of the empty tables, empty chairs, the closed umbrellas, the big outdoor grill unmanned at that late hour. And when Black Suit had swung his gun at Ozburn, Holdstock had put him down with two shots and missed by a fraction of an inch with the third.

Sitting in the regional director's office and staring at his hands, Jimmy Holdstock replayed the scene for what seemed like the thousandth time.

But by now the scene had changed. It started one way and then it became different. Now, when Jimmy saw it again, the black-suited gunman—his name turned out to be Victor Davis—wasn't swinging the gun on Ozburn, he was lowering it.

Holdstock closed his eyes. Janet Bly had held fire. Sean Ozburn and Charlie Hood had held fire. So Jimmy had been outvoted three to one on deadly force and killed an innocent boy, too. Since it happened, he had been telling himself that the toolmarks on the boy's bullet would prove him innocent, but really, he knew that no one else had fired and what were the chances of some other shooter having taken out Gustavo Armenta?

He took a deep, wavering breath. *I've killed a young man I never saw alive,* he thought. *Leadeth me beside still waters. Please.*

"We've talked to Ozburn and Bly and the deputy," said Soriana. "Sean and Janet thought Davis could have been preparing to fire. Charlie Hood didn't say that, but he did say that Davis was not lowering the gun as ordered. So, three out of three witnesses are standing with you, Jimmy. And I'm standing with you, and Agent Mars is, and all of ATF. The boy was an accident. He was collateral damage. It breaks my heart to see the innocent die and I know it's breaking yours, too, Jimmy. But don't let it break all the way. We need you whole again."

Holdstock sobbed without sound, head hung, big hands still folded on his lap. It felt good to let those tears out. He thought he should feel humiliation, too, but he didn't.

He didn't cry long. A moment later he had wiped his face on his hands, took another deep, wavering breath, and stood up.

"You want a couple of weeks off, take them," said Soriana. "You're entitled to them and you've earned them the hard way."

"I think I'd like to work, sir. Back on the horse and all that."

"The fact that Gustavo was the son of Benjamin Armenta gives us cause for concern," said Mars. "There are the Zetas. We can reassign you."

"I want to see this through."

"You want to do a couple of weeks of office work here in San Diego?" asked Soriana. "We could use you. You can bring Jenny and the kids, stay in a motel with a pool, enjoy the summer."

"No, sir. But thank you."

Soriana and Mars stood and all three men shook hands.

"We'll get your sidearm back to you in good time," said Mars.

"I appreciate your support, you guys."

"You acted properly, Jimmy. You did the right thing."

"I really, really appreciate that."

Holdstock bought small gifts for Jenny and the girls in a San Diego Target and made El Centro by two o'clock. He ate his sack lunch on the way home but he was starved, so he drove to the Denny's and pulled around back and parked with the other locals in a patch of scarce afternoon shade. He stripped off his tie and when he got out of the car he buttoned the suit coat over his hip holster and walked around to the entrance and into a blast of conditioned air.

He got a newspaper out front and sat at the counter and ate a large lunch and a piece of pie for dessert.

He read the front page and sports and slowly he felt the terrible tension lessen in his body. *You did the right thing*. Funny what a few words could do. Words from men you respect.

He left a big tip for the waitress and pushed outside, thinking that was how he had met Jenny. He could still picture the little café where they'd met, the bud vases on the tables, Jenny beautiful. He'd go in for lunch whenever he could afford it, wait for her station if he had to.

He was smiling when he got into the Ford and started up the engine and hit the air, and when he turned to back out he saw the bright orange flyer on his rear window. The print was facing him—something about losing weight. Could actually stand to lose a few pounds, he thought. He glanced at the cars on either side of him and saw the orange sheets flapping in the hot desert breeze.

Holdstock sighed and got out and went around to the back. The flyer was held in place by a rock. He reached for the rock and heard something behind him, and when he turned, the first man hit him on the head with something small and hard, and a huge second man drove him down to the asphalt with a choke hold and didn't let go. The first man stripped away his pistol and hit him again over one temple. The last thing Holdstock knew for sure, they were stuffing him into the backseat of his own car.

6

Bradley Smith and Ron Pace braced themselves against Smith's Cyclone GT convertible while two gunmen frisked them and two more stood by and watched. Smith looked over at Pace. The gunmaker had been blindfolded since the outskirts of Tijuana, and he was still blindfolded now. He was grinning.

"Wipe the smile off your piehole," said Smith.

"I smile when things get intense."

"I told you the people who run Favier and Winling are intense."

"They don't even trust you, and you work for them."

"He who trusts ends up on the dinner table."

"They frisk me for guns, but I *make* guns."

"They know what you do. Speak when spoken to." Smith looked at Pace, and the idiot was smiling again.

As the cartel pistolero felt his boots for weapons, Smith looked out at the pale green Pacific. It was afternoon, and the summer Baja wind had whipped up battalions of whitecaps and sent them marching toward shore. The last time Bradley was here on the beach at Baja was early spring, when he had brought his fiancée, Erin, to an old hotel down here to celebrate her first recording contract and their engagement. Quite a party—fifty friends and family down from L.A., Erin's band, of course, some producers and soundmen and session guys, Bradley's gang of outlaws, and all the roadies and dealers and hangers-on, catered by an upscale restaurant in TJ, booze courtesy of a friend with a San Diego tequila distributorship. Bradley and Erin, in a Max Azria runway dress, had snuck off with blankets and made love on the sand dunes. He missed her right now. Business was business, but Erin was his heart.

When the gunman was finished with him, Smith turned and looked up at Herredia's hilltop retreat. It was a white Castilian two-story buried in a lavish oasis of pools and fountains and blue palms and big terra-cotta pots overflowing with protea and plumeria and flowering tropical vines. A helicopter hovered high above, swaying in the currents like a kite.

"Where is it?" asked the gunman.

"In the trunk," said Bradley, handing him the keys.

They walked single file up a winding stone path toward the house, then along the shady western flank of the home, then descended into a grotto of gurgling pools and flowers. The pistolero carried the lacquered box with the stainless steel Pace Arms insignia on the top. Bradley saw two uniformed Mexico Federal Judicial Police officers with combat shotguns standing motionless beside a man-made waterfall. He was impressed that Herredia was now employing *Federales*. He'd never seen that before. He knew that local and state police were defecting to the cartels for better pay and benefits, just as the federal soldiers were defecting to the Zetas. Calderón was pitting both police and soldiers against the cartels as never before—thus the spiraling body counts and savagery as the cartels warred for share in a tougher market. The men who had once upon a time pursued Herredia now drew much fatter salaries for protecting him. Herredia's answer to the Gulf Cartel's Zetas, thought Bradley. He glanced back at the stone-still soldiers. The times they are a-changin'. Spooky. Maybe Erin could write a song about it.

From this height Bradley saw a swatch of desert far below and an airplane hangar painted to match the desert and an ancient transport helicopter hunkered beneath a canopy of camouflage net. A soldier stood guard outside the hangar. A man squatted beside the big helo, welding away at its flank.

Then the path dropped steeply and a handrail appeared and when he rounded a wide turn, the wind pushed against him. He saw the cove of black rocks below and heard the ocean pounding onto the white crescent of beach. It took a few minutes to get there.

Bradley jumped down from the last step and felt the sand give beneath his boots. He saw North Baja Cartel leader Carlos Herredia waiting in the shadows where the black rocks met the sand. There was an old cable spool upended for a table in the shade. Two pistoleros sat on plastic buckets. Nearby stood old Felipe with his combat 10-gauge, drum-fed shotgun. Bradley had never seen him without it. It was like a limb. Felipe was white-haired and walnut-faced and wore a black eye patch.

At the far side of the cove, Bradley saw that pallets had been leaned up against the rocks, each one with a paper human silhouette target affixed. A hundred feet offshore bobbed a sleek sportfisher manned by two men who were now sitting on the fighting chairs and smoking. Down at the waterline was a small dock beside which five men squatted on their haunches. As Bradley and Pace and the four gunmen walked out onto the sand, the squatting men stood up and studied them.

Bradley introduced Herredia to Ron Pace as Señor Mendez, deputy chief of worldwide operations for Favier & Winling Security.

Herredia offered his hand and considered him with a black stare. Pace swung his hand in a big arc like a rube and told Señor Mendez he'd heard a lot about him.

Bradley flinched inwardly as he shook Herredia's hand and received a brief, formal hug.

Old Felipe gave Bradley a partially toothed smile and thoroughly ignored Ron Pace.

One of the pistoleros set the wooden gun box on the spool table, and Pace unlocked it and opened it.

He took out the Love 32 and presented it to Herredia. Herredia was a big man with big hands, but his index finger fit through the trigger guard with room to spare.

"It's heavy."

"Yes, sir," said Pace. "I'll show you why."

Herredia's eyebrows were bushy and when they rose upward in the middle he looked soulful, and when they lowered into a glower he looked capable of anything. Now they were level as he looked to the men at the shoreline.

Bradley watched them shift their weight uneasily, as if they wanted to walk away but also wanted to stay together, their attention divided between the men in the boat offshore and what was going on around the big cable spool. He could not hear the words but their voices were anxious and speculative.

"What is this?" asked Herredia. He stabbed a finger at the widened cooling comb atop the barrel of the automatic.

"Let me explain," said Pace. "It's called the Love 32."

"A gun named Love?"

Bradley listened as Pace launched into the same presentation he'd given a few days ago at Pace Arms. He stated the gun specs, then explained the name of the Love 32. Herredia looked at Bradley blankly at the mention of Murrieta.

"The thirty-two-caliber bullet is weak," said Herredia.

"You can say that one thirty-two-caliber bullet is weak," said Pace.

"I did just say it."

"Watch, Señor Mendez."

Pace set the pistol on the spool and tapped out the frame pins with his pocketknife punch. He opened the frame and made the small adjustments with the needle-nose pliers. He reassembled it, then ejected the regular clip and replaced it with the big fifty-round magazine.

Bradley noticed the sharp twinkle in Herredia's eyes as it dawned on him what he was seeing.

Herredia was nodding as Pace released the telescoping graphite butt from the back side of the frame. Bradley saw that Pace was ignoring his audience now, having drawn them so completely into his drama. Pace pulled out the butt and it clicked into place with authority and he held the gun as anyone would hold a pistol, but the graphite brace fit firmly into the crook of his elbow. Pace raised and lowered the weapon to make sure the brace was the right length. The fifty-shot magazine protruded from the handle with an artful, lethal curve.

"Fifty thirty-two-caliber bullets are never weak," said Pace. "Señor Felipe, do you know about muzzle-rise in a full automatic weapon?"

"He knows everything about all weapons," said Herredia.

"I doubt that, but keep your hand on the top of the barrel, old man, or you'll blow yourself into eternity. Which I suspect will feel a lot shorter than most of us like to believe it will."

Bradley winced inwardly again, but Felipe was smiling. Pace handed the weapon to him. He grasped the pistol grip and worked the retractable brace into his elbow, and he lifted and lowered the gun as Pace had done.

Then he led them across the sand and stood fifty feet or so away from the pallets. The old man spread his feet and swung the gun up and braced his left hand on the barrel comb.

Bradley listened to the five-second volley and saw the chips of wood and paper flying and the middle of one of the targets grow a hole outward. Through the hole he could see the sunlight hitting the black rock behind. The smoke rose quickly into the breeze. The men down by the dock watched unmoving. Bradley saw that they wore ankle irons linked to a chain fastened around a dock stanchion. The boatmen waved their baseball caps, and their laughter rode the breeze to shore.

Herredia looked at Bradley, nodding.

"There's one more feature I think you will like, sir," Bradley said.

Pace took the Love 32 and screwed the sound suppressor into the end of the barrel. He popped out the big magazine and clicked home a full one.

"Now you can mow down your enemies without waking the baby," said Pace.

Bradley saw the quick menace in Herredia's face, but Felipe cackled.

Pace presented the newly loaded and silenced weapon to Felipe, and Felipe presented it to El Tigre.

Herredia looked out toward the dock and waved. Bradley's heart fluttered and he took a deep breath and felt intensely present and bad. The men in the boat weighed anchor and the engine started with a gentle cough and a puff of smoke. Some of the five men near the dock turned to watch the boat.

Then the muffled groan of a helicopter became a full roar as an old Vietnam-era CH-47 transport chopper slowly lifted over the rise from the desert behind them. Its markings and numbers were Red

Cross. It passed by above them, and Bradley could see the scars on its belly left by Herredia's welder. Then it was far out over the sea, banking to the south.

"A gift to me from my Colombians," said Herredia. "They stole it but wanted faster ones. It can carry more money and weapons than any vehicle."

Herredia smiled at Bradley, then he cradled the Love 32 against his elbow and motioned for Ron Pace to follow him. Pace gave Bradley a proud grin, then he followed Herredia until they were sixty feet from the dock. The boat had swung north, and Bradley saw both boatmen watching intently.

He watched as Herredia asked something of Pace but the words were lost in wind and distance. Herredia appeared to press his case, offering the gun. Pace stepped back, shaking his head, and he raised his hands as if trying to keep something away. Herredia nodded at the five men and continued speaking and Pace continued shaking his head. Herredia spat out a final statement, then swung the machine gun on the men. Bradley saw the vibration of Herredia's big forearm as he pressed down on the gun, and he heard the metallic clatter of the gun as the prisoners struck out with their fists or tried to shield themselves with their hands, and the air shimmered with their blood and Bradley heard screams while the bullets cut through them, some bullets stitching the placid cove water behind them, and he heard more screams as they twisted and buckled and fell gracelessly, then he heard no screams at all and it was over.

Ron Pace collapsed to the sand and Herredia stepped over him and came up the beach. Bradley watched the smoke rise and vanish, heard a groan, saw the boat heading toward the dock fast, the men with their hat bills low and serious.

"Zetas," said Felipe.

"Not anymore," said Bradley. He walked back to the spool table and took a red plastic bucket and carried it down to the water and let it fill halfway. Then he came back over and poured the cold seawater over Pace's face. Bradley dropped the inverted bucket to the sand and sat on it and lit a cigarette and waited for Ron to come to. He took out his cell phone and checked it, then heaved it out into the ocean. He watched the boatmen load the bodies into the boat, swinging the dead by ankles and wrists high until their own weight carried them over the gunwales and they hit the deck with thumps that became less hollow as their numbers mounted.

"Holy shit," said Pace.

"Little holiness here," said Bradley.

"Five men."

"A hundred a week. Two hundred. Heads on stakes. Mendez against the Zetas. We don't know how many are dying."

"I may vomit."

"No one cares about your vomit. Stand up and shake it off, Ron. It's time to negotiate with Mendez."

"He's Herredia."

"Herredia, then. Stand up. Clear your brain. We've got a deal to make."

Late that night they sat on a tile veranda overlooking the Pacific. Bradley watched the moonlight shiver on the water and heard the palm fronds rattle in the breeze. He felt culpably brutal but he was not a man given to self-doubt.

Pace proposed to manufacture one thousand guns, two large-capacity magazines for each firearm and one sound suppressor each, for one million cash dollars. He pointed out that this was roughly one-half the cost of used Chinese- and Indian-made submachine guns in God-knew-what condition, and only one-third the cost of new ones—few of them concealable and none of them silenced. They would be warranted free of defects for one year. The guns would bear no serial numbers or manufacturer's marks except for *Love 32* on the right side of each barrel.

Pace handed Herredia some Polaroids of the Pace Arms building, the mold and dye bays, the assembly lines, the firing lines, the offices. Herredia looked at them patiently in the light from a tiki torch.

"I think the thirty-two ACP is a weak load," he said.

"Tell the five dead men that," said Pace.

"I want to rename the gun," said Herredia. "Something about death or the devil."

"I'm sorry, Mr. Mendez, but it's the Love 32. This is nonnegotiable. History . . . ," he added absently, staring out at the water. Herredia brooded and glowered and tried to ply Pace with fine tequila and wine and fishing stories but Pace responded with a series of knock-knock jokes until Bradley finally butt in and suggested that he shut the fuck up and make a deal.

Pace came off his price a hundred grand, while making clear that all transportation and shipping was one-hundred-percent Mr. Mendez's responsibility.

"Shipping is not an interest of mine," Herredia said, with a look at Bradley. "Mr. Jones here is very good at moving things from one place to another. Between us, the transport will go smoothly." At first, Bradley hadn't liked El Tigre's quip about the stolen Red Cross helo carrying more cash and guns than any vehicle. Bradley had no patience with men who didn't value a good ally when they were lucky enough to have one. If Herredia wanted to move his own dollars and guns, then let him. But now it sounded like Herredia was offering to share the machine. A helo. Interesting.

"And I'll need one-third of the nine hundred thousand dollars up front so I can order materials, hire my crew back, retool the lines for a totally new product, and make enough molds and dyes to crank out the units fast," Ron said.

Pace had told Bradley this a few days ago when he'd made his proposal over martinis, so Herredia was prepared for it. Herredia told Pace that there would be three hundred thousand cash in small bills waiting for them in a Compton warehouse just as soon as they could get there to pick it up.

Pace told Herredia that, once operational, he would run one assembly crew—his finest—on seven twelve-hour shifts per week, with two hundred and fifty units ready for pickup in ten days. The full one thousand would take until midsummer, three weeks out.

"Your enemies will never know what hit them," he said.

Bradley was prepared for Herredia to pitch smug Ron Pace off the balcony and be done with the *pendejo*. Ever since the death of Gustavo Armenta, El Tigre had expected vengeance on Americans from Benjamin, which meant American retaliation, which would be very, very bad for business. Herredia was irritable enough without being cajoled by a wiseass gunmaker. He just wanted his thousand machine pistols, value priced, and he wanted them soon.

"Tonight I will say a long prayer that I am not in business with a fool," said Herredia. "*Ándale*. You have work to do."

He stood and shook hands with the gunmaker. Felipe watched from a corner. Two pistoleros left the darkness and escorted Pace and Bradley to the car.

7

Two days after the Buenavista shoot-out and one day after the disappearance of Jimmy Holdstock, Hood and his Blowdown team let themselves into Victor Davis's townhome in Yuma, Arizona.

They were looking for guns. They searched the living room, kitchen, and small dining room without success. The master bedroom entertainment center yielded pornographic DVDs but no firearms. Hood noted that the framed picture of a lovely woman on Davis's nightstand was actually the sample photo sold with the frame. The Frame Shop sticker was still on the back. The dream girl had cost Victor $9.99. In the master closet hung two dozen dark suits, at least a dozen white shirts, and maybe thirty ties.

But the guest bedroom held pay dirt: four plastic bins under the bed, containing forty-eight used small-caliber handguns. Many were in poor shape, Hood saw. Six more bins stacked neatly up on a closet shelf held the big stuff: six .357 Magnum Smith & Wesson revolvers, four .44 Magnum autoloaders, ten .38 Detective Special revolvers, twelve Pace Arms nine-millimeter automatics, and two FN 5.57s. They were used but in fine condition.

Bly pointed to the FNs. "They penetrate body armor. The cartel gunmen call them *asesino de policía*—cop killers."

Hood immediately thought of Holdstock again. He looked at Ozburn and Bly and knew that they were thinking of him, too. Hood feared the worst. Holdstock had vanished somewhere between San Diego and El Centro the day before. His car was missing, too, suggesting willful flight. But Holdstock had a family. Holdstock was stand-up. Hood thought he'd been murdered or abducted in retaliation for the shooting of Gustavo Armenta. Zetas. Abducted was worse.

"Okay," said Ozburn. "We're having another Jimmy moment. I'm gonna think a prayer for him right now where we stand. You two can join me or not."

Hood bowed his head and closed his eyes. He sensed Bly doing the same. He asked for Holdstock's safe return. He pictured Jimmy flipping the burgers at the barbecue he'd hosted for Hood before Hood had moved to Buenavista. It was a nice afternoon, and those few hours between them made Jimmy the best friend Hood had in this vast desert. His wife and daughters were a delight. *Help him, help him.*

"Amen," said Ozburn. "You didn't think that ATF could be so much fun, did you, Charlie?"

"It never stops." Hood smiled to himself. He liked these people. He liked the way they refused to call themselves ATFE, just the old ATF was what they said. Ozburn had quipped once that it was ATFE but the *E* was silent.

There were four shotguns stacked in one corner of the closet and long rifles stacked in the other. The closet floor was lined with green military surplus ammo boxes, and when Hood toed them, he could tell they were full. He squatted and opened one and looked at the neat boxes of .44 Magnum loads, factory made.

Hood had quickly learned that Arizona was the widest and deepest part of the Iron River. It was legal to buy guns in Arizona with minimal ID, a cursory background check, and no wait. Then a gun owner could sell, trade, carry, and conceal with almost no paperwork. Many dealers both licensed and unlicensed worked out of their homes, just like Victor. Hood had seen handguns for sale in scores of gun shops in Arizona towns, in liquor stores, even in the convenience stores of gas stations along the scenic state highways.

"We yanked Victor's license a year ago," said Ozburn. "He sold to some straw buyers plugged into the Tijuana Cartel. He sold to young mothers in east L.A. We couldn't build a case, so we closed him down. But Victor didn't miss a beat. Gun heaven, man, pistol paradise. Most of this iron would have hit the streets in the next three months if Victor hadn't run up against his own product. He'd sell the beat-up shit guns to the inner-city bangers. The heavy stuff he'd sell to the cartels. The badder the bad guys, the better their guns are."

Bly ran a metal detector through the house in search of more. Ozburn safed and photographed and logged the guns and put them into ATFE lockboxes for transport.

Hood found a briefcase stuffed with ATFE Firearm Transaction Records and appointment books under the living room sofa. He'd seen such forms before—each dealer was required to complete and sign one for each sale, then keep it in his possession. If the dealer went out of business, he was supposed to send the forms back to ATFE for storage, but Victor Davis was noncompliant. Hood wondered at a system that trusted the crooks to follow the procedures.

He set the briefcase on the kitchen counter and rifled through the forms. They'd been thrown in loose. He found dates ranging from 2004 through June of 2009, when ATFE had pulled Victor Davis's federal firearms license. Hood knew that 2004 was when the Iron

River began to swell—cartel competition, another surge of Mexican law enforcement, another hike in the prices of street drugs across the United States. Now it was a flood and he was part of the levee.

He ran one hand through the piles of forms. Hundreds of them. All makes of guns, all calibers, from .22-short derringers to 10-gauge riot guns. The buyers were mostly men, but not all. The prices ranged from fifty dollars for a used Lorcin .25 to seven hundred and fifty dollars for a new Colt .45 ACP. The names were Dalrymple and Johnson and Gutierrez and Hoades and Valenzuela and Milliken and Djorik and on and on and on. Hundreds and hundreds more.

Hood pulled up a barstool and flipped through, arranging the sales by year.

A Beretta nine for Wilson of Oceanside.

A Taurus .38 for Foxx of Commerce.

He thought about Holdstock and his car. The car gave Hood hope, but not much hope. Holdstock had had enough? Run out on his wife and daughters? Run away to Mexico in order to stretch a modest federal paycheck? What quality of hope was this?

A Savage Arms 12-gauge for Mendoza of Yuma.

A Ruger .22 for Pfleuger of Santa Ana.

A Colt .45 for Lochte of Tempe.

Mendoza of Yuma, the Ruger for Pfleuger, Lochte of Tempe. Like poetry, thought Hood: bad fucking poetry. Maybe Holdstock ran his car off the highway and CHP hadn't found it yet. Was this hope at all?

A Pace Arms for Gowdy of Phoenix.

A Bryco for Stevens of Alpine.

More likely the Zetas had grabbed him and used his own car to take him across. If that was true, Hood thought, then he was probably beheaded by now and someone would find his body in one place and his head in another, and the Iron River would have swept away another life. The cartels had never come north to grab a U.S. lawman. Now they had accomplished what before they had never dared. The old rules were gone. The word *unraveling* came to Hood's mind. He saw the ends of fresh-cut ropes twisting in a bitter wind.

A Winchester for Lopez of L.A.

A Lorcin for Barret of . . . who cares?

A Charter Arms for . . .

A .40-caliber derringer for Allison Murrieta of Norwalk, California.

Hood looked away and took a deep breath and let it out and looked back at the FTR.

Allison Murrieta/Suzanne Jones. Take your pick. He recognized her bold handwriting. It conjured her voice and the shape of her face and the feel of her body and the taste of her breath. She had been shot with that derringer in her hand, not quite ready to use it against a boy. It was ivory-handled and beautifully tooled. Now it was Hood's gun, bequeathed wordlessly to Hood by Allison's son.

Hood held the form and looked at her signature and in spite of everything he felt at this moment, he smiled.

As he put the FTRs in chronological order, Hood looked for patterns. His ATFE task force trainers in Los Angeles had been pattern crazy. Most of Victor Davis's customers were male, though there was a group of females aged twenty-two to thirty-five, all with east L.A. addresses. This pattern was common: Inner-city moms afraid for their children were often targeted by gun pushers. But an opposing pattern existed, too: Inner-city moms were also often straw buyers purchasing weapons for homies and husbands and boyfriends. Hood had learned that once a buyer purchased two or more handguns in five or fewer days, the dealer was supposed to file an

ATFE Multiple Sales Form. These were kept on file in regional ATFE offices, and a pattern of heavy MSF filings suggested organized trafficking. Of course straw buyers knew this, so they would change to the "lie and buy" method, which was to use a counterfeit ID. These IDs not only disguised the true identity of the buyer but easily passed the brief Arizona state background check because fictitious people aren't listed in databases. If a licensed firearms dealer was scrupulous, he would report any suspicious sales to ATFE. If not, or if the bogus driver's licenses were convincing, then dealers could sell deadly weapons to criminals with records of violence, underage buyers, the insane, the undocumented, the drunk, the high, or the furious—or to anyone wanting to make money as a middleman for the cartels. A dealer with a pattern of sales to such people always sent up red flags in the ATFE computers, but by the time the flags waved, it was often too late.

Hood saw that Victor Davis's source lay along the Arizona-Mexico border. And most of his sales were there, too, with some customers to the north in Orange and Los Angeles counties. He pictured the U.S.-Mexico border between San Diego and Corpus Christi, all two thousand rugged miles of it, and he wondered that some 6,700 gun dealers were licensed to do business along it. *That's more than three gun dealers for every mile of cactus and rattlesnakes,* one of Hood's instructors pointed out. *What's that a pattern for? Fucking death and destruction is what.*

Patterns upon patterns, dollars upon dollars, guns upon guns.

And that was the legal end of it all, not counting the hundreds of unlicensed profiteers who bought and sold on the blackest of markets.

Hood examined the appointment books. They were nearly identical, plastic-covered, with calendars and space for notes, differing only by the dates. There was one for each of the past five years. The entries were cryptic and heavily abbreviated but neatly written. Davis had been prone to doodling tight, crosshatched designs that sometimes grew to encompass entire days.

Hood flipped through, reading the entries with one track of his mind and worrying about Jimmy Holdstock with the other. Using the Firearm Transaction Record date on the derringer sale to Allison Murrieta, Hood found the corresponding appointment book and looked up the day. It was August 2, 2006. In the date box was scribbled in black ink, "*Allison M./x-small 2-shot/.40 cal & ammo/6pm IHOP in Escondido.*" The entry had been circled in blue ink, and Hood followed a blue line across the page and into the "Notes" section. Here he read, "*Chick brought son & when she used head he said he needed six pieces/light & short/no #s/has buyers!/will call.*"

Hood did the math: Bradley Jones, studying Outlaw 101 at the age of fifteen. He scanned through the remaining months of 2006 but found no sale. He figured even bold Victor Davis wouldn't record an illegal sale to a minor anyway.

He found the appointment book for 2009. This was the last year that Davis had sold firearms legally. ATFE had revoked his license in March. Hood saw that his sales activity actually increased, beginning in April. Working harder, thought Hood, getting lower prices for the same iron, spending longer hours getting to know his customers enough to determine they weren't undercover cops. The handwriting had degenerated with the extra work. It was cramped and sometimes illegible.

On April 4, Davis had written "*R. Pace/noon/El Torito N.B.*" The entry caught Hood's eye because it was circled in bold black ink and had a bold red *X* through it. He wondered if R. Pace was of the Pace Arms company in Orange County. They'd been bankrupted by then, hadn't they? One of their guns had gone off unexpectedly and killed a boy—a design flaw. Was Davis trying to buy inventory at Chapter 11 prices? Hood flipped forward and saw another "*R. Pace*" date in May. Another in June. And a final date for 2009, November 4. All of them were circled, as if in hope of great things, and all but the last had been dramatically Xed out. In the space below the last date, Davis had written "*F.U.*"

Hood was surprised to get a Pace Arms listing from the operator and a woman's voice at the other end after he dialed.

"Pace Arms."

"Chuck Reynolds for Mr. Pace, please."

Hood was put on hold and a few moments later a young-sounding man spoke.

"Ron."

"I'm calling about Victor Davis."

A pause, then, "We're out of that business."

"Davis was killed two days ago during an illegal firearms sale down in Buenavista."

"I'm sorry. Are you a cop or ATF?"

"Neither."

"We're out of that business."

"You made four appointments with him last year."

"I rescheduled three times and honored the last as a professional courtesy. I never did business with Victor Davis. He was not a friend or an acquaintance. He wanted to buy inventory, but we didn't have any inventory. We were broke by then, Mr. Reynolds. We're still broke now. We haven't made a gun in over a year. We still owe the family of Miles Packard eleven point two million dollars. Good-bye."

They were loading the lockboxes and the FTRs into the task force van when two El Centro PD cruisers barreled down the street and double-parked beside them.

A plainclothes cop hopped from the second car, brandishing his shield holder, introducing himself as he trotted to the van. His name was Atkins.

"Let's go inside," he said.

They stood in the good light of the kitchen, and Atkins brought a freezer bag from his coat pocket. Inside the bag was a standard-size letter envelope.

"The desk got a call at ten a.m. from a woman saying where an important letter could be found. It wasn't on PD property but it was close by. An officer found it five minutes later and I received it five minutes after that."

Atkins spilled the envelope onto the granite countertop.

Hood read the handwritten print on the front: *BLOWDOWN*, all capitals, confidently rendered in red marking pen.

"It wasn't sealed," said Atkins. "The officer opened it and the desk sergeant opened it and I opened it. So . . ."

He took the envelope by a corner and held it up and shook loose two Polaroids.

One showed Jimmy Holdstock's face. It was puffy and pale, but his eyes were open and focused on the camera. He looked hungover.

The other was a picture of three items resting side by side in a dirty blue plastic tub: a pair of pliers, an electric circular saw, and a long-nozzled barbecue lighter.

Janet Bly raised a hand to her mouth, and Hood heard her breath catch but she said nothing. They all stared down at the pictures.

Ozburn whispered something that Hood couldn't make out.

"Yeah," said Atkins.

"Have you seen the PD security videos?" asked Hood.

"Nothing. The envelope was placed inside a newspaper that was set on a bus bench a hundred feet from us. Our cameras don't go there. I'm really damned sorry they don't."

"A bus bench," said Hood. "What about transit security?"

"They don't have cameras at that location."

"Greyhound might."

"Greyhound is around the corner."

"A witness?"

"We're working on that. That whole area is dead at night. Especially when it's up above ninety degrees."

"We can get some information from the Polaroids," said Ozburn. "Did you guys touch them?"

"None of us touched them. They're yours."

Atkins slid the envelope and pictures into the plastic freezer bag and gave the bag to Ozburn.

"You haven't called any reporters, have you?"

"No reporters."

"Because the people who have Jimmy will play for attention. That's the whole idea. It's a form of terrorism."

"Nobody knows but us and his wife. I haven't told her about the pictures. It's up to you now."

Janet Bly walked outside and slammed the door.

Ozburn was already on the phone to the regional director by the time Atkins followed her out.

"They've got Jimmy," he said. "They took him right off American soil."

8

That evening, Hood sat in the shade of his modest courtyard and watched Bradley's green Cyclone stream up the hill toward the house. The music blared and the dust danced. Bradley's fiancée was riding shotgun and Hood could see her red hair flying behind a black scarf.

He waved them into the carport, and Bradley goosed the car into the shade. It looked good next to his IROC Camaro. Hood had always loved the single-minded power of muscle cars, their half wildness and partial comforts. The music stopped and Erin turned and looked at Hood, then the doors opened at the same time.

Bradley was wearing plaid shorts and flip-flops and a white guayabera and a narrow-brim hat. His hair was cut short and his face clean shaven. "Why'd you pick this place?"

"Location," said Hood.

"We can't stay long. Just came by to give you the good news."

Erin got out and stretched and tossed the scarf into the car. She pushed her sunglasses up into her hair. She wore a white dress with black polka dots and no shoes. "I've got dust on my dust. Good to see you, Charlie."

Hood showed them the house, then they sat in the courtyard at a round rough-hewn table and benches without backs. The courtyard faced east to get the cool of evening if there was any. Hood brought out a pitcher of ice water and glasses. The desert spread in a flat infinity below them. Hood thought of Holdstock.

"There have been some changes since we talked to you," said Bradley. "Erin? Want to get this show started?"

He watched Bradley and Erin exchange looks. Erin went to the Cyclone.

"So, how's the Iron River?" asked Bradley.

"Quiet for three whole days."

"Not a shot fired?"

Hood shook his head absently. He couldn't get Holdstock out of his mind. *Pliers and a circular saw,* he thought. *Christ, what have we come to?*

"You glad you came down here?" asked Bradley.

"Oh. Yeah."

"You don't look too glad."

"That was your word."

"Okay, friend. Just talkin', just filling up space."

"Do you know Victor Davis? Your mother bought a gun from him four years ago. The one you gave me after she died."

Bradley shook his head. "She had more than one gun."

"You tried to buy six."

Bradley looked at Hood and nodded. "It never happened. I was fifteen."

"That's what worries me."

"Worry about yourself."

Erin was back with a plastic garment bag on a hanger slung over one shoulder and a square envelope in her other hand. She laid the bag over the low courtyard wall, then sat back down and handed the envelope to Hood.

It was heavy and cream colored, and on the front in beautiful cursive writing, it read: *Charles Hood & Guest.*

"That's your handwriting, Erin."

"It sure is. Open it."

The wedding invitation inside was classy and brief, though Hood read it twice to make sure he hadn't made a mistake.

"It's a three-day wedding celebration?"

"We hope it's enough," said Erin. "The Valley Center ranch is where I first saw you. Bradley and I were moving out. Remember?"

"I remember."

Hood pictured the Valley Center compound where Suzanne Jones had lived, now partially owned by her son, Bradley. It was eight acres in the hills near Escondido. Hood could see the big house and the outbuildings and the grassy expanse of the barnyard and the small creek that formed the south property line. It was tucked back into Cahuilla Indian land.

"It's going to be like the rancho days," said Erin. "The Californios, you know, they'd party for a week at a time. They'd feast and drink and dance and crash and wake up and keep going. Music, music, music. They wore beautiful clothes, old-world fashions because a lot of them were Spanish. They were generous and gracious and maybe a little dangerous. Anyway. Hope you can come."

"I'll be there," he said.

Erin looked at her fiancé. Bradley was drumming his fingers on the old wooden table.

"You're on," she said.

Bradley set his hat by the invitation, then collected the suit bag and disappeared into Hood's house.

"Congratulations again," said Hood.

"He's coming around, Charlie. The old ghosts are clearing out. He's growing up well."

"Good."

"He's nineteen."

"I hold him up to high standards," said Hood with a smile. "I demand the best for you."

"I'm a happy woman."

"You deserve it."

"You'll be doing the same thing soon."

"Is that right?"

"Yes. And thank God it's over with that prosecutor of yours. Ariel?"

"Don't diss Ariel."

"As your guardian angel, I must. She was too intense, too . . . what's the word, Charlie? *Prosecutorial*? No. You're going to meet your match one of these days. Don't be in a hurry, though. Be picky. Extremely picky."

"I like getting advice from twenty-two-year-olds."

"Thirty is not old, Charles."

Hood saw the small smile on Erin's face.

Bradley strode back into the courtyard, wearing a Los Angeles Sheriff's Department Explorer uniform. It was khaki and slightly baggy for his athletic shape. The nameplate on his chest read JONES. He laid the garment bag back over the wall.

"They accepted me into the Explorers program, Hood. Without your help or your recommendation or anything else from you. They took me because of who I am and what I can be someday. I start next week. Can you believe it? I'm gonna be one of the good guys. I'm proud of me."

"Congratulations. I mean it."

"Accepted."

Hood saw a brief darkness pass through Bradley and it reminded him of the darkness that would sometimes pass through the boy's mother. Bradley had loved her powerfully, and had despised Hood for intruding into their lives. Just a few weeks later, she had died in a holdup, shot by a boy named Kick. Bradley vowed to kill him. Kick had been murdered last year and Hood suspected Bradley had kept his word. Bradley had an alibi that the LAPD believed and Hood didn't—Erin.

"But I still think you took out Kick," said Hood. "And used Erin to cover your ass. And that is something we should acknowledge here, no matter what costumes we wear and who calls who friend."

In the silence, Hood felt the wind come up behind him, then roll on over like a wave, lifting wisps of dust on its way down the slope toward the desert floor. Bradley's hat started across the tabletop, but Hood caught it and sailed it to him.

"You tell me I'm a murderer and Erin is a liar. Why am I standing here? I told you this visit was a dumbass idea, sweetie."

"I guess," she said quietly. "Hood? Charlie? *He was with me.*"

"I hate the sight of you lying. I hate the sound of it."

"I'm going to be an LASD deputy, Hood. Get used to it. You don't own the department. You don't own me. I'll probably be your boss before you know it."

"I might have killed him, too," said Hood.

"You don't have the balls. Well, I've had enough of this beautiful desert for now. Erin, get in the car."

Bradley grabbed the suit bag and jumped the wall. Then he stopped and turned and smiled back at Hood. "But I still want you at the wedding, Charlie. I want a big expensive gift, too."

Erin stood by the table. She looked at Hood, then back at Bradley waiting by the car now, then at Hood again.

"We didn't deal those cards, Charlie. We played them."

Late that night, Hood was back in his courtyard, writing a letter to his mother and father. Only his mother would fully understand it, but she would read it out loud to her husband, a once warm and energetic man now nearly incapacitated by Alzheimer's disease. Hood's father loved getting the letters he only partially comprehended, and Hood did this mainly for him. He had bought high-cotton stationery and an expensive pen and a book of stamps. He thought before he wrote and tried to say what he thought.

Dear Mom & Dad,

I hope this note finds you well. I've moved into my new home here and I like it. I can see all the way to Mexico if I look south. Buenavista is kind of pretty, though dusty and very hot. Some of it is a sleepy Western town, with a beautiful old church and stone streets in old town, and saloons and outdoor markets, but it has Rite Aid and Dairy Queen and a big new hospital, too. In the old square up on the hill, you can hitch a horse or park a Porsche, and you see plenty of each.

Things have not gotten off to a good start. I don't mean to worry you, but I promised to be truthful. My second day here, our task force unit killed two young men. On my fourth day, one of our task force agents was abducted on American soil and I fear that he has

*been executed but fear more if he has not. This has
never been done before. Mom, Dad, there are headless
bodies piling up all around Mexico, thirty-four in the
last ten days. Nearly 6,000 people have lost their lives to
the cartel wars this year alone and the year is far from
over. Some are innocents—some are women and
children. Things are unraveling here. It's something
larger than the guns and the murders and the
mutilations. We're losing the rules of human beings. I
feel like there's a big storm coming, something terrible
and cleansing. In some very mysterious way, I feel
needed here. What this says about me I don't know. But
I do know I miss you. I hope this note helps in some
small way to bridge the miles between us. Give my love
to all my brothers and sisters.*

*Love,
Charlie*

Hood readied the envelope and put it in his pocket and slipped his
jacket over his gun and drove into Buenavista. This late the town
was quiet. Hood parked near the zocalo and walked past the church
and the fountain and civic buildings to the post office and dropped
the letter in the slot.

He was surprised to find a postcard in his post office box, likely
from his mother. It was a picture of Imperial Mercy Hospital taken
on a clear day under blue skies. On the back was a brief paragraph
about the state-of-the-art medical facility, and a handwritten note
that appeared to be slowly and painfully accomplished:

Dear Deputy Hood,

*We have some things to talk about. Mornings and nights
are best. My daughter vanished six weeks and one day
ago and my heart hurts much more than my body.
Please come.*

Mike

Hood pocketed the card and walked up the street where they had
chased Tilley and Victor Davis, past the shops and the galleries and
the market, all closed now. He stopped within the shadowed columns of the colonnade and looked at the Club Fandango, where a
doorman stood outside with his arms crossed and his feet spread as
if against a crowd of onrushers, but there was only a blond girl who
looked too young to get in and the man was shaking his head no.
Music pulsed faintly from inside, and the light behind the shaded
windows randomly changed colors and depth.

As Hood watched, three black Escalades rumbled up the stone
street and came to a stop in the No Parking zone at the entrance. They
were almost new and the windows were blacked out and the roof-
tops bristled with antennae. California and Mexico plates, he saw,
Sonora and Sinaloa. Two of the men who got out of the middle
vehicle were young and black-haired and trimly dressed. The two
others were older and larger and they dressed in looser clothes
meant to conceal. There were two women, young and stylish, hair
up and earrings dangling and high heels sounding on the street
stones, and the trim men offered their arms to steady them for the
walk to the door. A similar contingent exited the SUV farthest from
the entrance, and Hood heard a quick shriek as one of the women
stumbled and was caught by the other. Men commented and laughed.
No one left the first vehicle.

At the door, the young men had words with the doorman and the girl, then the doorman swung open a tall wooden door and the men went inside. Hood watched the girl say something to the doorman, then sling her bag over her shoulder and saunter to the nearest Suburban. Her hair flashed golden in the light of the streetlamp. A back door opened and an arm came from the black interior and helped the girl climb inside. Hood stood unmoving for half an hour and watched, though he didn't know for what. Then he walked back to his Camaro and drove home.

9

Mike Finnegan sat nearly upright in his ICU bed. Hood saw the twinkle of his eyes deep in the gauze. His TV was tuned to the morning news, where a meteorologist called for very warm weather in Imperial Valley, midnineties and humid with subtropical moisture.

"Why won't he use the word *hot*?" asked Finnegan. His voice came tightly from within his wired jaws. "Ninety-five is not very warm. It is hot."

"The power of suggestion."

"Yes, weathermen come to believe they influence the weather, like craps players with dice or you policemen with crime rates. Her name is Owens and she's twenty-one. Five seven, one fifteen, brown and gray. She didn't get my cramped little body and brain. She's beautiful and smart. Her mother died six years ago. A heart attack."

"Did Owens run away?"

"Vanished. She didn't run away. She didn't pack anything. She had just finished her junior year of college with a GPA of 4.25. She was working part-time at a bedroom store and volunteering at a

Skid Row soup kitchen in L.A. on Saturdays. When she disappeared, it made the local papers. I filed all the proper police reports."

"Was she living with you?"

"She had an apartment in Glendale."

"Boyfriend?"

"No. Some casual male friends. Nice young boys."

"You've talked to them?"

"Absolutely. No calls. No ransom demand. No contact whatsoever. . . . I read about the mishap in Buenavista. Two days after you get here, boom—the body count jumps by two. Gustavo Armenta? I shuddered when I read his name in the paper, then I thought, no, certainly he can't be related to Benjamin of Gulf Cartel fame. But then again, he certainly could be."

Hood considered Finnegan. The patient in the next bed lay intubated and unconscious. The other bed in the three-bed pod was empty. Hood used the remote and turned up the volume on the news a little.

"Why would you shudder?"

"In anticipation of vengeance."

"Gustavo was his son."

"Amazing how little we know of the Zetas."

"What do you know of them?"

"Only what I read. Paramilitary. Magnificently armed. Lavishly cruel. Heads over here, bodies over there. I wonder what they dream about. I'd sure keep a weather eye for myself and my task force brethren, too. Benjamin's honor will demand vengeance for his son. Blowdown. I like the name."

Hood listened to Finnegan's clear and sometimes animated voice. He liked pronouncing words. Hood studied the bedside cart. On the top shelf were three good stacks of hardcover books—history, biography, current events, science and technology, *Dog Cartoons,* and a novel that Hood was pretty sure had won a big literary prize last year. The second shelf of the cart and the bottom were filled with neat piles of newspapers. One pile was the *New York Times,* the other the *Los Angeles Times,* the third stack the *Imperial Valley Press.*

"Do you know how tiring it is to hold a hardcover book in one hand, up high enough to read because you can't raise or lower your head? Then move the book back and forth to read the lines because you can't move your head back and forth? Then set it down and struggle just to turn a page, then lift it back up? I do not recommend it, Deputy."

"What are you doing down here in the desert if Owens went missing in Los Angeles?"

"She called me five nights ago. She was sobbing. She said she was sorry for putting me through this. I only demanded one thing—an address. It's just inside the *Secret Wars of the CIA* volume on top there. Get it."

Hood moved around the bed to the cart and lifted the cover of the book. The address was written on a Hamburger Hamlet bar napkin: 181 Skylar Road, El Centro.

"And you were on your way there from L.A. when the tire on your pickup truck blew?"

"Exactly. Go to that address. Tell her what happened to me. Tell her she is loved beyond her wildest dreams. *Beyond* them. Don't try to get her to come here. She will not do anything unless she wants to. She's always had a mind one hundred percent her own."

Hood took the napkin and slid it into his coat pocket. "Why do you care what the Zetas dream about?"

"In dreams, men are uncontested. They're free. A man alone with his soul is pure man. Oh, very revealing what he dreams. Human nature on display. Did you dream last night?"

"Not that I remember."

Finnegan chuckled softly. "They say that both God and the devil can place dreams within a sleeping human. They say it is done less often than you would think. It's risky because they don't know how a man will react to it. A dream can be rejected, like an organ. Somewhat prosaically, they call a dream placed within a sleeping human, well, a placement."

"Who calls it that?"

Finnegan lifted his right hand, indicating the book cart. "Oh, some writer in some book in some century in some language. It's impossible to keep everything straight anymore. It's all just conjecture, isn't it? No man has seen God. No man has seen Lucifer. No man that I've ever talked to! It's just a useful way of looking at the world. And seeing into it."

Hood wondered if this was Finnegan's brain damage showing through. It was surprising how lucid and even humorous the little man was, given the severity of his injuries. Hood's sister had suffered a brain tumor as a teenager, and the first hint that she was afflicted were meandering, dislocated, illogical ruminations on her faith and religion. They happened with growing regularity. Then she had a seizure and they scanned her brain, and the surgery was done, and his sister never warbled on about God and his angels after that.

"How did you get my name and address?" he asked.

"I told you. Coleman Draper."

"When? How did you know him?"

"Last winter. He worked on my car."

Hood had investigated Draper, a reserve sheriff's deputy, for Internal Affairs, and discovered that the man had done some remarkably terrible things using his reservist's uniform, gun, and shield. Draper had owned a thriving German auto repair shop in Venice Beach.

"He told me of his association with the sheriffs. I told him that my daughter had disappeared. This was the first time Owens had done this, and I had reason to believe she was in Antelope Valley. He gave me your name as a contact at the LASD substation in Lancaster. He spoke highly of you."

"But Draper died sixteen months ago. He couldn't have given you my new address."

"No. I cajoled it out of a friend at the USPS. I have my contacts, Deputy, just like you have yours."

"What do you do for a living, Finnegan?"

"Bathroom products, wholesale. It's not as exciting as it sounds."

"Which manufacturer?"

"Most of them. I'm a broker."

"What's the name of your company?"

"Just Mike Finnegan Bath. I'm known. Bathroom products is a small world once you've been in it for a while. I'm in several Los Angeles Yellow Pages if that impresses you. So, has Benjamin Armenta demonstrated his displeasure with the Blowdown team?"

"Do you know Armenta?"

"We've never met."

"That's not your business, what happens with Blowdown."

"No. My business is Mike Finnegan Bath."

"And that's how you earned the ninety grand in the toolbox in your truck?"

"That's how."

Hood said nothing for a long moment. He saw a momentary blackness within the gauze before the reappearance of the twin glimmers.

"Much can happen in a blink, can't it, Deputy?"

"So, Owens vanishes with regularity?"

"This is the second time."

Hood looked at motionless Finnegan, listened to the TV news and the hum of the ICU and the voices coming from the nurses' station just outside the pod. He felt someone behind him and turned.

"Dr. Petty," said Finnegan. "You melt my plaster in that trim white doctor's coat."

"You have too many broken bones to be flirting with me. Good morning, Deputy."

"Doctor." Hood watched Beth Petty scan the bedside chart.

"I've managed to offend you again, Dr. Petty," said Finnegan. "I apologize."

"No offense taken, Mike. I enjoy flattery, even if it's from a bandaged-up little man whose face I can't see. Okay, as of one hour ago, you've got the resting pulse of a Golden Gloves boxer and the blood pressure of a healthy twenty-year-old. How do you do it?"

"Now who's flattering?"

Petty looked from the chart to Hood. She was almost his height and her dirty-blond hair was clipped back and her eyes were brown. "Deputy, I'll be two minutes here. Can you wait for me in the hallway outside the unit?"

"I'll wait."

Finnegan cleared his throat. "Thank you for talking to Owens, Deputy Hood. I think you know how important it is." Hood waited in the hall. Two uniformed U.S. marshals stood outside a room and gave him a hard look.

In the cafeteria, Hood and Petty got coffee and sat across from each other in plastic chairs at a small table by a window. The window was covered with sunscreen peeling at the edges. Two more marshals and two other men wearing suits and ear sets with speaker wires came in behind them and went straight to the coffee dispensers.

"So you don't know Finnegan?" she asked.

Hood shook his head. "He claims to have known a man I used to work with."

She looked at him, and Hood wondered what Finnegan had told her about Draper and Draper's death.

"He claims to have known Wyatt Earp, too," she said. "Claims to have had drinks with him in San Diego. Earp ran a saloon with a prostitute named Ida Bailey, says Mike. I checked it out and it's true. At least according to Wikipedia, it's true. Anyway, I talked to Gabe Reyes and he's found out not much at all about Mike Finnegan. Gabe ran his name and numbers through Tucson, Sacramento, and the FBI and they don't have anything criminal on him. He's never been fingerprinted. No social security number. No birth record or education records. All he really had was a California driver's license and a home address in L.A. Sacramento told Gabe that the license was genuine and current. And I'm sure you know that Mike had ninety thousand dollars in a toolbox in his pickup truck."

"How long can you keep him here?" asked Hood.

"As long as he can pay. I'm not supposed to know or tell you this, but his ninety grand is now down to thirty-five. It'll last about three more weeks if he doesn't require more surgery or exotic tests. Then he either comes up with more money or insurance or we transfer him over to rehab for a month on the county. At the rate he's going, he'll be ready for rehab in three weeks. He's tough as leather. I was doing an ER shift when they brought him in that morning. I stabilized him and assisted the surgeons who set the broken legs and arm, wired the jaw, and repositioned the cheekbones. We fitted him with the cranial rods and collar because two neck vertebrae showed fractures. We didn't do anything with his broken ribs—four fractures, thank goodness. The big worry was his skull—two fractures, deep and long on the X-rays. We peeled a portion of his scalp and stapled his skull, loosely. There has to be some give if the edema gets bad. We loaded him with antibiotics and steroids, and so far, no infection and no swelling. Well, very little swelling. That man was busted up something bad, Deputy. I didn't expect to hear a peep out of him for three or four days, and now, well, you've seen him in action. He rarely sleeps. If someone is in the room and conscious, he talks to them. If not, he reads. Those are all library books you saw in there. He talked two day nurses into making a run for him, gave them a list of books he wanted. He offered them each a hundred dollars for their time, but they didn't take it. He keeps telling me how hungry he is, wants us to cut his jaws free so he can eat. He's slurping down the liquid diet like you wouldn't believe."

Hood tried adding up all of this but couldn't even get ballpark.

"Oh," said Beth Petty. "There was a bullet lodged in his face, behind the left cheekbone, below the eye. It looked like it had been in there quite a while. We cut it out. I gave it to Gabe Reyes."

"Small caliber, large?"

"You really are a cop, aren't you? Can't a bullet in a man's face just be a bullet?"

"Yes."

"I'm sorry. My father was a cop. He . . ."

Hood waited for elaboration but got none. "Where?"

"San Diego."

He nodded and looked at the doctor, then out the window. The morning was bright, and still early enough for shadows. On the patio outside were tables with built-in metal umbrellas, but the only diners were blackbirds pecking at a syrup tub on an abandoned breakfast plate.

"Why all the uniforms here?" asked Hood.

"To protect bad guys from other bad guys. The uniforms are federal and so are the suits. The bad guys are cartel heavies. There's a deal between the U.S. and the Mexican governments. We treat their VIPs because the Mexican hospitals don't have the facilities. We do level one trauma here, the only hospital for a hundred miles. It's hugely profitable for us, I hear. But there's a lot of security involved. There was an incident."

"Incident?"

"A man with a gun, a criminal record, and a cartel affiliation. There was a rival cartel captain up in the ICU where Mike is now. No shots fired—security did its job. You probably didn't hear anything. Imperial Mercy does a good job of keeping things upbeat and quiet. We have a PR staff for that, actually. And of course the feds don't say much to anybody but each other. There's talk of new security here—scanners and wands, like an airport."

Hood looked at the four men across the room.

"I'm sorry about what happened over in old town," she said. "Were you there?"

Hood nodded but said nothing.

"Just like Dad," said Beth Petty.

"It was one of those situations where everybody does their jobs and an innocent man dies anyway. Maybe like the ER."

"Completely none of my business. I'm sorry. I could *never* get anything out of Dad, either. I think it scarred me for life. Terribly." She smiled and blushed. "So I keep trying."

"I'll talk to you anytime, Dr. Petty."

"Beth."

"Charlie. But watch what you ask for. You get me going and I'll make Mike Finnegan seem quiet."

Her smile was tentative, then full. "What *about* that little dude?"

10

A small padded envelope arrived in the U.S. mail that afternoon, addressed to Blowdown. The senders had the correct task force field office location in El Centro. It contained a DVD.

Hood, Ozburn, and Bly sat in their small conference area with the bad air conditioner and the TV and DVD player. Ozburn dialed his cell phone while Bly fed the disc into the machine and pressed PLAY.

A warehouse maybe, one wall visible in deep background, no windows, the light fluorescent, chilly and bright.

Jimmy strapped into a chair, wrists taped tightly to the armrests, fingers red and bloated.

Jimmy, eyes wide at the camera and sweating hard as someone stepped into the picture—a man in a Halloween werewolf mask and pliers in one gloved hand who roughly lifted one of Holdstock's swollen fingers above the others. The werewolf mask was blue-faced and black-haired. Then the camera zoomed to steel teeth on a fingernail. Hood watched. What he saw and heard scalded through him like a dose of venom and it briefly left him short of breath.

In a break between Jimmy's inhuman screams Hood could hear Ozburn talking softly into his cell phone.

The government Bell landed ninety minutes later in a patch of desert behind the task force office, blowing sand into an opaque fog from which emerged four men. They leaned low and single file beneath the rotors as Hood watched through a window. He recognized ATFE agents Soriana and Mars from his Blowdown training.

Soriana threw open the door of the task force office and marched inside. Mars followed him, carrying an oversize leather briefcase strapped over a narrow shoulder. It was heavy. Soriana introduced government consultant Dan Litrell from Washington, and Baja state police sergeant Raydel Luna. Litrell was red-haired and freckled and looked to Hood like an athlete. His handshake was powerful. Luna was taurine, both tall and large, with a thick neck and rounded shoulders and bowlegs. His head was shaved and tanned to the very top, where the hair was tapered up to form a short black mesa. His temporal and jaw muscles were pronounced. He shook Hood's hand softly and his smile was not a smile and he said nothing, then turned his black eyes on Janet Bly.

They brought in chairs, and everyone but Luna fit around the small conference room table. Luna stood in a corner like a punished schoolboy or a minor deity. The air conditioner wheezed loudly and produced a small amount of cool air. The men took off their jackets, and Janet Bly put her thick brown hair up under an ATFE field cap.

Mars produced a small digital recorder and placed it in the middle of the table and turned it on. He established time and location and participants, but Hood noted that he said nothing about Raydel Luna.

"Look, Sean," said Soriana. "You start us off with the Blowdown buy at Guns a Million. Just walk us through all that because it sets the table for the rest of it. I'm going to record this whole meeting and I'm ready to roll when you are."

Ozburn told them the story up to the arrival of the Polaroids, which he then displayed. In his biker's vest and black T-shirt he looked like a roadhouse gambler dealing poker. Then on to the DVD. The seven law enforcers watched the DVD in silence. Not one word. Hood thought that by him watching, Holdstock had to feel the pain anew, though this was preposterous.

There was a moment of quiet after the last of Jimmy's screams was cut short by the cameraman.

"We need to go get him back," said Bly. "They'll kill him if we don't."

"We can't invade Mexico," said Soriana. "We have to go through diplomatic channels. This is our only way."

"Bullshit," said Ozburn.

"I second that," said Bly.

Hood said nothing, but he watched Mars tap his fingertips on the table.

"I had a long talk with the Homeland Secretary yesterday," said Mars. He was thin and pale and he looked to Hood like an undertaker. "I've never heard her so heated up. She talked to our consul in Mexico City, he talked to the State Department, he talked to anybody in the White House who would talk to him. They're not listening. Their hands are tied. Tied to each others', as happens in our republic. They can't rewrite international law for Jimmy Holdstock."

"But they can leave him to be tortured and murdered?" asked Bly.

"I'll be in Washington by late tonight," said Soriana. "We've got meetings with State and the Mexican Consul first thing tomorrow.

I'm still on hold with the Senate Foreign Relations Committee, but it's looking better."

"Go to meetings while Jimmy suffers and dies," said Bly. "I have a badge. I'm really tempted to shitcan it right now."

"What good would that do?" asked Litrell. "Even your conscience would lose, eventually."

Ozburn stood and pushed the VCR PLAY button, but as soon as the blue-faced werewolf appeared, he hit PAUSE, then OFF. Hood watched as two white SUVs with blacked-out windows rolled to a stop near the Bell.

"I'm not turning in my badge," Ozburn said. "And I'm not sitting on my hands while Jimmy's down there. So, bosses, what do you recommend?"

"You'll do exactly what we order you to do," said Mars. "ATF will not sanction cross-border measures. It's beyond our mandate. ATF follows the letter of the law. ATF will not set foot in Mexico until we are invited by the federal government of Calderón. Dan?"

"Ditto. You can't go there unless the Mexicans say you can. They will say no such thing. This breaks my heart. I remember Kiki Camarena and I will never forgive our system for not being able to go down and get him. Pray for the diplomats to work out something with Mexico. Calderón is different. He is committed. Please be patient. Please believe in our country and our system."

Soriana crossed his arms and sat back. "Sean, Janet, Charlie—I hope we're clear on this. You can't go south on us. Literally and figuratively. It's not set up to work that way. I need assurances now, ladies and gentlemen. Something audible for my superiors. Rules are rules."

"Aye aye, sir," snapped Ozburn.

"Yeah, yeah, yeah," muttered Bly.

"Yes," said Hood.

Mars looked at each of them in turn, then turned off the recorder. He placed it in his coat pocket rather than back into the briefcase from which it had come. He stood and hefted the briefcase onto the table and left the room without it. Soriana shook hands with the Blowdown soldiers and walked out.

Hood watched through a window as the two men strode to the helo. But they boarded one of the white SUVs, then the vehicle spun a dusty U-turn and bounced stiffly on its struts across the desert toward the road.

At this, Litrell rose and went to the window and watched the SUV drive away, then he turned to face the others. "Raydel?" he asked.

Luna nodded and stepped to the table. He unzipped the main compartment of the briefcase and looked inside, then at each of the Blowdown teammates. His voice was clear and sharp.

"The Zetas have Holdstock outside of Mulege," he said. "They will keep him alive for another forty-eight hours. Then they will behead him. I have men I can trust and men I cannot trust. If we do this, you will have to kill and keep from being killed. All I can promise you is someone's death."

Luna reached into the briefcase and brought out a clear plastic freezer bag with a semiautomatic handgun inside it. Five magazines had settled to the bottom. He set it on the table near Ozburn and then likewise set other guns before Bly and Hood. Hood looked down at the Glock, a simple, dependable Austrian killing tool of polymer and steel.

"No numbers," said Litrell.

Luna continued to pull dark treasures from the briefcase: six fifty-count boxes of forty-caliber ammunition, three used-looking passports, three fat stacks of used U.S. twenties held with rubber bands.

"When do we leave?" asked Bly.

"Now."

"We'll need clothes and toiletries."

"They are in the helicopter. We can fly almost to Cataviña. After that, the helicopter will draw suspicion. We need to go now. But before we leave, you need to understand that this is my operation in my country and I am in charge. There will be no dispute or discussion. There may be unusual circumstances. I am supported by some powers within my government and hated by others. Mexico is in a state of change. Mexico is a state of change."

Luna stood before Ozburn. He looked him over from toe to head, and Hood saw him peer into Ozburn's eyes. Then Luna did likewise with Bly, and when it was Hood's turn, he looked back into Luna's hard black eyes and he nodded but didn't look away.

"Sean, Janet, Charlie," said Litrell. "The Calderón government knows but it does not know. Washington knows but it does not know. They have taken an extraordinary step. You are the first. If you are successful, it will mean something even beyond the life of Jimmy Holdstock, maybe a new way of fighting this ugly war. If you fail, you will be denied and denied absolutely. Mexico and the United States have washed their hands of you. Those hands are already dry. Good luck."

A few minutes later, the Bell engine wailed and Hood felt the machine corkscrewing backward up into the sky, felt the untethering of his body and his soul from the laws of gravity and of men.

II

He watched the rusted brown earth of Baja California scrolling under the chopper, rimmed by a vast curved horizon that defied measure. He could not tell by looking if this was an expired land or one still waiting to be born. There were occasional farms and there were sandy washes squiggling down from the hills where water had once raced, and the farmhouses had corrugated metal roofs and the tiny outbuildings huddled under stands of paloverde and mesquite. The dirt roads were etched in pale paths, and Hood saw only one vehicle moving there, drawing a cloud of dust behind it and moving so slowly, it looked to be not moving at all.

The Bell put down in the desert ten miles from Cataviña, just east of the Baja spine, a few miles south of the 30th parallel. Two rental cars were waiting. Hood and Luna took the lead. Luna drove the two-lane fast, passing the old cars of the natives and the ponderous travel trailers of the gringos, and he passed an eighteen-wheel semi on a blind curve negotiable by faith alone. Hood looked out at the boulders and ocotillo and cardón. A long red snake with its black head high off the ground whipped across Highway 1 in front of them and Hood looked over his shoulder and saw it serpentining over the shoulder gravel toward an outcropping of rocks. Behind the snake came the Ford containing Ozburn and Bly.

Half an hour later, Luna and Bly played table tennis in the rec room of the La Pinta Hotel in Cataviña while Hood and Ozburn inquired about lodging. The hotel was full, as they knew it would be, but they raised their voices and complained loudly, establishing themselves as gringo tourists who were now inconvenienced by a long drive south to Guerrero Negro.

The boulder-strewn beauty of Cataviña gave way to an incline at the top of which lay a great dry lake bed. It stretched on for miles, flat and hard beneath the blue sky. Gradually the barren landscape became generous again and Hood looked out at the sharp yucca and the spine clusters of the cholla deceptively backlit by the lowering sun to appear downy, and the elephant trees squatting among the boulders. The highway gradually lowered as they entered the Vizcaino Desert, seething with wind, immense. The thermometer read ninety-three degrees and the road ahead of them became a wavering mercurial slick. Two vultures ate at a roadside carcass, and as the car approached, one hopped cumbersomely away and the other withdrew its poached pink head from the spoil and blinked. Hood saw buttes rising flat in the east and for a moment he could see the Pacific Ocean, then it was gone.

They crossed from Baja California to Baja California Sur just above Guerrero Negro. The Blowdown team found lodging there at the Nationale. Luna checked in later and ordered food to his room while the three Americans demanded the six-top in the middle of the dining room and spoke loudly through the dinner, as suggested by Luna. They continued loudly in the cantina after dinner and the men took turns dancing with Janet, her movements infused with anger. She was strong-bodied and pretty when she smiled, but there was no smiling at all that night and Hood thought how easy it was for them to look like miserables straining for fun.

In the morning they drove south into the oasis town of San Ignacio. The date palms planted by Spaniards nearly three centuries ago rose dense and cooling from the arroyo floor, and Hood could see the rolling hills of figs and grapes and oranges. There was a breeze and on it Hood smelled the citrus and the sweet green smell of fresh water.

"The water comes from a river and the river is underground," said Luna. These were the first casual words he had offered since Hood had gotten into the car with him the day before. The tone of his voice implied great volume unused. "It comes to the surface here and there is a dam."

"It's tranquil," said Hood. He looked out at the thatched-roof dwellings and the tree-lined plaza and the magnificent domed mission rising above the palms.

"It is the last tranquility you will see. On this assignment."

"Are you hopeful, Sergeant?"

"What does it matter?"

"Hope counts."

"Does hope or lack of hope cause anything that happens?"

"I think it can."

"But maybe this is a superstition, that men can influence events by what they believe. The gambler. The priest. That ills can be remedied by a hoped outcome. That American hope can be expressed through power, and that this power is deserved and eternal."

"Luck comes to the hopeful. Luck comes to those who are ready for it. I've seen it happen."

"Oh, we will be ready, Mr. Hood. You see the mission? Its walls are four feet thick and made from lava blocks. The blocks were not made with hope but with the opposite of hope. They were made with fear that they might not last."

Hood thought about this. "That's fine, Sergeant. But I'm going to hope we can get Jimmy out of here and back across the border alive. I'm going to hope that real hard and I'm not going to stop hoping it until it happens."

Luna cracked the smile that was not a smile but did not take his eyes off the road. "A discussion of hope is a small thing. If you want the killing down here to stop, you must stop the guns. Simple."

"That's why I'm here."

"My country is being torn apart by yours. America supplies the guns and the need for the guns. I don't understand your people. You are insatiable for power and luxury. You are insatiable for improvement. You are insatiable for drugs. You take drugs to wake up and drugs to fall asleep. You take drugs in the morning to become alert and drugs at night to sleep. You take drugs to have sex and drugs to not have children. You take drugs to keep your legs from twitching. For your children it is an easy step to the pleasure drugs that come up through Mexico. But we of the police cannot defeat this way of thinking. We cannot eradicate your degeneracy. So it's the guns. You need to stop the guns."

"But you need to stop the dope, Sergeant. The cartels crave the guns and the money just like our people crave the coke and smack. Your poisons are made for our young. Your people profit from what you yourself admit you can't change. And if you want to use the word *degenerate* you can apply it to the cartels and the Zetas. Mankind doesn't suddenly become pure south of the border."

Luna looked at Hood, then back to Highway 1. "So," he said. "This."

Hood waited, but Luna said nothing more. "Yep. This."

Near Santa Rosalia they pulled off onto a dirt road that led back into a narrow valley. There were white boulders and cardón cactus reaching sedately into the air, and their arrangement was harmonious enough to have been planned. The breeze had become a steady wind now, and across this vista dervishes of sand whirled with sudden fury, then collapsed. Hood and Luna came to a gate made of barbed wire and old branches grayed by the sun. A uniformed officer walked it open, his pant cuffs trailing in the dust.

Hood turned to see the second car follow. When they came over a rise, he saw the low pink stucco building at the end of the road. There were four satellite dishes and various antennae sprouting from the roof. And there were six beaten white sedans and the six black-and-white radio cars parked without order in the circular dirt driveway.

Luna waited for Ozburn and Bly, then led the Blowdown unit into the building. There was one main room and it was heavy with cigarette smoke and filled partly with uniformed police and the rest with what Hood took to be plainclothes officers. He counted twenty. They sat in folding metal chairs around two long tables set end to end in the middle of the room, and when the Americans came in, they all pushed back their chairs in a clamor of metal on concrete and stood. The men wearing hats doffed or tipped them to Janet. The smokers crushed out their cigarettes in ashtrays and on the floor. Luna introduced the Americans, then rattled off a few sentences of such rapid Spanish that Hood caught only a few words. There was another table against a far wall, with two ancient spiral-corded landline phones and charging stations for six satellite phones, and a computer, monitor, printers, faxes, and a large tilting stainless coffee percolator with the spigot near the bottom.

Along another wall were racks of M14 and M16 rifles and Mossberg 12-gauge combat shotguns. The older M14s were fitted with night scopes and the M16s and shotguns had flashlights mounted on their barrels. There were vests and night-vision headsets and binoculars hung from hooks on the pegboard wall, and dozens of canisters of ammunition stacked knee-high on the floor. Hood studied the gear and thought of his tour in Iraq and wondered if he was drawn to the hardware of death or if it was drawn to him. *We cannot eradicate your degeneracy.* The wind lashed the windows and he looked outside to see a nearby paloverde break into a shiver of spines and small green leaves.

One of the uniforms brought over four folded chairs, and Luna and the Americans sat. A slender gray-haired man in a desert camo suit rose and handed out maps. Hood studied his. Mulege was a village of six thousand. It sat beside the Rio Mulege. It had an airstrip and a museum and even a U.S. consular building. It was one hundred sixty-one kilometers from here.

Hood looked down at the ink-heavy copy, noted the hand-drawn rectangle with the black X marked through it, south of town, five kilometers from the shrine of La Virgen Maria. The gray-haired man discussed the map first in Spanish, then in English. He said the black X was an abandoned hacienda where the American was being held captive. When he said this, he looked one at a time at Hood and Ozburn and Bly, and Hood saw gravity in his eyes. The man explained that the crosshatched pathways around the hacienda were dirt roads passable by four-wheel-drive vehicles. None of them passed within two kilometers of the hacienda, he said. Lookouts would be deployed throughout the area, but there was no way of knowing where, so the sooner they stopped the vehicles and proceeded on foot, the better.

Luna stood and spoke again in Spanish, then English. Just after sunset, five of their men would set out in two cars along the north dirt road. They would use their global positioning units to halt four kilometers from the hacienda, then continue on foot. They would have one satellite phone. He named the five. Eighteen minutes later, five men in two cars would begin their approach from the west on the dirt road accessible from Highway 1. They would end their drive within three kilometers of the hacienda and continue on foot. They would carry the battering ram and one phone. He named these five, too. When they were one kilometer away, they would travel only on their hands and knees and stomachs. Simultaneously, another group of four would drive the south road to within two kilometers before setting out on foot with one satellite phone to communicate with the rest. They would go to the ground one kilometer out. He named these.

Hood watched and listened and he thought that Luna looked like Jimmy, the same big neck and shoulders and the stout bowlegs. And Hood saw the shiny smooth mounds of muscle of Luna's neck and jaws and temples all shaved clean and he thought that the man was very much like a bull in his strength and density and great available power. Jimmy had that, too, he thought, and in him it was tempered by a full and willing heart, and that was why Hood would use all of his tools, even lowly hope, to keep Holdstock from being tortured to death on alien soil at the age of twenty-six.

Luna said that he and the Americans would drive in from the east, then travel by foot and then by hands and knees. They would arrive ahead of the others by a few minutes—it would be ten P.M. by then. Luna would kill the guard at the generator and disable the generator and when the lights went out, they would take the house. The mission was to get the American out alive, he said. He said that certain things were in their favor: surprise, the cover of the wind, the new moon of two nights ago, the satellite phones for communication, the brand-new mounted lights on the rifles and the shotguns, the fact that the Zetas might be tired and perhaps drunk. He said certain things were not in their favor: The American might already be dead, the distances they would have to cover would leave them vulnerable to the lookouts, they didn't know how many Zetas were there though his information said eight, they were unfamiliar with the hacienda and couldn't know where the fire would come from or exactly where the American was being held.

Luna ordered first in Spanish, then in English, that they would take any man prisoner who cooperated fully and they would kill the rest without hesitation. A human silence rippled through the room, but there was the wind outside.

Hood wondered where the other two men would be. He looked at Ozburn and Bly. As if reading his mind, Luna said that Officer Blandon would be staying here to guard the armory and the communications gear, and Dr. O'Brien would be here also, waiting to treat the wounded and do what he could for the American.

"His name is Jimmy," said Hood. "Jimmy Holdstock."

"Jimmy Holdstock," murmured someone.

"Right on," said Ozburn.

Luna now left his place and slowly walked around the table. He looked at every face. Then he softly spoke another command in Spanish. Hood heard it clearly and it surprised him not for what it demanded but for what it implied.

He watched as the Mexican officers shook their heads and grumbled and cursed. They reached for their belts and pockets and deposited their cell phones on the table before them. Luna said something, and each man arranged his cell phone faceup directly in front of him.

The gray-haired man in the fatigues moved around the table with a dirty pillowcase and he and Luna watched them drop their phones into the bag. A uniformed cop with blue eyes and a drooping mustache caught Hood watching him, and his face colored in shame.

I have men I can trust and men I cannot trust.

• • •

Hood carried the combat 12-gauge slung over his right shoulder. The wind nudged him forward. The sky above was black and clear enough that the stars stood in relief, some near and some far and some in a dense middle belt. The night-vision headset was hot and tight and it cast the world in the same green highlights through which he had seen the murderous alleys of Anbar province. Hood listened to the rhythms of his boots on the gravel and to his breathing, and he felt the grit of the headset against his face and he could hardly believe he was doing this again.

They trod across the desert four abreast and fifty feet apart, well off the rough dirt road, picking their way around the boulders and the cholla and watching for rabbit holes and western diamondbacks. Sand drifts passed them from behind, then settled, then rose and hurried past them and settled again. To Hood's right was Bly and beyond her Ozburn. They advanced methodically and Hood sensed their eagerness. To his left, Luna moved through the desert with a lightness that belied his size. He carried an M16 muzzle down in his right hand, and over his left shoulder hung a compound bow with an attached quiver of six arrows. They were big-game arrows, tipped with cross-blade heads with razor facets designed for penetration and the letting of blood, and in the green-limned world of the night-vision goggles, they glittered like huge emeralds at the ends of the shafts.

Hood topped a rise and the hacienda came into view. It was a kilometer away. The main house was large, two stories, and made of adobe brick. It was lit inside and out. There was a barn and three outbuildings visible in barnyard lights that twinkled in the wind. These all sat on flat ground in a small valley from the edges of which rose steep hillsides covered in mosaics of enormous pale boulders grouted with black desert scrub. Hood glassed the hacienda and saw two SUVs parked beneath a metal sunshade. There was a compact car tucked close to the barn, and three dirt bikes leaning against what had once been a chicken coop. The door of the coop stood open in the wind.

Just a few hundred yards away stood the spotter. Hood looked to Luna, but Luna had already seen him. Hood tossed a rock at Bly and pointed out the spotter and Bly turned toward her right. Luna signaled Hood to down and stay, and Hood passed this on to Bly, and she to Ozburn. Up on his elbows Hood could see Luna crawling forward on hands and knees, the bow and the M16 strapped crosswise to his back in a lethal X.

Through the binoculars, Hood saw that the spotter was young and slender. He wore a baseball cap backward. A satellite phone was clipped to his belt, and the blued steel of his AK-47 shone slightly in the faint moonlight. The collar of his black shirt flapped in the wind and his pant cuffs rippled.

Hood saw Luna moving slowly through the desert, watched the distance between the men close by inches, wondered at the punishment being taken by the sergeant's hands and knees, wondered at his slowness and his silence in the wind. In the night far beyond, a shooting star dropped and crumbled and vanished. Then another. To Hood they appeared to be sliding down the last plane of creation, but he knew they were close.

Half an hour later, Luna stopped and very carefully sat back on his heels and unraveled his weapons. He was a man in slow motion. He set the assault gun on the ground. He unslung and brought up the bow and pulled an arrow from the quiver and notched it. He drew the string, and the bow arms flexed acutely and the pulleys turned and when Luna rocked upright, his string hand was already steady at his jaw. Hood felt the wind gust, then subside. Through the glasses he saw the squeeze of Luna's finger on the trigger. The spotter cocked his head alertly, then turned toward Luna and collapsed. The arrow had flickered across the desert. Within seconds, Luna was standing over the man, and Hood saw the big knife in his hand, but Luna knelt and put the blade tip to the ground while he genuflected. Then he raised the knife into the air and motioned to the others.

At 10:10 P.M., Luna shot the generator guard, the arrow fixing him to the chair in which he sat, and when the guard looked down to the fletching at his chest, he fell to one side and the chair fell with him. Hood watched Luna slip through the night to the garage and turn off the generator. When the lights in the ranch house flickered out, they attacked. Hood saw the south team streaming toward the front door with a battering ram. The north team at the rear breached the windows, and Hood could hear glass breaking and shouting and gunshots popping from inside. He heard automatic gunfire from the west side opposite him.

He switched on the mounted flashlight and followed Luna and Ozburn into the garage. Jimmy's Ford Five Hundred stood dust-covered at the far end. There was a door leading into the ranch house. Luna lowered a shoulder and shattered the door and sprawled to the floor inside. Hood leveled his shotgun for cover and when he saw the two gunmen, he blew one off his feet with a scorching boom, and Ozburn and Bly dropped the other with bursts from their M16s, but as they fell, two more emerged from the darkness of the house, and Hood and Ozburn and Bly killed them, too. They advanced through the mudroom and down a hallway to the spacious black of the kitchen, into the far end of which suddenly backed two more Zetas, firing in retreat. When the pistoleros turned into the beam of his flashlight, Hood watched their guns and not their faces and as the barrels swiveled toward him, he unleashed the 12-gauge again while Ozburn and Bly fired, too, and two roaring seconds later when Hood stepped over the bodies, his night-vision goggles were so heavily splattered he shucked them to the floor. They ran down another wide hallway and into the great room lit faintly by moonlight through the high windows and by candles flickering above the tremendous stone fireplace, and there they met most of the west team clomping dazedly in from the far darkness, their flashlight beams skittering and jerking from the old wooden floorboards to the white adobe walls to the rough ceiling timbers of the cavernous room. Then three of the north team ran in from the rear of the house and joined the others roiling up the wide wooden stairs leading to the second story. As he ran the stairs three at a time, Hood heard furious engagement outside the ranch house to the south.

Hood crashed through a locked door. In the beam of his light he saw the bed pushed up against the wall and the bedsheet knotted to the headboard and trailing out the open window. A man holding on to the sheet looked at him through the window opening. Then the man's face dropped from sight, but his hand came up with a machine pistol and Hood blew the hand and the pistol outward into the night. At the window, he looked down and saw the man stumbling zigzag into the darkness, clutching his handless wrist at eye level. Hood heard more fury to the south and he could see the wavering orange edge of fire coming from the other side of the ranch house. He glided down the bedsheet to the ground and rounded the south corner. Two of the south team officers were down, engulfed in flames, barely moving. The other two, both uniformed officers, staggered backward and dropped their weapons, hands and elbows up as a geyser of fire drove them backward into the dark. The Zeta turned the flamethrower on Hood, but not in time. The man lifted off his feet as if yanked, and the flame roared skyward, then stopped. Hood smothered one of the uniforms with his body and then rolled him over into the desert sand. When he got up, he saw the other burned officer had recovered his weapon and now stood facing the pale desert from which ten men loped toward them.

Hood took cover behind one of the SUVs, racked the shotgun, and slid in four new shells. His hands felt thick and cold, but they obeyed his will. The burned officers retreated behind the other SUV, and Hood watched the Zetas closing steadily from a hundred yards out. He heard voices behind him and when he turned and looked up, he saw the glimmer of gun barrels from a second-story window. To his left, Bly and Ozburn slid into position behind a slouching concrete fountain.

The Zetas came faster now, firing methodically. Hood pressed himself tight to the wheel of the vehicle. He heard the bullets clanking through the sheet metal and slapping against the house wall, and he heard the far-side tires blow, and when he looked over to the fountain, he saw the sand jetting up and lead-smeared divots pocking the concrete. He lurched from his lie and hit the ground hard on his elbows. The Zetas were fifty yards out. Two of them carried flamethrowers and they sent intermittent fire through the dark for effect and when the first of them was forty yards away, Hood aimed the short-barreled shotgun three feet above his head and squeezed off the shot. The man screamed and dropped the flamethrower and jammed his hands to his face, then fell to his knees in the sand. The Zetas came at full run. To Hood's left, Bly and Ozburn opened fire. Hood heard the barrage from the second-story windows behind him. Four Zetas were down and the remaining six pulled up and stopped and Hood saw them veer away from the gunfire and each other. Luna and four of his men emerged from the desert on one side of them, and three more uniformed cops corralled the Zetas from the other. For ten seconds, Hood on his belly watched as the last attackers were shot to ribbons in the three-way slaughter.

They found Holdstock in one of the outbuildings, a former smokehouse that reeked of meat and smoke. He was ankle-ironed to an ancient ring set into the adobe wall and the chain was just long enough to allow him to lie on a soot-caked mattress on the floor. He lay on his back, everything but his head covered by a filthy blue blanket. He looked up at Janet Bly's flashlit face, theatrical in the darkness, and Hood saw him smile as the tears flooded from his eyes. He started to move, then stopped. Someone pulled back the blanket. Jimmy's hands rested on his naked chest, the stumps of his de-nailed fingers and thumbs bloated with infection and vibrating with pain.

12

Dear Mom & Dad,

I apologize for not writing the last two days. I won't go into details, but we were part of a diplomatic mission south of the border. We were successful at great cost. Jimmy is back with us, but eighteen are dead—all fourteen narcotraficantes and four Mexican policemen. Jimmy was treated very badly, but he's going to heal up. Blowdown departed Mexico that very night and left it to Baja authorities to make some sense of it. I'm trying to make my own sense of it. At a certain point, fighting is your only choice, and I brought myself to that point willingly. I now own a full soldier's soul, something I never quite earned in my months in Iraq. I don't know what the cost will be to me. Right now I am numb and very tired. I've been here for ten days now, and they have been the bloodiest and deadliest days I've ever seen. I still don't know if I'm shaping my life or if my life is shaping me. I suppose most of us never answer this question finally. I met a little man who claimed that God can put dreams into the minds of sleeping people and the devil can, too. But they don't ever know how the person is going to react to the dream. That stuck with me though I'm not sure why. Maybe because I used to believe that God and the devil are in competition for us. I believed that when I was a kid, anyway. Or maybe because I've had some very strange dreams lately! I continue to believe that I belong here. What this says about me, I honestly don't know. Yet.

Love to all,
Charlie

13

"This makes my heart glad, Marcos," I say.

"Yes, Mr. Pace."

We're in production for one thousand units of the Love 32. Today is Friday, August tenth—one year almost to the day since Pace Arms made its last gun. I watch from the third-floor security window as the machinists and assemblers and finish men punch in. They were rounded up by Marcos. Some have come from as far as Mexico City to take this work. I know most of them from before. They're skilled and honest and hardworking men, and mostly undocumented, too, so I don't have to pay them much. As I watch them file into the manufacturing bay, I realize how much I've missed them. I don't think a single one of them genuinely likes me, but that's not the point.

I've decided to start with just the night shift—four to midnight—which will allow our activity to blend in with the other assembly plants in this manufacturing zone. We'll increase to two shifts once the bugs are out. I say *bugs* somewhat guardedly because these production lines have a proven track record for speed and efficiency. During my finest year as production manager, we turned out 139,554 weapons. Recalls were slight. And Marcos has fielded the cream of the crop, just as I asked him to.

"I have work," says Marcos, turning for the stairs. Marcos was happy to commence work again, but since learning that our thousand-unit lot is to be produced without serial numbers or an identifying gunmaker's symbol of any kind, he has been somewhat subdued. He knows it's illegal. He knows there are bad people waiting for these lovingly crafted products. He knows that they are paying his salary.

I sit in my third-floor office to enjoy a few minutes of nostalgia. I can hear the muffled sounds of sidearm manufacture two floors down, and the loopy Mexican music the crew always plays. As always, the building smells of cut steel and bluing agents and gun lubricants and ignited gunpowder. I think of coming here as a little boy, seeing Mom and Dad in their professional worlds—Mom in marketing and Dad in contracts. I think of Uncle Chester, too, immense in his cream linen suits, pink-cheeked and small-fingered, his head a bald immensity. I remember the respect he demanded and got, and I wish that of all the Pace family traits, I could have gotten his confidence and gravity instead of the general squirrelishness with which I try to make do. Yes, it was pure Ron Pace to faint when Herredia slaughtered the five men down in Mexico. No, it was not the first time I've fainted at the sight of gore: viewing a car wreck when I was ten, seeing a neighbor saw off two fingers at his garage workbench when I was twelve, watching a lung surgery video as part of a smoking prevention program when I was fourteen. Etc. I faint but I do not look away. This is my smidgen of bravery. The incident in Mexico was by far the worst.

I enjoy the view through our freshly washed windows—one of the first things I did after getting the start-up capital from Bradley and Herredia was to recontract with the janitorial service. So right now, just after four o'clock on a hazy warm Orange County afternoon, I can see South Coast Plaza rising profitably out of what was once a lowly bean field, and I can see the graceful maze of the freeways and boulevards and interchanges, and of course to the west I see the sacred holy ground of the evangelical Trinity Broadcasting Network, rocked recently by a scandal of homosexuality. I feel bad for the scandalized minister because I know what it's like to be hated by the media and a large portion of the public. And I thought his broadcasts were sometimes moving though often corny, too.

And of course I think of Sharon Rose Novak, to be married tomorrow at noon in Newport Beach. It's fitting that Pace Arms is born again and Sharon Novak dies a symbolic—to me—death within the same twenty-four-hour period.

So I walk out to the lobby and sit where she has worked for the last five years and where she will continue to do so—I truly hope—after her Maui honeymoon, for many, many years to come.

Here is where she sits.

Here is where she works.

Sharon and I are almost exactly the same age. We were born on the same day of the same year. I'm actually two and one-half hours older. Soon after we discovered this coincidence, we began making lists of differences and similarities between us. It was a way to test astrological theory. Well, the list of differences got real long real fast, and there were not many things we had in common besides basic human nature. She is generous and I am selfish. She is outgoing and I'm reserved. She is open with her words and feelings and I am closed. She is ignorant of the past while I like knowing what has happened before. She hates making plans and I love making plans. She resists commitment and I'll commit to practically anything. She thinks astrology is total bullshit but I believe it has certain truthful aspects. So far as unusual things in common, we both love bagpipe music and loathe walnuts and we both constantly dream of having siblings though we are only children. And that's about it. A few weeks after she started working here, I told her I loved her. We were seventeen. I presented her with a brand-new, never-fired Pace Hawk autoloader chambered for the .22 Long rifle cartridge, arguably our finest gun. I had it engraved for her: *For Sharon, safe forever in the arms of Pace,* smug that the arms would be my own. It was in a presentation box. She heatedly scoffed at this and didn't really speak to me for almost half a year. I nearly cracked. Gradually, we became friends again and I was always very careful not to exhibit affection or desire of any kind though I'm sure these things showed through. I compensated with a tireless work ethic and what I thought was a haughty cool. I became aware of certain nicknames and gossip being circulated here at Pace Arms, mostly on the second and third floors, but I had to admit I deserved them. She kept the gun but never referred to it again. Sharon will be married in less than twenty-four hours and I still think she's the most delightful and desirable woman in the world as I know it.

It's nice to sit in her chair for a few minutes. Like walking a mile in someone else's shoes, though more comfortable. Here in her work area, I look at the pictures of her cat and a pop singer whose name I don't even know, and of course the snapshot of her fiancé. And when I finally stand up, I remind myself that it is time to let her go. It really is. This is not a new idea for me. As always I am wholly, utterly, spectacularly unenthused about it.

Down on the assembly line, I walk along with my hands folded behind my back, just watching the men work. Assembling weapons is difficult because the tolerances are unforgiving and most of the parts are small and rigid. It's hard on the eyes and on the back and neck. There's not much chatter. Pace Guns aren't really made on an assembly line at all, because eighty percent of the work on each firearm is done by one person, by hand. There are no moving lines. Each gun is built individually. It's more a craft than a job. Through the PA speakers plays a loud and oddly syncopated Mexican unrequited-love song that of course reminds me of Sharon.

When I go back upstairs to do some paperwork in my office, Sharon Rose Novak is sitting at her desk.

I actually do a double take. My jaw in fact drops.

"Don't say anything," she says.

She doesn't look at me. She's slumped down in the chair. She's looking down at the desk, and her arms are crossed and her pretty blond hair is hanging down and partially hiding one of the world's great faces.

"I said don't say anything."

"I didn't."

"Act like I'm not here."

"But you are here."

"Don't get literal with me. I don't need anyone or anything. I'm here and that's all. If you say one more word, I'm leaving."

I walk past her and go into my office. Half an hour later, I'm still sitting there at my desk and she walks in and sits where Bradley Smith had sat just a few fateful weeks ago. She's dressed in sweats and running shoes and a long-sleeved T-shirt with a peace sign on it. Her hair is a mess and her nose is as red as an apple, and her cheeks are flushed and her eyes are rimmed in pink. There's a smear of eyeliner between one eye and the cheekbone.

"What's going on down there?" she asks.

"We're in business again."

"We haven't made anything in over a year."

"The first twenty units will come off by the end of shift."

"Units of what?"

"Nothing you've seen. Nothing you know about."

"Where's all the paperwork, the bids and counters and best and finals?"

"That was all done with a handshake."

She looks at me with suspicion, then her eyes erupt with tears. "He left me a note. He said he couldn't do it. He said he loved me. He's driving to Colorado. My family is here from all over the country. His, too. We've got wedding gifts piled up in the extra bedroom. He said he couldn't do it. I am totally humiliated and I miss him so much."

I sit, stunned by the enormous turn of events. It takes me a moment to speak.

"Sharon. I'm . . . very sorry for you."

"Please don't say anything right now. All you can say is the wrong thing. Do you know what I feel like doing? This is terrible. But I feel like shooting him. I'm not sure if I want to shoot him all the way to death or not, but I want to put at least one bullet in him. I think I should wait until I've settled down to answer the death question. When I can think clearly."

"I know I'm not supposed to say anything, but don't shoot him. He's not worth ruining your life over."

"He's already ruined it."

"That's absolutely not true."

"I know it's not. But you weren't supposed to say anything."

"I'm going to say just one more thing, Sharon Rose."

"I hate my middle name and don't call me that ever again."

"Okay. Now, I won't say anything else, but *you* have to. You have to keep on talking. If you keep talking, your feelings will become clear. If your feelings are clear you can proceed to . . . um, well . . ."

"To where?"

"Checkout?"

She looks at me. I didn't know a human nose could become so red and shiny. It looks waxed. Above it and on either side, her eyes are blue lagoons.

"Marriage was my idea," says Sharon. "I couldn't ever make a commitment or keep a promise until I met Daryl. Then I met him and I fell in love with him. I did *everything* in my power to make him ask me to marry him. I loved him and worked hard at loving him and I gave him all the rewards and punishments I could think of. But after six full months, nothing. Then I simply told him that we were getting married. He agreed. It was easy. Maybe not as romantic as being asked, but the result is the same. And I was aware of who I am and what I could expect on the open market. He was much more desirable than I am. He was handsome. He was talented—he wrote me the most beautiful love poems a girl could want. He writes technical manuals on the installation and operation of marine waste systems— you know, yacht toilets—and he wants to be a real writer someday. But the closer we got to tomorrow, the further away he went. In his mind and in his heart. Even with his body. He was drinking a lot and no sex. Almost none. I mean, really lousy sex. I didn't know there was such a thing. When I asked him what was wrong, he'd say nothing. Nothing was wrong. Nothing, nothing, nothing. And I believed him because I wanted to believe him. And, well, yes—I might have a stronger will than his and a clearer idea of what I want and less reservations about getting what I want. But what I wanted was *him*. And last night I threw all my houseguests out of my apartment because I wanted to be with only Daryl and make all his problems go away so I could see his smile on our wedding day, and I tried so hard to do that, but nothing worked, so I just said Daryl you fucking dweeb you fucking wimp you fucking fag just tell me what the fucking fuck is wrong with you or get the fuck out of here. Out he went. I threw myself around and drank some vodka and called a girlfriend and she came over and I conked out before midnight. I just shut down. And in the morning, this was taped to my front door. He could have just texted but not Daryl. Mr. Written Word, practicing to be Tolstoyevsky."

Sharon leans over and pulls a folded sheet of paper from a rear pocket of her sweatpants and flies it to me. My heart flutters because the paper is warm and contoured by her butt.

I unfold the cooling letter and read aloud the handwritten words:

Dear Sharon,

I cannot express the sadness through which I write this letter, and I can never be absolved for what I have done to your innocent heart. I cannot go through with this. I cannot be a husband now. I do not fully understand this nor do I expect you to. Know that I love you and know that if I could remove this pain from you, I would gladly hand my soul to the devil. I know that in a few short years you, Sharon Novak, will think of these words from time to time and realize that what happened between us happened for the best. I'm driving to Colorado because I don't know a single person in that state. Last night with a heart both heavy and hopeful I prayed that in your future you would receive all the happiness that heaven will allow.

Your Daryl

"That's sad," I say. I fold the letter and set it toward her on the desk.

"I don't want it."

"Keep it. He's right about your future."

"You apes are all the same."

"You'll come to see that he was right."

"When I hear his words, I hear his voice and don't want to shoot him." She pockets the letter.

"I'll make coffee," I say.

"I don't want coffee." She stares at the carpet for a long while. She chews both thumbnails. I can feel that something in her is giving up, trying to give up, but it's going to be a long time before it gives up all the way.

"Let's go down to the test range," I say. "We'll get some fresh silhouettes up, name them Daryl, and you can blast them to smithereens. We can tape that letter over the heart if you want. Pretend his words are his guts. Sound good?"

She looks at me. "Do we have any of the big guns around, the forty-calibers?"

"Sure. And a new one I invented. I think you'll love it."

"You invented it?"

I nod. Sharon has always been drawn to inventions. I remember trying to impress her with my own inventions over the years. There was a battery-operated toilet bowl sweep based on the sweeps used to clean swimming pools, a device that kept umbrellas from folding up backward in the wind, a pepper-spray attachment that would fit any cell phone, and a better mousetrap that actually *was* better but far too expensive to build. I never sold any of them, though I came close with the toilet bowl sweep.

I can only imagine what she'll make of the Love 32.

"Come on," I say. "Rise and shoot."

"I want to go say hi to some of the guys. Marcos here?"

"You bet. I'll go with you. It's really great having this place up and running again. And, Sharon? I'm really glad you're here."

"I realized this is the one place I can go where I have something to do and don't have to explain myself."

"It's good to have a place like that."

She sighs and stands and shakes her head. She looks at me for a good long time and I look back at her.

Of course I blush and of course she knows why.

"Ron, that's insane."

You get what you take, my man.

"No, Sharon. It's the definition of sanity. I love you and always will and we both know it. It's a simple truth. It has nothing to do with what you say or do. Deal with it."

By then I've allowed myself to acknowledge the happiest truth of my life: Sharon Rose Novak has come to *me*.

"Coffee. Thanks."

Sharon and I make a provisions run and return to Pace Arms with a six-pack of Bohemia, a cold bottle of Stoli lemon vodka, ice, one pound of peanut butter–filled pretzels, and two cheese enchilada dinners from El Matador. Down at the firing range, we sit at stations four and five and eat the dinners from their foam boxes. Sharon dusts two beers and pours a stiff vodka over ice. She pulverizes dinner.

"I haven't eaten since I got that letter," she says.

After dinner, we set out a new silhouette target and run it back to fifty feet. If you've ever tried to hit a human-size target with a handgun at fifty feet, you know it's harder than it sounds. Sharon blasts away with one of our .40-caliber Hawk automatics and she gets three of nine rounds in the black. Two hit outside in the white and one misses the paper altogether.

I motor in the target and examine it. "You can do better than this. Remember, it's *Daryl*."

Sharon gives me a dark look, and for a second I think she's going to cry again. "Slap on a new one," she says.

"You might want to try a different gun," I say. From the station four gun safe, I remove the lacquered gun box given to me by Mom. I remove the Love 32 and show Sharon how it transforms from a rather homely .32 semiautomatic pistol to a silenced machine pistol. She watches and frowns as I effect the transformation. When I finally slam home the beautifully curved fifty-shot magazine—no rounds in it yet—Sharon takes the weapon and shakes her head.

"It's beautiful."

"Thank you. I've named it the Love 32."

"Why?"

I explain the Murrieta angle. Predictably, Sharon has never heard of and is not one bit interested in Joaquin or Harry Love and is somewhat grossed out by the severed head.

"Whatever, Ron."

"You won't say *whatever* when you've fired it."

I load the weapon and lecture her on the muzzle-rise tendencies of machine guns. I show her how to press down with her left hand on the air-cooled comb. I run the target back to about thirty feet so Sharon can wallop Daryl hard. She drains her second sizable vodka rocks and takes her position behind the firing line of station five. Let me say for the record that I've never seen a more beautiful sight in my life than Sharon Rose Novak standing ready at the firing line with the Love 32. She looks back at me still red nosed and hostile, then she turns and unleashes a full-auto, five-second, fifty-round fusillade that makes very little sound beyond the metallic chiming of empties on the carpet and the quick rip of paper and the smacking of bullets hitting the sandbags that line the far wall. She saws Daryl pretty much in half. She safes the gun and points the barrel to the floor and looks at me. Strangely.

"Again?"

"Of course."

"Goodie."

She pours and drinks most of another glass of vodka while I load the Love 32. When I bring in the line for a new target, Sharon hands me the letter from Daryl.

"Head," she says.

I find some tape in the station four tool bin and fix the letter directly on the target's head. "Sharon, don't forget the muzzle rise."

"You think I'm drunk."

"You should be drunk by now."

She gives me a wicked laugh and sweeps up the Love 32 and takes her position. I send the target out to forty feet.

"Ten feet more," she says.

So it is done. I sit back and cross my arms and watch Sharon lay serious waste to Daryl's poetic good-bye letter. She keeps her head steady, but her hair bounces with the vibration of her body. As do her small but lively breasts on either side of the peace sign. She holds down the barrel with her left hand, just like a pro. Scraps of letter jump into the air—all of imbecile Daryl's pretty adjectives and big-bore nouns and elegant verbs, his *cannot* and his *devil* and his *soul*. The poor windbag has obviously made the biggest mistake of his life.

Then Sharon lowers the gun and just stands there looking out at the target. She sighs and sets the Love 32 on my station bench and goes back and slumps into the seat at station five. She finishes the vodka and pours another. She tears into the peanut butter–filled pretzels and eats a handful.

I break down the Love 32 and stow it back in the gun box. I bring the target forward and unclip it, and with the tatters of the letter still taped on, I fold it in half a few times and set it on the firing bench. I collect the brass in a plastic bucket—range rules.

All the while, I keep half an eye on Sharon. She sits unmoving except to raise the vodka to her lips, staring downrange. Her expression is glazed and her hair is in her face. The pretzel bag slips off her lap and spills to the carpet. Time passes. To help pass it, I check my cell for messages and text Bradley that the first run is coming off as I write. I tell him the units are exceptionally beautiful, though I haven't seen a production line gun yet. It never hurts to beat the drums ahead of time. I stare at station two for a long moment while I think of Dad. He wanted me to follow Mom into marketing, but Chester said that I would head production and later graduate into R&D. So much for that. I did my own R&D and came up with the Love 32. All Pace Arms had to do was go bankrupt to give me my opportunity.

"I wish I had a sister," says Sharon. Her voice is low and thick. "If I had a sister, I wouldn't be so fucked up."

"You're only temporarily fucked up. If you were chipper right now, you wouldn't be normal."

"I don't want to face all those people tonight."

"Then don't."

"I don't want to shoot Daryl anymore."

"Then don't shoot him."

"I don't know what to do."

"Do nothing."

"I don't feel so good."

"I'll help you up. You can have the penthouse. The water pressure in the shower is terrific. It can blast a potential hangover right out through your pores. I've done it."

"I don't feel so good. Did I already say that?"

"Sharon, let's stand up and hop right over to that elevator."

We ride the elevator with her head on my shoulder. I pretty much hold her up. I get her to the penthouse couch and change the bedsheets. When I come back to the living room, she's curled up, breathing fast. Then she starts in with those high-pitched moans that flutter on the ends, and I shoulder her up and to the bathroom and lay her gently on the cool marble floor and get some good hot water going in the shower.

I shut the door and wait outside. A few minutes later, I hear her banging around. Then she gets sick. That takes a while but there's still something feminine, almost dainty about it. Then the shower door slides open and shut. She sighs hugely. She mutters. Nearly an hour later, I'm sitting in the living room and I hear the bathroom door open and the meaty pad of bare feet on hardwood. Then the bedroom door shuts.

I hustle downstairs to the range and collect the pretzels. Back in my office, I make myself a drink and set up the sleeper couch. I eat and drink on the foldout bed and read Winston Churchill's *The Gathering Storm,* then watch some true crime reruns on TV. When the show is over I read until late, but even with lights out I can't get to sleep.

I smile in the dark and I know why I can't sleep. I've got a nine-hundred-thousand-dollar deal working downstairs and the only woman I've ever dreamed of asleep in my bed a hundred feet away.

This is the happiest night of my life, so far, and I want it to last.

14

Hood introduced himself to Owens Finnegan through the security screen door of her El Centro home. He held up his shield wallet and said her father had asked him to look in on her. He couldn't see her through the small perforations in the steel. Her voice was pleasant and soft.

"Dad's okay?"

"He's in the hospital in Buenavista."

"Please come in."

She was on the tall side and slender, just as her father had said. Her hair was brown and wavy and cut above the shoulders, with bangs almost to her eyebrows. Her eyes were light gray and calm. She wore a crisp blue pin-striped dress shirt over a pair of jeans and she was barefoot, with a silver or stainless steel chain around one ankle. There was a pearl on each ear. Her skin was pale. She was beautiful and she had neither the air nor the appearance of joy.

The living room was small and had two director's chairs with blue canvas seats and backs facing the door. There was no other furniture and no pictures hung or plants growing. There were half a dozen cardboard boxes against one wall. The carpet was dark green and old.

"Just moving in?" asked Hood.

"I've been here two weeks. I don't have a lot."

"Do you move around?"

"When it's time. I'd offer you coffee, but I don't have any. There is water."

"Please."

Hood looked around the barren room and listened to the water running in the kitchen. She came back with two cups, and when she handed him one, he saw inside her shirt cuff the end of a scar that wrapped out of sight beneath her wrist. The cups were foam and the water was room temperature.

She regarded the room. "I dislike confined spaces. There's a picnic table in the backyard and it's in the shade this time of day. We can sit out there."

The lawn was a stubble of tan crabgrass, but a peppertree shaded the table and benches. Hood sat across from her and told her what had happened to her father, and how he was doing now at Imperial Mercy, and how they had found ninety thousand dollars in cash in a tool chest in his truck.

She nodded as if she had heard all this before. "Did he tell you the bathroom products story or the wealthy family from Napa County story?"

"Bathroom products."

"There are other stories, too."

"Any of them true?"

"Everything he says is partially true. You haven't really seen him, have you—his face as he speaks to you, I mean."

"No. His whole head is wrapped up."

"Well, to understand my father, you have to see him. I learned to watch his face as he talked to me. When you do that, something about him slowly becomes evident. It can take quite a while to realize it."

"And what's that?"

"He's insane."

Hood considered. He had once browsed the *Diagnostic and Statistical Manual of Mental Disorders* and been impressed by the sheer number of them, and the way they were classified and differentiated. He thought again of his sister, whose sanity seemed to be dwindling until her brain tumor was discovered, and how quickly her sanity was salvaged when the tumor was removed. He thought of the bullet taken from behind Mike Finnegan's cheek and wondered if it could have caused mental disturbances.

"What's his diagnosis?"

"Paranoid schizophrenia. He's been treated for it most of his adult life."

"In institutions?"

"Occasionally. He's not a danger to himself or others. No violence."

"Does he take medications?"

"I truly don't know. He's always been sensitive and secretive about his condition."

"What can you tell me about the bullet in his head?"

In the outdoor sunlight, the gray of her eyes looked like polished nickel, and Hood had never seen eyes of this color.

"You said he was hit by a car," said Owens.

"They found a bullet lodged behind his cheekbone, below his left eye. They said it looked like it had been there quite a while."

"He never told me he was shot. That's Dad for you."

"That's just a little hard to believe, Ms. Finnegan."

"You don't know how many things about my father are hard to believe, Deputy Hood."

"He must have a facial scar."

"There is a small scar below his cheek. But he always said it was caused by a boyhood injury in the vineyard in Napa."

"Did your father and mother get along?"

"She died of a heart attack not long after I was born. My father remembers her fondly. He loved her."

"Did he ever take you to her grave?"

"She was cremated and scattered in the Pacific."

"What was her name?"

"Bernice."

She looked away and Hood found her scar, a raised and jagged thing lying in wait inside the buttoned cuff.

"Where did they get the name Owens?"

"Family. Way back."

"Where'd the ninety grand come from?"

"I don't know. I would ask him, then believe ten percent of what he says. As a starting point. I don't mean to be facetious or dismissive of him. But I do find it necessary to keep some distance between us. Madness is contagious. Truly it can be."

Hood looked out at the small backyard. There was a concrete-block wall on three sides, and the tree was the only living thing in the yard. Far overhead, three vultures circled perfectly like a baby's mobile hung high in the blue.

"So you pack up and leave when you need to," said Hood. "That's the distance you're talking about?"

She nodded.

"Then I can tell him that you're all right and that you will be in contact with him when you're ready?"

"Yes."

"He asked me to tell you that you are loved beyond—"

"My wildest dreams. *Beyond* them. He's been telling me that since I was a little girl."

Hood's turn to nod now and he saw the faint lines of a smile at the edges of Owens Finnegan's mouth, then they were gone.

"Can you give me the name of his doctor?"

"He doesn't refer to them by name. He rarely refers to them at all. He's ashamed of his illness."

"How does he support himself?"

"He does have the bathroom products business, which he works at only part-time. When he's clearheaded. He has family money, though his father was not a wealthy Napa County viticulturist. It appears that he grew up in San Bernardino County and that his father sold new General Motors cars."

"'Appears'?"

"Dad's history is vague and subject to Dad. He was adopted, an only child. His father and mother died before I was born. As for his birth mother, Dad never knew her. He never cared to know her. He loved the parents who raised him and that was enough."

"Do you have siblings?"

"None."

Hood looked up and saw the vultures gliding in synchronized orbits, orderly as the works of a wristwatch. When he looked back to Owens Finnegan, she was watching him with nickel eyes.

"Why don't you just go see him?"

"I might. You ask lots of questions."

"It's part of the job."

"I'll bet you always did, even as a boy."

"Yes. Asking questions was a way to avoid answering them."

"A personality flaw?"

Hood nodded. "Luckily, in my line of work, it can be a plus. Are you going back to college in the fall?"

"Oh, that's another one of Dad's beliefs that is independent of the facts. I've never set foot on a college campus except for the theaters. I'm an actor. Sometimes I do various work to support myself."

"What kind of work?"

"Cocktails. Pet sitting. Personal shopper."

"Not much acting work here in El Centro."

"I always wanted to live in a desert. I can still make auditions in L.A. I like driving."

Hood stood and she walked him back inside. In the kitchen, Hood noted the emptiness of the place, not a dish or a dish towel or a bowl of fruit or a toaster or a coffeemaker.

"Look at this," she said. She led him down a hallway to the door at the end. She swung it open and Hood looked in. The shades were drawn, but a lamp with a pale orange shade cast a warm glow over the room. The dresser and mirror looked expensive. So did the area rug. The sleigh bed was blond maple and high, with a rich leather-and-fabric spread and matching pillows piled against the sloping headboard. The air coming at him smelled sweet.

"I have a few nice things," she said.

"Very nice."

"There is always more than meets the eye, Deputy Hood."

"You are right, Miss Finnegan."

She walked him out to his car. The neighborhood looked like it was built in the late fifties, small identical houses with attached garages. There were For Sale signs, and the home across the street had boarded windows. Hood noted the black late-model Mercedes convertible in her garage.

"May I see your cell phone?" she asked.

He worked the little holster off his belt and handed the phone to her. She opened it and began pressing buttons expertly, and Hood watched her fingers and the scars. A moment later, she snapped the phone shut and gave it back to him. "I want you to call me."

"Why?"

She stepped to him and took his face in both her cool hands and turned it so Hood was looking away from her. Then she turned his face the other way. He felt like an animal being examined. She came closer and turned him back to her, and Hood stood before her metallic eyes.

"You will have a reason."

Dr. Petty intercepted Hood at the nurses' station and veered him away from the ICU.

"He's taken some kind of turn. He's having seizures and talking nonsense—murders and criminals and God knows what. He says he saw Bobby Kennedy die at the Ambassador. He talked about Manson and the beautiful smoggy sunsets at Spahn Ranch. We gave him sedatives and a dose of steroids and ran an MRI. The swelling is pronounced."

"Can I see him?"

"He's finally stable, so don't wear him out. Come."

Hood and Beth Petty stepped inside the privacy curtain drawn around Finnegan's bed. The monitor readout showed a pulse of seventy and normal blood pressure.

"Charlie. Hello, Doctor. I'm so glad you came to visit." Finnegan's voice was a drawl and slightly lower than usual. Hood figured the sedative.

"They finally hung him in San Jose," said Finnegan.

Hood looked at Petty and she glanced at him but said nothing.

"Who?" asked Hood.

"Tiburcio Vasquez. He was a bandit and a good guy. Ladies' man, gambler, hell of a shot. I stood in the crowd, way in the back, and I could see the gallows in the shafts of sunlight filled with the dust the horses kicked up. A free drink for every white adult male at Henderson's Saloon, Henderson himself an ass, but a free drink is a free drink. You should have seen the women. They were dressed up, hundreds of them, the ladies loved Tiburcio. He had his way with them, that's for sure. Dr. Petty, you look very much like one of those women and I think you brought this whole memory on. Beauty is changeless. Only the bodies that house it change. Tiburcio's buddy Abdon Leiva was the betrayer. He ratted out Tiburcio after catching him with his wife. I told Tibby it would happen, but he didn't listen. They almost never do. There were a bunch of kids inside General Livery and you could see their faces lined up along a crack in the door, getting a look at the hanging. And Sheriff Brewster, he asks Tibby if he's got any last words and Tibby says, '*Oh yes, yes yes.*' See, he's got a little statement all ready to go. I encouraged him to do this, but the composition was all his own. He said, '*A spirit of hatred and revenge took possession of me. I had numerous fights in defense of what I believed to be my rights and those of my country-men. I believed we were unjustly deprived of the social rights that belonged to us.*' And Brewster says, 'Anything else, Tiburcio?' And Tibby says, '*Pronto!*' and the hangman springs the trap. It's hard to write a story with a better ending than that."

"That is a good story," said Hood.

"He's been talking on like that all morning," said the doctor. "Frank James and Sirhan and Manson and even O.J."

"Vasquez and Manson had revolutionary potential. Vast egos and the indispensable ability to believe their own lies. Foundation of the statesman and the dictator. Actually believed they were righting wrongs by robbing and murdering people. Otherwise, there would have been no reason to monkey around with them, now, would there?"

"Explain," said Hood.

"When you choose a friend or an enemy, don't you look for the strong?" drawled Finnegan. "For people with ambition? People with appetites and talents and profound, profound energy?"

"Sure."

"Dr. Beth hit me hard with steroids and Seconal."

Hood glanced at the monitor. Finnegan's pulse was up to ninety, but his blood pressure hadn't changed. "I saw Owens this morning. She said she'd come see you. She didn't say when."

"Bravo, Charlie. Thank you so much. Quite a woman, isn't she?"

"She's lovely, but she didn't smile, not one time."

"She's never been happy."

"I saw the scars on her wrist."

Beth Petty looked at him, and Hood held her look for a moment.

"They found her just in time," said Finnegan. "No note. It was a serious attempt, not a cry for help."

"Why?"

"She genuinely believed she had no reason to live. She loved nothing and was interested in nothing."

"Didn't she love you?"

No one spoke for a long moment. Hood could see the shine of Finnegan's eyes deep within the bandages. "I wasn't a good father. I was gone a lot. Bathroom products. Family affairs in Napa County. My father and mother . . . well, that's a long story. Owens felt abandoned. She was thirteen, terribly overweight, bad acne. She was almost totally inscrutable to me, a man lost to commerce and pleasure and to his own demons. After that dark day when she tried to end it all, I tried my hardest to be there for her. Gradually, she found herself. As if she were born again into the world. It was a long and sometimes painful awakening. So, all the more difficult for me when her vanishing acts began. Which is why it was so important to me that I know she's all right. Thank you, Deputy. Now please describe her home to me."

Hood described the house and yard and asked about Owens's acting career.

"Well, not much of a career because she's still in school. But she's gifted in that way. It took us some years to discover those gifts. . . . I just had the thought that, Dr. Petty, you also remind me of a prostitute who worked for Ida down in the old San Diego red-light district. They called it the Stingaree. Ida ran the ladies around town in horse-drawn buggies, and the johns would come to Wyatt's saloon on Sixth and go upstairs. Nice place. Fantastic sin zone then, the cat's pajamas. San Diego was really the place to be if you had a wicked streak. A busy port means horny sailors. Still true today. I don't know what it is about you, Beth, maybe that nice round forehead and cute little nose, or maybe something in your eyes, just makes me think of women I've met before. I guess if you get old enough, everyone reminds you of someone else."

"I'm so happy to remind you of a whore."

"Please don't take offense. The canvas is limitless and impersonal. It is a meeting of time and space, and your place on it is not much larger than a dot and not much longer than a moment. The prostitute's name was Marie. She carried someone's beauty and you carry hers and someone will someday carry yours."

"Oh."

"How old are you, Mike?" asked Hood.

"Fifty-one. Did Owens appear to be well fed? She's prone to letting her nutrition go and simply living on energy drinks."

"She looked healthy."

"Eyes like the moon, eh?"

"Somewhat."

"I'd like a full report on Holdstock, but I'm too tired right now to remember anything. Later, Charlie? This evening or tonight, maybe?"

Hood now felt something that he had felt only one time before. It was like surprise and like recognition and like dread, but he didn't know a word for it or if there was a word. Once when he was a boy in Bakersfield, walking to school, he watched a tiger cross the street in front of him and trot off toward the park. It glanced back at him. Its size and coloring and movement were not within his experience of the world. Later he learned it had escaped from a private collection. He felt now as he had felt then, and it was indescribable.

"You can't know about Holdstock," Hood said.

"I can't know or you can't tell?"

"I've never said his name to you," said Hood. "Nothing has been written about him recently and he hasn't been mentioned in any news media. How do you even know his name?"

"Sources."

Hood racked his brain. He wondered if Finnegan's source who had supplied Hood's new home address was a USPS employee and had gotten his hands on Hood's recent letter home. Had he been lax enough to use Jimmy's last name in that letter? The nurses could tell him if Finnegan had had a visitor.

"When you tell me your sources, I'll tell you about Holdstock."

"Don't be boorish, Charlie. Butting heads is never good policy. When you come back to see me we can discuss Holdstock as he deserves to be discussed. My number one concern, if I were you, would be that the Zetas will simply storm the hospital and take him again. Now, you come back and bring a good zinfandel, something peppery. It will cut right through the hoof-and-mouth disease I feel developing. I like the Bonterra organic. Of course I'll need a straw."

"You know nothing about Jimmy but his name."

"A Badger tight end. Lapsed student of divinity. Married the waitress. Took the Blowdown gig for a shot at better weather. El Centro. My. It's all available."

Hood considered. "Then you can tell me about the bullet, too."

"I was wondering when that would come up. You did not have my permission to remove it, Dr. Petty."

"We judged it best," said Petty.

"I wonder what caused the swelling in my brain to increase. My enormous intellect? The removal of the bullet? Really, I don't feel right. Where do these false memories come from? They're obviously only fantasy and hallucination. Dr. Petty, maybe you can discover in me a new mental illness. Can you name it after me? Finnegan by proxy? Mike's syndrome? Well—it's exhausting to see Tiburcio dangling again. Doctor, it's not your fault you look like a whore from another century. There is no expiration date on the kind of beauty you possess. This has been an exciting day, but I'm very tired now."

Hood looked at Petty, who swung back the privacy curtain and followed Hood out.

"Don't forget my straw," called Finnegan.

Hood took the elevator up to the sixth floor but one of the uniformed deputies outside Holdstock's room said that Jimmy was sleeping. The deputy said Jimmy was doing okay—his wife and kids were in earlier. He looked okay. Right now Holdstock was in dreamland.

Hood asked to just peek in and when he did, he saw Jimmy on his back with his hands bundled into gigantic white appendages that lay beside him. His face twitched and it was a color between white and blue and covered with sweat. Hood got the nurse to look and she said it was good, always good when they can sleep through pain like that.

Hood took the stairs down, and on the third level he saw two U.S. marshals standing guard at the landing door. The stairwell air was hot and still, and Hood's footsteps echoed flatly. The marshals recognized Hood and stood in deference as he came down the steps.

"Deputy Hood," said one.

"What's this?"

"A Gulf Cartel heavy who got himself shot up last night. We have to give the creeps top-notch medical care and protect them from their enemies, right?"

"When did he come in?"

"Early this morning. Hey, terrific work down there. I heard your guy had it pretty hard."

"Yeah. They tell me he's doing better."

"When they start letting marshals join the war parties, I'm signing up. Take some scalps. What are you guys going to do next—Blowdown, I mean?"

"Just our jobs."

"Keep up the good work."

Hood nodded and headed down the stairs. He called his mother and they talked for a few minutes, then Hood asked her to get the two letters he had written and read them out loud to him.

Standing in the shade of the Imperial Mercy entryway, Hood listened to his mother's voice as she read. He remembered that same voice reading stories to him when he was young, remembered the Bakersfield living room in which they sat, remembered his mother as the young woman she no longer was.

The name Holdstock was not in the letters.

Then Hood talked briefly with his father, who sounded clear and rational and before hanging up said, "I love you, Anderson," Anderson being his father's friend shot down over Khe Sanh in 1968 and never heard from again.

15

Holdstock in fact was dreaming he was in Imperial Mercy Hospital. In his dream the deputies outside his door talked quietly, Hood looked in on him, a nurse spoke to Hood just outside his door. He was aware of everything in his room. It was exactly like the one he occupied when not dreaming except that lying back flat against the ceiling was a blue-faced werewolf that looked down on him, affixed to that surface by the logic of terror. He couldn't open his eyes and look at it. Even from within this dream, Jimmy was sure he was dreaming and he knew the blue-faced werewolf wasn't really there, but he couldn't bring himself to open his eyes and look because he might be wrong. He knew the cost of being wrong. He tried to muster a dream-shattering scream, one that would explode him and the monster out of it—his body shook and his mouth gaped and his lungs heaved from their very depths, but not even a whisper of sound came out.

Earlier in the dream, Jenny and the girls were standing above him and he looked up into their faces. Gustavo Armenta stood between the girls, holding their hands, pale as death. Their expressions were searching, as if he were a river and they were looking for something on its bottom. Jenny. Patricia. Matilda. Gustavo. They were talking about him as if he weren't there. The blue-faced werewolf was stuck up on the ceiling, and Jimmy had to face his family and smile while the beast stared down at all of them from just a few feet away.

In the dream, when he couldn't take it any longer, Jimmy sprang out of bed and lunged up at the ceiling with both hands, but he felt his fingers wither and his hands melt and his arms dissolve until they were only short stumps that smoldered at the ends like wet firewood as he waved them impotently at the werewolf. Jenny and Patricia and Matilda pressed him back into the bed and told him everything was all right now and they looked down at him again with their searching expressions and continued talking about him as if he weren't there.

Later a nurse shook him awake. It seemed to take hours for Jimmy to swim up through the heavy sedated layers of sleep. Then he burst into the world. It was like being born. She told him it was time to eat something and she raised his bed with the control. Jimmy felt the blood rush from his head and his heart pounding hard and fast and he smelled the high-pitched stink of fear coming up from the blanket. He glanced up at the ceiling and felt the dry approximation of a smile crack across his lips.

16

Hood walked into Gun Barn and felt the cooled air hit his hot, damp shirt. There were customers at the counter and in the aisles. Hanging fluorescent tubes cast a nervous light on the men and the racks of long guns. He noted three security cameras without even really looking for them. He smelled gun oil and steel.

"Help ya?"

The man before him wore a Glock on his hip and a black leather vest and star-shaped badge that read DALLAS.

"Charlie Hood for John Crockett."

"Appointment?"

"Eleven."

"Good, because he's the owner and you have to have an appointment."

Hood badged Dallas. A man behind the counter, black-vested and star-badged also, looked over at Hood, then went back to his customer.

"Mr. Crockett will be right with you."

Hood browsed the racks of long guns, mostly used, mostly old American military guns. The prices were good. Some had the bayonets still on. The semiautomatic rifles and carbines were lashed together with locking cables through the trigger guards. He browsed the counter, looking down at the handguns, everything from two-shot ivory-handled derringers to a Casull .50 caliber. He saw some nice Colt 1911s similar to the one his grandfather had given him and that he occasionally carried on duty. There was an archery section that had bows very similar to Luna's. The crossbow section was large. Hood saw blowguns and throwing stars and throwing knives and high-powered slingshots similar to the ones he had owned as a boy. The knives ranged in size from huge bowie knives to tiny dirks. There were battle swords and Japanese fighting swords and decorative swords and lances and scimitars and dueling foils and medieval execution axes and scythes for the Grim Reaper. Farther back in the store, he found open crates of surplus antipersonnel bombs and neutered hand grenades and brass. There were government-issue flashlights and wristwatches and helmets and flak jackets and combat boots and K rations and parachutes. The clothing section featured everything from underwear to sports coats in a variety of camouflage patterns. The security cameras watched him.

The man from behind the counter appeared beside Hood. "Sorry. We're busy. I'm Crockett."

"Can we talk in your office?"

"I can talk anywhere I want."

Crockett led them around the pistol counter and checkout stands, down a short hallway, and through swinging saloon doors with a KEEP OUT sign with a picture of a gun barrel pointing out at you. Crockett let the doors swing shut, but Hood had his hand up in plenty of time. Crockett was short and big-eared and wore his hair in a crisp flattop so that, viewed from behind, his head looked like a wing nut.

The office was spacious and carpeted and lit with the same jittery fluorescents as the showroom. One wall was a bank of video monitors, ten in all, each fed by a separate camera in the showroom and one at the rear exit. There was a big steel desk behind which Crockett sat and began to trim a dark-leafed pyramid cigar. He snipped a hole in the small end, then lit it with a lighter shaped like a hand grenade. Hood waited as he puffed and rotated the cigar and the smoke wavered out and up.

"Shoot," he said.

"You know the deal. You see us here every other month. Suspicious sales, suspected straw men, bad guys. It's your responsibility to report all of that to us, but since you almost never do, we have the pleasure of coming out to where you are."

"I love you feds. You make doing your jobs sound like the twelve labors of Hercules."

"Don't flatter yourself, Mr. Crockett. You're just a small man. Maybe you can offer me something meaningful today."

"You're new."

"To Blowdown."

"Something meaningful? Sure. Maybe you can tell me what this means. A couple of years back, I sold guns to a couple of guys I didn't like the looks of. They cleared the FBI check. They had valid ID. They did the wait period, and their check cleared, the whole deal. But I had second thoughts, so I called the feebs. The FBI. The ATF. I left messages and I e-mailed them, too, just to make sure there was some kind of paper trail. Well, guess what. I never got so much as a call back. No e-mail, no nothing. And that, Mr. Hood, is why I don't relish you coming in here and hassling my ass while there's paying customers waiting for my help."

"So in the last two months you haven't sold a gun to anyone who raised your suspicions?"

"That's right. We get our share of dumbass crazies who can't even pass the background. But if I called you guys every time one of them walked in here, you'd have to set up an office in the parking lot. I mean, look at that guy on camera six. You count from upper left across, then down, to arrive at six. Good. See that guy? He's come in every week for five years trying to buy a Desert Eagle. Look at his clothes. Look at his hair. He lives under that bridge on Firehouse Road. Eats out of Dumpsters. He's crazy as a shithouse rat and I won't sell him anything in my store. So don't tell me I don't do my job."

"I had more sophisticated buyers in mind. There's a war going on down in Mexico right now, Mr. Crockett. It's left six thousand people dead. Five hundred of them have been cops and judges. Some are women and children. They're getting those guns from us. Every time the Mexican government asks us for a weapon trace, it comes back to a U.S. dealer."

Crockett turned his cigar and puffed and blew a plume out at Hood. "Whatever you say. You're talking about six thousand pistoleros, not everyday people. Bad guys kill other bad guys. From where I sit, it's Mexico's fault. They hardly check cars coming into their own country. You ever think of that? I sell a legal product for self-defense. I sell to people who pass the background and have legal ID. I can't control what happens later. In case it's never occurred to you, my taxes pay your salary. Those animals down there are the killing machines, not the guns. Not me."

Hood watched the video monitors for a moment. He watched the blue smoke drift across the screens.

"No suspicious sales?" he asked.

"Not one."

"Look at these pictures, please. Tell me if you recognize any of the men."

Crockett looked at his watch and sighed. "Okay."

Hood pulled the folded sheets of images from his shirt pocket. There were four pictures per page. Most were made from digital surveillance videos, some from old VHS tape. Some were clear and some were not. All were unidentified. But ATFE had gotten tips that put these men under suspicion, and all had been seen along this stretch of the Iron River.

Crockett flipped through them, shaking his head. He set one aside. Then another. He held them up and pointed. "Here. I've seen this guy and this guy in my store."

Hood collected the hot list. "When?"

"Impossible to say. Last six months, probably. Or I'd have forgotten them by now."

"Did they purchase?"

"I've got a brain up here, not a computer. I can't remember every buyer. Impossible. I've got all the Firearm Transaction Records, just like you require. You can go through them anytime you want. See? I cooperate. I care."

"I'd like to see the FTRs for the last sixty days."

"I'll get Dallas to help you. I've got better things to do than sit here and watch you sound out the big words."

"You're funny."

Crockett smiled around his cigar at Hood and called up front for Dallas.

Hood read through the records and wrote down information on buyers who didn't look quite right. He had little more to go on than their names and addresses and their handwriting. They had cleared the backgrounds and shown good ID and paid good money for their guns and ammo. He tried to think in patterns, as his ATFE instructors had drilled into him. He saw no patterns, just men buying guns.

Dallas tried to help, giving his opinion on some of the buyers, prying ATFE hiring information out of Hood. Dallas was fixin' to join up someday.

Hood drove toward Calipatria through the ferocious middle day, heat wavering up from the horizon like fumes, the asphalt before him pooling with liquid nonexistent but appearing as smooth as mercury. He thought of the lives he had taken near Mulege. In the dazed aftermath of the shoot-out, Hood had retraced his steps and found the last of the four men he had killed. He had knelt beside him but he didn't know what to do. The older man's body lay heavily in the desert sand and it seemed to Hood to be as individual and as important as himself, more advanced on its earthly journey and therefore worthy of respect. But Hood still didn't know what to do. He wanted to believe in an accessible and generous heaven awaiting most men, but this was not the Christian arrangement that he had been taught, so he did nothing. He found the three others and did nothing also and he told himself fuck it, they chose this life and I chose the flip side of it and we all signed on with our eyes open. There was no way Hood could feel superior of soul in this wind-blown, bullet-ruled patch of torture and death.

The manager at Rudy's Gun Room had not sold guns or ammunition to any suspicious buyers. He was a pleasant but vague man with a large mushroom cap of a mole growing from his right cheek. Hood had the feeling that as a seller of firearms, he was neither observant nor discriminating. He walked Hood to the door and waved him off like a relative discharging an obligation.

Then down to Brawley, where the owner of Tracker Joe's was eager to point out that he had filed two reports of suspicious buyers with ATFE one month ago, but there had been no questionable activity since.

Driving east from town to scorching town, Hood hit the Firing Line and the Shoot Shack and the Gun Locker and Freedom Arms and Floyd's Surplus and the Bullseye, but nobody had sold a gun to a suspicious buyer. There's no such thing as a suspicious buyer, Hood was told, because if they're suspicious, we don't sell to them. Laughter. He wondered again at the idea of an industry left to regulate itself. With guys like Crockett in the deal, it was a wonder ATFE could enforce anything at all. Crockett had opened something in him and he felt sick in his soul and he couldn't erase Mulege. Jimmy's fingers. Jimmy's face. He drove fast, but not even the motion that he had craved as a boy could put distance between him and what he had done and seen.

Then it was dark and he was hours from Buenavista, so he got take-out food and water and bourbon in Yuma and took the prison turnoff. Near the river, he found a dirt road and he wound his way down it in his Blowdown SUV. The headlights cut through the dust as gravel cracked off the undercarriage. He came to a broad turnaround and he shut off the engine and got out. There was a bank lined with cattails and beyond it he heard the Colorado running fast and deep. The smell was as sweet as any he could remember, and the cattails were black slashes against the lighter black of the sky. To the east the walls of the old Territorial Prison rose in the blackest shade of all, and Hood could make out the watchtowers and the old adobe ramparts. He had visited the prison as a kid. It was by then a museum, and Hood had been surprised by how small the cells were, and his father had taken a picture of him sitting on one of the tiny steel bed frames built into the floors, Hood making a face to get his brothers and sisters to laugh.

He sat on the tailgate of the SUV and ate the tacos and drank the water and bourbon separately. He found some music. Later he stripped down to nothing and waded out through the cattails and lowered himself into the fast cold water and, holding on to the cattails, realized how swiftly he would be carried away if he or they were to let go. He stood by the car in the darkness and let the hot desert breeze dry him and then he put on only his underwear and hung his pants and shirt by the garment hooks and spread the coat over the back of the driver's seat. He lowered both rows of backseats and opened all the windows and set his holster close, then stretched out there but was not comfortable. He listened to the river and to the bugs tapping around him. As a shield against Mulege, he got out his cell phone and called Owens Finnegan.

"You were right," he said. "I have a reason to call you."

"What reason is it?"

"I want to know why you held my face like that. What were you looking for?"

"A face is a map of the heart."

"What did you see on the map?"

"Innocence."

"You must have seen violence and death, too."

"Innocence is their measure. I love that you can still be measured."

Hood said nothing for a long moment. "When I saw your scars, they made me want to save you."

"All men want that. I don't need saving anymore. Where are you now?"

"By a river near a prison. Where are you?"

"In my bed. It's late, Charlie."

"Your father was relieved that you're okay. He wanted me to describe your home. He was concerned about your diet because you're prone to living on energy drinks. He insists that you are going to college."

She laughed softly.

"Then he hallucinated about the hanging of an outlaw, and the assassination of Robert Kennedy and drinking with Wyatt Earp in San Diego."

"Dad. What an imagination."

"It's like he was really there. Details, sensory stuff."

"He never told me about drinking with Wyatt Earp, for whatever that's worth. Don't buy into what he says, Charlie. But be forgiving of him. He must have suffered head trauma when that car hit him."

"There was sudden swelling. The doctor says it's not unusual."

"I'll visit him soon."

"That would make him happy."

"When will you visit me?"

"Soon."

"I know I'm frightening. I can't hide the scars. So, Charlie, you come see me again when you're ready."

He slept lightly and went back to the river once but didn't go in.

At eleven o'clock the next day, Hood stepped into Dragon Arms in Quartz, California, population 1,200, elevation ten feet. It was 104 degrees according to the hardware store thermometer across the street. Even after the just-bought deodorant, he smelled strongly of the river, a dank mix of water and vegetation and mud.

Dragon Arms was a small, cool basement store that appeared well cared for. A man and a woman stood behind the counter when Hood walked in, both watching him enter, and Hood knew they had been waiting for him. The man was stocky and silver-haired, and the woman was a big-haired brunette in a green silk dress. They looked early sixties. The man came around the counter and swung his hand into Hood's.

"Ivan Dragovitch," he said. "You are the new Blowdown agent."

"Yes, Charlie Hood."

"This is my wife, Sheila."

She offered her hand from behind the counter, and Hood shook it over the pistols.

"I respect ATFE," said Dragovitch. "I admire agents Ozburn and Bly and Holdstock. Come, sit. I have some new faces for you."

The Blowdown crew had told him of Dragovitch's selective contempt and adoration for his customers. He'd shot a biker-robber dead the week his store had opened, then chased the man's accomplice outside and shot him dead, too. He was openly disdainful of anyone who looked off-center to him. If you were clean-cut and had decent manners, Dragovitch could be courtly and deferential. If he offered coffee, he liked you. He adored law enforcement and made no secret of it. He had had Ozburn, Bly, and Holdstock for drinks once at his home in the hills outside Quartz, and Ozburn said he was gracious. Ozburn also said he was borderline paranoid, but so what.

Dragovitch led Hood to the counter and found him a stool. He was thick-necked and blue-eyed and he styled his silver hair in the jutting prow of a TV evangelist or NFL head coach. Hood sat and smiled at Sheila, who remained standing near the register. She was heavily made up and pretty.

"Coffee, Deputy Hood?" Dragovitch asked.

"Sure. Black is fine."

Dragovitch went through a door in the back and shut it.

"Do you like the ATFE?" asked Sheila.

"They're good people. I'm a sheriff's deputy on assignment."

"The gun sellers get a bad rap. Ivan tries his best to comply and be helpful."

"If all the dealers were as helpful, we'd have a much easier job."

"There were rumors about Agent Holdstock."

"Oh? I didn't hear them."

"That he was taken to Mexico and tortured, but the Baja police rescued him."

"That's quite a tale. I saw Jimmy just yesterday and he didn't say a thing about it."

She smiled and shook back her hair. Her fingernails were red and carefully kept. "You wouldn't tell me anyway."

"Naw. I wouldn't."

Hood looked down through the glass countertop at the handguns, price tag strings looped through the trigger guards. Dragovitch's prices were on the high side, but his wares were polished and tastefully arranged and the countertop glass was etched with use but without a smudge. Hood looked up and around for the surveillance cameras but saw none.

"There are four of them, all hidden," said Sheila. "It makes the customers more relaxed. I do the faces."

Dragovitch came back with a mug of coffee and two black three-ringed binders. Sheila produced a Dragon Arms coaster from behind the counter, and he set the coffee on it. He handed Hood one of the black binders. Hood saw that the contents were sectioned off by month. He turned to June, the last month that Blowdown had been here for a routine field interview. As Hood patiently flipped through the pictures, Dragovitch flipped correspondingly through his binder, which was thick with FTRs. Hood was impressed by the quality of the images. Although taken from the digital video cameras, the stills were clear and focused. Sheila had spent some time on this.

Dragovitch narrated. "There, the first, a man who bought two very nice Ruger twenty-twos. It just took a while for the background to come through. I don't know. They say the computers are slow, but maybe there's a problem with this man, eh?"

From the FTR, Dragovitch rattled off the buyer's name and age and address.

Hood, sharing none of Dragovitch's suspicion, nodded politely and turned to the next page.

"Then, this man came in three days later and he bought two more of the same Ruger twenty-twos. This is strange. This seems like more than coincidence to me. When he purchases, I realize his home city is the same as the man who bought the two twenty-twos three days before—Oceanside. Why Oceanside? Why so many Rugers?"

Hood nodded politely again and turned to the next page.

"Now that next man was a human scum. He was rude. He smelled badly. I refused service to him according to the sign above my cash register. He cussed me vividly and made a gesture to Sheila and walked out. I have no FTR, so I don't know anything about him. But I suspect one thing—he will not be back."

Hood continued. Most of the pictures were of shoppers who did not buy. They were simply people whom Dragovitch suspected of being suspicious. Hood did see a pattern here: younger buyers with facial hair, biker or hippie types, Hispanics of all description, blacks. Dragovitch made his judgments on an odd array of detail: One buyer had an eye patch, one wore a Che Guevara T-shirt, one claimed to be of Croatian descent but didn't know Zagreb, one used an inhaler, one had a broad forehead and thick black eyebrows and a swatch of bleached hair combed back.

"Meet Silenced Automatics," said Dragovitch, looking down at the picture. "Silenced automatics are all he talks about."

"But you won't sell him silenced automatics," said Hood.

"A man who looks like that?"

Hood flipped the last picture over and closed the binder.

"Thank you, Mr. Dragovitch."

"Deputy Hood, I do have something for you today. Something solid. I've been eager for you to see the picture and hear the story."

Ivan looked at Sheila. Hood saw her nod and color. She reached behind the counter and offered still another picture to Hood.

"Here," she said.

Hood took the sheet. It was a rather nice portrait of Bradley Jones. He was wearing a leather cowboy hat and sunglasses, but it was unmistakably Bradley, from the leather vest to the goatee to the lanky posture.

"His name is Kyle Johnson," said Dragovitch. "He has been in here several times the last year. He has not purchased anything, yet. Yet. He implies some connection to law enforcement. He said he was looking for something small and automatic. I said you mean semiautomatic and he said no, I mean fully automatic. I told him there was no such gun that I can legally sell. These are military weapons. He would say it was all a joke, that he wasn't serious. But he would return a few weeks later and we would have the same conversation. He would attempt to be charming, but he is only arrogant. He would look at me and Sheila and smile with some wickedness and he would suggest that we could produce such an automatic firearm if we wanted to. I said the world is awash in AK-47s and M16s and all manner of MACs, so why not find an unscrupulous dealer to sell full automatic? Why keep coming here? And this young man, he would ask questions and examine everything in the store and then he would leave. We were uncertain whether to make his picture. He never bought, true. But he is young and proud of himself and dresses with subversion and he stands against everything I believe in. He brought Sheila a flower in a vase. He brought me a quality bottle of vodka. Still, I do not like him and he does not represent America. But now that he has agreed to purchase, we believe you should be aware of him. We have run his background check and he has passed it, of course. His driver's license is valid. He is a legal customer."

"What does he want?"

"Ammunition only. No firearms."

"What round?"

"The thirty-two ACP."

"How many?"

Dragovitch raised his eyebrows. "Well. This will be of some interest. He wishes to buy, ah, fifty thousand rounds."

"Fifty thousand rounds."

"New shells, U.S. made. I know a wholesale supplier in San Diego. Kyle has agreed to a cash price of eighteen thousand dollars."

Hood looked at the picture. "When?"

"This depends on the source of the supplier. The quantity is large. Perhaps one more week."

"Where?"

"All specifics will be discussed. Everybody trusts everybody, yes, of course. But there are always cautions with such things. There will be transport and logistics and security. Many details."

"When was he in here last?" asked Hood.

"Saturday. He has shaved and cut his hair short since that picture. He looks more clean. He wore clownish clothing—plaid shorts and flip-flop sandals and a very bright flowered shirt. I intermediated the agreement and negotiated a proper fee for myself. But now I report my suspicions to law enforcement. Sheila and I looked forward to bring you this good news, Deputy Hood. We hope you are pleased. And we hope that your investigation will be successful. We wish our part in this to be invisible. Dragon Arms cannot continue to do business if we ourselves are suspected."

Hood sat, flabbergasted to the core of his hope, but in other places not surprised at all. He stared down at the picture of Bradley and the array of guns floating in the background beneath the counter glass. A finger with a shiny red nail rotated the picture. Sheila looked at it intensely, her expression hard to read.

17

Bradley sat cross-legged on the floor of the Whittier Explorer Academy weaponless defense gym and listened to the training sergeant explain the wrist break. He watched the demonstration without paying attention to it, imagining instead Erin last night onstage at the Whiskey and later in their bedroom.

"Daydreaming, Jones?"

"Absolutely not, sir."

"Then get up here and show us what you've learned."

The other Explorer sat down and Bradley took his place, bowing slightly to the instructor, then waiting relaxed. The gym was well lit and the floor was padded and there were speed and heavy bags along two walls, and body-size attack targets and huge medicine balls along another.

"Grab my wrist," said the instructor, whose name was Grgich. He was stout and short-limbed, midforties to Bradley's eye.

When Bradley took his wrist, Grgich did a slow-motion twist-grab-turn and easily moved Bradley around and down to one knee. Bradley tapped out and Grgich waited a moment, then let go.

"Again," he said. "Half speed."

Again Bradley was forced to one knee, but when he tapped out, Grgich waited, keeping the pain up. Bradley was a second-dan black belt in hapkido, and the last time he'd used the art, he had badly broken two men. Again, Grgich wrenched him around and down and held him past the tap.

"Your turn."

Bradley rose and felt the heat of the pain in his face. One of the other Explorer trainees was a pretty young woman, and Bradley caught the worry in her expression.

"Your app said you have some experience at this," said the instructor. "But I'm here to tell you that on the street, everything changes. Whatever you think you know, forget it now."

"Right."

"You bet it's right."

Grgich took Bradley's wrist, and Bradley did the twist and grip, but the man used his strength to break it and with his other hand he spun Bradley and bent his arm sharply behind him and forced him to the mat. Bradley tapped out and Grgich held fast, then let go and backed away.

"Don't go easy," he said.

Bradley righted himself and took a deep breath. Again, Grgich clamped down on his wrist. Bradley faded very slightly to draw Grgich off balance and to judge his strength. Then he kihaped loudly, as Master Paulson had taught him, the kihap having several purposes—an exhale that focuses energy, a battle cry, and a summons of focus and power. Bradley's twist and grip came as fast as a gunshot. He turned the heavy man's weight against him and drew back on his arm and eased him to his knee upon the mat. Grgich didn't tap out, but Bradley released him and stepped away.

"That was good," huffed Grgich. "Again."

"There's no reason to do it again."

"This is training and you are the trainee. Again."

Grgich gripped his wrist, and Bradley felt the ungoverned strength of the man. He kihaped and locked the instructor's wrist in his hand and twisted up the arm and turned him. But he felt the continuance of Grgich's rotation and he felt him lower and pivot fast so that the instructor was facing him again, their wrists still locked, Grgich off balance, leaning in. Bradley's instinct told him to turn and throw his enemy, but his desire to succeed as an Explorer overrode it and instead he allowed Grgich to throw him over his back to the mat.

Bradley rolled once and bounced to his feet and continued to bounce like a boxer waiting for the bell. He thought of Erin and this kept him from attacking.

Grgich stood panting, face flushed, hands up in a fighting stance. Then he let them down.

"Next."

After the weaponless defense class, Grgich approached Bradley at the water dispenser.

"I was there when you met Coleman Draper. At the recruiting booth."

"I remember."

"When I saw your name on the trainee roster, I was surprised. I didn't think a little shit dribble like you could make Explorer."

"I'll make Explorer."

"I can't believe they let you in."

"They let you in."

"You and Draper hit it off?"

"We had beers and that was it."

"I'll be watching you, Jones."

Bradley dropped the paper cup into the trash and headed off for the firearms safety class.

• • •

The pretty trainee sat down next to him and introduced herself as Caroline Vega. Her handshake was firm. She was dark-haired and brown-eyed, and even in the unflattering Explorer uniform, she appeared to be built with strength and good form. She had had no trouble learning the wrist break. They watched the handgun demonstration, then shotguns, rifles, and pepper spray. Bradley daydreamed about Erin. He felt a strong physical desire to be near enough to smell and hear and see her. The first time she had looked at him, Bradley felt like he had walked into a beautiful room. Three years now. They were children then. Erin was the only goodness in the world that interested him now that his mother was gone. He had large appetites for pleasure and for beautiful things, but what he wanted most was to be near Erin and to see her. Nothing else mattered that much. Bradley was not an introspective man, but it amused him to know that only one person on earth owned his heart and that if she were to leave him or vanish or die, he would become nothing more than a scourge upon the land.

"Why are you doing this?" asked Caroline. It was break time and they stood in the shade of an olive tree in a campus quadrangle.

"It might be a decent job someday. You?"

"I want a place to start. Base camp."

"So you can what, boldly go where no woman has gone before, explore strange new worlds?"

She laughed, but Bradley could tell she felt belittled, which is what he had intended.

"I guess."

"I know what you meant," he said. "You meant there's more to life than a cotton-poly uniform blouse and ten-hour shifts."

She looked at him with a skeptical lift of an eyebrow. "I'm going to burn through L.A. one way or another. This is just the beginning.

There's money and pleasure and a thousand ways to get them. That's what I'm doing here, looking for a *way*. And you want to know something else, Bradley Jones? I know you. I know who you are. Allison Murrieta had it right. And you're doing the same thing here that I am. Good luck, hombre. By the way, I liked you better with long hair."

She started across the quad.

"Wait."

"I don't *wait*," she said over her shoulder.

He watched her walk back into the classroom. When he took his chair, he saw that she had moved to the back of the class. He turned and found her and nodded and she stared him down. She had scribbled a phone number on the cover of his LASD Explorer class syllabus.

For the rest of the firearms safety class and all the way through criminal law, police procedures, and community relations, he pictured Erin at different moments. He could remember the moments clearly, her clothes and her scent and the way she wore her lovely red hair, and he could rerun a particular smile or expression, and he could hear the sound of her clothes sliding off her skin and the sound of her voice onstage as she sang. And as he remembered these things, Bradley smiled inwardly at his outlandish luck. Thousands of young men had seen her perform, and half of them fell in love with her on sight. Bradley had fallen, at the Whiskey on Sunset, before the first song of her first set was over. On his third straight two-show night, he finally caught her eye and she had looked back wholly at him. He was sixteen with good fake ID and a solid vodka buzz on.

— When you look at me it's like walking into a beautiful room. I'm Brad Jones.

— That's a pretty thing to say.

— I'm short on words right now.

— I'm Erin McKenna.

— After the last set tonight, we need to talk.

— Oh do we *need* to, Brad Jones?

— Yes.

— What are you going to talk with if you're short on words?

— I'll find something.

She smiled and that was her first real smile only for him and that is what Bradley pictured as he listened to the last remarks about next Saturday's training sessions. There were to be 184 hours of instruction over eighteen weeks.

Two weeks down, thought Bradley, and less than a million more to go.

Still in his Explorer uniform, Bradley slouched in a chair in the women's shoe department at Nordstrom. He listened to the music and smelled the medley of perfumes and shoe leather wafting over, and stared at Erin. She was modeling stage boots. She wore a tan miniskirt and her legs were long and pale and the heels of the boots elongated them and coaxed the muscle beneath the skin. She passed so close, he could smell the lotion on her legs. He sighed.

"Too high a heel?"

"There's no such thing."

"Too rhinestony?"

"More the merrier."

"Too something. These are too something."

Erin strode away from him and left a soft feminine eddy of scent behind her. She pointed out three more pair, and the salesman carried the boxes back to the stockroom.

"Four pairs and no dice," she said. She stood in front of the floor mirror, turning her legs to it this way and that, examining them as if they were accessories and not a part of her.

"It's impossible to watch you do this," he said.

"Oh?"

"You know it's impossible. That's why you're with me."

He heaved up from the chair, went to the couture department and found three beautiful dresses in her size and carried them back to shoes and laid them over the seat beside him. He sat and watched her finger one.

"They're beautiful. I know what you're doing."

"Yes, you do."

She looked down at him and set her hand on the back of his neck as she flexed her legs again for the mirror. The current boots were black and lightly studded.

"Keepers," said Bradley.

"I found these, too." She knelt on both knees in front of him and pulled from a box a short red boot in faux crocodile with little chains for laces. She leaned in and set one hand on Bradley's leg and held up the red boot with the other.

"It was made for you," he said.

"I think so, too."

She looked at the boot, then up at him. The most beautiful room in the world. Bradley felt the surge of emotion, stronger than adrenaline, stronger than violence, stronger than drugs or alcohol.

He took her hand and stood. "We'll take these two pair," he said to the salesman.

Erin took off the black boots and handed them to the clerk and followed Bradley to the fitting rooms in couture. He held out the three hangers with the expensive dresses as if bearing a flag or the colors of some exotic authority. He nodded crisply to the couture saleswoman and stood aside to allow Erin to enter first the hallway of fitting rooms. The door to room seven squeaked as Erin pushed through. Bradley hung the dresses on the wall hook, then closed the door and slid the lock. Erin turned his head hard with both hands and rose on her toes to lock her mouth to his.

An hour later, Bradley sat in Rocky Carrasco's new lair in El Monte. Rocky was Herredia's California distribution chief, a second-generation *Eme* captain, compact and knotted with muscle, and covered head to toe in tattoos. He had bullet scars on his arms, and knife scars on his stomach, and a twinkle in his eyes.

"El Tigre will be happy," he said. "I'm always happy to make money. How about you, Bradley? Are you happy?"

"Fully satisfied and happy."

"You'll make a good husband."

Bradley studied the illustrated Rocky. There were numbers and letters and an Aztec warrior and a sacrificial maiden and a dripping heart between two hands and knives and the sun, all in color. The chain links around his biceps were etched in rough black, prison-style, and Bradley figured were probably the first tattoos Rocky ever got.

"Did you ever think that you put too much faith in one thing?" asked Bradley.

"You mean like Jesus or money?"

"In a person."

"Like a brother, man?"

"Like a woman."

"A woman? Sure, when I was your age. A young man needs to believe. He needs to worship with all of his big heart and small brain. So he dies for love or for his god and country. But can all love and all gods and countries be worth dying for? No. Then you get older and you become disappointed. In her. In yourself. The Mexicans have a saying—it's not what a woman is worth, it's what she costs."

"I don't understand that. It sounds clever, but I don't know what it means."

"It means that you will pay a price for your lovely red-haired *tesoro*."

"I believe she really is a treasure. I'd pay everything for her."

"Then you will pay everything, if that's what she costs. Simple!"

Rocky drank rum and Coke, and Bradley drank iced tea, as they weighed and pressed and vacuum-packed the cash. Rocky played *corridos* and love songs on a commercial-grade jukebox brightly illuminated by colored neon lights. From the far corners of the warehouse, gunmen watched.

The cash was drug payment from throughout Southern California, Herredia's largest market, earned a few dollars at a time by thousands of young homeboys and passed up the line to Rocky's soldiers and lieutenants and captains until once a week it was consolidated here in the old El Monte warehouse, the last stop before heading south to Mexico. Bradley and Rocky used two expensive digital scales to do the weighing. A pound of twenties was worth $9,600. A pound of hundreds was worth $48,000. Bradley's first and only partner in this business had once told him that the weights and values made him believe in a just and merciful god, though Bradley saw no god in them at all.

"You need a partner to help you with this job," said Rocky.

"There's too much at stake for one man. I'm surprised that Herredia doesn't supply you with one. I can."

"I don't work for you."

Rocky smiled and shrugged. "It's no less for me. I'm thinking of you, my friend."

"I understand, Rocky. And I respect that. But I don't have anyone quite right for this job."

"You have other partners."

"They have other skills."

Bradley thought of Clayton the forger and Stone the car thief and Preston the phone fraud master. Good men but not action men. Men with criminal records, in fact, lightning rods for trouble. Not who you needed sitting next to you on a run through the border into Mexico with hundreds of thousands of dollars at hand. You needed someone capable and calm, someone who would not arouse suspicion. Someone distracting, even. Someone manifestly not guilty. And of course, someone who could pull a trigger if they had to. He thought of Caroline Vega, with her uniform and badge and her avowed passion to *burn through L.A. one way or another.*

"You need the help," said Rocky. "If you get tired or sick or late, you can become careless. One mistake and El Tigre is out a lot of money. And he loses trust in you and loses trust in me and we know what happens when trust is gone."

They compressed and sealed the bills with a vacuum packer made for game meat. This minimized scent and bulk. Finally, they stashed the packs in three large rolling suitcases, then buried them with brand-new clothing still tagged and folded, in case the *Federales* decided to snoop. Bradley always took several more tubs of the new clothing as a donation to various Baja parishes, along with a note on Los Angeles Diocese letterhead forged by Clayton and identifying Bradley Jones as a representative of All Saints, an El Monte Catholic charity. He had never had a problem heading south through the border, and now that he could wear his Explorer uniform and present a replica LASD badge also made for him by Clayton, he felt even more confident.

Shortly after dark, he left El Monte for Tijuana in a Ford Freestar with twenty-five pounds of cash worth $384,000 and ten plastic tubs of new clothes. Already hidden in the van were the first five production Pace Arms Love 32s for Herredia's perusal, a deal separate from Rocky and about which Bradley had said nothing. Two carfuls of Rocky's pistoleros trailed him through the surface streets to the freeway, then fell away. Bradley now wore street clothes instead of the conspicuous and uncomfortable Explorer uniform.

Bradley drove within the speed limit and signaled his lane changes and listened to the radio. His mind was clear and he was alert from the caffeine in the tea. He thought of the Love 32s nearby and could not fail to think of the five men whom Herredia had extinguished using the prototype. He knew that they were Zetas and had chosen to be killers, but he also knew that as men they were conscripted not only by their free wills but by history and the complexities of luck. He believed that those men had died at that time so that he did not have to, and for this they had his respect.

His phone buzzed and he saw the call was from Owens Finnegan and he let it ring. He didn't know what to make of her and he did not trust her, but he was not in the habit of turning down help from people who offered it. That was how you filled out your team, grew your people, expanded. Clayton. Coleman Draper. Israel Castro. Rocky. Ron Pace. Owens and Mike Finnegan. Caroline Vega? You never knew where you'd find them or where they would find you. He'd met Clayton in jail and found Coleman Draper at a sheriff's department recruitment booth. Draper introduced him to Israel Castro, Mike Finnegan had introduced himself and his daughter, Owens, at one of Erin's performances up on the strip. And Caroline Vega was training for Explorer, just like he was.

He pulled over at a rest stop and called Erin and they talked for nearly half an hour. She was performing tonight and this pricked his longing and his anger at having to miss the performance.

Back in the car he thought of her and his heart tripped because his distance from her was growing, but he reminded himself that ten hours from now, befriended by the early morning darkness, he would be driving into his garage at home up in the desert of L.A. County with $15,360 stuffed into a hollowed body panel in the van, his share for the night's work, his base paycheck for the week, and plenty to cover the stage boots and the couture dress and some of the mounting expenses for the wedding, and Erin would be standing backlit in the doorway between the house and the dark garage, radiant and his.

18

Holdstock tried to smile at Hood as he walked in. He was unshaven and his hair was aslant, his eyes vacant. His hands were heavily bandaged, each finger thickly delineated by gauze, and they rested beside him like the root balls of trees upturned.

Hood held up the music CD he'd bought for Jimmy, then commenced opening it with his pocketknife. It was a collection called *The Bakersfield Sound* and Hood thought Holdstock would like its emotional straightness and down-and-out humor.

"Thanks," said Holdstock. "Isn't that where you're from?"

Hood sat in a visitor's chair and yapped about growing up in Bakersfield for a minute or two. Heat, wind, oil fields. Good music and good people. It was late Sunday afternoon, and Imperial Mercy was quiet. He could see Holdstock's interest drifting, so he stopped talking and looked along with Jimmy through the window to the blue Buenavista sky. They were six stories up.

"The deputies are still here, right?"

"Yeah, Jim. Two of them outside and two inside the stairwell. They checked my badge before they let me in. Don't worry."

"When I dream about my family, Gustavo is with them. He holds the girls' hands. He's white. He's in charge of them. He's going to escort them to either the grave or heaven. I can't tell by his expression what he's thinking."

"You won't dream about him forever, Jimmy. It was an accident. No one on earth blames you."

"Benjamin does. Honor. That's why they'll come to get me."

Hood had learned that in his seven days of capture and torture, Jimmy had been injected with adrenaline and other stimulants so he would remain conscious and endure more pain. A doctor said this would induce a psychotic state that would take some time to abate. Not only had his fingernails been pulled out but they had crushed two of his molars and hobbled him by breaking both of his big toes. A psychiatrist had told Ozburn that Jimmy was more devastated emotionally than physically. The doctor had treated prisoners of war and said that in some ways this was worse because Jimmy had been singled out, perhaps by chance only. No fellow soldiers had gone through this with him. He had been utterly alone. He had only himself to blame. That was why it was important to visit him often and let him know that there were other people who were on his side. It was going to take time. Much longer than the fingernails that would or would not grow back, depending on the damage done to the germinal matrix, or the healing of the bones, or the building of crowns to fill the place where his teeth had been.

"Charlie, can you get me a gun?"

"I can't, Jimmy. Oz and I asked about that, and they turned us down."

"You've got yours."

"I'm not a patient here, Jimmy."

The truth was that Holdstock had no way to fire a handgun with the gauzy stumps of his fingers, and the psychiatrist had said that if he could, Jimmy might use it on himself.

"Because if they come after me here, I'm going to need a gun," said Holdstock.

"They won't come after you here."

"I have no defense."

"You're not ready to shoot yet, Jimmy."

"These bandages won't be on forever."

"I'm not going to bring you a gun."

"Well, then fuck you, Charlie. And fuck everybody who looks like you."

"I had a friend in high school who used to say that to me all the time."

"I'm sorry, man. But you try lying here, can't pick your own nose. And your wife cries when she looks at you and you know she notices other men. And your kids stare at you like you're some kind of pathetic freak. And you pray and you pray and you pray, and so what?"

"I know it's bad, Jimmy."

"Bad? I'll tell you what's bad—I think those Zetas are going to come through the damned door any minute and drag me back down there. It's irrational. It's crazy. It won't happen. But none of that matters. I spend the night with my eyes wide open, and sleep a few minutes during the day. They got into my head, Charlie. I keep hearing 'em."

Out of respect for what Jimmy believed and heard in his mind, Hood said nothing.

"Would you ask Jan or Oz to bring me a gun?"

"They won't. It's not about guns now, Jimmy. It's about you getting healthy enough to go home."

"I won't go home. They'll break into my house and kill me in front of my wife and girls."

In fact, Hood knew that this had just happened to a Baja policeman, and that such things were happening to cops and prosecutors throughout Baja, and now that Benjamin Armenta and his Gulf Cartel had crossed the U.S. border to capture Jimmy Holdstock, the rules had changed.

And again, out of respect for Jimmy and the newly possible, Hood said nothing.

"I asked Jenny not to come today," said Holdstock. "It's too hard on me."

"I understand."

"How can you understand?"

"Sometimes it's better not to see people. You have to be ready."

"I love them."

"They know you love them."

"I want my life back, Charlie."

"You can get it back."

"How?"

"Want it. It'll just take time."

Hood heard Luna's powerful voice: *Does hope or lack of hope cause anything that happens?*

"I'd still rather have a gun."

Hood looked out the window to where the vast horizon met the blue heat of the sky. "You know an L.A. guy named Mike Finnegan?"

"No."

Hood told Jimmy about the small man hit by a car while changing a flat out on Highway 98, and how this man had Hood's name and his new post office box number written on a piece of paper folded in his wallet.

"Why would I know him?" asked Jimmy.

"He knows your name and a little about you, and who you work for." Hood immediately regretted his words.

"Then he's probably a fucking Zeta," said Holdstock.

Hood saw the fear on Jimmy's face and it was genuine. "He's in bathroom products. He's in a cast pretty much head to toe. His daughter is an actress."

"Or maybe a reporter snooping around Blowdown, looking for a scandal."

"I don't think he's that important, Jimmy."

Jimmy looked at Hood, and Hood could see his fear subsiding. Holdstock sighed and shrugged. "Charlie, just tell me some Blowdown stuff. How are the field interviews going? You tried Hell on Wheels? Did you meet Dragovitch and his weird-ass wife yet?"

Beth Petty and Police Chief Gabriel Reyes sat on either side of Mike Finnegan's bed. There was one window to the north, and Hood could see the distant hills corrugated by centuries of rain now shaded to blue by a great white cloud. He noted the stack of books on a stand by the bed, not one title the same as last week. And a fresh stack of magazines with the latest *Scientific American* on top. Finnegan's new head bandage revealed slightly more of his face, but the rest of him was still encased in plaster, and his head was still immobilized by the steel skull clamp and rods.

"Come in, Charlie," said Finnegan. "They're interrogating me about the bullet."

Petty smiled at Hood, and Reyes nodded. They were both in street clothes. Hood had never seen Beth Petty without a white doctor's coat and a stethoscope. A nurse rolled in a chair, and Hood sat at the foot of the bed.

Finnegan's eyes were blue and his nose and cheeks were freckled. An orange stubble covered his face. His lips were full, and Hood thought they might be swollen still from the accident. He saw the clench of the wired jaw and the difficulty with which the man spoke.

"There is some problem with the age of the thing," said Finnegan.

"He means the bullet," said Petty.

Reyes looked at Hood. "It was manufactured sometime between 1849 and 1862."

"A cartridge can remain viable for centuries," said Finnegan. "This idea confounds Chief Reyes."

"What confounds me is how the bullet got into your face," said Reyes.

"Isn't that self-explanatory?" Finnegan smiled fractionally, a labored maneuver of lips and stationary jaws.

"He said he was shot by his lover," said Reyes. "He said she just happened to be packing an ancestor's thirty-one-caliber Colt repeating revolver."

"Percussion repeating revolver," said Finnegan. "Which was introduced by Colt in 1849. It helped settle the West."

"Why did she shoot you?" asked Hood.

"Failure to leave my wife. The bullet was deflected by a stout grapevine. Cabernet Franc. Marie was plotting an al fresco suicide scene, I realized later. At any rate, after hitting the vine, the bullet flew with reduced velocity. It knocked me ass over teakettle, but I righted myself and kept running. I made it to a fire station and they took me to a hospital. The doctors believed it would be more dangerous to take it out than to leave it in. That was thirty years ago. In the wilder days of my youth." Finnegan chuckled.

"The FBI told me that bullet is over a hundred years old," said Reyes. "You don't find 1849 thirty-one-caliber Colts just lying around. You find them in museums and collections. Nobody carries them."

"Marie dug it out of an old trunk," said Finnegan. "There are thousands of old trunks in this world. And don't forget that a good gun is eternal. There are harquebuses and snaphaunces still every bit as deadly as they were the day they were forged. In gun years, our history is much shorter and condensed than any of you seem to realize."

Hood stood and leaned over the bed and on Finnegan's cheek found the scar attributed by Owens to a Napa vineyard mishap. The little man stared at him.

"No, you misunderstand," said Finnegan. "The bullet entered from behind. I was running for my life."

Hood looked into Finnegan's clear blue eyes. The light that had shone from behind the layered gauze was still as lively now as it was when the darkness had amplified it. He remembered what Owens had said about learning to read the insanity in Mike's face, but if such a thing was possible, Hood saw none.

"You said Marie was the whore I reminded you of," said the doctor. "At Wyatt Earp's saloon in San Diego."

"Is that so?"

"Charlie was in the room."

"I think you can solve this mystery, Doctor. We're talking about women living roughly a century apart."

"Two Maries."

"You're a sly one."

"I think almost everything you say is a lie," said Reyes. "You're just making it up."

"I didn't make up the bullet," said Finnegan.

Reyes shook his head, then looked at Petty and Hood and back to Finnegan.

"I don't mean to exasperate law enforcement," said Finnegan. "And back to the other night, Gabriel, you must offer all the love you have to your son. All sons need a father's love. He needs it more because he is a homosexual and the world has little love of them. But you are his father."

"I never told you he was homosexual."

"I listened carefully."

Reyes sighed. "We got to talking a few nights ago."

"There's nothing to be ashamed of," said Finnegan.

"No, there isn't. But if that thirty-one-caliber slug entered from the back of your head, it had to pass through your skull and brain to get where Beth found it."

"I like the way you chew on things," said Finnegan. "Good lawmen are always good chewers. But it's common for a foreign object to migrate through the body over the decades."

"No, really," said Reyes. "Your X-rays should show a hole where the bullet went through."

"I'm sure they would," said Finnegan.

"I'll get them," said the doctor.

A minute later, she was attaching them to the reader that hung from the wall. She clipped a series of three across the top and stood back. Hood looked at the contours of Finnegan's skull, the gradients of light and dark and density.

"There," said Petty. She pointed out a very faint circle of darkness on the anterior left side of the skull.

"What do I win?" asked Finnegan.

Reyes stood and stepped up close to the X-ray film. "Are you sure that's a bullet hole? Kind of faint, isn't it?"

"The bone will heal over time if the wound is small. What we see here is probably regrowth."

"How much time?"

"I don't know exactly. Years."

"What about damage to the brain tissue?"

"There is some evidence of disturbance. It appears slight. See the pale finger here?" She tapped her own finger to the film.

"Only slight damage from a speeding bullet?" asked Reyes. "Account for that, Doctor."

"I can't. But there must have been very little brain damage to begin with because brain cells don't replicate. The brain is a miraculous organ in the sense that we can live without relatively large parts of it. The compensatory powers are impressive. People live normal lives with bullets and other objects lodged deep in their brains. I've seen it."

Reyes looked at the little man, then back to the film. "You've got the worst luck in the world, but you've got the best luck, too. You get shot in the back of the head, bullet goes through both skull and brain and should have killed you, but instead the hole heals up just fine. Then you get hit by a two-ton Mercury doing sixty. It breaks your neck and half the other bones in your body and messes up your lungs, kidneys, and liver. It breaks your skull and batters your brains, but you crawl a half a mile through the desert. Now ten days later, you're offering me advice on how to talk to my son. You're a strange man."

"I like you, too, Gabe."

Reyes took another long look at the X-ray, then turned to the doctor. "So, Beth, how is Mike's overall recovery coming along?"

"Very well. The swelling was a setback and I can't account for it."

"You told me his resting pulse is seventy and his blood pressure is in the normal range for a twenty-five-year-old man in good physical shape."

"Grandma called that an iron constitution. She said it was fresh vegetables, low salt, no tobacco, prune juice."

"You subscribe to all that, Mike?"

"Don't ask me about food. I haven't eaten real food since I got here. Even prune juice sounds good. I've never smoked anything in my life."

"I'm going to ask you about that ninety grand again," said Reyes. "Where'd you get it?"

"I earned it. I saved it for this, a rainy day. Mike Finnegan Bath."

"I got the number and address in L.A. from information," said Reyes. "I've called four times. All I ever get is a recording."

"The landline and office are formalities, really. I mostly use the cell. My clients all know how to reach me."

Reyes exhaled, shaking his head. "Is the key in your wallet for the office?"

"None other."

Reyes stood over Finnegan. "I still don't believe your story, Mike."

"Which one?"

19

Hood and Beth Petty stepped into the elevator and when the door shut, Hood felt the sudden pleasure of their aloneness. She wore a yellow dress and her skin was brown with summer and her scent was subtle. In the heeled hemp sandals, she was almost Hood's height. She smiled at him and looked away.

The elevator stopped at the sixth floor, where two patients in wheelchairs and two nurses and the two deputies who had been outside Jimmy's door waited.

"We'll make room," said Beth Petty and she tugged Hood by his cuff and led him out of the elevator car and around a corner toward the stairs. They came to Jimmy's room and the door was open, but the privacy curtain was drawn around the bed. Hood stopped and saw the faint shadow of a person leaning over the bed and he heard a woman ask about leg cramps and then Jimmy's husky response. He heard the swish and ringing of water. Two new deputies stood talking to a pretty woman at the nurses' station, and the men gave Hood the law enforcement look as he and Petty passed by.

They entered the stairwell. It was very hot. Hood saw that the deputies here had finished shift and vacated their posts and he heard the voices and the sounds of possible replacements coming up at them through the space below the sixth floor.

Hood listened to his and the doctor's footsteps sound on the metal steps and echo in still flat air. Beth stopped behind him and Hood turned. She looked down at him from five stairs above. She looked inquisitive and lightly irritated.

"I like being where you are," she said.

"I like it, too. I've thought about you."

She smiled and flushed but didn't look away this time.

Hood turned and watched the new men arrive on the fourth-floor landing below him, a slight bespectacled older deputy and a big younger man with a head of bleached hair. The size difference made them seem comic. The older man looked up at Hood and nodded and wiped his forehead with a folded handkerchief, then they clanged through the door out of the heat and into the building proper. As the door shut, something Hood had just seen triggered a memory, but the memory was too dim and vaporous to identify. When he got to the landing where the deputies had just stood, the air hung electric and wrong. Hood opened the door and saw the two men walking purposefully down a hospital hall toward the elevator.

"What?" asked the doctor, coming up behind him.

"It's nothing."

"Dad used to be like that. Always suspicious. He says it kept him alive."

"Maybe it did."

"He's sixty-five and long retired. His god is golf."

They descended through the echoes of their own footfalls, poly-rhythms on the steel steps. The deputies still tugged at Hood, but they were only doing their jobs by any rational accounting he could apply. Just some overtime to protect the vulnerable and to guard

prisoners, a commonplace paycheck booster for deputies, the bane
of administrators in cash-strapped departments. He thought that
what Beth Petty had said about liking to be where he was was beautiful. He would tell her that. They continued down.

Hood, like Reyes, was a chewer of things.

The older deputy's handkerchief, he thought, *sureno* red. No.
The glasses?

No, not the glasses, the other guy's hair.

When he reached the fourth-floor landing, Hood saw the brassy
bleached swirl of hair from one of Sheila Dragovitch's suspect pictures. *Meet Silenced Automatics. Silenced automatics are all he talks
about.*

Hood wondered if the bleached deputy had been working the
Iron River undercover. Certainly Imperial County Sheriff's had a
hand in. Other task forces, other lawmen.

And of course he wondered if the bleached deputy was a deputy
at all.

Silenced Automatics.

"What floor is your office on?" he asked.

"Three, down one."

"Go there and call security for assistance in Jimmy's room. Lock
the door and stay there or get to your car and go home."

"Charlie?"

"This is probably nothing."

"What is nothing?"

"The man in the stairwell."

"The old guy or Pompadour?"

"Pompadour. *Go.*"

Beth hurried down toward the third floor, her sandals soft on the
steel steps. Hood watched her stride across the landing to the door
and look up at him before pushing through.

He took the steps three at a time back to the fifth floor and when he looked up to the sixth, the two deputies were not there. He made the landing and popped the strap of his hip rig before going through the door.

The hallway was deserted except for one older man pushing a drip trolley. He wore a hospital gown and white socks and he gave Hood a wintry look. Hood rounded the corner to the hallway and walked fast. It was a big hospital and seemed bigger now on this calm Sunday, and Hood went through double doors that stood open, then past a display of children's art in a glassed wall case and he continued in a quiet trot. Then he came to a dark round woman in a white dress and a brightly stitched rebozo across her shoulders and a bowler with a beaded headband and she held across her chest in both arms a bouquet of immense paper flowers in purples and oranges and blues and reds and she was telling Hood flowers, beautiful flowers, as he passed her. Far down the hallway, he could see that there were no deputies outside Jimmy's room and when he asked the pretty nurse where they had gone, she said to the cafeteria for coffee, really good lattes for a hospital if you haven't tried them, and when Hood came to the closed door of Jimmy Holdstock's room, he palmed his sidearm against one leg and pushed through.

Holdstock lay partially upright, head back against the pillows, sleeping. His lips twitched lightly and his eyebrows were raised as if he were surprised and his eyeballs quivered beneath their lids. He was cleanly shaven and there were comb lines through his hair and Hood could smell aftershave and shampoo. Hood shut the door behind him and felt for the lock, but the door could not be locked from inside except with a key. He used his cell to call Ozburn and Bly and told them that he was alone with Jimmy and there were a couple of deputies coming on shift who didn't look right. From the room phone, he called security and described them. He went to the window and looked down at a portion of a side parking lot. He swung one of the visitors' chairs to the door and worked the back of it up under the knob. At this, Jimmy opened his eyes and lifted his head and found Hood here on the outskirts of his dream. He looked frightened. Hood touched his face with one hand and slipped his gun into his holster with the other.

"It's okay, Jimmy."

"Are the guards still outside?"

"It's okay."

"I was in Baja again. In the dream."

"You don't ever have to go to Baja again," said Hood.

"What's the chair against the door for?"

"I'm not sure of some men."

"Oh, shit, it's happening."

"It's probably nothing, Jimmy."

"Nothing is probably nothing."

"Be calm, Jimmy. I'm going to be here for a while and when I like the way things are, I'll leave."

"Don't hurry. Don't hurry, Charlie. Sorry I cussed you out, man."

"It's okay."

"I can't describe helplessness. It's the worst feeling in the world."

"You're not. You're needed. Here, Jimmy."

Using his penknife scissors, Hood cut away part of the bandage on Holdstock's right hand. In a minute the index finger was exposed, pale, then darkly stained with Betadine from mid-knuckle to tip, which was gnarled purple and deeply slotted by the violent extraction of the nail. It looked alive and discrete, an appendage to no thing. Hood was surprised by its ugliness and seeming incurability. In Holdstock's gaze was a short history of pain. Hood raised one knee and withdrew the eight-shot .22 AirLite from his ankle holster and fitted it snugly into the gauzed palm of Jimmy's hand. Jimmy concentrated wholly as he passed his trigger finger through the guard without touching the nerves to the steel, then curled his finger very gently to the trigger. He nodded and withdrew the finger and let it rest safely alongside the guard and the lower frame of the small revolver. He smiled slightly. He exhaled and lowered the gun to lay against his leg and covered it with the corner of the sheet. They waited. With the door shut, the antic noises of the hospital were dulled. Hood heard the padded volume of someone walking past the door outside, then it was gone.

Then a louder shuffle outside and a sudden rapping on the door.

"Security. I'm coming in."

"This is Deputy Charlie Hood. Enter with your hands up where I can see them."

"I'm Lucas. I'm not armed. You in there, Jimmy?"

"I'm in here, Frank."

"Keep your hands where I can see them," said Hood.

"Nobody get excited and shoot, now."

Hood hooked the chair away from the door with his boot and the door slowly opened. Two empty hands appeared to their forearms, and the security guard elbowed in. He was tall and stately and wore rimless spectacles. His eyes went to the gun on Hood's thigh pointed up at him, then to Jimmy.

"I got a call from a doctor to come to this room, and another call about two men of interest somewhere on these ten floors. I'm half the Sunday shift, but the other half called in sick. I can't be in two places at once, so I came here."

"You're agent in charge here, Jimmy," said Hood.

"I can handle it."

"I know you can."

Hood holstered his gun and went to the window again and looked down. There was a young couple walking toward the building and a taxi in motion. He walked out and shut the door behind him.

At the elevator banks, he pushed the DOWN buttons on both sides and waited. Over the next minute, two cars opened empty and one stopped, and the flower woman looked at him. He waited another minute and heard cars pass down and up, the sounds of their hoisting machineries muted within the shafts. Then out came the two replacement deputies for Jimmy's room. Each held a large white beverage container with a black top, and Hood intercepted and badged them and explained what was happening. They argued briefly. Then the deputies set their drinks on the floor, and one broke off toward Jimmy's room and the other followed Hood to a waiting area. There Hood looked down to a different part of the lot, the front lot, and he could see the great concrete overhang that shaded the main entrance and the curving entryway and the palms towering up on either side. Up close to the building, the lot was filled with cars, but farther back were empty places. A black-and-white police cruiser was parked midway, and the two deputies walked briskly toward it. From these six floors up, the bleached hair shone like a small brass coin. Then Hood saw a yellow Charger sweep into the lot and he knew it was Janet Bly's.

He was on the speed-dial in an instant, but her recording came on just as the Charger parked at the red curb near the entrance and Janet got out and disappeared beneath the overhang, running.

Leveraged by the handrail, Hood flew down the stairs, the deputy clambering loudly after him. It seemed to Hood that he hit the ground floor in seconds, but as he sprinted across the lobby, he saw that Janet had apparently already made the elevators, and when he ran outside into the concussive heat and rounded the concrete planters into the parking lot, he saw that the prowl car was gone.

He ordered his new partner to call it in, then ran to his Camaro in the rear lot and gunned it for the exit. He had to guess which way they had turned on B Street. So he guessed and turned, but he saw nothing of them or their car.

He was cursing when he saw Ozburn's raised black Land Cruiser roaring toward him down Third for the hospital. Hood circled back.

They all sat in the cafeteria. No one was sure who the two stairwell deputies were: The door team never saw them, and the off-shift stairwell team had either known them to be legitimate or not laid eyes on them. One of the first stairwell team deputies confirmed by phone that he and his partner had departed their posts a few minutes early because of the sweltering heat. They had not seen their replacements and didn't know who they would be. Neither of the door team said they knew a fellow deputy with a head of upswept bleached hair. The terrible question of what had happened to the authentic replacements, should this fleeing pair prove to be the impostors they seemed, went loudly unsaid. Hood felt the hostility in the deputies and he didn't blame them for it.

Later, Blowdown huddled in the first-floor prayer chapel for privacy. There were holy books in several languages on a shelf, and on the wall were framed photographs of religious sites around the world. Hood said the bleached deputy could be a genuine deputy working both sides of the iron trade. He had worked with profoundly corrupt deputies in L.A. and he knew that L.A. was not unique. Not all men were immune to money and power, and far fewer immune to the survival of their family or themselves.

Four hours later, Hood and Beth Petty emerged from the Imperial Sheriff's Department station in El Centro. He held open the heavy door of his Camaro and Beth got in. The night was cool and the sky was flat and heavy with stars. Hood felt only a small ripple of contentment as the V-8 and the glasspacks rumbled beneath him.

They had seen pictures of the two deputies assigned to the stairwell during the shift in question and these men looked nothing like Glasses and Pompadour.

Over the next three-plus hours, they had viewed HR photos of every sworn male deputy and had not been able to identify them. At Hood's request, they also looked at pictures of all male reserve deputies and this had been fruitless, too. A strong but nameless tension had mounted in the conference room. Hood felt the currents of it shifting and changing as various ICSD brass came to check progress and left to make cell calls and muttered quietly among themselves out of earshot.

As Hood and Petty were getting ready to leave the room, the ICSD captain who had run the show told them that the two deputies who were supposed to guard at the stairwell had apparently thought it was the midnight shift. They claimed they were told it was the midnight shift. There had been a communication glitch, and the captain said he'd get to the bottom of it.

They sat across from each other in a brightly lit booth in the Buenavista International House of Pancakes. It was late and the dining room was nearly empty and Hood heard a vacuum being run on the other side of the register. He was tired and nervy with hunger, but he felt again the pleasure of being with Beth Petty alone. Surrounded by the claret vinyl of the booth cushions and the geometric polyester carpet and the rose-colored laminate tabletop, she looked to Hood like life itself. He watched her study the big illustrated menu. She lowered it.

"It's different."

"What."

"Everything. The world now. The guns and drugs. The heads. The cops that aren't cops. All the slaughter. It's no longer occasional. Thousands of abortions every month and women leave babies out back of the hospital all the time. Something got out of its bottle. I'm not sure I want to know what it is."

"Okay."

"I don't believe in the end of the world. I believe it keeps going and it becomes what we make of it. Approximately."

"I hope you're right."

"I saw you check my ring finger that very first second in Mike's room."

"You nailed me, Beth."

She put the menu back up and talked from behind it. "I'm starved. That was a long, long night at the cop house. Cops are slow people. Deliberate people. The German plate sounds good. Either that or the chocolate chip pancakes on the kid menu, side of bacon. And I'll be honest with you, it felt good to have that finger checked."

"I'm sure it happens a lot."

She moved the menu to see him. "I was married through med school and it was a disaster. We about ruined each other. Should have never done that. Live and learn and no hard feelings. You?"

"No."

She positioned the menu over her face again. She said nothing for a long while, then, "I hate having to explain myself. That's why I don't date much. When I do, I pray for a guy who talks about himself the whole time. I escape with my privacy intact. Not that I have secrets. I've had a very ordinary life. Maybe a quirk or two, sure, everybody's got those. I can't guess what kind of date you would be. But then, this really isn't a date."

"Want me to start in talking about me?"

She spoke again from behind the plastic sheath. "I'm going kid menu and side of bacon, large milk. Guilt free. I love this place because there's not a single health-conscious thing in it. I used to fast once a week for a day. All I can say is, it's hard to sleep that night. I love to eat. There's an overweight woman inside me, just waiting to get out."

"You talk a lot for a person who doesn't talk a lot."

Menu down: "Wrong. I don't like to explain myself but I love to talk at certain times. I talk when I'm hungry. I talk when I've had a hard day, and men with guns have been creeping around in my hospital. I talk at meals because for eight hours a day most everything I see has to do with blood, guts, illness, and death. I talk to my dog. I like saying words such as *violet* and *Saskatoon*."

"You want a guy who can listen to you blather on and on without a comma and never even get tired of it."

She raised the menu again. "He's bound to get tired of it, but he still has to listen. I value good manners very highly. You know, I could do the German plate *and* the kid plate. And I'll bet you right now, if I ate all that I could still have dessert. Which begs the question of what's a good dessert after chocolate chip pancakes? What do you think?"

"I think it means you were raised in a large competitive family."

The menu stayed up. "Five kids."

"Ours, too."

"Then how come you're not talking *your* fool head off?"

"I'm letting you."

When Beth Petty lowered the menu, there was a straw in her mouth aimed at Hood and she blew a spitwad into his chest.

20

Hood sat on his stool in Hell on Wheels, the ATFE Dumpster modified for surveillance. The tow truck he had used to transport it was now parked over near the restrooms. Hood was borderline claustrophobic and disliked being caged. He ate a candy bar and drank a can of odd-tasting iced tea.

Twelve hours ago, Ivan Dragovitch had called Hood about the ammo sale, and Hood was now near ground zero of the deal, a rest stop on Interstate 8 midway between San Diego and Yuma. Ozburn and Bly had given him hell and their blessing, but this was still a legal deal, and bad as it smelled, it didn't warrant the whole Achilles team. Within the ATFE ranks, small individual operations were encouraged because they often got results and were an important method of finding possible informants. Hood told them nothing of his relationship with Kyle Johnson. He wanted to see Bradley buy fifty thousand rounds of .32 ACP with his own eyes.

Dragovitch had suggested the rest stop. Here, in the far corner, at nine P.M., Kyle Johnson would inspect and legally purchase the product from an unlicensed munitions dealer named Wesley Savage. Ammo sales were not federally regulated, and the state forms were cursory at best. Dragovitch would preside and Hood would witness and record. Hood knew that Bradley could have gone online to any number of sites and had the quantity drop-shipped to his home, but this would have subjected him to the security protocols of the company and to their suspicions and possible relationship to ATFE. Savage's prices were higher because he had no questions and filled out no forms.

Sitting now on the stool in the Dumpster in the middle of the immense desert, leaning forward with his elbows on his knees and his fingers crossed, Hood saw himself from the outside for a moment. *There I am on a stool in a cage. All the many paths have led to this.*

He thought of Beth Petty and her nervous chatter and the tone of her skin against the yellow dress. He wanted to touch her.

He held the video recorder up to one of the holes. He had positioned Hell on Wheels way out on the edge of the parking area to give himself a generous field of vision. With the zoom he could see across to the "Dangers of the Desert" display and the vending machines and the strip of ground with the NO DOGS sign above it and the sun-blackened turds dry in the dirt. Past them were a flat expanse of desert in which the creosote and ocotillo and cholla stood disparate in the windless evening. At the end of everything, the sun lowered into a lake of red.

Dragovitch pulled into the rest area at eight o'clock. Hood watched his black Dodge pickup lap the parking lot once, then roll to the far corner, closest to the desert, where pets were allowed. Dragovitch got out and left the door open, rolled his shoulders, looked around with casual alertness. Hood expected Sheila to get out next, but she didn't. Instead Ivan whistled sharply and a white blur sailed from the pickup cab and into his waiting arms. Dragovitch held up the wiggling papillon, then set it down, and it pranced sharp-footed to business in the dog patch.

Hood sat on his stool and noted the final lengthening of shadows before sundown. He rechecked his recorder settings and the clamp holding the concave mike dish. He watched through a peephole. The rest area was getting busier, cars pulling in and out, and families hustling for the bathrooms and lining up for the vending machines, the big rigs moaning into their dedicated area and moaning out again.

The meeting time came and went. Dragovitch paced and the papillon lay on a cushion on the tailgate. Hood was tired of sitting in the Dumpster and he had the feeling of things going wrong.

A kid ran all the way from the vending machines to throw away a wrapper. Hood lowered the mike and backed away from the spy hole. He watched the boy lift the top and he felt the wrapper tap his head, then fall to the floor of the bin beside him. The kid brushed his hands together with a job well done, then turned and sprinted away.

Nine fifteen.

Bradley and his gang unloaded the ammunition in the Jacumba garage of Israel Castro, a friend and confederate. Jacumba was a smuggler's roost between San Diego and El Centro, a hilly warren of trails and tunnels and dirt roads straddling Mexico and the United States, and Bradley liked this rough country and the lawlessness that hovered over it. He had met Castro through Coleman Draper, the reserve deputy shot dead by Hood. Castro had offered to store and later transport the ammunition, and get Savage's truck down into Mexico for sale. Bradley knew it would fetch a good price from any *narco* with horses and acres to enjoy, or simply product to transport. The men worked quickly and silently, and when the heavy crates were arranged on the pallets, they said good-bye with the touching of fists. Car doors opened and closed and the metal garage door rumbled down and the motion lights at the gate held the dust for a moment, then even that was gone.

Bradley set off east and fast. The new Cayenne Turbo was a dream, four-hundred-plus horses throbbing through him as he penetrated space like a bullet. He thought of his mother again, a woman who loved speed and was sometimes possessed by a reckless abandon that had thrilled him from a very early age. But now he was driving away from Erin, and this pulled at his heart like gravity and he believed he could feel the distance growing between them, and it seemed unnatural and perilous. He had never asked his mother if speed felt good when it was taking her away from what she loved. He had never asked her about her love of anything but himself.

At nine thirty he sped past the rest stop where the deal was going down and he caught a glimpse of Dragovitch's big black Ram far back in the parking lot. Smiling, he gunned it. Forty minutes later he pulled into the driveway in the hills outside of Quartz.

She was waiting for him on the front porch. Her dark hair was up and she wore a red chiffon dress and stood partially hidden by a porch column, her arms bare and her neck bepearled and her nails lacquered. She was barefoot.

Bradley left the engine running and made the porch in a few long strides and dropped a black suede Harley-Davidson purse to the boards.

"You're beautiful tonight, Sheila. Yes. Here's five thousand for you."

"You said nothing about money."

"Burn it if you want. You earned every penny of it."

"I never asked for a penny."

"And I thought you'd like the Harley bag."

"What else have I earned?" She stepped forward and lifted her face to his, and Bradley kissed her on the cheek. Her perfume was strong and enticing. "Please come in. We have time for a drink."

"No. He'll be back."

"It would mean very much to me."

"As it would to me, Sheila. But we can't let love make us foolish. Ivan would shoot us both."

"Don't belittle love. I've seen it in your eyes. You can't hide it."

"No, I can't."

She took his face in her warm soft hands and he kissed her deeply and with some feeling, but foremost in his mind was to leave this place unshot and make it back to Erin as soon as possible. He felt Sheila's body against his and the wonderful offered weight of her. She was more than three times his age and amply beautiful still, but this was Erin's moment as were all moments, and in this thing that resembled unselfishness Bradley put stock and took pride. He broke away.

"You take my breath away, young lady."

"I want something beautiful to remember you."

He took her hand and looked into her eyes as he spoke. "'Love is a war of lights in the lightning flashes / two bodies blasted in a single burst of honey.' You can have that."

She looked and he could see the pulse in the pale trunk of her neck. "You wrote that for your fiancée."

"Neruda wrote it for my fiancée."

"But you gave it to me."

"The more you give away, the more you have."

"So it is only about you having more?"

"I hope to be a better man than that someday. Until then, enjoy the five grand. And you might want to do something about the lipstick before Ivan comes home. I don't think he'll be too happy. Sheila, I thank you for bringing such a treasure to me."

"You're nothing but a criminal. But I know I'll dream of you again and again."

Bradley touched her cheek and got back into the Cayenne and drove hard.

At almost ten, Dragovitch hoisted himself off the tailgate of his truck and flipped open his cell phone with a fast flick of his wrist. The dog sat up. Hood watched the man shake his head and grab a handful of his own hair and pull on it. A moment later, Dragovitch came lumbering across the parking lot toward the Dumpster.

Hood climbed out, his heart sinking, pissed off.

"Tragedy, Deputy Hood. Mr. Savage was kidnapped by four masked men at gunpoint while loading the product into his truck. He was blindfolded and his money and cell phone were taken. He was driven far into the hills and released without his shoes or socks. It took him two hours to get to a phone and call me. His truck is gone. The ammunition is gone. He tore apart his shirt to make shoes. He is furious."

This tale confirmed what Hood had felt, and now he was angry at himself for not feeling it more strongly and more clearly. "Ivan. I'm looking at a real short list of suspects who knew about this deal."

Dragovitch spread his arms wide, hands open. "And of course Mr. Savage said the same thing about me and the armed robbers. But I will tolerate no suspicion. None from you and none from Mr. Savage. My reputation with law enforcement is perfect. Mr. Savage has his enemies and they have delivered him to this. I take no blame. The world has many ears and many pockets, Mr. Hood. You know this."

"Fuck, do I ever."

He stepped away and called Ozburn. Halfway through his explanation, he thought he understood Sheila Dragovitch's intent stare at Bradley's photograph. On this hunch he asked Ozburn for directions to the Dragovitch home in the Quartz hills.

He caught up with Ivan in the pet area, where the papillon sniffed and lifted his leg with an air of discrimination.

"I want you to stay here for half an hour, Ivan."

"Why?"

"Stay put. Don't move. Direct order."

Hood pushed the tow truck hard, but it did him little good. It was all torque and no speed. He fruitlessly watched for Bradley's Cayenne coming from the other direction. Forty minutes later he rumbled slowly down a dirt road until he came to the Dragovitch driveway. He switched off his headlights. He saw no cars, and the garage was closed. The house lights were dim inside. He drove past and up the hill opposite and parked. He could see the front of the house and the drive and garage. TV light shifted inside. Someone moved within the living room window, and Hood followed the shape behind the loosely closed blinds. Through his binoculars he saw Sheila carrying a drink toward the TV light. She sat. She was wearing a light blue robe and her hair was down. She set the glass on a side table and curled her feet up under her and settled the robe over her legs. Her face was shiny with cream. She pulled the robe collar up closer to her neck and hung her head, and it looked to Hood like she was nodding off or sobbing or both. Twenty minutes later, Ivan's truck turned onto the driveway. Hood waited a few minutes, then left.

21

To my surprise, Uncle Chester is standing in front of my third-floor desk. For a huge man, he's always been quiet, and he's staring down at me before I can even guess why he's here. He's wearing his usual unstructured cream linen suit, wrinkled and world weary. Blue dress shirt, no tie.

"Ronald."

"Uncle Chester. Terrific to see you."

"If you say so."

I stand and come around and we hug. He feels unnaturally strong. With my arms around him, my hands won't even come close to touching. As always he smells of baby powder. When I was growing up, it was said that Chester had once crushed a two-hundred-pound mastiff that had attacked him without provocation outside a campground bathroom in the Sequoias. I have no reason to doubt it and I can feel that he could do the same to me here right now if he wanted to.

He lets me live and I step back. I haven't seen him in over a year, since just before the judgment that finally flattened Pace Arms. He has never changed: same overlarge body, same shiny shaven head, same blue eyes, same baby-skin face with the pink blossoms on his cheeks, same trim white teeth. If I paint him as a grotesque, he is not quite. There is something leonine about him, something graceful and powerful and feral. He might be twenty-five or seventy. There's just no way to tell by looking. I know him to be fifty-two, two years younger than his brother, my father, would be, and four years older than my mother, whom Uncle Chester married a year after my father's suicide. Dad committed the act here at Pace Arms while seated at firing station two, down in the basement, using the same model Pace Hawk .40-caliber autoloader that would later discharge and kill eight-year-old Miles Packard when he dropped the gun while playing with it.

I move a good chair into place for him.

"I didn't come halfway around the world to sit down."

"We can stand."

"Let's stand in manufacturing."

We take the elevator down. Uncle Chet stands with his hands folded before him and his head bowed and his eyes closed. He takes up more than half the space in the elevator car.

"I enjoy familiar sensations," he says. "Your mother says hello. She's stable as she can be, it seems."

"She likes the new room."

"I'm glad it makes her happy. It destroys me to see her like she is. Literally destroys."

Which makes me wonder if that's why he's been gone for over a year. My mother, Maureen, was institutionalized not long after Miles accidentally killed himself. She's a 295.30—paranoid-type schizophrenia, episodic with interepisode residual symptoms. She is only occasionally violent and twice suicidal. The doctors said that the boy's death probably contributed to her sudden break, but they couldn't say how much. Certainly she had already been destabilized by my father's act. As if all that wasn't enough, there is also a lineage of madness in her family. Chester said that she died when Miles died, that it just took a little time to become apparent. He said this often. Mom started out at a nice private sanitarium in Tustin, but with the death of Pace, Chester had her committed to a group home run by Fairview State Hospital here in Costa Mesa. It's not a grim place, and she has her own room. Through longevity she recently graduated to the best and largest room in the home, first floor, corner windows, southwest exposure. The window glass is reinforced with steel mesh.

"I see her twice a week," I say.

"Of course you do."

We step out and I key us into the manufacturing bay. Chester holds his small hands together behind his back and strolls. This was a posture I imitated during my head-of-production days and I feel compelled to use it now. I fall in beside him. He moves down and around the long tables, towering over them, looking down at the wheeled chairs, the task lights and the table magnifiers, the power buffers and grinders, the trays of hand tools, the piles of new red shop rags, one per workstation, the spray cans of oil and solvent, the bins of pins and bolts and springs and all parts machined, the files and tweezers, needle-nose pliers and nylon hammers, the waterless hand soap and the unempty ashtrays and the coffee mugs.

He stops. He wipes an index finger across the worktable and shows me the gray metal dust. He wipes his finger on a clean shop rag, then picks up a coffee cup and holds it upside down over the floor and waits. It takes a few seconds, but finally one milk-heavy drop of coffee rolls to the rim and hangs there.

"What are you making?" he asks.

"It's called the Love 32."

"I asked what are you making."

"It's a thirty-two-caliber full-auto pistol, silenced. I'll show you."

Down in the basement range, I pull out the lacquered box and unveil the Love 32. Uncle Chester sits at station five. He's nearly my height when sitting. I assemble the gun. His blue eyes watch without blinking. His petite hands rest on his massive thighs, and his head is cocked. He has the same stillness that I remember. I release the brace rods and set them at full length though I know they won't be long enough. I leave off the noise suppressor for now. I hand him the gun.

The last person to occupy his seat was of course Sharon, and I think of her sitting there with the peanut butter–filled pretzels sliding off her lap, and her sad beautiful face hidden behind her tangled blond hair. Right now she's on break, off to South Coast Plaza for lunch with her mom and dad. She's better. She has slept nine straight nights in the penthouse. That's every night but one since her wedding day. During her one night of absence, I couldn't sleep but I didn't ask her about it. I don't know what she does at night in the penthouse after I leave. I hear her lock the door after we've talked and watched TV or sometimes read. She sleeps late. But during her workdays, she has shampooed two stories of carpets, replaced the plastic electrical outlet faceplates with more fashionable models, purchased cheap but attractive framed photographs and area rugs for the vestibule that once held the Catlins and the mounted bear and buffalo, painted the bathrooms on the second and third floors, and replaced every bulb of recessed lighting with the new fluorescent minis that she found on sale at fifty cents each through a power company promotion. She has the energy of a .44 Magnum. Even without measurable evidence, I believe she will invite me to join her in my bed soon, and the idea of this momentarily obliterates Chester's presence in my world.

When I become aware of him again, he's holding the Love 32 in both hands, lightly, as if it might be hot or very delicate. He gently hefts it for weight. He removes from his handkerchief pocket a small tool which he applies to the gun. In a few seconds the thing is in parts on the bench, fully decomposed by Chet's precise fingers. He examines the parts where they lie. He rearranges them slightly. He could be divining the future. He becomes still again and ponders. Then from a brief entanglement of fingers and tool and parts, the Love 32 emerges whole again, fitted into Chet's hand.

I hang a silhouette and send it out fifty feet, and Chester steps to the firing line with the machine pistol. His appearance there is the polar opposite of Sharon's. Whereas Sharon standing there with the Love 32 was one of the most beautiful visions I have ever had, Chester with the same gun and standing at the same firing line looks only menacing. He stands the line sideways rather than face-on, and rather than using his left hand to brace the gun against muzzle rise, he curls it behind his back like a fencer, his whale strength superior to that of any machine gun he's ever fired, or so he has told me. He fires the five-second burst with the barrel so steady that the group in the middle of the torso is no larger than a softball.

He lowers the gun and turns to me. "The run?"

"One thousand."

"Shifts?"

"One. Our best people only."

"Customer?"

"Private security firm, Paris, France—Favier and Winling."

"Price per?"

"Nine hundred."

"That pains me. More to come?"

"A thousand maybe."

"How long until delivery?"

"Eight days. Ten."

"I assume this is all off the books. No contract, no permits, no licenses. Cash payments to suppliers and labor, no taxes, no ATFE."

"That's right."

"And no serial numbers on the guns."

"Right again."

"Ron?"

"Yes."

"I'm somewhat proud of you. Reload it and put on the silencer."

I screw on the noise suppressor and click in a fresh magazine. He fires left-handed this time, the group slightly looser than before. The bullets tap through the paper and patter against the sandbags two hundred feet away. Chester looks back at me, then past me. His smile is, as always, disturbing. I turn to see Sharon standing behind the partial wall of Plexiglas that fronts the spectators' area. She comes around it and down to the stations. She frowns at me, then trains her eyes on Chester still at the firing line. She's wearing a sleeveless white lace top and black trousers and nonsensible shoes. Her hair is swept up over her ear on one side and falls freely on the other.

"Hello, Mr. Pace," she says to Chet.

Chester turns and faces her with all his mass, the machine pistol dangling from his left hand. "Sharon. I have never in my life seen you so beautiful."

She looks at me, then back to him. "Well, thanks. Sorry. I saw the light on my camera console and wondered what was going on down here."

"Join us for lunch," says Chester.

"I just had lunch," says Sharon.

"We need your participation on a key front."

She hesitates, cuts a look at me.

"We do," I say.

She nods unhappily.

I get Chinese delivered and we set the little white boxes out on a card table in the third-floor conference room. We sold off the conference room furniture months ago, but last week Sharon presciently purchased a folding card table and four chairs. They are miniaturized by the big room and the tremendous size of Uncle Chester, who stands because the chairs are too small to support him. He cups a box in one hand and works the chopsticks with the other, a paper napkin tucked into his dress shirt and spread across a very small portion of his chest. I see the distress on Sharon's face.

"First things first," says Chester. "We need to raise the price per unit. Our design is simple and efficient. The materials are sound. The gun performs well. We will not sell it for that price."

"It's been contracted at that price," I say.

"There is no contract. There is only our word, and our word can be changed. Offer an incentive for an early commitment to the next thousand units. I suggest three percent off the renegotiated price of twelve-fifty. Next, we will renegotiate the cost of the sound suppressors separate from the gun. This feature is worth far, far more on the world market than you have guessed, Ronald, and good business is never guesswork. Believe me, your buyer is cackling to himself over the deal he's made with you. I do not enjoy the sound of that cackling. Now, with the design work complete and some start-up capital coming in, we need to produce in much larger quantities. In spite of what you may have heard, fortunes are not made one penny at a time. They are made hundreds of thousands of dollars at a time. True opportunity does not whisper. It screams. We must answer it loudly. Sharon, this is where you come in. We need to contact all of our former like-minded customers. By *like-minded* I mean anyone who might be interested in such a clean, dependable, and value-priced killing instrument. We have designed a beautiful thing. There is nothing like it in the world, at such a price. The market out there is vast, I promise. I've seen it this last year. Our world is a different place than it was when I began with Pace Arms back in 1978. It's even different than it was a short five years ago when you came to work for me, Ronald, and you, Sharon. Our world has blossomed. It has matured. It is famished for something like the Love 32. Sharon, you must find the people who need us. They are legion. It's time you move from the reception desk to marketing and sales. Your salary will be increased commensurate with your performance. You can accumulate wealth, Sharon. You can do this job."

She shakes her head and stands. Her face is calm, but I can see the anger in her eyes. "No. I can't and I won't. Good afternoon, gentlemen."

She marches from the conference room and lets the door huff shut behind her.

Chester stares at the path of her departure, then at me. "Fire her or I will."

"I'll handle it."

"Yes, you will. Is there a chance she'll take one with her and try to sell the design as vengeance?"

"She wouldn't do that."

"Would she contact the authorities?"

"She's completely trustworthy."

Chet considers the door through which Sharon had gone, then turns back to me. "Consider the best ways to implement the other orders I've just given you, Ron. You have much to learn. I'll be in close touch."

With this, Uncle Chester sets his tub of pork and his napkin on the card table and places the chopsticks on the napkin.

I walk him to the elevator and ride down. No words, just the faint smell of baby powder and gun smoke and Szechuan pork.

He keeps half a step ahead of me across the first-floor lobby and he pushes through the doors and into the soft Orange County sunshine without looking back.

Sharon is at her desk, aggressively tapping away on the keyboard. She does this when she's angry, much as Mom used to slam pots and pans around in the kitchen.

I stand there and she glances at the security monitors on her desk. "Here's what I think," she says. "I think he can't march back in here and take over. The Love 32 is yours. This buyer is yours. You've kept the doors open here for a year while he's been out in the world doing, truly, God *knows* what. You pay his taxes on this place. Pace Arms is yours as far as I'm concerned. I want that man out of here. '*We have designed a beautiful thing.*' You designed it, Ron. Not him."

"He owns the building and the fixtures. He owned the company."

"*Owned*. There wouldn't be anything left if it weren't for you. I won't let you give this away, Ron. You've worked too hard for it."

"Mind if I sit?"

"Please do."

"Coffee?"

"Sure."

I pour coffees and make hers as she likes it, cream and sugar. I pull up a reception chair close to her desk and sit.

"What are you going to do?" she asks.

"I don't know."

"He knows. He's going to take over the deal and take over the company."

"I see that."

"I will not work for him."

"Why not?"

Sharon continues to look at me, and I see the anger come back to her eyes. She has good outward control over her emotions, but her eyes are a dead giveaway, status indicators, like the LEDs that tell you what your TV is doing.

"You haven't seen the way he looks at me, have you, Ron?"

"Oh?"

"It's an ugly thing. He looked at me that way the first week I worked here when I was seventeen. It felt like he was injecting a virus into my bloodstream. He's looked at me that way a thousand times over the years. He looked at me that way today. But he held it longer. Ron, your Uncle Chester is an evil man."

In fact Chester was once questioned in a rape but never arrested. This was hush-hush. It never got below the third floor. It was a long time ago. "Describe the look."

"It's a show of strength. Like an army. Weight and power. He sees that compared to him, I have little. He knows that I know it. He loves my fear."

I feel my own anger stirring now, low level but with potential, like a nest of wasps feeling the first warmth of spring.

"And, Ron? I think he drove your mother insane. She was reeling from Tony's death. She was a little nutty, sure, it runs in her family, but she was smart and lovely and right there in the moment. She had spirit. She worked hard, but she was always ready to have a good time. He bludgeoned her down. He crushed every last bit of hope out of her. He sat on her so long, she forgot how to breathe."

"I think that, too."

"Everybody did. But nobody said anything and nobody did anything."

"She married him."

"It wasn't a marriage, it was a surrender. She was empty by then."

We let a moment of silence be. The brothers—my father and Chester—were very different men. Suicide points many fingers and whispers many rumors.

"Don't let him have this company," says Sharon. "If you do, I'll walk out that lobby downstairs and never come back."

"That's clear."

"Stand up for yourself, Ron. Stand up for me, too. Change the locks. Keep him out."

"I'm capable of doing that."

"I know you are."

It's hard to describe what I'm feeling right now, but as usual I try, not necessarily a good idea. "Sharon, I can feel different rivers and streams of history coming together here. They will move on without us, but they're here now."

"I don't see a river. There's no river within miles of here. I don't know what you're talking about."

"This all matters."

"Of course it does. May I have the rest of the afternoon off?"

"Of course."

She shuts off her computer and flips her desk calendar to tomorrow, then rises and slings her purse over her shoulder. She comes around to where I'm now standing and she raises her face to mine.

"Good. Because I'd like to spend it in your bed with you."

It's not comparable to anything else that's ever happened to me. Two minutes after we lock the penthouse door, we are in bed, but seconds later I'm uncontrollably spent though still half dressed. I'm not a veteran of love. I feel humiliated, but Sharon finds humor in all this and assures me that things will be looking up soon. And up they do look. An hour later we're finished again, and two hours after that, again. I call up a sushi place that delivers, then make hot fudge sundaes, and after that we're back at it. We are electricity. By midnight, we lie in each other's arms, and Sharon snores on my chest. I look out the window at the lights of the mall and the Christian compound and the freeways red with taillights going one way and white with headlights coming the other, and these are the rivers of the here and now, the rivers I tried to tell Sharon about. I know that we are waist deep in them and getting deeper. I press my nose onto the top of her scalp and breathe deeply. Human female sweetness beyond words. For the first time in my life, I feel absolutely responsible for another person. I know that her welfare is more important than my own. I realize that I am no longer the most important person on earth. In fact, I barely rate a distant second.

Early that morning while Sharon is sleeping and long after the manufacturing team has gone, I let Bradley Smith into the building through a rear fire exit and we make our way to the manufacturing bay. Here I unlock and open the steel safes that contain the first five hundred Love 32s.

"You look like you've been worked over by the sultan's harem," says Bradley.

"Better than that," I say.

"Sharon?"

I smile and feel myself blush.

"She's pretty quick on the rebound," says Bradley.

"I take it as a sign of healing."

"Well, congratulations. All your tail wagging paid off."

I watch Smith examine the weapons. I must admit they are beautiful. Not like a woman is beautiful, or a sunset, but as a car might be, or a laptop. Even with his hair cut short, Smith looks familiar to me. I know I've seen him before.

"You still look familiar," I say.

"You've said that before, Ron."

But the longer I look at him, the less it helps. I have a good memory for faces, yet it does me no good now. I feel drained but in the best of ways.

"If Herredia will commit to another thousand now, I can come off the price," I say.

"How much off?"

I think Uncle Chet is wrong. You keep your prices down. You build relationships. You make friends. "Three percent. It would save him twenty-seven grand."

"Indeed. And put another eight seventy-three in your hot little pocket. How much commitment?"

"One hundred K. I can deliver them by the end of September. Tell him he can name them something else. He didn't like the name."

Bradley looks hard at me. "What about Harry Love and all that bullshit you call history?"

"He can name his own gun is what I'm offering."

"He'll want *muerte* something. I'll see what he says."

Bradley extends the brace rods on one of the Love 32s, sets the gun into the crook of his arm, and sweeps it across the room.

"He'll use them against the Zetas, won't he?" I ask.

"Wouldn't you?"

"I think—"

"Do not attempt to think. Stay far away from your customers,

Ron. You are a gunmaker. That's all. If you go sticking your nose into other people's business, they'll chop your head off and mail it to Sharon. I'm serious."

The mention of Sharon's name sobers me. Bradley counts the guns. They're packed ten to a wooden case in twenty stacks of five. Each gun is housed in a foam envelope and the layers are separated by pasteboard sheets. Of course the lids aren't nailed on yet. There are four hundred and ninety-five weapons, not counting the first five production-line guns I fronted him last week. The cases smell of freshly milled steel and gun oil and grip rubber. There are little blotches of new-gun oil on the pasteboard packing sheets, a sight that has always pleased me, something akin to a job well done. The noise suppressors are packed separately.

Bradley steps into a corner of the bay and makes a short phone call. When he's finished, he wraps his phone in one of the red shop rags from a workstation, then picks up a hammer and pounds it to pieces within the rag. He drops the package into a trash can, then pulls another phone from a pocket and pushes it into the carrier on his belt.

We sit on patio chairs on the third-floor balcony and watch the sun rise. Highway 55 is already busy and the Santa Ana Mountains to the east are rimmed with light. We drink coffee spiked with whiskey, and Bradley has two good Cuban cigars, so we light up. Breakfast of champions. This is our third such celebration. The first was when he delivered the three hundred thousand start-up money, and the second was when Herredia enthusiastically accepted the production model last week. Now we can celebrate the halfway point.

What a way to start my first day of being Sharon Novak's man.

22

Mike Finnegan's Los Angeles apartment building was on Aviation Boulevard near LAX. Hood stood outside and looked at the complex, fifty years old at least and in disrepair, with peeling paint and a grassless dirt courtyard littered with plastic toys and brooded over darkly by a large magnolia.

Hood climbed the stairs and opened the door with Reyes's key. He entered and stood in a rhombus of soft L.A. sunlight while the jets rattled the window glass and vibrated the floor.

The carpet was blue shag and the walls were white. There was a worn red vinyl sofa that sagged and was stretched in the middle, and on the wall behind it a framed print of a big-eyed Mexican girl holding a puppy. The TV was a vintage black-and-white with a rabbit-ear antenna set on top. The walls were taken up with bookshelves that went to the ceiling, mostly inexpensive and unmatched but full of mostly hardcover volumes of history, biography, warfare, natural science, and drama. There were two small stools so the little man could reach the upper shelves. In the middle of the room, between the TV and the sofa, stood a small card table and one folding chair. The table was stacked with books and spiral notebooks.

The kitchen was neat and foodless. The refrigerator had ice cube trays in the freezer and that was all. There was a small kitchen table and two chairs, and on the table was a telephone and answering machine. Hood pushed the PLAY button and listened to the one new message, from Owens, saying she was sorry to have left so abruptly but she was in a good place in a desert and happy and not to worry. Hood pictured her lovely face and arresting eyes and the scars on her wrists. *You will have a reason.* There were no old messages.

The bedroom was curtained with bamboo-look plastic blinds and contained a twin bed neatly made up. The olive-colored bedspread was without wrinkles and the pillow was plump and perfectly centered. Hood saw his own military training in this, wondered if Uncle Sam might have more information on Mr. Finnegan. There was a small dresser and more bookshelves. In the closet were pants and shirts on hangers, a heavy canvas jacket with fleece lining, a few pairs of shoes.

Hood saw an odd glint beneath the canvas jacket and he lifted it open for a look. Hanging under it was a garment of dull gray mesh. Hood lifted out the coat and the gray garment. They were surprisingly heavy. Hood peeled off the jacket and tossed it to the bed. The garment was a vest, apparently made for a tall and slender man. Hood held it to his nose and smelled the flat metallic scent of steel. Down one side were buttons made from large silver Mexican fifty-peso coins. Down the other were thickly braided steel loops. Hood let the hanger drop and shrugged on the vest and buttoned up the side. It was snug and weighty but also supportive, the tail firm against his lumbar vertebrae. The arm holes were small, so the vest rode up almost to his armpits. He could imagine no use for such a thing except to repel bullets or blades. He wondered if it would work.

He walked back and stood in the patch of sunlight in the living room, and when he looked down, he could see rounded indentations roughly the size of bullets. The steel mesh had spread and flattened but held. One mark was right over his heart. There were sharper dents that could have been made by knives. He took off the vest and read the date on the top button: 1851. In the bedroom he hung it back up, then photographed it with his cell phone, then hung the canvas jacket over it and set the hanger back on the dowel.

Hood thought about the 1849 bullet in Mike's head and the 1851 vest in his closet and Mike's detailed recounting of the hanging of Tiburcio Vasquez and Mike's tales of drinking in Wyatt Earp's San Diego saloon. Here was a pattern that Hood's ATFE task force trainers would have loved. But a pattern establishing what? Mike the history buff? Mike the collector of Western lore and things? But there were other Mikes. Such as Mike the bathroom products guru who knew far too much about Operation Blowdown and Jimmy and Benjamin Armenta. And Mike who wondered what Zetas dream about. And Mike who had been at the Ambassador Hotel when Bobby Kennedy was murdered and could describe a sunset viewed from Spahn Ranch with Charlie Manson. And of course, perhaps the simplest and most definitive Mike—the Mike pronounced insane by his own daughter.

But in the second bedroom, Hood found no evidence that Owens or anyone else had recently lived there. The cot bed was neatly made, but the dresser and closet were empty of clothes. There were eight pasteboard boxes stacked in the closet and Hood found them full of books. The walls were bare and there was no TV and no reading lamp and no radio and no clock. He took more pictures.

Hood walked into the bathroom, wondering what a bath products broker would have in his own home. There were mismatched bath and hand towels, some old enough that threads dangled at the edges, a faded green oval rug, shaving products, and a large bar of blue soap in an upturned clamshell on the sink. The shower had a sliding glass door, frosted and clean, and inside was nothing but one economy-size bottle of shampoo. There was an ornate brass towel hook in the shape of a horse's head on the wall near the shower, but this single item was the only thing in the room that wasn't commonplace.

Back in the living room, Hood sat at the card table and browsed the top notebook. Inside he found a handwritten ledger that was cramped but legible—billables and receivables, dates and dollar amounts, notes. The most recent entry was two months ago and the oldest dated back to early last year. The largest transaction involved $5,999. There were illustrations of various bathroom products, such as shower curtains and rings, soap dishes, standing and built-in toilet paper dispensers, bath mats for tub and shower, medicine chests and wall cabinets, towel racks. These drawings were rendered in the same small tight hand as the notes, but they were simple and expressive. The other ten notebooks stacked there contained nothing but blank pages and folded clippings from newspapers and magazines. Hood opened and read through them. Finnegan had written the source and date on the top of each clip. Most of the stories were from small California towns, many of which Hood had never been in: Ravendale, Tollhouse, Ivanhoe, Trona. He made a note of these.

Some clippings dealt with small-time crime, most of it whitecollar—embezzling, fraud, forgery. Most of the perps were women. Some dealt with violent criminals and most of these were men, and educated. Some were about precocious children. Some dealt with quirky inventions such as a personal jet pack, a machine that could synthesize water from the air, a time-released multivitamin and mineral tablet that had to be taken only once a year. One was a feature titled "Saturday Night Special," about Ron Pace, a seventeen-year-old high school dropout manufacturing/design whiz who was running his family's hugely profitable gun company. This was Pace's second unscheduled flight into Hood's airspace in the last two weeks, so Hood read the article slowly and carefully. Pace was quoted as saying that "making guns is harder than making pizza but what I'd really like to make is history." Company president and CEO Chester Pace said that Pace guns were "the workingman's equalizer." The article touched on the suicide of Ron's father. There were pictures of Ron and Chester and Ron's pretty, unhappy mother, Maureen. Hood rose and stood back from the table and he took pictures of it and of the room.

He heard the knock on the apartment door and he rose and answered it. A small boy stood outside. He looked ten. He wore a Kobe jersey and shorts to his skinny calves and basketball shoes that made his feet look gigantic.

"Where's Finn?"

"In a hospital."

"Been gone a long time. He okay?"

"He's doing fine. I'm a friend."

"You look like a cop."

"What about you? Are you his friend?"

The boy looked past him into the apartment, then at Hood. "Yeah. He's gone a lot so this is no surprise. He gave me this."

The boy pulled his hand from his pocket and showed Hood the knife. It was an old-fashioned pocketknife with an elk horn look handle and blades at opposite ends.

"It needs sharpening. Mike sharpens it. He says a dull knife is more dangerous than a sharp one. He's got a sharpenin' stone in the kitchen drawer where the forks are."

"Come in."

Hood found the stone and whetted the knife, circling one blade then the other across the grinding surface while the boy watched.

"Mike does it slow like that."

"There's no hurry. I'm Charlie. What's your name?"

"Marlowe."

"Your mom know you have this?"

"She's dead so she don't know anything. Dad's cool."

"How long have you known Mike?"

"Since forever. He sleeps all day sometimes. Mostly he's gone at night. Sells them towel holders and dishes you put your soap in."

"He got hit by a car down in the desert. Lots of damage but he's healing up."

"Mike's good at healin'. I seen him with a cut on his lip once, and it was so deep you could see his teeth through it. Said he got punched. Two days later it was almost all healed up and after that no scar or nothing. He don't hardly eat. He's read every one of these books and more. I've been coming up here for maybe five years now, yeah, 'cause I'm ten, and let's see . . . three . . . no, four times Mike's packed up all his books in boxes and took 'em away. Because he read them all. I helped him load up his truck. Then he gets all new books and reads those. We watch TV sometimes. My dad and uncle come over and Mike gets beer. He listens to stories, but he almost never tells one. He asks a lot of questions. He wants to meet certain people. He says he likes getting people together. He brought over a kid one day for me to hang with. We're friends now. Mike understands kids. He told me if I got straight A's next year, he'd give me a hundred bucks for each one, and if I don't get straight A's, he won't give me nothing."

"Have you met his daughter?"

"I can't because he doesn't have one."

"Does he ever have friends over, or family?"

"Sometimes I seen a person here. But not much. He's mostly alone, sleeping all day and doing his bathroom things at night. He says there's certain kinds of people he can't be around."

"What kind of people?"

"I never ast."

Hood handed Marlowe the knife. The boy licked his forearm and shaved off some thin hairs with the long blade, then the short one.

"Mike's got red hair. When the knife is sharp, it leaves an empty spot with freckles. And guess what, the next day all that hair is back. Every hair of it. He doesn't know I know it."

Hood thought about this.

"Thanks, man. You did a good job on this. It ain't as good as Finn can do, but it's still good."

"Don't take it to school."

"A knife ain't nothing."

"It's enough to get you kicked out. Then you won't make the big money from Mike."

"Oh, I'll get that money. I'm getting all A's and Mike always docs what he says. He's never lied to me, not once."

Owens Finnegan answered the door of her El Centro home. Her face was made up and her lipstick was red. She was wearing a sleeveless white dress and wide carved African tribal bracelets and she was barefoot again. Hood stepped in and saw no change: same boxes stacked, same bare walls, same director's chairs. The kitchen was still bare as she led him outside to the picnic table.

"I made some iced tea since I knew you were coming."

She poured two tumblers from the glass pitcher. There was a sugar bowl and spoons on the table.

Hood brought up the image of the steel mesh vest on his cell phone and set the phone on the table in front of Owens. She turned it and shaded the small screen with one hand.

"That's from your father's closet in L.A. What is it?"

"A vest of some kind. I've never seen it."

"You never lived in that apartment on Aviation, either."

"No."

"But he's been there since the 1960s, when that black-and-white TV was new and he was ten years old?"

"That's always been his place of business, Charlie. Since seventy-something. He buys old stuff because he likes it. That old TV never even worked. We lived in various places—Sierra Madre, Glendale, Los Angeles—not on Aviation."

"I don't enjoy being lied to. It wastes my time and it pisses me off."

"I never told you I lived in that apartment. I can't control what Dad said. I'm sorry if I've never seen that article of clothing before."

"What about the clips? The stories from the small towns in California? All the inventors and promising children and small-time criminals?"

"Dad's interests are across the board."

"No shit, Owens."

Hood drank some tea and put his glass down, then stood and walked across the dead brown grass and looked out to the desert beyond the wall. To the southeast, thunderheads loomed out of Mexico, great white anvils climbing the blue.

She stood facing him and handed him his tea.

"Mike knows way too much about Mexican drug cartels, and the ATF," said Hood. "He seems almost fixated on a man I work with. Mike knows things about him he just shouldn't know. Did he do investigations? Do you have law enforcement in the family?"

"None that I know of."

"Government, military, intelligence?"

She shook her head, and the dry desert breeze lifted her hair. "It was always passion and bluff. He wants to be an insider. He has an extravagant and sometimes powerful mind. I've never known anyone as intelligent as he is. Or as crazy. I've seen him lie in bed for days, crying and never eating. I've seen him stay awake for days, making phone calls and doing sketches and reading, reading, reading. He doesn't invent stories or friends or incidents. He invents entire *worlds*. They are populated and specific."

Hood looked into her eyes, now almost silver in the bright sunlight. She took his glass and flung the tea and ice against the wall and dropped the glass to the dry grass. He felt her hands cool on his cheeks again and the warmth of her breath on his face, then the softness of her lips on his. He lifted her hands off his face and felt the risen cords of scar-flesh under his fingers.

"They're me, Charlie. Past, present and future, all in one. Don't be afraid of them."

"I respect them."

She took his face in her hands again and kissed him again. Hood broke it off and lifted her hands away and kissed the underside of the left wrist, then the right wrist, and as he did this she closed her eyes and exhaled quietly.

"There might be another day for this," he said.

"Tell me when you find it, Charlie."

23

Holdstock lay awake and listened to the late-night sounds of the hospital. His door was closed. He was taking less medication for pain and to sleep, so his native energy had started to flow again.

He got up and used his crutches to make the toilet, clumsily balancing on his armpits while parting his gown with the thick gauzed trunks of his fingers. His broken big toes were operational for indoor distances. The crushed molars had already been replaced by crowns, and his swollen face had almost returned to normal size. Frank the security guard had confiscated his gun, and two nurses had rebuilt the right-hand bandage that Charlie Hood had so trustingly modified. Jimmy's hospital gunslinging days were over and this left him feeling naked and defenseless again.

He managed to get the gown closed, then he worked his bandaged hands back into the crutches. With his weight born by his palms and the crutch handles, his fingers throbbed with pain, but it was a bearable pain. On his crutches he shouldered his way through the half-open door and into the hallway. There was only one deputy on duty at this hour and he sat with his head bowed to the *Car and Driver* spread across his lap, but he was asleep.

Jimmy labored down to the nurses' station and talked with Lourdes for a minute or two. Standing at rest he used his armpits to bear his weight and was able to lift his hands upright to let the blood drain back down from the infernal fingertips. With his hands up like that, Jimmy thought he must look like a man being arrested. There was a Dodgers game on the little TV in the station, so Jimmy somewhat illogically told Lourdes about a touchdown he'd scored for Wisconsin, a last-second reception and twenty-three-yard run that put them past rival Indiana 21–14. When he was done, Holdstock felt a little short of wind and he made a joke about getting more tired talking about the touchdown now than actually scoring it. He breathed deeply and noted the simple pleasure of feeling fresh air coming into him.

He continued down the hall. Slow going. This was his fourth exercise session in four days. Ever since Hood had spotted the two fake deputies, Jimmy had understood that he'd have to get his strength back in order to survive. He needed to get out of here. He needed to be home with his wife and daughters, no matter how much of a burden he might be, no matter that their pity shamed and angered him. It was only in the last four days that Jimmy had begun to truly want to live. He had not dreamed of the blue-faced werewolf in five nights. Sometimes he would lie in the bed smug and satisfied that the beast wasn't there. Then he'd glance up at the ceiling to make sure.

He passed through the open double doors and stopped at the children's art display, breathing hard again. He transferred his weight to his armpits and raised his hands and felt the pain drain down. He looked at the display. T. Ford's airborne skateboarder was still his favorite, with A. Anthony's cotton field and M. Gonzalez's fire-breathing monster right up there, too. He wondered what Patricia and Matilda would come up with when they were a few years older. Hopefully not their father lying in a hospital bed. He wondered if Gustavo Armenta had made drawings as a boy, if he had made his father proud. What would a son need to do to make a drug trafficker feel pride? Jimmy had heard that Gustavo was college-bound, a business major, a good young man. He repositioned his hands on the crutches and continued on.

At the far end of the hallway, he came to the waiting area alcove. There was a suite of chairs and two tables of magazines and good windows. This was as far as he'd made it in the past. He was tired by now, so he hobbled over and plunked down into the orange fabric chair he liked and he looked down through the big window. The sky was black and pricked by stars up high. No moon. Lower in the window, the hospital lights were strong and Jimmy could see the big concrete overhang that shaded the main entrance below, the palms uplit, the sweeping drive. There were no cars parked in the drive now, no admissions or discharges in this early morning.

Jimmy lifted his feet one at a time and put them on the matching orange ottoman. It took only a few minutes upright to send the blood hard south and inflame his broken toes with pain. Now they cooled. He read the magazine titles. He looked down at the driveway. He dozed. A big silver tour bus lumbered onto the drive from Second Avenue. It was covered with bright pictures of red hibiscus flowers and dancers in colorful dress and a jumping marlin and a beach at sunset. Holdstock knew that Buenavista was an alternate border crossing to busy Tijuana but he'd never figured Imperial Mercy Hospital as a point of interest. The tour buses always passed through but never stopped. Maybe doctors, he thought, part of a convention or professional program of some kind. He thought he was dreaming, but his eyes were open.

The bus pulled up to the curb just short of the overhang and it parked. He could barely make out the letters on the side: AMERIGO. The graphics were bright and clear in the driveway lights, and the windows were darkened for privacy and coolness. Holdstock saw the tall door buckle open and watched men bristling with armament pour from the vehicle and flow thick-booted and single file across the concrete toward the hospital lobby one after another, man upon man, ordered and many.

"Zetas," he said.

Holdstock lurched up, his feet hitting the floor with shocks of pain, hoisted himself onto the crutches, and nearly lost his balance as he made the difficult pivot. He strained forward recklessly but managed to look back out the window at the line of men still trotting into the lobby. He took the floor in big crutchfuls. There were no patient rooms along this section of hallway, and Jimmy had no cell phone, and there were no pay phones or house phones or fire alarms and no doctors or nurses or patients or janitors, not even Frank, here at this hour, only the wide empty hallway and the shining floor before him. He saw the open double doors and the children's art exhibit far ahead and he committed himself to this distance just as he had done as a Badger tight end running a downfield pattern. The aluminum crutches creaked and rattled as he whapped them to the floor and he was thankful for the rubber grips.

He lunged past the art. Looking down to his left he could see the back end of the bus but he couldn't see the door, so he turned his attention back to the hallway and stretched out his stride, reaching far ahead with the crutches and holding them down true with his big strong arms while he swung his legs between them like a pendulum, landing on his heels and rolling forward upon his toes, ignoring the pain, then butterflying the crutches through the air to begin again.

He made the turn at the elevator bank. He pushed the DOWN buttons on all four cars, but this took time. He heard automatic gunfire below. Coming back to the hall, he could see the nurses' station far away, but he saw no nurses. At the first patient room he came to, Jimmy swung in, yelling at the man in the bed to call security. The man raised his head and when he saw Jimmy, he scrunched back on his elbows in surprise and he reached for the phone on the stand beside the bed but knocked it to the floor. Jimmy couldn't grasp it with his bandaged hands, and the man said he couldn't leave his bed, just a day out of surgery, and Holdstock could hear the dial tone humming up at him, but there was no way he could punch a number, so he heaved back out into the hallway. He heard gunfire again, much closer now, probably on the sixth floor. Lourdes ran toward him with a cell phone to her ear and the sheriff's deputy from outside his room followed her, broad-shouldered, his hands held out from his sides like a gunfighter and Holdstock could tell from his posture that the man had no idea what to do.

When Lourdes got closer, he heard her say *"Frank where are you we hear guns."* Then the deputy was upon them, guiding them into the nearest patient room, where a woman with a tube in each nostril stared at them while her young roomie announced that she had 911. Lourdes and the deputy lowered Jimmy into one of the visitors' chairs; then the deputy pulled it to the far wall between the beds, facing the door. He commanded Lourdes to lie down behind the same bed, then he drew his sidearm and stepped out of the room and shut the door. There was another volley of automatic fire, jagged and brief. It came from the far side of the sixth floor. Then more shots. Holdstock realized they'd found his room empty and were now going room to room down the hallway, looking for him. The fire alarm shrieked to life and the patient told the 911 operator that Imperial Mercy was under attack and slammed down the phone. The woman lay back and stared at the ceiling and prayed out loud.

"They want me," said Holdstock.

"They'll kill you," said the young woman.

". . . into the valley of the shadow of death," said the older one.

Jimmy climbed up onto his crutches and lurched across the room, banging hard into a steel bed stand and clanging into a wastebasket. He couldn't open the door, but the young woman got it for him, and when Jimmy had cleared the threshold, she closed it hard.

He stood still in the hallway while people ran past him, going both directions, some screaming and some grimly silent and some with cell phones pressed to their ears and some pushing drip trolleys before them like stubborn children, but all with their hair wild and their eyes wide and their gowns flapping. Another burst of automatic fire rattled from around the corner. People reversed direction at the sound and surged back toward Jimmy, knocking him to the floor and stampeding by. Getting back onto the crutches was one of the hardest things he'd ever done in his life, with his ruined hands and throbbing toes and his heart pounding and the treachery of the aluminum crutches as they shirked his weight and skittered out from under him. A woman helped him and finally he was up and wavering. He clambered forward into the storm. Three Zetas rounded the corner, then three more. They wore camouflage fatigues and military-style boots and black handkerchiefs over their mouths, and Jimmy could tell by the sudden cocking of his head that the lead man recognized him, and Holdstock swung faster toward the man, thinking they can kill me but they can't stop me, and he roared forward on the crutches ready to die. The Zetas knocked him down again and swarmed him and they held his arms and legs and head and they carried him to the stairway and into the stairwell, then down the steps. Their boot echoes were faint as they rapidly descended, swiveling him on the landing and descending again and rotating him again on the next landing, down and down, until Jimmy looked up to see the high ceiling and the dramatic lobby lights above him and he realized now that they were taking him again and that the death he had just accepted would have been a far better thing than the days of life to come.

24

The monsoon struck well before first light, the sky opening like an enormous black blossom, and great torrents of rain slanting down through the wind. Rivulets poured through the serrated arms of the fan palms along the hospital driveway and cascaded silver down through the lights. The downsloping drive was a smooth rapid that threw up wakes against Hood's boots as he ran.

He was drenched by the time he made it up the long Imperial Mercy driveway. He passed the police and sheriff's cruisers and the paramedic squads pushing the gurneys into the building.

Reyes led him into the lobby. A gurney stood near a pool of blood on the polished granite floor where Frank the security guard had been slain. The blanket was up over him now and his hand protruded from under it, and Hood saw the wedding ring still on the old man's finger. Reyes took Hood to the staff elevator and they headed up.

"They've got Holdstock. They knew right where he was and they took him."

Hood's heart sank to have this confirmed. In his call, Ozburn hadn't been willing to believe it. He heard Mike Finnegan: *My num-*

ber one concern, if I were you, would be that the Zetas will simply storm the hospital and take him again.

"Five dead," said Reyes. "They threw enough lead to stop an army, but only five are dead. Maybe that's a miracle by today's standards."

"Was Beth here?"

"No. She was not. They killed Frank back down where you saw. They went straight to Jimmy's room. Up on the sixth, they killed two nurses and a patient and the deputy who was guarding Jimmy's room. One of the first-floor nurses looked at her watch when they came in, then she called nine-one-one. She looked at her watch again when they carried Jimmy out—it was one minute and forty seconds later. They were in a tour bus, Charlie, a fucking tour bus. It stayed parked right out there until they loaded Jimmy in. My officers got here thirty seconds after it left. ATF got Customs to close the border heading south, but I haven't heard a thing about any damned bus. They won't use the crossing. They'll use the dirt roads and the tunnels and the secret trails the traffickers always use."

Hood and Reyes stepped around two bodies that were still on the floor but covered with bloody sheets and blankets. The patients had been moved to the cafeteria. There was blood on the floor and the walls, and Hood could see where the bullets had left lines of holes in one wall and shattered the safety glass around the nurses' station. A nurse lay dead and covered on the station floor, with her feet showing under the blanket and her white nurse's shoes and her ankles smeared dark red. Paramedics pushed the deputy past in a gurney, and Hood saw his handgun lying on the floor near a wallow of blood. Farther down the hallway, he saw a crutch in the middle of the floor and another flung up against the wall and he knew Jimmy had fought.

A Buenavista cop with a video camera began shooting and narrating. Ozburn and Bly came marching down the hallway toward Hood. Ozburn had a phone pressed to one ear, and Hood heard him asking *"How the fuck can you fucking not find a tour bus with twenty fucking gunmen in it?"* Bly looked equally furious, biting her lip, her gaze downcast and shifting.

"Get me four helos and twenty agents," barked Ozburn. "Fuck the fucking monsoon!"

Ozburn's Land Cruiser exited Highway 98 and ran west along the frontage road. The rain had stopped, but the wind was ferocious. Besides their sidearms, they had two combat shotguns and the M249 SAW machine gun that in the hands of the warrior Ozburn was reputed to pack hellish fury. Behind them were two sheriff's SUVs and Reyes's police Jeep, a total of fifteen lawmen, counting Blowdown.

They came to a locked gate to which Bly knew the combination, and when Hood heard the lock click open, he shoved hard on the pipe rail gate and swung it out. A county-maintained fire road lay beyond. Ozburn drove through and picked them up and descended a long stretch south. The road was recently bladed, but the grade made the truck slip and slide even in four-wheel low, and Ozburn used first gear to negotiate the steep descent. At the bottom he turned left onto an even steeper road, and as Hood leaned forward, he saw that it was rutted and narrow, part of the warren of traffickers' roads that spread throughout the Buenavista hills on both sides of the border.

Ozburn stopped and waited. In the dashboard lights his face was beveled and his heavy features reminded Hood of the comic book heroes he had read about as a boy. Hood turned and watched the vehicles rumble one at a time down the steep muddy road behind them, then split off, one left and two right, Reyes and the deputies both familiar with this, the stateside branch of the labyrinth. They had all agreed to stay as close together as was reasonable and still cover the roads, in case good luck or a benevolent god ruled this night and they were actually able to overtake the tour bus and Jimmy. Fifteen well-armed fighters coming from different directions was a decent match for twenty Zetas. Less was not. Reyes had reminded them twice to avoid the gullies and low washes.

At the bottom of the slippery slope, the Blowdown team found itself in just such a gulley, with steep sandstone walls and the bottom already running six inches of water, fast. Ozburn picked his way up the wash and fishtailed up a hill, tires hurling red plumes of water and mud until the vehicle hopped over the crest. From here Hood could see the lesser hills spread before him and the lights of Buenavista.

The wind had blown out the monsoon clouds and now the sun rose yellow in the east. In the new light the roads throughout the hills looked like the scratchings of some huge child, playthings. Hood saw one of the sheriff's SUVs spinning up a steep hill to the south. Reyes's Jeep trundled along a ridge top, and the officer in the passenger seat ran the beam of a mounted floodlight in front of them in search of tracks. The wind hissed and whistled and shook the ocotillo and made chevrons on the rainwater that stood in elongated puddles alongside the road.

Ozburn threw the truck into park, and the Blowdown team simply watched. The cholla vibrated in the wind. Hood saw a jackrabbit stretch between patches of creosote. On the downhill side of the dirt road the water was running hard, bubbling with sand and rocks. But the longer he stared south across the border, the less movement he saw until finally at the horizon's end, there was nothing moving at all, certainly not a tour bus alive with red hibiscus and dancers and jumping marlin, only the newly rinsed land motionless under the fickle sky.

"It's his mind," said Bly. "Once you lose it, it's gone. It breaks like a rubber band. I saw it happen to my grandmother. Just poof, gone and never to come back again. She was old. Jimmy? I think he almost lost it in the hospital. He barely hung on, then he turned the corner. If they take his mind, we'll never see him again."

"I want that bus," said Ozburn. "Right out there on that wide muddy road, stuck to its axles, a bunch of Zetas running around for us to mow down."

"That was cool what you did, Hood," said Bly. "Giving Jimmy your weapon and cutting away his bandage so he could shoot it."

"Thanks. The doctors weren't too happy."

"Yeah, well, an hour ago if Jimmy had had a piece and his bandage cut right, there might be less people dead," said Ozburn. "Or would it be more? Fuck it."

"It was the butts 'n barrels game to see who got Hell on Wheels," said Bly. "Jimmy's luck turned when he lost it. He spun the gun and nailed himself and nothing's gone good for him since. One damned spin of a gun. Which got him stuck in the Dumpster that night. Then later he took out Victor Davis in the restaurant because he saw a threat that none of us did. Did you ever think that—that Jimmy saw what we did not? He's got twenty-twenty uncorrected, you know. You know? Then it was one hundred percent pure bad luck that he misses with one shot and kills some poor guy trying to get his girlfriend out of harm's way. And the guy is Gustavo Armenta. And the Zetas grabbing him? What could be worse luck than that? Why not grab one of us? Benjamin Armenta doesn't know who shot his son. It could have been Davis returning fire, it could have been me or one of you. Or both of you. But no, they take Jimmy. *Twice.*"

"Don't blame yourself for Jimmy," said Ozburn. "It's untrue and destructive. Jimmy isn't about you."

"I know."

"Then *do* know it, Janet," said Ozburn. "We'll get him back. Somehow we'll get him back. Find that tour bus, Hood. You're the one with the eagle eyes."

Hood continued to stare out the window and said nothing. Something broke into the cloudless western sky and he saw the ATFE helo swooping in on the wind, tipping wildly. It rose and dipped and sped up and slowed down as the gusts had their way with it. Then the helo was hovering above them, nose to the wind, rotors digging for purchase in the treacherous currents, searchlights blinking their greeting and their devotion. In this precarious thing, Hood saw everything good and hopeful and hopeless about the work that he had chosen.

When they got back to Buenavista and into cell range, Ozburn called Raydel Luna, but the Mexican policeman didn't answer his phone.

Two hours later they still had not been able to raise Luna.

The tour bus had long vanished and there was no word from Jimmy's captors.

Neither Soriana nor Mars was available by phone: Both had been ordered to ATFE field divisional headquarters in L.A.

Sitting together in a Buenavista lounge for a late and bitter lunch, the Blowdown team watched in mute defeat as the Humvees and trucks filled with National Guardsmen rolled through the narrow streets on their way to secure the border, and the news network helicopters came drifting in from all of the four directions.

They'd been told that there would be one thousand Guardsmen

in Buenavista by evening, and another three thousand deployed along the border from San Diego to Corpus Christi. Army and Marine units were standing by, but the president had yet to take this large step. The border had already been closed in both directions. Blowdown also knew that the coming public uproar and media tumult over Jimmy would leave any covert rescue operation without sponsors at the higher levels. So now almost worthless were their own secrecy and ability to surprise.

"Whole new fucking game now," said Ozburn.

"We're bit players," said Bly.

Hood knew that they were right.

Jenny Holdstock appeared on the TV that hung over the bar and pleaded through tears for the return of her husband. He was the best man she had ever known, the best father. She looked truly hopeless. The girls sat on either side of her, nervous and bewildered.

25

That night Hood walked up the Imperial Mercy driveway with a bottle of the peppery organic zinfandel that Mike Finnegan had requested, and a straw. The broad semicircular drive was now a parking lot of media uplink vans and portable lights and camera crews and generators and miles of cable. He saw vehicles from all the big news networks and from stations he'd never heard of and affiliates from all over the American Southwest. Network helicopters crisscrossed the sky above. Reporters and videographers roamed and gave Hood the curious eye. He recognized two New York network anchors he'd been watching for years and several reporters, amazed that tiny Buenavista had spawned a tragedy of such interest.

He dodged the reporters and showed his badge to a deputy at the lobby entrance, then showed it again to another deputy when he got off the elevator on the ninth floor.

He walked toward Finnegan's room, stunned by the day. Hood had seen the TV evening news, already bristling with angry citizens wanting to go get Jimmy back from people who were supposedly our friends. The American president had just finished a televised news conference reassuring the American people that they were safe from criminals from all nations, urging patience, and pledging to secure the border "decisively and by any means necessary." The Mexican president had warned the United States that any form of "retaliation" across the border would, under international law, constitute the invasion of a sovereign state.

Finnegan held the lidded blue plastic hospital cup with his good left hand and raised the straw to his mouth to drink.

"Oh, that is good," he said. "I haven't had a glass of wine in months. What did you think of the president's words?"

"How do you know so much about Jimmy?"

"Oh, straight to the point tonight. You've had a dismal day, I know. Web searches mostly. I once purchased access to law-enforcement-only sites but realized I didn't need to. I'm pretty handy with a computer, Charlie."

"So you hack in?"

"It's easier than that. Passwords and protocols are not created by geniuses. They're just people. I've never used my information for anything but good. I really have no one to discuss my findings with. I've never compromised an operation or an investigation or an undercover agent. Nor will I. Ever."

"You haven't been around a computer since you came here. But you've discovered things about Jimmy that have occurred lately."

"Discovered or imagined?"

"True things, Mike."

"Imagination is often truthful. Truth can even come from those who were not there—Homer and Matthew and Hawkings."

"How did you know the Zetas would come for him again?"

"How could you not know it?"

"What will they do with him?"

"Bring him great pain."

Hood studied the little man's face. He had round cheeks and a pink tone of skin and his whiskers were red and getting longer, and with his cheerful blue eyes, he looked like an aging cherub.

Finnegan raised the blue cup, and the straw found his mouth. He sipped and swallowed. "I know who you are, Charlie. I closely followed the exploits of Allison Murrieta as did so many Angelenos. Video of the funeral was all over the Web, of course, so imagine my surprise when her arresting officer—shown so very briefly on a late news clip—turned up as a mourner, too. Turned out to be you. Certain law enforcement and courthouse blogs were revealing. You were much talked about. How is Bradley, her son?"

"Fine."

"Getting married, I hear."

"This is what I mean, Finnegan—just exactly how *did* you hear it?"

"You're getting exasperated. The same as Reyes."

"How did you hear it?"

"He told me weeks ago, Charlie!"

"Where? Why?"

"I was right there in the Viper Room. Owens was with me. It was the night the band changed its name to Erin and the Inmates. I was very much minding my own business. But Bradley Jones is immensely vain and immensely proud of Erin McKenna. He told me everything—the date, the location, the early Californio fiesta theme. I couldn't shut the boy up."

Hood drank some of the wine.

"Charlie, I'll let you in on a little secret: I can't hold my liquor. Nor can I resist it. May I?"

Mike slowly extended the cup, and Hood refilled it and handed it back. Finnegan took a long sip, then let go of the straw and sighed. "In Napa we grew a grape called carignane. It was a filler grape, like merlot, and we mixed it with the big cabs and petite syrah and some zinfandels. A very strong, very opinionated varietal. Personally I loved it better than all of them. I wanted to bottle and sell it. But commercial wine making is driven by marketing, and the marketers could never even pronounce *carignane*, let alone sell a bottle of it to a blockhead in a supermarket. So merlot won out. Merlot got to be the new star. Largely because the name is easy to pronounce and fun to say. It's got that subversive little *t* at the end, silent and suggestive and a little French. But as a grape, it's gutless next to my beloved carignane."

"You never lived on a vineyard in Napa, Mike. You made it all up. Even Owens stopped believing that story years ago."

Mike stared at Hood for a long beat. In his eyes Hood saw broad contemplation but of past or future or of this moment he couldn't guess.

"True, to a point," said Mike. "But it's a good memory, made up or not. I need all of those I can get. Don't you?"

Mike sipped again. Hood saw a sparkle in his eyes now, the joy of getting caught in a lie and truly not caring.

"Tell me another story," said Hood.

"Once there were two powerful brothers who lived hidden in a forest. From there, they and their loyal helpers watched over a village. No one in the village ever saw them, but the brothers and their helpers made the sun rise each day and the rain fall and they caused every seed to grow or not grow. The brothers loved the village and every person and animal and plant and every living thing in it.

"These brothers were not equal in their powers. The stronger was not the smarter, and the smarter was not the stronger. The stronger called himself the King, and the smarter called himself the Prince. They argued constantly about the best way to guide and watch over the village. The King believed that his rules should be revealed and followed, while the Prince believed that the villagers should be free to discover and be true to their own nature. One day they fought, and the King drove the Prince and all of his followers out of the forest and into the desert beyond.

"Now the strong King from the forest revealed his rules to the village, and many believed and followed. Unbelievers were tortured and slain though the King did not approve this. So the smart Prince from the desert sent his followers into the village, disguised as citizens. These helpers tried to sway the villagers away from the King, using words and song and dance and art of every kind. Many men and women came to believe what the Prince's helpers said—that the King was nothing but a cruel old fool and that men were noble enough to make their own good rules. And the King, seeing that his might alone was not enough to rule the village, likewise sent his helpers disguised as citizens to persuade with words and song and dance and art of every kind.

"And the village became a city, and the city became a state, and the state covered the earth.

"So life on this earth became a contest between the King and the Prince, each unseen but each represented by his helpers. They compete for the hearts and minds of humankind. They are envious of humankind. Neither King nor Prince is powerful enough to defeat the other absolutely. This, Deputy Hood, is a way to understand what you see around you and what you do not see."

Hood sipped his wine. "Stories are lies."

"Through which we see the truth."

"It's a Christian parable."

"Christ is neither mentioned nor implied."

"It reminds me of some Native American myths."

"A very insightful people. Doomed by trust, disease, and alcohol."

"I suppose there's more you want to tell me."

"Surely you're curious, Charlie."

Hood had the thought that he could indulge Mike Finnegan's fantasies in exchange for whatever truth Mike might offer about himself, and about Jimmy Holdstock. "Which are you, Mike, the King's helper or the Prince's?"

Finnegan chuckled, raised the cup again, drank, and lowered it to his belly. "Why not a simple villager?"

"I'm appealing to your arrogance so you'll tell me who you are and what you know about Jimmy."

"Charlie, I can't tell you who I am. Nondisclosure agreements, you know. Most organizations have them. But I can tell you what I *do*."

Hood waited, sipped the wine. "What do you do?"

"First you have to understand that I'm part of a huge bureaucracy. There are high levels and middle levels and then just basic workers. I'm a journeyman, a midlevel pro. Mainly we influence. Mostly we just talk. We certainly listen, very closely, I might add. We encourage. We dissuade. We cajole. We will at times frighten. We arrange meetings between key villagers without their knowing it. But we have no huge powers. We can do dream placements, which I told you about earlier, which are risky because they are unpredictable. We can cause or cure minor illnesses—colds and headaches and some allergies. Our senses are keener than those of most villagers, so it appears that we are prescient but we are not. We can read a villager's thoughts so long as those thoughts are clear and strong and we are physically close to the person. For example, if I am within eight feet of someone, I can hear what they think and see what they see. Sometimes very clearly. It's like hearing a radio or looking at a video. There is much clutter to sort through, I will tell you; on a crowded street, for instance, one thought intrudes upon others just like conversations going on at once. That's why we live and work only in our assigned geographical divisions—because often we need physical proximity with our contacts. We develop relationships with some villagers, though far fewer than you might think. We can't waste our time with the petty, the small-minded, the insane. We can easily use them when we need them, but they have no lasting value. We seek relationships with those of ambition and force and monstrous desire. We like to begin with children. Our relationships can become what we call partnerships. These partners come to accept who we are and what we stand for. My division, of course, is California. I got lucky, because I really love California—its geography and history and its various peoples. I inherited Hollywood and all its glorious powers of persuasion and suggestion. See, our only real power is our influence over the villagers. Villagers run the village. Their will is free. Nothing is fated nor preordained. No one is possessed. Men and women are in most ways much stronger than we will ever be, much more capable of tremendous good and tremendous evil. You are our work."

Hood felt the same odd and indescribable sensation that he had felt when he saw the escaped tiger walking the street in Bakersfield. It was the feeling of being unprepared for this experience, ignorant and surprised and awed.

"We're six feet apart, Mike. I'll think a clear thought and you can tell me what it is."

"I don't do parlor tricks. More wine?"

"It's gone."

"For the best. I've already talked too much."

Hood took Finnegan's empty cup and poured some wine into it from his own. "Do you go to hell when you die?"

"We don't die. We heal. It's the one small advantage we have over humankind. There is no hell."

"So you saw Tiburcio hang. Personally. You were there."

"Oh, yes. Half a century before that, I was helping Father Serra teach agriculture to the Cahuillas. *Trying* to teach them, I should say. The missions were important to both the King and the Prince because faith is amplified by numbers, but it is also very easy to manipulate and to corrupt. But you know this. I took part in Fremont's Bear Flag Rebellion, though, to be honest, I was little more than a spectator. Two years later Mexico gave up Alta California and the fun really started. I was at Sutter's Mill a week after gold was discovered. I rode with Harry Love and the California Rangers and was there at the shoot-out at Cantua Creek. Love never killed or beheaded Murrieta. The severed head that Bradley now possesses belonged to a bandit named Chappo. I knew Bradley's mother, Allison Murrieta, fairly well. What a woman. She had courage and beauty and such . . . appetites. In fact, I introduced her to the man who first seduced her, Bradley's father. Nature took its course from there, as it usually does. She shot him in a bit of a rage, though not fatally. I can relate to that, the being-shot part. I've kept an eye on Bradley over the years, from a distance. When I introduced myself to him in the Viper Room that night, he had no idea I'd helped his parents meet. But Allison lacked vision. She was a solo artist, not a team player. I know her mother, too, who has vision but no courage and no talent. Their progenitor Joaquin, El Famoso, was blond-haired and gray eyed, nothing like swarthy Chappo. I intercepted Earp late in his days in San Diego, as I did Frank James in L.A. Ditto Bugsy, Dragna, Mickey, Bompisiero, all the gangsters a few years after Frank. Later, Sirhan Sirhan, Manson, I knew them all, some well, some not. Small, selfish criminals don't interest us because they're of minimal utility and they're everywhere. I'm not allowed to go gallivanting across the nation in search of partnerships. I have to look for them nearby. I've never been east of Utah. I mention these individuals because they have become known. They were the apparent stars. But the overwhelming majority of my partners you, Charlie, have never heard of. The men and women who make the history books are simply the ones who manage to commit the final act, stumble across the finish line. Unseen machinations both large and small are the stage on which they act. Making history is like painting the inside of a house—it's mostly prep work."

"You're with the Prince."

"Isn't it *interesting* that you're not quite sure?"

"Then what's your goal?"

"Annihilation. The annihilation of the King's law and all his followers."

"You just made a hash of that nondisclosure agreement, Mike."

"It was the wine."

"No, it wasn't. So why? If you're who you say you are now, why tell me all this?"

Finnegan was quiet for a long moment. "First, because I know you won't believe me. I'm completely safe with you. I've told the truth to law enforcement officers before, but you refuse to listen and hear. Which is half the reason we're able to get anything at all accomplished—people in general just will not believe. Second, I tell you all this because you are just the kind of person I would love to form a relationship, then a partnership, with. It likely wouldn't happen—you're much too strong-willed and law-abiding for the likes of me. Unless, of course, there was something that you wanted very, very badly . . . something I could help you with."

Hood thought for a moment. "What about the King's helpers? Are they like you?"

"By and large. We follow the same rules. They outnumber us badly. They are not terrifically intelligent, more like frat boys in a way. We have opposing goals, of course. We don't mix. To us, the

King's men and women smell bad. And we smell bad to them. It's an evolutionary thing, rather doggish actually. I can ID one of Bigfoot's helpers just by smell alone from ten, maybe fifteen feet away."

"Bigfoot?"

"We make up other nicknames for the King because we don't enjoy saying his true name, and to bring some sense of humor to things—Bigfoot is popular now. The Fist, Big Bore, the Fat Lady. These days, Bigfoot's helpers are calling the Prince the Queen, or the Shitbird, or Slimebucket, things like that. Some of those names they got from you in law enforcement. We all love TV and crime novels. You'll hear some pretty colorful language fly when we get to drinking."

"Like a bar full of you?"

"Exactly. We socialize some, trade information, mostly just get sloshed and complain about the hours and the bosses. I have my sympathies for the workingman and -woman, I can tell you."

"I'd like to sit in on one of those," said Hood.

"Those are private, Charlie," Mike said quietly.

"What did you do while the Zetas stormed in here?"

"What do you mean, *do*? I can't move."

"Did you know when it would happen?"

"Only that it had to. The nature of things. When I heard the first shots, I summoned the nurse with the CALL button and tried to dial the phone for security, but with one hand it took a while. Five dead. It sounded like many more. I'll give you some advice if you want it. Don't count on Luna for help again. Don't count on him at all."

Hood got the tiger feeling again. "How do you know about Luna?"

"Oh, that's funny, Charlie. My beat doesn't stop at the border!"

Hood took Finnegan's cup and poured the last of his wine into it. "Has Owens heard all this?"

"Bits. Hints. I don't want to burden her. She believes fully in my alleged madness. She's beautiful, isn't she?"

"I don't believe she's your daughter."

"She is not. But she believes she is my daughter, Charlie. And my heart sinks every time I see those scars."

"Then what is she to you?"

"Do the scars draw you to her or push you away from her?"

"Is she a partner?"

"She's too damaged."

"I went to your place on Aviation. You're not running a bath products business out of there. If you are, it's small and disorganized and occasional."

"It's all of that. It's one of many stories, Charlie, all partially true. The story of the carignane is not totally false."

Hood nodded. He watched Finnegan. The little man slurped the last of the wine like a child finishing a milk shake. Then he sighed.

"What's that steel mesh vest in your closet for?"

Finnegan stared at Hood. "It's to be a gift. It's bullet- and knife-proof. It belonged to an acquaintance, handcrafted by a Frenchman in Bakersfield. This was some time ago. I know someone who should have it now."

"What about the clips in your notebooks—the white-collar criminals, the precocious children, the inventions? All in California, weren't they?"

Finnegan exhaled loud and long. "You can lead a whore to culture, but you can't make her think."

"Did Bradley tell you he has the head of Joaquin?"

"Oh, yes. As I said, I could hardly shut the boy up. He thought he was dazzling me."

A tiger on the march, thought Hood. His scalp crawled. "Tell me about Ron Pace."

"I've met him. The last of the Ring of Fire, Ron, a gunmaker extraordinaire. Just a kid. I don't think I have to explain his potential to a Blowdown agent."

"Do you have a partnership with him?"

"No. He was immature, suspicious, reactionary. When Pace Arms ceased manufacture, I moved him down on the roster. Injured reserve, so to speak. Do you really believe these things I'm telling you?"

"Why would you help me get Jimmy back?"

Finnegan stared at him for another long moment. "Mere killers must not always prevail. Our goal is that chaos and strife and enmity prevail. Some good competition. Personally I'd like to see you go forth and kick some ass, Charlie. I understand your problem. You are suffering under the rules of play. I *know* how badly you'd love to run down there and behead a few of those bad men. And rescue poor Jimmy. I'm on your side."

"Then help me do it, Mike."

Finnegan's eyes twinkled back beyond the wraps. "I think I'm beginning to convince you. We have partnerships with law enforcement all over the planet, you know."

"I'm too old and stubborn. Old dog, new tricks, all that. What if I got mad and pitched you out a window or something?"

"I'd come crawling back up." Mike cackled softly. "Charlie, good partnerships between two beings, whoever or whatever they might be, can be built upon only one thing—truth. We are all of us saddled by this, men and women, the blessed and the damned. Thus do I stand in truth before you. Lay before you, actually."

Hood picked up the empty wine bottle and set it in the small wastebasket beside Finnegan's bed. "Where's Jimmy?"

"I'd tell you if I knew."

"What good is drinking with the devil if I can't get some good intel?"

"Not *the* devil. *A* devil. A mere journeyman. But let me see what I can do."

From home, Hood called Soriana and told him there was a patient at Imperial Mercy who knew more than he should about too many classified things. He asked Soriana to file a federal request-for-information between ATFE and the FBI, DEA, CIA, military intelligence agencies, the postal service—any federal bodies that may have employed the man. Soriana said that, given the current situation, the request would be low priority and weeks in the filling. He'd try. Hood made a note to petition Sacramento and all Southern California county governments tomorrow morning early.

He went outside and cracked a beer and sat in the dark heat and watched another Guard convoy rolling in from the west. He thought that Mike Finnegan was probably insane and possibly dangerous. Information could be a weapon. Hood did not believe that armies of devils had worked for centuries on earth to win the hearts and minds of frail and temporary humanity. *Stories are lies that lead us to the truth.*

The navy helos prowled above, their searchlights straining to reveal an event that had happened and was now both over and ongoing.

26

The next afternoon, Bradley steered his Cyclone GT up the dirt drive toward his mother's ranch house. It was now two years since her death, and his heart turned heavy and full as his old muscle car rumbled slowly along.

The ranch was in Valley Center, northeast of San Diego. It was eight acres of savannah and rolling hills, with a stream and a pond, a pasture and a paddock and a barn, and citrus and avocado trees loaded with fruit. It was wedged between two different tribal reservations. One road in, and this road was gated and locked. Upon his mother's death, the ranch had become the equally held property of her three sons, Bradley, Jordan, and baby Kenny. Bradley had very generously cashed them out six months ago and made it very clear that they were welcome to come back and live there whenever they wanted, rent free, as his guests, in the home that the three boys had spent six happy months before their mother had been killed. He was in negotiations to buy twenty-five adjacent acres, beautiful acres, he thought, acres the color of lions.

He looked into the rearview and saw Erin in the Cayenne Turbo eating his dust. Her vehicle was loaded to the top with boxes of valuable things, as was his Cyclone, the bulk of their possessions to be coming later by moving van from their former home up north of L.A. Bradley glanced up again at his fiancée and smiled. Without trying in the slightest, she moved him.

He parked in front of the house, and Erin pulled in beside him. Clayton and Stone wandered in behind them in their own vehicles, also loaded with personal possessions. Two of the casitas at the far end of the barnyard were theirs. Always attuned to appearances, Clayton the forger had already painted his to match the barn—red with white trim. The other three remained pink as Suzanne had liked them.

Bradley climbed the stairs to the porch and unlocked the front door. This porch needs dogs, he thought. He swung open the door for Erin and he stepped in behind her. The new tiles were in and the house smelled of new paint. Sunlight barged through the windows, no drapes or blinds or curtains needed in this remote place. It had a rambling, open-floor plan thanks to his mother's knocking out of walls. Her last live-in lover, Ernest, father of baby Kenny, was a full-blooded Hawaiian who was good with his hands and had converted the living room to a kind of tiki room with wood carvings and masks and torches and a bar and a corkboard wall displaying all manner of Hawaiian clubs and axes and spears and knives. She called it the party pit.

Bradley walked into this room and saw people in it, drinking and eating and carrying on until the early hours. Loud. He saw himself stealing beers and selling them to the other kids. He saw Ernest, on a bet, hurling one of the great spears through a beer can taped to the corkboard wall. Bradley had grown up enamored of the primitive weapons, and Ernest had left the tiki room intact as Bradley had asked him. Ernest was living in Oahu with Jordan and baby Kenny now, and on Bradley's last visit, two-and-a-half-year-old Kenny was already getting the hang of the skimboard. They would all be at the wedding.

Erin turned and looked at him. "You okay, Brad?"

"Perfect."

"She's everywhere. This place has her crazy energy."

Bradley found the spear slit in the corkboard, pushed a finger into it. "It came out the other side."

"I know."

"Mom was pissed. Not because of the hole but because she bet against him, that he'd miss the can from across the room. Lost five hundred bucks."

"We'll have good times here, too."

"I wouldn't mind if my brothers came back. Ernest, too, for that matter."

"Just bet *on* him, not against him."

They carried boxes into the big master bedroom in the back. They helped the movers get things into the right rooms, and for every box he carried and every possession the movers brought in, Bradley felt his old life in L.A. growing smaller and his new life in Valley Center growing larger. The only downside was Erin's long drive for gigs, but like Bradley, she enjoyed fast cars, and a performer's hours would keep her out of workday traffic.

The movers were finished by evening. Bradley gave them beers and fifty bucks each for not busting anything. When Clayton and Stone headed out for dinner and gambling, Bradley and Erin ran naked down the dock and dove into the cool pond, then wrapped up in blankets and climbed into the tree house hidden high in the enormous barnyard oak tree. From here they could see the minor lights of Valley Center and part of an Indian casino miles away and the black foothills to the east. Along this skyline, the palms dissolved into the night. Bradley had had the foresight to cache a bottle of tequila and two glasses, so they sipped the agave drink and sat on the old tree house couch, watching an inverted quarter moon float up over the hills like a capsized dinghy.

Later they set up Erin's studio in one of the big rooms that Suzanne had made by knocking down walls between three smaller bedrooms. Bradley had installed skylights that opened and closed by remote, and screens to keep the bugs and birds and leaves out, so when they opened them, the warm summer air unfolded down on them, and looking up, they could see stars. The baby grand had been moved in and tuned the day before, so now came the guitars and amps and mikes and recording equipment and, as always in a musician's life, the miles of black cord needed to energize them all. Bradley knew nothing of this gear, so he simply put things where she wanted them and stole looks at her and felt as he had felt a hundred thousand times before that he had been lucky in her, the luckiest ever.

"I've got some things to move into the barn," he said. "I won't be long."

"Take your time."

He unlocked and pushed open the sliding barn door. He turned on the lights. It was one big and mostly unbroken space, no stalls, his mother never having gotten the horses she wanted. She always used to say she was too busy for horses. She had been a hard worker, he thought with a wry smile. Two jobs: schoolteacher and armed robber.

Pigeons fluttered in the new light, and a handful of feathers sashayed down from the rafters. This would be his version of Erin's studio, a place for working on his cars and daydreaming and being alone. A place for hatching plans. Maybe a place for becoming a poet.

His phone buzzed on his belt. He took the call from Owens, listened to what she had to say, hung up. He pictured her face, the lunar eyes, the raised serpents of scars intertwined upon her wrists. She made him uneasy, but she had helped him before and now she was offering to help him again. Her father was an interesting little man, likely insane, but he raked Bradley's nerves when he was around, and Bradley's instincts told him the man could help him. He knew things Bradley couldn't believe he knew. Bradley tried to trust people as little as he needed to, and Owens, with her vague history and uncertain circumstances, made this easy. He thanked her and rang off and holstered the phone.

Then Bradley looked at the floor where a double murder had taken place, and a sharp anger arose inside him. Bradley himself had discovered the bodies and in that moment had shed his boyhood. He was sixteen. His mother had been the target and the two men who had died, brothers, were men he had known and liked. Innocents, generous men. Later his mother had had the concrete replaced because the blood had soaked into it and left its eternal smudge that no bleach or broom or high-pressure hose could remove, but when she had seen the new wet gray concrete, she had them shovel it back out and replace it with the broken-up blood-stained slabs. Respect, Bradley knew, though his mother had never explained herself.

He drove his Cyclone GT into the barn, the Cleveland 351 rumbling low through the glasspacks. It was a perfectly restored 1970 and it shone beautifully under the fluorescent lights suspended from the rafters. He closed and locked the barn door. From the trunk he took a JVC television box and carried it over to the far corner. He set it on an old wooden table, then reached under the table and retrieved the key fob hung from a nail.

He again collected the TV box and walked to the opposite end of the big room, which was separated by sliding shoji screens. He used his foot to slide one open and walked in. This area was finished off with hardwood flooring and some comfortable furniture and a big-screen TV and a good stereo. There were bookshelves, mostly automotive pictorials and histories, and hundreds of car magazines, and many volumes of poetry, which Bradley enjoyed. Poems were the opposite of cars. Cars went fast, while nothing stopped time like a good poem. He had tried writing them. There were notebooks filled with them, almost one entire shelf of notebooks, but he had never written one he liked. Too much emotion. Not enough. Too much detail. Not enough. He kept trying. But he also knew that at his wedding to Erin, he would recite from Neruda and not himself, though she had asked him to read something written in his heart.

There was also a Ping-Pong table. He carefully set the TV box down on the floor, then took the paddles and ball off the Ping-Pong table and tossed them onto an old leather sofa. With the table clear, he hit the fob button. The concrete slab and the hardwood flooring that was cut away around the Ping-Pong table and the table itself, all rose six feet into the air and locked into place on four staunch hydraulic lifters. Bradley hustled down the steep narrow stairway with the JVC box and hit the fob again, which lowered the slab above him. He listened to the hiss of the hydraulics and then the final clunk of the concrete settling back into place. He smiled. He had built the door using the powerful lift assemblies from two trash trucks he had stolen in nearby Escondido. Driving the trash trucks away fast at night had been surprisingly good fun. It had taken him six backbreaking months to excavate the vault, using pick, shovel, and bucket. The labor and the thousands of trips up and down the ladder had left him ten pounds lighter and considerably stronger than when he'd last played football two years ago. And there was no feeling like the satisfaction of having done something with his own hands. Welding and cutting and working the steel had come easy to him, through his passion for working on cars. This trapdoor and the vault below were a secret that he had shared with no one.

He set the JVC box down and turned on the lights. The room was generous—twenty by twenty, eight feet from floor to ceiling. One wall was lined with three steel combination safes with a total capacity of forty-two cubic feet. The safes were bolted to the concrete floor and they were fireproof. There was a workbench along another wall, and a metal rolling shop chair. The worktop was orderly and sparse: two expensive digital scales, a vacuum packer designed for use on game, a rolled lariat, a Colt single-action revolver, an oily red bandana, a handmade Indian arrow with a small obsidian head, two rough-hewn wooden boxes in which Bradley could see the leather-bound book with no title on the cover and old clothes and old newspapers and photographs and a bandoleer with some of the bullets still intact.

Bradley picked up the TV box and moved it to the workbench amidst these oddities, then cut the packing tape with his switchblade. He folded open the top flaps and reached inside and pulled out a black velvet hood, which he set aside. Then he gently lifted out a heavy glass jar. He held it up to be face-to-face with the head inside, a man's head, severed cleanly at the neck, a pale and lonely thing. The head was bald, and a layer of black hair lilted just off the bottom of the jar. The face could have once been handsome. Joaquin Murrieta. El Famoso. Bradley's great-great-great-great-great-great-great-grandfather. Although history said the bottled head was lost in the great San Francisco earthquake of 1906, Bradley had read in his mother's journal that in fact it had been stolen from an exhibition hall one week before by Ramon Murrieta, one of Joaquin's grandsons. The leather-bound journal said that the head had been spirited down through the generations by Joaquin's most kindred descendants.

Now it was here. Bradley believed the head. He believed that it had had power over his mother, the power of the past, the power of blood. Now it had power over him. She had kept it right here in the Valley Center barn, stashed in a hidden attic space that Bradley had discovered when he was fourteen. She had never told him about it or how it got here, but she had tried to. He remembered her sitting him down for important talks that failed to contain the important. She would begin but couldn't finish. The journal had told him more than its writer ever could, and Bradley had spent hours with it before and after her death. Now when he read the words, he heard them spoken by her voice. *I anguish over my oldest son. He is clearly Joaquin's spirit, as I am. But I don't know if I want him to grow up Joaquin's way or just be a normal boy, a normal man. What am I supposed to do with the legend of Joaquin? Does it continue through me to Bradley? Does it end with me? Do I give Bradley his truth? Do I hide it from him? Do I let him search for it? Talk about a pickle. I've thought about it and prayed about it and even tried to just forget about it but I can't. Carrying history is a burden. I'd rather be robbing a fast-food place.*

Bradley knew that she had died not knowing what to tell him of his history, but when he had seen the head and put the pieces together, he understood.

He set the big glass jar on the workbench beside the Colt revolver and watched the head bob slightly and the hair begin to settle.

"*¿Cómo estás, el Famoso?*"

He rolled the work chair over and sat in it and looked at the tableau upon the bench. He got up and took his mother's journal from the wooden box and laid it down beside the head and the gun, then opened a drawer and took out a feather duster and swiped it over the bench top. He put the duster back and sat back and viewed again. As he thought about his mother and Joaquin and his coming wedding to Erin, Bradley's heart felt full and sad and joyful all at the same time. These powerful emotions were exactly what all those notebooks were filled with, he thought, lame attempts all just to say what he felt.

Later he opened each safe and inspected the bales of vacuum-packed cash. He liked to run his hands over the packages. Because his payments from Herredia were often in small bills, they took up lots of space. He had laundered some of the money through Israel Castro, in Jacumba. Israel had several legitimate and illegitimate businesses and he was happy to work with Bradley and his money. Israel, as a notary public and a loan originator, had helped Bradley buy the Valley Center ranch for cash. Of the approximately one and a quarter million dollars that Bradley had earned in the last year and a half, only one hundred thousand remained in the safes. But he'd learned that fifteen grand a week, base pay, adds up fast. There was also money from stealing cars, but he had not been doing much of that with the wedding to plan and his new position as an arms procurer for Herredia. The deal for the Love 32s would earn him ninety thousand if everything happened like it was supposed to. Erin would be making better money now with the recording deal, but as Bradley had seen, musicians almost always either starve or succeed hugely. Clayton and Stone were freelance and they worked their asses off forging payroll checks and stealing cars, and as their land-lord and mentor and occasional muscle, Bradley took a nice tribute from them.

He smiled and shut the safe door and spun the locks. Proximity to cash and Erin made him feel secure and full of heart and wicked horny. He put the hood on Joaquin and took the empty TV box and hit the fob. He stood and proudly watched the door ascend into the barn light.

27

The seven hundredth Love 32 is finished and I sit at the bench beside Marcos and take the weapon from him and feel its wonderful weight and balance in my hand.

"The crew is tired," he says. "Twelve hours a day, thirteen days in a row. No rest."

"They can take a day off if they want."

"They want the full bonus at the end. Is why they work hard."

"Six more days should do it. Five point six, actually."

"They have a request."

I set the gun on the bench and look at Marcos. He's a heavy, jug-eared Baja Californian with a family of five, all of whom were born here and are citizens. Unfortunately, Marcos and his wife are not citizens and not legal workers, though why they haven't become naturalized, I can't tell you. His English is good and he is more than smart enough to learn the basics of our history and constitution. Over the years I've told him several times that Pace would pay for his citizenship classes, and for any work he might miss in order to attend. Same for Teresa, his wife. The first time I told him this was five years ago, around the time I took over as production manager.

Marcos had smiled amiably and nodded and said he would consider this, and he's been smiling amiably and nodding ever since.

"They would like a larger bonus," he says. "They ask you for sixty-five dollars per day if the job is finish in eighteen days or less."

"I offered them a fifty-dollar-per-day bonus if the run is finished in twenty days or less. And they agreed."

This is even more important now than it was when the agreement was made because Herredia wants the guns ASAP. With the National Guard stationed all along the border, and the American military itching to charge south, and the Mexican military ready to repel boarders, Herredia doesn't like feeling outgunned by the Gulf Cartel and the Zetas. All this chaos is a handy cover for him and Benjamin Armenta to blast away at each other and the other cartels and not draw the full wrath of the Mexican government.

"Yes," says Marcos. "But you know, the gas is very expensive for they driving to work. They cannot live in Costa Mesa, so they live in the Santa Ana and drive far. They live cheap. They have children. Jesus needs the tires for the van. Lauro he has the baby, and Juan he has the two babies. They send money home."

"They agreed, Marcos."

"Yes."

I do the math in my head. A bonus of fifty bucks a day for each worker would cost me a thousand dollars per worker if the thousand-unit run is complete in the agreed-upon seven days. A bonus of sixty-five will cost me eleven hundred seventy dollars per. There are twelve gunmakers, so the total difference to me would be two thousand forty dollars. If I agree to the larger bonus, I know full well that they'll finish within eighteen days. So my total production payroll, with the higher bonus, would be seventy-four thousand five hundred and twenty dollars, with extremely good odds of finishing up quick.

My personal net from this run, after overhead, payroll, and materials, will be around seven hundred grand.

I look down at the handsome weapon that lies before me on the bench.

"Okay," I say.

"Thank you."

"Five more days."

"It will be finish."

"Three days would be better."

"We are working very hard. Thank you. Thank you, Mr. Pace."

Marcos barrels away and I sit alone for a moment to feel good about myself. Generosity is a gift to the giver, too. In my expansiveness I reflect on how my life has changed in three short weeks. I have never really seen myself as the captain of my own destiny. This idea always struck me as specious and self-referential, what with gods and fate and governments and history and luck. I still *don't* see myself that way, but I'm not about to turn away from life's blessings no matter how mysteriously arrived they are. I've just blundered into things, into a fresh new business and into the chance to love the love of my life. To my small credit I have realized a few key things. I realized that I'm not as gutless and ineffectual as I thought I was. I realized that Mendez is actually Herredia, which has put me into business with one of the richest and most ruthless men in the Western hemisphere. And I've also realized that Bradley Smith is of course Bradley Jones, the great-great-great-great-great-great-great-grandson of Joaquin Murrieta, the great and terrible El Famoso. It came to me a few nights ago just where I'd seen his face. Thirty seconds later, I'd found a short video of his mother's funeral online and spotted Bradley prominent among the mourners. If I said that I was not personally thrilled to be marching through history beside a direct descendant of El Famoso I would certainly be lying.

• • •

Sharon and I have just made love for the third time today when there's a ring on my security monitor near the front door. I put on my robe and go to the monitor to see Uncle Chester standing outside the lobby entrance.

"Hello, Uncle," I say.

"I did not give you permission to change the locks," he says.

"We had a break-in."

"We need to talk."

"In fact we do. Come on in."

By now Sharon is in the living room in her indigo silk robe, glowering at me.

"You let him in."

"He's my uncle."

"We didn't change the locks to beam up Chester whenever he wants us to."

"We need to talk. You know that. He's coming up, Sharon. That's what is going to happen here."

She stares at me because she knows that she is partially responsible for my new assertiveness, and she knows she could ruin it if she wanted to. I derive a new strength from her. But I'm utterly in love with her and I tell her this often and I show it constantly in the most glaring and obvious ways: I bring flowers and gifts, I take her on short creative outings such as a day on Catalina and a pleasant lunch with Mom on the sunny lawn outside her mental hospital Victorian, and just yesterday I bought and boxed up a complete sushi and sashimi dinner, including a thermos of martinis, and we took it all to the end of the Newport pier and sat on the benches, watching the fishermen, and ate and tossed balls of rice to the gulls. She knows I'm a fool for her, complete and total. I can't fake that I'm not.

But I also can't let my uncle stand outside in the dark. It's time for me to tell him the new rules here at Pace. And Sharon knows this, too.

"We better get dressed," I say.

We tour the production floor. Chester in his pale linen suit glides along ahead of me, hands behind his back, and despite the new rules here at Pace that I'm dreading telling Chet about, I can't resist falling into his slipstream and holding my own hands behind my back and adopting his patient, noble stride. Sharon walks beside me, arms crossed. I have come to know her well enough over the years to understand that the slight tightness in her mouth and the odd flatness of her eyes and the barely detectable clenching of her jaw indicate uncut fury. You don't mess around with Sharon when she looks like this. The gunmakers steal looks at Chester. Among them he was a man to be feared, and he still cultivates and enjoys their fear immensely.

The shift is almost over and the eight hundred thirty-seventh gun has just come off. Chester lifts it in his hand, aims up at the lights, and dry-fires. When Pace Arms was still in full production, Chester was known to fire men and women who dry-fired a Pace weapon. It's hard on a semi.

"You would have fired you for that two years ago," I say.

"The pull is too heavy."

"Four and a half pounds."

"That's easily four and three-quarters. Consistency is everything, Ron. Consistency is the physical manifestation of trust. Sloppy workmanship will doom us and I cannot allow it. It's time for us to talk."

"Okay."

He sets the gun on the bench and looks down on me and Sharon. The lights shine off his bald dome of a head, and his cheeks are flushed pink. He lifts his nose very slightly, then lowers it, and I guess he's picked up the smell of our sex. He smells of baby powder. He gives Sharon a small-toothed smile but says nothing.

In my office, Chet sits in my chair behind my desk. Sharon and I sit before him like a couple consulting a doctor. I can feel the anger coming off her.

"What is the renegotiated price for the first one thousand Love 32s?" asks Chet.

"I haven't renegotiated," I say. "I made a deal and I will honor it."

He cocks his head and leans forward. "Again?"

I repeat myself.

"Certainly you've renegotiated the price of the sound suppressors."

"No, sir. The whole deal stands. One thousand units, complete, at nine hundred dollars each."

"Then you insist on giving our product away."

"I've never seen nine hundred grand in one place in my whole life."

Chester leans back, and my executive chair wheezes. The headrest doesn't even come up to the tops of his shoulders. "And the incentive discount on a cash commitment for the next thousand from Favier and Winling? I remember us agreeing on a discount of three percent off the new per-unit price of twelve hundred fifty dollars."

"It's three percent off the current price of nine hundred per gun, Uncle Chet. You and I agreed to nothing. I haven't heard back yet."

Chester studies Sharon. "Have you had any success finding us some customers?"

"I have a list of possibilities. At nine hundred dollars per unit, the Love 32 is going to sell briskly at the very least."

"CC me on the list, please. Sooner than later."

Sharon says nothing.

"Ron, is the crew on a twice-monthly payroll cycle as before?"

I nod.

"So they've been paid for just three days' work so far?"

"Yes. Their big payday will be the last day of production, if they can finish in eighteen. I'll actually have to pay them a day early, because payday is on a Friday. They'll be getting bonuses, too."

"Bonuses? Oh my, Ronald. Not like the old days, is it?"

"They'll earn them. Believe me."

Chester eyes me with something like amusement. "Now, I've given some more thought to our endeavor," he says. "One, on a go-forward, we will change the name of the gun because nobody wants to confuse love and death. Two, there is no Favier and Winling of Paris, France. I suspect these extravagant and dire events in Mexico may be linked to our order—this is merely an intuition. I expect you to tell me the true name of our customer by the end of the work shift tonight. Three, Ron, you can't simply pocket seven hundred thousand dollars. The three of us will receive the monies, distributed per our old salaries and according to the old percentages, then share the balance, greatly increased by the reduced number of employees, according to the same established model. Of course. Ronald, as designer and production manager, you will draw a handsome salary for the time you have spent on the project. Sharon, you will continue to draw your current generous salary. I love all the new money-saving lightbulbs, by the way. I of course will be compensated as CEO and president. We will all be quite happy on payday. Now, lastly, and I think you'll like this—on the morning of the big payday, you will call the United States Immigration and Naturalization Service and the United States Border Patrol and anonymously report the undocumented workers who will be arriving that afternoon on floor one. At that time we will be having appetizers before a king crab dinner at the Charthouse. My treat. The workers will be arrested and deported without pay and we will save the labor payroll. Don't worry. I still have friends on the labor board. Our chances of prosecution are nil."

It's so quiet I can hear the tap-tap-tapping of the finish men two stories down. I look at Sharon, and her face is blank fury but somehow very specific about what it wants me to do. I sigh and stand and go to a window and look out. South Coast Plaza is sparsely lit and empty. The Christian compound is dark. Only the freeways buzz with life eternal. My heart is pounding and I feel a stiffness in my knees. My legs are weak as I return to my chair and sit down beside Sharon. I lean forward.

"Uncle Chester," I say. My voice wavers and I clear my throat, then clear it again. "Sharon and I have put some considerable thought into this matter. When our business plan is finished, I'll be able to be more specific. But for now . . ."

"Business plan?"

"Ron and I have talked about it," snaps Sharon. "We think that after this first recovery deal puts some cash back in Ron's pocket, we should reincorporate the old Pace Arms operation under a new name and with new investors and new directors. We'll apply for all the necessary permits and pay the fees and taxes. We foresee a completely legitimate new firearms manufacturing company before the end of the year. You and Ron's mother will receive ample proceeds if we make ample money. We've talked to our lawyers and they are drafting a buyout for the property and machinery and furnishings."

Chester, always pale, has now lost even the pink flush of his cheeks. "We're having a bit of a power struggle here."

"Uncle Chester," I say. "You brought this upon yourself. When I looked up from that desk a week ago and saw you standing here, I thought, terrific, Chester's back. He knows the business like nobody else. Maybe he can help. Maybe we can work together again. He is a Pace. He is my mother's husband. Maybe, just maybe, with all of us working toward it, Pace Arms can sail the seas of commerce again, under a different flag. This is what went through my head, all when I first saw you. But instead of helping, you try to take over my work. You try to take everything I own. You try to cheat my men and rename my invention. You visit my mother a total of one time— she told me this, Chet. And you look at the woman I love as if she were a picture in a jack-off magazine. You even take *my* seat at *my* desk in *my* office. So, Chester, there's no struggle here at all. This is ours now."

To make the point more dramatic, I stand, which puts me more or less eye to eye with Chester across the desk. I think of the mastiff he crushed, which outweighed me by twenty pounds and had larger teeth. But surprisingly, or perhaps not, my knees feel fine and my balance is good and I feel a lightness and a readiness and a sense of physical and mental well-being. Chester is impossible to read now, just an immense, unmoving, pale, bald, infant Buddha with battalions of rage apes lurching around inside his head, no doubt.

"I'll be in touch," he says.

"I'll be here."

"There is no problem unsolvable by reasonable people," says Chet.

"You have to find them," says Sharon.

28

Hood sat in his Blowdown Tahoe across from the Pace Arms building and watched huge Chester Pace come lumbering from the entrance. Hood turned down the radio news. Chester's head shone in late-night security lights, and his pale suit rippled as he walked and he was looking down as if in thought.

There were lights still coming through the blackened windows on the first and third floors, but from this distance Hood couldn't see in. The building was ringed by a metal fence. Eight vehicles were parked in the Pace lot, mostly older economy cars, one nicely lowered Chevy Malibu, and one battered van. Hood recorded the license plate numbers in a small notebook.

Chester Pace strode into the parking structure, and a moment later a black Lincoln Town Car came into view, listing to port, tires whistling on the concrete ramp. The Lincoln lurched to a stop at the pay booth, and Chester punched something into the keypad and the arm raised. Hood wrote down the plate numbers in his small notebook and slipped the notebook back into his coat pocket. He turned the news back up.

Four hours later, just after five A.M., twelve men came from the building in a loose group, all Latino, early twenties to sixties. They looked tired. One of them placed a card in the fence gate and then opened it. He held it open for the rest and they walked into the parking lot in loose formation, then spread out to the various cars. Through his open window, Hood heard one of them laugh and a *buenas noches.*

When they drove away, the lot was empty. The lights on the first floor went off. Hood looked up to the third. Two of the corner windows were not blacked out but sheltered by blinds, which were now only partially open. He could see part of a ceiling lamp, and this and the blinds suggested a residence. Hood saw two figures inside, a man and a woman, moving slowly and closely as if in conversation.

He sat there in the dark for a few minutes. The lights on floor three went out. He kept waiting for his cell phone to ring with news about Jimmy, but it did not. Twenty-four hours since his abduction, thought Hood, Buenavista crawling with Guardsmen, and the president still holding up the possibility of a military surge into Mexico. Hood hated that idea, but he'd take it if the U.S. Marines got Jimmy back. Fat chance of that, he thought. The only way to get Jimmy out of Mexico was to deal with the people who took him. Simple. But if the Gulf Cartel wanted Jimmy's headless body found on a road somewhere as a warning to law enforcement or other cartels, then there would be no word from them, ever. Hood's hope was growing dimmer and his anger was burning brighter.

Late afternoon the next day, Hood was back. It was five o'clock. Same lights on the same floors, same vehicles in the lot. No Chester Pace. Hood's background check of Chester had revealed no criminal record. He had paid back taxes of nearly three hundred thousand dollars last year, which on top of the legal fees to defend himself and Pace

Arms had all but wiped him out. He had no children, an engineering degree from Cal Poly, and according to his CDL, he wore no corrective lenses and weighed three hundred and eighty-four pounds.

The background check on Ron Pace had revealed a twenty-two-year-old high school dropout with no criminal record, either. He was single and held two patents, one for a toilet bowl sweep and one for a device that would keep umbrellas from being ruined by the wind. From a smattering of articles written on the Pace family over the years, Hood had learned that Ron's father had committed suicide right here at Pace Arms when Ron was ten. Ron's mother had married Chester the next year. Two of the articles touched upon Maureen Pace's hospitalization for schizophrenia.

Around five thirty, Hood watched as Ron Pace and a pretty young woman came from the Pace Arms building. They walked arm in arm across the entryway and into the parking structure. A moment later a red Mini Cooper zoomed to the pay booth and the arm went up. Pace waved to the attendant, then sped out. Hood followed. The Mini weaved through the traffic up Baker and turned north on Harbor Boulevard. Hood stayed back. Pace signaled a turn into Fairview State Hospital. The Mini stopped at a guard gate, and Pace talked to the guard. A moment later the gate swung open. Hood waited for the Mini to clear, then he pulled up to the gate and showed the guard his federal marshal's badge. He tailed Pace to a parking lot shared by three of the smaller buildings of the complex. When Pace parked, Hood found a spot at the opposite end but facing the same direction. Hood watched Pace and the woman walk into what looked like a large Victorian home that stood apart from the other buildings and was surrounded by a trim green lawn.

One hour later they came back out. Hood waited half an hour, then walked across the lot and the grass and into the old Victorian.

Inside, it was dimly lit and quiet. It smelled lightly of mildew and disinfectant and age. The foyer had a sign-in log. Hood printed the name Sam Fischer beneath Ron Pace's entry and wrote in the time of day, and in the "to see" space he wrote "Maureen Pace" and under "relation" he wrote "friend."

Confessing that this was his first visit to Maureen, Hood was given her room number by a helpful young patient with black curly hair and ice blue eyes who was watering the plastic palm in a brass pot in the hallway. She smiled beautifully. When she tilted the big red plastic watering can back up to continue her task, Hood noted that not one drop of water came out.

Hood stood outside Maureen's room and looked past the open top of the Dutch door. When he knocked, she came into the small foyer with an inquisitive look on her face.

"Good evening, Maureen. I'm Sam Fischer. Do you remember me from Pace Arms?"

"Of course. How are you? Come in."

Hood waited for her to open the bottom half of the door. She smiled at him and stepped aside, then led Hood down the short hallway and into a sitting room. There was a fireplace with no fire and a braided rug on top of the carpeted floor and a bentwood rocker and a love seat facing each other over a small pine coffee table. There was a small kitchen. Two walls had tall corniced windows that offered views of the lawn and beyond. The glass was reinforced with steel safety mesh.

Maureen took the rocker. She was slightly built and pretty although she took no pains with her appearance. Her hair was pulled back into a ponytail, and her face was pale and lined. There were ribbons of gray in her dark brown hair. She wore a denim dress that looked two sizes too big for her, and a pair of athletic shoes with no laces in them. Hood thought she looked incomplete.

"I was hoping you might be able to put me in touch with Ron," he said. "I'm unemployed. Guns are what I know. Manufacturing, sales and marketing, admin—I can do it all and I'll take any work I can get. When I ring the bell at the old building, nobody answers."

"Oh, the company is long bankrupt," said Maureen. "They don't have a penny. But I see Ron almost every day. He was here just a few hours ago."

"How is he?"

"Good. Good. He took up with that girl he was so crazy for the whole time—Sharon."

"Of course, I always liked her. What's Ron doing for employment, then, if Pace is completely defunct?"

"I don't know, really. He *says* he has an office there. He *says* he goes in to work. Just a couple of weeks ago, he said he had a big project starting up. But I don't believe him. I think he makes up good news to give me something to be happy about. Ever since I told him about the caves, he's been quick to make things up."

"The caves?"

"Exactly."

Hood paused and looked out the mesh-reinforced windows to the shady lawn. There was a round vinyl dining table with chairs around it and a birdbath with a mockingbird splashing and drinking. In the evening light, the grounds seemed bucolic and hopeful.

"How's Chester?"

She studied Hood. "The caves rim the Pacific coast from Chile to Alaska. Not far offshore. Some believe they're inhabited. I say believe what you want because the Mayan calendar only goes up to the year 2012. Just do the math on that one. Chet? Oh, he's back, of course. I don't see much of him for how much of him there is to see."

Hood nodded. "What did Ron tell you about the big project starting up?"

"He didn't say much. He called it a secret job and he'd be able to give me details someday but not yet. I can tell when Ron is excited about something. He glows. He always did, even as a little boy. The first Slinky he ever got in his Christmas stocking? You could have lit all of Seattle with the light on Ronnie's face. He's got two speeds—zero and full blast. And when something excites him, look out."

"I wonder," said Hood.

"Wonder what?"

"If he might be making guns again."

"That's prohibited by the terms of the judgment."

"Yes, I guess it would be."

"But who's to say he's not making guns in one of those caves?"

"I doubt that, Maureen."

"Well, making guns is the only thing he knows how to do, so . . ."

Hood nodded.

"How did you know I was here?" she asked.

"One of the newspapers had it. From years ago."

She studied Hood again. He sensed in her a patience that might be endless. "What did you say you did for us?"

"Down in manufacturing mostly. Built a whole lot of Hawk twenty-twos and a fair amount of the nines."

"Oh, that twenty-two Long was a sweet pistol."

"Still is."

"I carried one until they took it away. Never used it except once at a restaurant. I was seated outside and I put it on my place mat to hold it down in the wind. They frowned on that!"

"I'll bet."

"But really, we're responsible for our actions. Finally, finally, we arc." Her gaze held Hood for a long beat, then she looked outside. "The kittens are in the fountain again."

"Nice."

"I don't remember you."

"I worked nights and swing, so I didn't see much of the higher-ups."

"You wouldn't be a lawyer, would you, sniffing around for some money that isn't there?"

"No. I'm just a gunmaker looking for a job."

"Good luck, Mr. Fischer. The Ring of Fire is dead and gone now. Too bad. There were six different companies at one time, and Paces ran four of them. There was Tony, my first husband, and then Chet, and all their brothers and sisters. Seven impressive Paces. Chet was huge and Barb was tiny, so figure that one out. They all got married and had kids and made guns by the skil-dillion. Pretty much all the upper management were Paces by blood or marriage. Good jobs and good pay and good products. The liberals killed us. They think guns run out on the streets and shoot people. They think guns rape women and sell drugs. They think guns walk into classrooms and kill students. They don't have the guts to look into their own souls and blame human behavior on the humans. They think . . . well, I don't know what they think. But they kept looking for a way to shut us down. When that gun went off accidentally and little Miles died, it was the end of everything. He was a beautiful little boy. It gutted the Ring of Fire. Scattered the Paces. Look at me. A crazy lady in a nuthouse and I'm all of forty-eight years old. Can you believe that? Look at me, Sam. I feel like the ruins of civilization itself."

Hood looked. "You're still young and lovely."

"Of course you say that. But I detect dishonesty in you. It's time for you to go. I hope you find employment."

• • •

Hood drove back to Pace Arms and resumed his stakeout. His conscience muttered to him about lying to a crazy woman, but he told himself it was for the greater good. He knew this was the first refuge of the scoundrel but tried to believe it anyway.

Again he waited for the call about Jimmy, but there was no call. Forty-eight hours now. His muttering conscience went silent and his heart filled with uneasy anger.

Then the phone finally rang, but it was Buenavista PD captain Gabe Reyes reporting that he'd found a cell phone and a charger under Mike Finnegan's pillow an hour ago. None of the nurses had ever seen the phone or heard him talking on it, and when Reyes went to the messages and call logs and contacts, they contained not a single name, number, or message.

"He said he never used it," said Reyes. "That it was just for emergencies. It's one of those prepaid models. I think he was whispering or texting. That's why they never heard him talk."

"Whispering or texting who?"

"I doubt it was somebody wanting to buy a shower curtain. You don't hide a phone and not use it. And I checked—if you lie in that bed where he does, and you can use your right hand, there's an outlet within reaching distance. He could have been using and charging that thing late at night when the nurses were changing shift, not paying such close attention."

Hood thought that all of Gabriel's police work added up nicely, but he wasn't sure to what. "Thanks, Gabe."

"I want to get Father Quang to talk with Finnegan."

"Explain."

"He's a priest out of El Centro. Vietnamese, you know, a lot of them are good Catholics. Quang has a deep sense of evil because he has seen things. He is bright. I think he might help us cut through some of Mike's bullshit."

"I'd like to be there for that."

"Sure. One more thing, Deputy. Beth said IHOP was terrific. She had a light in her eyes. Treat her well."

"Yes, I will."

Around nine o'clock, Hood got out of his truck and shut the door quietly and trotted across the street. He climbed the fence and strode across the entrance walkway and the little perimeter of flower bed. He followed the edge of the building until he found a dark and sheltered place, then he squatted amidst the shade-tolerant begonias and rhododendron and African violets and looked through the smoked glass. An early article about Pace Arms said that manufacturing was done on the first floor, and this appeared to be true. In the faint light within, Hood saw the twelve men working diligently at their benches, all fingers and elbows, all working on what appeared to be small-caliber semiautomatic pistols.

Back in business, he thought.

He was almost all the way home to Buenavista when Ozburn called: Raydel Luna was here in California and Jimmy was alive somewhere down in Mexico, and there was a plan.

29

They set off in their own vehicles, Hood in his black Tahoe and Ozburn in his Land Cruiser still caked with dry pale mud and Bly in her black Suburban, a dark posse charging down the highway through the deeper dark of night.

Hood brought up the rear, keeping his eyes on the divider and on the back of Janet's ride, but along the peripheries of his sight the spindly ocotillos rushed by and the paloverdes marched full and rounded, through the headlight beams and to the north the quarter moon sketched the outlines of the distant mountains against the sky.

Luna was waiting at a bar called the Corral on Highway 98 just outside of Quartz. The Corral came into view ahead on Hood's left. There were cars out front. He watched Ozburn drive by without slowing, then Bly and Hood did the same. The restaurant sign was dim and read only CORRA. A mile past, Ozburn signaled and flogged it, then skidded into a smoking U-turn across the highway and came back at Hood with a merry flashing of brights. Hood smiled, and when it was his turn he did the same. They parked noses-out in the lot, Bly and Hood near each end and Ozburn in the middle. Hood could hear music playing inside, a loud *corrido*.

Hood pushed through the door first. The music jumped in volume and he saw the pool players and the drinkers and the smoke drifting into the rafters. Faces turned his way, washed in the red light of candles in red glass domes on the tables and along the bar. Luna sat in the depths of the room with two other men.

He stood as they approached and he shook their hands strongly and his small eyes bored into Hood's. He wore a vaquero-style sport coat with leather-trimmed pockets and yoke that was too small for him, and this made his thick neck and shoulders seem even larger, like a bull disguised as a mariachi. Amador was Luna's physical opposite, light and slender and long-necked and angel-faced. He was dressed in the uniform of the Baja State Police, and an AK-47 was propped against his chair. Hood guessed early twenties. Esteban Vogel was also nothing like Luna. He was light-skinned and blue-eyed and sandy-haired and he wore slacks and an open-collared dress shirt and a blazer that draped expensively. Early thirties. Along the wall beyond them stood two uniformed Mexican *Federales*, both young.

Luna said that Jimmy was alive and being held somewhere in the mountains. But there had been developments. And everything in Mexico was "not usual" since the bloody kidnapping at the hospital. The slaughter in Mulege was bad enough, he said, but now things were very, very not usual.

"Let me explain," said Esteban Vogel. "You know that originally the Zetas were defectors from the Fifteenth Battalion of Mexico's Special Forces—GAFEs. These men were great soldiers, our bravest and best. They specialized in airborne operations, counterinsurgency, counter–drug trafficking, and, as we saw at Imperial Mercy, rescue operations. At first there were only twenty defectors. They were led by a man named Humberto Vascano, known as Z1 and El Verdugo, which means the Executioner. He sold their services to Benjamin Armenta's Gulf Cartel and began recruiting in the poor Mexican states of Veracruz, Oaxaca, and Puebla and Chihuahua. Vascano is charismatic and ruthless. The recruits were trained in the special forces tactics, and armed heavily. Because of their counter-drug trafficking training, they became very effective drug traffick-ers. Because of their counterinsurgency training, they became accomplished insurgents. They were paid three hundred dollars a week to start, and could earn up to one thousand. The pay for the GAFE soldiers is two hundred dollars per month and this was the reason for the defections."

Vogel looked at each of the Blowdown team while he removed a silver cigarette case from his coat pocket. He offered cigarettes around the table. Bly and Hood accepted. Vogel lit their smokes, then his own, and clipped the case shut.

"This was three years ago. At that time, Mexican desertions were approximately one hundred soldiers per month. Now it is twelve hundred soldiers per month. The Zetas have grown to over one thousand. They grow faster than we can count. They have out-grown Armenta, though some of them still work for him. They have branched out into Quintana Roo, Coahuila, Tamaulipas, Si-naloa, and Baja California states, establishing territory, controlling smuggling routes, reaping profits, destroying the opposition. They have been extremely successful in Guatemala and are now draw-ing recruits from the once legendary special forces known as the Kaibil. The Kaibiles are defecting at twice the rate of us Mexicans. The Kaibiles and the Zetas have aligned themselves with the Mara Salvatrucha, which gives them street-level numbers and footholds in American cities. They consider themselves superior to the cartels. They have bragged about overthrowing the government and murdering President Calderón. They have been unleashed. I can tell you that the worst is yet to come. Gentlemen, and lady, of Blow-down, we have a crisis in our country and now it has moved into yours."

"We want Jimmy back," said Ozburn.

"This long preamble was necessary," said Vogel. He exhaled curtly. "The Zetas have Jimmy. But they are not Benjamin Armenta's Zetas. It is Vascano himself. The Executioner is offering Jimmy to Armenta for one million dollars. But more important than the money, he is using Jimmy to destroy the trust between our two governments. Both sides are humiliated by the hospital raid. Because the kidnapping makes Calderón and his government appear inept and lacking in control, Vascano believes he is closer to destabilizing it. And, if he can infuriate the United States against Mexico, this is good for the Zetas. This was an act of terrorism not only against the United States, but against Mexico. However . . ."

Vogel drew deeply on the cigarette and slowly let out the smoke. He tapped the cigarette out in a black plastic ashtray. "However, at the powerful urging of my advisors, and Sergeant Luna, I asked Vascano, through intermediaries, to also offer Jimmy to you. He has agreed."

"What price?" snapped Bly.

"Five million dollars."

"The United States government doesn't pay terrorists," said Ozburn.

"Nor does ours," said Vogel. "And it will not be seen to. But we are hoping to defuse the crisis that began at Imperial Mercy. We are hoping that the return of Mr. Holdstock, perhaps made possible by certain sympathetic elements within the Calderón administration, will ease tensions. We are hoping that the sight of Mr. Holdstock returned to American soil, reunited with his family, viewed by millions of Americans, will reduce this strife between our two great nations."

Hood sat back and figured his net worth if he cashed out everything he had. It was about forty grand if he kept the Camaro.

"We'll get it," said Bly.

"You tell Vascano we're going to get it," said Ozburn.

"You already have it. It's a gift from our people to Jimmy Holdstock. You just have to deliver it to Vascano and bring Jimmy back across the border. The Zetas will call Luna at noon tomorrow. Only two persons can be present to transport the money and collect Jimmy. One must be Sergeant Luna. If a third is suspected, they will murder Jimmy on the spot. They have said that the Executioner wants this exchange done quickly."

"What if Armenta offers more?" asked Hood.

"Vascano will sell to the highest bidder."

"We could easily be walking into a slaughter," said Ozburn.

Vogel leaned forward and spoke quietly. "Agent Ozburn, this is possible. But my people have used the very best of their skills in negotiating with Vascano, and they tell me that he is more interested in collecting the ransom than in killing a Mexican policeman and an American ATFE agent. He has already pitted our government against yours through Mr. Holdstock. It is a worldwide event. It cannot have gone better for Vascano. Now all he wants is the money. We have all the assurances we can have."

"From a man called the Executioner," said Bly.

"The situation is perilous but not hopeless," said Vogel. "And even so, it is the very best we can do. So discuss this among yourselves and decide who will take the money down with Sergeant

Luna. My people have talked to Soriana and Mars, but that is all. We are a very small group of men and women trying to accomplish a large thing. Now, my ATFE friends, I suggest you follow me."

They trailed the two soldiers through the small kitchen, then out the back of the bar, then across a flat lot. Waiting near a windbreak of greasewood trees were two more soldiers and two military jeeps and an American SUV and an armored half-track. The half-track had a Mexican army logo on the machine-gun station, and a third soldier seated before the .50-caliber gun.

"Bring your vehicle around," said Vogel. "The sooner we finish this, the better."

A minute later a soldier lifted a large canvas backpack from the storage hatch of the half-track and hefted it over his shoulder for the short walk to Ozburn's truck. The weight bent him. Vogel said it was all hundreds, as demanded by Vascano, just over one hundred and four pounds of them, packaged in one-pound bundles of forty-eight thousand dollars. Confiscated cartel money, he said, weighed and packaged in the United States and smuggled down into Mexico by car and sea. The soldier backed against the truck and shrugged off the pack onto the tailgate. Bly insisted on inspecting it. As she did, Hood watched the bundles accumulate on the tailgate of the vehicle.

"The bills are not short and not marked," said Vogel. "There is no transmitter hidden in them or in the pack. We will give them no reason to keep Jimmy from you."

"No, you won't," she said.

Bly continued her inspection unhurriedly, then replaced the bundles in the big pack. She had to lean a shoulder into it and push with both legs to move it off the tailgate and into the back of the Land Cruiser. When she had finished, Vogel and one soldier climbed into one of the jeeps, and the other two soldiers dispersed into the other.

Hood watched the half-track roar to life and the gunner lock down his weapon. The big machine pivoted madly and lurched forward through an already flattened section of greasewood, then powered off across the desert toward the border like some enormous warthog. The jeeps screamed along behind, throwing clouds of dust into the dark, and even through these clouds Hood could see the world of stars above.

The Blowdown team and Luna stood beside him and watched. "I belong to you until the Executioner calls," he said. "After that, one of you will belong to me. But when we cross that border again, we will both belong to the devil. After all, we have made a deal with him."

There behind the Corral among the empty booze boxes and beer kegs and the foul trash cans and the slumping garbage bags and the dripping hose and the sticklike mantids fixed to the screen door beneath the naked lightbulb, Sean Ozburn spread an old newspaper upon the hard ground and weighted its four corners with rocks for butts and barrels.

Because of his seniority, they used his gun and he spun it first.

Ozburn defeated Bly.

Ozburn defeated Hood.

Hood eliminated Bly.

Hood beat Ozburn twice, the barrel of Ozburn's gun locating Hood with the seeming confidence of a compass hand swinging north.

Even though Hood had prevailed, in deference to Ozburn's age, he offered to let Ozburn go get Jimmy. Ozburn said a deal was a deal and so it was.

Luna looked on with his hands folded before him and his shoulders stretching the fabric of the vaquero coat, his neck a taut column, his shaven scalp shining except for the flat black berm on top, his eyes lightless, and at Hood he smiled his smile that was not a smile, and the chill imparted to Hood was as true as any he had experienced in the streets of L.A. or the alleys of Anbar or the tunnels of Jacumba.

Don't count on Luna for help again. Don't count on him at all.

30

Dear Mom & Dad,

I'll be out of the country tomorrow, hopefully for just an hour or two. But I thought I'd write to tell you I love and miss you and I plan on seeing you in October for Dad's BD.

I'm sure you've seen all of the chaos here on TV. It's much less focused and contained when you're in the middle of it: There are National Guard troops everywhere and more coming in every hour, and all the news media are scrambling around looking for someone to talk to, and patients are checking out of Imperial Mercy in droves because they're afraid it could happen again, and there's a hundred people at least outside the hospital entrance carrying signs that say "Take Back Jimmy" and "America Stand Up" and "Don't Tread on Me," and things like that. There's half-tracks and troop carriers and light tanks all over Buenavista and nowhere to park them so they pull up onto the old stone sidewalks, which busts them up pretty good. There must be a couple thousand Guardsmen here. They're billeting them in houses if people will take them, and they've set up a headquarters in the desert outside of town but that desert is a hostile place.

I saw Jimmy just a few days before they took him, and he was doing better. I'm fearful for him, though. His body was broken but bodies heal. It's his mind that worries me. Jimmy's mind was broken, too, and I don't know if it can survive more pain. Not an hour goes by that I don't think about how the Zetas could have kidnapped me instead, or anyone else on the Blowdown team. Because it was Jimmy I respect and thank him. I owe him. Dad, maybe you understand that because you always felt the same way about Anderson. I believe that we the living ride on the shoulders of the sick and the crazy and the dead. That sounds morbid but it isn't.

Know that I love you. I'll see you soon.

Charlie

31

The Executioner called at ten minutes after noon. Hood watched Luna step from the bustling lobby into the courtyard of the Hotel Majestik, cell phone pressed to the side of his head, nudging past a senior U.S. congressman, who turned and glared at him. Hood saw two other Southern California representatives and, briefly, the Secretary of Homeland Security pressing through the lobby, surrounded by a phalanx of her bodyguards. The Guardsmen and reporters were thick, and the camera crews were shooting interviews in every nook and cranny of the old hotel.

Luna stood by a fountain with his back to Hood. He appeared to be arguing. A moment later he lowered the phone and flicked it shut with a snap of his wrist and barreled back through the lobby. Hood followed. They walked to the parking lot of the ATFE offices, where Ozburn and Bly were standing guard over Hood's Tahoe. The vehicle had been outfitted with two GPU transponders so it could be tracked over long distances, and loaded with two spare gas cans that were strapped into the rear compartment beside the five million dollars. The cash had been divided into two backpacks, which would give each man a fifty-pound load and still leave them free to use both hands for weapons. Hood had chosen a drum-fed 12-gauge and he carried his usual Glock .40 on his hip and the AirLite eight-shot on his right calf. He also wore a pair of bull hide cowboy boots, and the left boot heel contained the ivory-handled two-shot derringer given to him by Bradley Jones. Late the night before, Hood had carved an exact place to fit the piece. It had taken him hours to create this opening and get the fit just right and still leave one side of the sole intact to fit back over the weapon and lock puzzlelike into place and not come open when he walked. Luna had requested an M16. He wondered if Luna would bring his bow and arrows, but he did not. Luna considered the weapons with what looked like amusement.

Ozburn handed Hood a thousand dollars in small U.S. bills, mad money, he said, and Hood folded it once and put it in the left back pocket of his jeans. Bly replaced the U.S. federal plates with Baja plates.

A few minutes later, Hood watched the Customs booths fall away in the rearview mirror. Luna directed Hood not west as he had expected but east along the border on Highway 2, out of Baja and around the Gulf of California, then down into the Mexican state of Sonora. Hood had never been here. He looked out at the mounded white desert and at the saguaros and the cardóns with their arms lifted to the sky. Then the towns fell away as if the land had refused the idea of towns and there was nothing but the intrusive road and the few cars on it. In the clear Sonoran air, twenty miles looked like ten and in his heart the impossible seemed not impossible. He wondered if hope could be as illusory as vision in this stark and untouched place.

"Where is Jimmy?" he asked.

"The Sierra Madre Occidental."

The mother mountains, thought Hood, centuries of violence—

murderous Apaches, scalp-hunting Comanches, bandits, kidnappers, rapists. The Aztecs couldn't control the Sierra Madre, and the Spanish couldn't. Now the drug lords and their armed hyenas had moved in. Even the Mexican military hadn't been able to bring order there. "Then it's going to be a while, Raydel. Talk to me. Tell me what you can."

Miles rolled past before Luna spoke. "Vascano is in the mountains. We will get instructions in Creel, the mining town. It is a place for the Tarahumara and vaqueros and cattle. The Tarahumara hunted deer by running them into exhaustion. Now there are fields of yerba and poppies. There is production of opium and heroin. *Narcos* everywhere. These are now the treasure of the Sierra Madre. In the mountains, a man isn't considered a man until he has killed another. Outsiders are killed on sight unless they are sponsored. We have Vascano's protection until he decides to revoke it."

"But Vascano's power is in the south."

"After the Buenavista hospital attack, President Calderón sent soldiers to Vascano's *plazas* in Quintana Roo and Tamaulipas and Veracruz. But they found nothing because Vascano is not in the south. He is in Chihuahua state."

"But he won't be for long," said Hood.

"If Calderón learns that Vascano is in the Sierra Madre, he will send thousands of soldiers. You and I will either be shot dead or arrested as allies of Vascano."

Hood thought of Jimmy and looked out at Mexico and felt the miles compounding and compounding. The mountains materialized before him and Hood saw the great parallel ranges of the cordillera stacked skyward and into the distance.

"Vascano is sick," said Luna. "An illness or an injury, no one says. His son is with him."

"How old?"

"Eighteen years."

Hood looked out the window. More time. More miles.

"This is not what you think it is," said Luna. "This so-called war against the cartels? The war is not about stopping drugs. Our country is corrupt. The rich hoard wealth for themselves. We have a few of the very rich and many millions of the very poor and no one in between. But now a new rich class is beginning. The cartels have created it. They have amassed money, which becomes power through violence, and later through legitimacy. The cartels crave legitimacy, and the ruling class will not surrender it. So the cartels use Zetas, and the ruling class uses government soldiers. This is a war of the classes. It is a struggle for power and privilege."

Nineteen hours later, they saw the lights of Creel high above them in the Sierra Madre. The last miles were a vertical struggle up switchbacks upon switchbacks that built pressure in Hood's ears and raised the engine temperature of the vehicle. The pine and juniper forests were fragrant in the still cold night, and the escarpments were black and bottomless. A chill morning fog dampened the narrow dirt streets. A train rolled into the station like an exhausted cyclops, its headlight steady in the mist. They took rooms at the Hotel Chavez and Hood slept a dreamless six hours.

In the afternoon they filled the tank and purchased one more spare gas can, which they filled and strapped in with the others, and two inflated spare tires only roughly the proper size. They bought food and bottled water, and Hood bought a thick red-and-white woven sweater that he immediately put on.

Then he drove south into the first immense gorge of the Copper Canyon. The afternoon smelled of wet rocks, and the junipers dripped mist, and the hot part of the day was cold. Luna said that they would not stop for approximately six hours, until they reached the tiny village of La Bufa. There would be instructions from Vascano. The road was bad but passable, and the government had confiscated the weapons of the police in La Bufa.

Hood drove down the steep rocky road in first gear, letting the transmission be his brake. He picked his way around towering columns of rock that blotted out the sunlight and looked too precariously assembled to stand for long but had instead stood for millennia. Tarahumara men and women labored uphill on foot, the men dark-faced in loose white blouses and shorts and scant sandals with tire treads for soles, some of the sandals laced high up their calves, their feet the same rough brown as the road. Hood imagined running down deer in a pair of those. The women's dresses were white and loose and buttoned high at the neck and some had piping across the shoulders and some of the girls wore necklaces of leather and beads and carved wooden crosses that dangled forward as they leaned into their steep ascents. The Tarahumara moved slowly and some had blankets and scarves against the cold.

They continued down. The pine and juniper gradually gave way to oak and to tan grasses that seemed to grow from the rocks themselves. Then yucca and scrub oak appeared as they descended farther into the barranca. The temperature rose. Hood wriggled out of the new sweater and threw it into the back. Hours later, Hood realized that they had dropped into the lowland vegetation of agave and mesquite and cactus and he smelled the Urique River below them, marked by the palm trees that grew along its winding course. The outdoor thermometer in the Tahoe read eighty degrees. Here, nearer the river, there was no wind and the air was humid and still.

Around a turn a blue mountain rose from the canyon floor, a blue softer than the sky. He had never seen such blue, much less a mountain of it.

"Copper tailings from the mine works at Bufa," said Luna. "La Bufa village is not far."

In La Bufa they met with *agente de policía* Evangelista Limones in a small office with a rough-hewn pine desk and three metal folding chairs and a timber-pole ceiling. There was a framed picture of St. Christopher on the wall and a bare lightbulb dangling from the ceiling, and bright afternoon sunlight rushing through a window. Limones was slender and wore jeans and a big buckled belt and a short-sleeve plaid shirt knotted over his navel, as did many of the vaqueros of the Sierra Madre. He spoke in English for the benefit of Hood.

"First there were rumors of Zetas in Batopilas. Then the government soldiers come here two days ago. They confiscate my pistol and ammunition. They were fourteen men in four vehicles. Three were . . . how you say, jeeps? Jeeps with machine guns on them. One vehicle was armored. They leave La Bufa after only one hour. They drive toward Batopilas. The soldiers they have not return. Since they leave here, no vehicles are coming from Batopilas. Two days, no vehicles. No Tarahumara. No burros. Nothing. And now no vehicles are leaving La Bufa for Batopilas. People are afraid of what has happen. When no one comes from Batopilas, they become afraid and they do not go down the road."

"We will go down the road," said Luna.

"Yes, I know."

"Were the soldiers *Federales* or Chihuahua police?"

"*Federales* from Calderón."

"Tell us the rumors of Zetas in Batopilas."

"A Tarahumara boy say he saw them. Maybe ten men. If this is true, then they come from another direction. Not through La Bufa. Through San Ignacio or Satevo or from the river. Or maybe they fly. Do Los Zetas have airplanes?"

"I have not heard that," said Luna. "But it must be possible."

"The Tarahumara boy is the only witness. If he is lying, then the soldiers have come for nothing."

Hood looked through the window to the narrow rock street where a pig snorted along the gutter and a shopkeeper swept the sidewalk outside her door. Two vaqueros walked by, looking into the police station silently.

Hood and Luna slept at the one *pensión* in La Bufa. Early in the morning they had eggs and tortillas and coffee, then set out for Batopilas.

32

The darkness gave way to fog, and Hood never got out of first gear. One hour into the journey, Hood saw that Evangelista Limones had been telling the truth. Not a vehicle came their way, no mules or horses, no man, woman, or child. He saw one cow and one coyote and one rabbit, then two hours later, as the heat of the day climbed out of the canyon around them, Hood saw vultures circling far away in the blank sky.

"Batopilas gave the world its silver and copper," said Luna. "The Spanish took it, then the Americans. An American named Shepherd developed the mines in the late nineteenth century. He built a castle and a hacienda and a foundry. He brought turbines from the United States and made hydroelectricity from the Batopilas River. At that time it was the only city in Mexico with the luxury of electricity, apart from Mexico City. After the big wars, the mining collapsed. Now Batopilas is a ghost town. There are mansions and buildings abandoned. There are tons of opium and yerba grown in the canyons. Occasionally the government sends in soldiers. The growers bribe the soldiers to leave them alone. If the soldiers find a grower who has not arranged his bribes, then the grower is given three choices. He can choose *bote*—prison for ten years. Or, he can choose *leña*—to be beaten half to death with wooden clubs. Or he can choose *plomo*—lead. This means the grower is given a head start into the bushes and then the soldiers cut him down with machine guns. He has a small chance of getting away. *Plomo* is the most popular choice. It is considered *valiente*. Valiant. Very Mexican. There are a few tourists but not now, with the violence and the summer heat. There are telephones, but they don't always work."

Outside of town, Shepherd's castle lay hollowed and crumbling by the river. It was three stories high, with Gothic windows through which Hood could see the walls of the opposite side. There were towers at both ends and these were partially engulfed by tree branches that grew through the window openings. The roof was gone, and the masonry had long sloughed off the walls.

Hood put the vehicle into park, then he and Luna hoisted their weapons from the back and checked their ammunition and placed the combat shotgun and the automatic M16 between them, barrels down on either side of the transmission hump, the butts resting against their seats.

Around the next bend, four vultures raised their pink faces from a dead man on the side of the road. They looked at Hood irritably but didn't move. Hood drove the Tahoe forward and they hopped away and managed to take flight. Hood and Luna got out and saw that the man was a soldier and he had been shot several times and beheaded, but they saw no head. Flies buzzed in the still heat, endlessly repositioning themselves on the man. One quarter mile closer to town they came upon two more soldiers similarly killed and mutilated. Still seated, Hood looked down at the bloating bodies, and their smell mixed with the sweet scent of the Batopilas River nearby, and these smells and the heat tried to sicken him.

He drove. Then there was a steep descent and another tight

switchback that straightened to reveal the three heads on the left side of the road, the faces eaten by the birds but still with expressions somehow forlorn and regretful. The vultures stood blinking twenty feet away in the scant shade of an agave.

"There's no excuse for this," said Hood. "What does this signify? Who is it for?"

"Us."

Just outside the village, another six soldiers lay dead and piled upon the road. The vultures stood atop them, fanning their wings in the heat. Hood saw that the men had been dragged and left there as a roadblock, and he wondered if the remaining five were blocking the road on the other side of Batopilas. They were abundantly shot but not mutilated.

Hood and Luna stepped from the Tahoe and together dragged three bodies to the side of the road so they could drive past. Hood thought his chances of dying in an ambush right there and then were very good. He was willing to strike a protective deal with any god or devil who would offer him one, but he heard no voices in this place or in his heart and he felt forsaken.

Two mules stared at them as they entered the village. In Batopilas plaza, two ancient men watched them from a bench. Their faces were dark and wrinkled and they squinted at the Tahoe as if facing a storm. One of the men lifted his hand and pointed them onward down the street of river stones. A woman in a bright-yellow-and-orange shawl refused to look at them, then scuttled quickly around a corner. There was a small store open and two Zetas with AK-47s stood on either side of the door and there were two more across the street outside a *carnicería*. They were young and dressed in uniforms of solid green, with black boots and black vests and helmets, and they had emblems of some kind on their shirtsleeves up by the shoulder. They bulged with ammunition. The Zetas stared at them with bored expressions, but their fingers were inside the trigger guards of their weapons. One gestured slightly with his gun and Hood drove. Outside the police office was a streetlamp and from it hung by his neck was a man with a badge pinned to his shirt pocket. His face was black and his eyes bulged on stems like a crab's and his neck was stretched obscenely, and beneath his dangling boots a black straw cowboy hat sat upturned on the sidewalk. Another Zeta stood in the open doorway of the office and he pointed his gun at Hood's face and tracked him in the sights as Hood drove by. He looked sixteen. He wore a pendant bearing the image of a bearded man, Jesus Malverde, Hood knew, patron saint of *narcos*.

"And he takes his bullets to Malverde shrines to get them blessed," said Luna. "So they fly straight and kill his enemies. And Malverde blesses his shipments, too, for safe passage to the United States. Look how eager he is to kill. It is his passionate desire."

Outside a cantina at the far end of town a slender, older Zeta waved Hood over and told him to park. Two more men came from the cantina with their guns lowered, and Hood now understood Luna's amusement at the weapons they had brought. Faint music played from inside the cantina.

Hood stepped from the vehicle, and the Zetas pushed him against the car and took his weapons except the derringer in his boot heel. They took the cash from his pocket. They dragged the heavy packs from the back of the Tahoe, and Hood heard them crunch to the street next to him. They opened the packs and looked in but did not touch the money. Then one of the Zetas motioned with his gun, and Luna and Hood each knelt and hoisted the heavy packs to their shoulders. Then Hood felt a gun barrel poke the back of his head, aiming him down the road.

There were three Zetas ahead of him and three behind. Past town, they came to the five dead soldiers strewn across the road beheaded and they stepped over and around them while the vultures scattered into the brush. A hundred yards farther were the heads lying beside the road. After half a mile, they went left onto a trail through the palms by the river, and the trail narrowed, then it opened on a broad flat beach of brown sand and boulders along the thin, slow Batopilas River, and there were four men on horseback waiting. One of them was Jimmy. He sat on the horse hunched and wavering, and he stared blankly at Hood and Luna. His wrists were tethered to the pommel and the big bandaged mitts of his tortured hands rested on either side of it. They had dressed him in a gold-and-blue Mexican football jersey.

"Hi, Jimmy."

Jimmy didn't look at him.

Vascano was a big man with a heavy face and curly black hair, and he wore the same uniform and armored vest as the other Zetas. Hood could see that Vascano's face was pale and sagging and dark around the eyes, and he could see that the teenaged boy on the horse beside him was a young version of his father, stout and alert and handsome. The son sat with an AK-47 ready across his saddle, and the fourth man brought his horse around and lowered the barrel of his shotgun at them.

Hood shrugged off the pack and let it drop to the ground and so did Luna. Two of the men on foot dragged the packs toward the horsemen and they opened the flaps and upended the packs and the one-pound bundles of drug money tumbled out into the sand. The men sifted through the packets, looking for dye and transponders.

Jimmy's horse snorted and lowered his head in search of grass, and Hood saw that Holdstock was weak and his balance was bad. Jimmy looked down as if to help the horse find something.

"Jimmy, look at me," he said.

After a moment he looked up, but Hood wasn't sure if Jimmy recognized him or not.

"Luna," said Vascano. He spoke Spanish, and Hood could follow his meaning if not all of his words. "I am pleased to meet you. When I heard your name, I decided to sell this man to you and not to Armenta. It wasn't only the money. It was because of you. You run your enemies down like dogs. You kill with guns and a bow and arrow. You accept no bribes. You are loyal. You are an unusual man. Step forward."

Luna stopped halfway to the horses.

"But you are poor as a peon and your family has nothing and your department is corrupt. Your government is corrupt. The soul of your country is corrupt. So what are you loyal to but your own foolishness? You are a dog chasing its tail. Come and work for me. I'll pay you ten times what they pay you now."

Luna looked up at Vascano but said nothing.

"Say something," said Vascano.

"We choose. We decide and that is final."

"Who says what is final?"

"Each man."

"Prove to me that you profit from your loyalty."

"There is no profit. There is want and need and humiliation at the hands of the weak. But that does not change things."

"But your wife wears old clothes, and one of your sons needs surgery and your daughters have no prospects because they are thick and bullish and built for fighting, like you are. I know these things, Luna. They are facts."

"My wife is still beautiful in old clothes and the bones of my son will heal. My daughters will marry warriors like themselves."

Vascano nudged his horse forward. Hood saw that it was black and beautiful and there were silver studs in the black leather of the harness and rimming the shiny black saddle. Vascano looked down at Luna and he coughed, and the cough multiplied itself until Vascano evacuated it with one deep convulsion. Vascano's face was white and his hair was a madman's. His son rode forward to wait beside him, and the Zeta with the lowered shotgun shuffled left to keep a clean line of fire.

"It is not you and me," said Vascano. "It is Mexico. Everything must be torn down. Everything must be rebuilt. The age of privilege and corruption is nearly over. There is always revolution in the hearts of men, and now those men have guns to match our hearts. We will cut the head from the snake. We will stamp the last life from the body and then Mexico will have new life and a new body."

"Then Mexico will be trading one generation of selfish tyrants for another."

"The bloodshed and confusion will pass. Help me make them pass, Luna. Be loyal to hope, not foolishness."

"Hope does nothing."

"Then be loyal to your family and the abundance you can bring them. Heal your son."

"I will not."

"Why not?"

"I don't work for the enemies of Mexico."

"Oh? Then who is this standing behind you? And who is this pathetic man on the horse? They are Americans, and Americans are the enemy of Mexico. They have the appetites of Satan and the money and guns to satisfy their appetites. They are rotting with luxury and godlessness and they have spent themselves into ruin. They have nothing in common with us but a border."

"You kill and kidnap."

"So that rotting America will help me drive this rotting government from our land."

"And to put five million into your pocket."

"It will finance the revolution as well as myself. Share it with me, Luna. For Mexico and for yourself."

"You are not a revolutionary. You are a murderer and a beheader. I will not work for you."

Vascano stared down at him white-faced and crazy-haired, then he pulled an overlarge revolver from his holster and shot Luna straight through the heart. The bullet twanged off a rock behind Hood. Luna rocked back, then charged, but the shotgun roared and caught him high, knocking him backward off his feet onto the sand. He rose slowly, his great head a bloody mask, tattered and featureless and grotesque. He charged again, but this time it was into the river, where he fell forward on the rocks and lay still in the shallow brown water.

Hood had moved toward Luna and now stood before Vascano. Vascano had lowered his gun, but it was still in his hand resting against the saddle blanket.

"Who are you?"

"Deputy Charlie Hood of Los Angeles."

"You volunteered for this?"

"It's my job to do this."

"Are you a friend of Jimmy Holdstock?"

"Yes."

"What do I do with two rotting gringos?"

"You let me take Jimmy back like you said you would."

"If you go back, you can say where I have been. You can fight another day. You are worthless to me alive. You are weak. You are nothing without thousands more of you. Jorge, what do I do with them?"

His son eased his mount forward and he stopped abreast of his father. Again the shotgunner maneuvered to his left for a clean sight line.

"You send them home so they can tell the tale of Vascano, the revolutionary who destroyed the puppet Luna. The world will fear you more, and the men and women of Mexico will love you more. These men are your prophets."

"This would be letting rattlesnakes go free."

"Their stories will help us. They will give us a face."

Vascano looked at his son. "You will be our face."

A cough erupted in his chest and continued, deepening. He turned and motioned to the shotgunner, then he raised his pistol toward Hood and fired. The bullet screamed by Hood's head, both a sound and a feeling.

Vascano lowered the gun. The shotgunner spoke into a satellite phone, but he kept his other hand on his weapon, the barrel aimed at Hood.

A moment later a helicopter suddenly surged over the top of the canyon and cut a sharp descent toward the water in graceful switchbacks and finally it pivoted itself down upon the rocks near where Luna lay. The water around the machine quivered as if rising to a boil, then burst into a chop, and downstream of Luna it was turned pink by the deafening and indifferent blades. Two of the Zetas carried the backpacks to the helo, and Vascano and his son dismounted and gave the reins of their mounts to the shotgunner and stroked their horses adios, then strode to the helicopter, ducking under the rotors and climbed in with the money. The machine rose back into the sky and within moments had vanished over the canyon rim.

The shotgunner barked something to his men, and three of the Zetas started back toward town. Three more came up behind Hood and he felt the barrel of a gun against his spine and he fell in behind the first three. He heard the others behind him and he turned to see one of the men leading Jimmy's horse. Jimmy slumped and swayed not quite with the rhythm of the animal. The bandages on his hands looked smaller than they had at Imperial Mercy and they looked clean, their whiteness jarring in this bloody desert.

A gun barrel found his back again and Hood turned to the trail and he listened to the clopping of the horses behind him. At first he thought of the heat and of the bodies ahead on the road and of Luna dead in the river, but these thoughts fell away by their own weight. With the sound of the horses, Hood thought instead of years ago, riding with his father and mother and brothers and sisters when he was a boy in Bakersfield, trotting past the oil pumpers that sometimes spooked the rented mounts, galloping along the smooth flat edges of the cotton fields with the morning sun warm on his back and feeling that life was good and it was going to get even better and he was impatient to get to all those better things. The world was a place of wonders.

Back at the cantina, the six footmen watched while the shotgunner tethered the horses to a hitching post and helped Jimmy down. The shotgunner pointed his weapon at a battered station wagon, once white but now eaten by rust. It was a Vista Cruiser with a large smoked roof window for viewing the sky and the sights. Hood let Jimmy drape an arm over his shoulder, then they slowly moved together to the car. The front seats were little more than loose foam, the vinyl having cracked away years ago. The windshield was cracked from bottom to top, a seam that glistened even through the dusty glass. Hood helped Jimmy into the backseat, where he could lie down, then he got behind the wheel and turned the key to check the gas.

The shotgunner came from the cantina with a plastic bag and a neatly folded amount of American cash. Through the driver's-side window he handed Hood the cash and the bag, and when Hood looked inside he saw a bottle of rubbing alcohol and a roll of white tape and a bottle of tequila.

"*Gracias*," said Hood.

"I was trained in the United States. They were decent men. Armenta is looking for Jimmy. They will be on the roads that lead to the legal crossings. Smuggle yourselves in, like we do."

33

It was dark by the time they made La Bufa. Jimmy lay in the back asleep. Hood filled the tank and bought food and water and began the steep ascent to Creel. The old station wagon was powerful, but the transmission was imprecise and the steering was loose and the worn tires slipped on the fog-slicked rocks. For a while, Jimmy slept, then he sat up. Hood could see the outline of his head in the rearview.

"It's good to see you, Jimmy," he said. "We're going home."

But Jimmy had said nothing to that point and he said nothing then. So Hood drove. He peeled tortillas off the bundle and ate them folded with one hand as he steered. He handed the pack back to Jimmy. The soft drinks had been warmed by the heat of the lower barranca. He told Jimmy how hard they had tried to find the tour bus and about the powerful monsoon that hit later that day and about the Guardsmen now stationed in Buenavista and the reporters everywhere and all the Americans who wanted to invade to get Jimmy back and all the tension between the countries and how even the president had acknowledged the idea of U.S. military action.

Jimmy's silhouette came in and out of view in the mirror in the darkness, but he said nothing, then lay down across the seat again.

Just after sunrise in Creel, Hood was able to call Ozburn on a pay phone. Ozburn screamed in joy when he heard that Jimmy was alive and free. He called back ten minutes later to say that in four hours a capable Mexican state police captain named Wilfredo Duarte and two of his officers would collect and drive them to the border at Douglas. Customs would be ready for them. They would be back in the U.S. of A. by midnight.

Hood and Jimmy slept through the morning in Creel on two double beds in a small pension room, Hood with his derringer under the pillow and Jimmy snoring. Music came faintly from a room down the hallway, and the air was cool and fragrant with juniper and pine.

They all left Creel at ten A.M. in Duarte's white Chihuahua police Suburban. It had a light bar on top and state emblems and green lettering on the sides. Duarte drove. He was middle-aged and had a somber face and a paunch. His men were younger, one muscled and bald and one slender, with thick black hair. One sat up front and one in back with Hood and Jimmy. The policemen spoke among themselves, and Hood snoozed with his face against a window until the heat woke him up. Jimmy watched the landscape roll past and said nothing.

Close to eight P.M., Duarte answered his satellite phone and a long discussion ensued. Hood caught some of it: Armenta's Zetas were targeting the Douglas crossing. Duarte said that Nogales would be better. Hood reckoned Nogales was another two hours west, which meant another two hours for Armenta's men to find them.

Jimmy looked at him. Duarte listened. He unleashed a string of sentences too fast for Hood to comprehend. He heard the word *Ozburn* twice. Then Duarte punched off and turned his head slightly to Hood and Jimmy in the back.

"Nogales," he said. "Armenta. Is good. Ozburn knows."

"I need to call Ozburn."

Duarte picked up the big phone and dialed. A moment later, Hood heard Ozburn's voice.

"It's okay, Charlie. Your guys know what they're doing. Douglas is a bust, man. Use Nogales. You'll be there in a couple of hours."

They approached Nogales in the thick of night. The two officers checked their M16s and set them muzzles-down and close by. The satellite phone rang again and Duarte answered with an expletive. He listened. He said if not Nogales, then where, and he listened for a long while after that. He said yes six times in a row, then cursed again and punched off.

"Nogales is not good," he said. "But we have a plan."

They drove west and north toward Sonoyta. The moon struggled up and dusted the desert with light. Hood knew this road by map only and he knew that it was the one paved road for miles and if Armenta's Zetas chose to patrol it, they would be easily found. The officers became nervous and held their guns close. Hood was pleased by their nerves because he knew that these Chihuahua policemen could deliver them to Armenta for more money than the officers would make in their lifetimes. They cleared a rise, and Hood saw the new border wall. This was badlands, the hills bald and deeply carved by sudden rain and scorched for months by the sun. In the faint moonlight, Hood saw the steel panels of the wall serpentining along the contours of the terrain until it came to a sudden end. Here at the end of the wall, security lights pounded down on the naked land in clusters of four lights atop portable trailer towers that washed the ground white. Hood saw stacks of steel panels and pallets of concrete and mounds of mixing sand and the Cat D4s with the augurs attached and the mixers and the big water trucks casting shadows.

Duarte slowed and eased off the highway onto a dirt road. The road was narrow and rough and the Suburban bounced gently on its long wheelbase. They descended into a gulley and stopped out of sight from the highway and Duarte flashed the lights twice, then left them off. A set of lights flashed an answer across the desert from the United States, from out in the darkness beyond the end of the wall, twice, then once again.

Duarte turned to Hood. *"Apúrate, gringos!"*

Hood climbed out and helped Jimmy to the ground. He thanked Duarte, then got his duffel off the seat and started down the dirt road with Jimmy beside him. Hood could hear the cars on Highway 2 behind him, but when he turned, he could see nothing of it. The Suburban still sat at idle, lights off, the officers watching them. The road narrowed to a path, and the path led toward the wall. Hood saw empty water bottles and tatters of clothing and plastic bags tied to rocks and bushes used to mark the way north. The pathway followed the low spots between the badland hills and for a moment they walked between the mounds, invisible to the world. But Jimmy slowed, then stopped, and he looked at Hood, then behind them, then ahead. He was breathing hard and very pale. Hood tossed his duffel into the desert and took Jimmy's arm around one shoulder and together they found a difficult balance and continued.

They followed down a valley and along its bottom, then they climbed again. They came to the crest of the rise and looked out at the wall and the building equipment bathed in the bright lights. He looked ahead to where the headlights had flashed and saw the glint of windshield and for the first time in two days, he allowed himself to taste the hope of making it out of here alive with Jimmy. Jimmy leaned heavily on him and breathed fast.

"There it is, Jimmy," said Hood. "That's home and we're going there."

With that, something caught Hood's eye and when he turned to his right, he saw the headlights coming through the desert toward them. They came from the Mexico side and they were two miles out at least, but he knew if they were Armenta's Zetas and they could see the Suburban tucked into the little gulley, they would drive toward it, and he and Jimmy would be stranded here in the badlands without cover or weapons. A second pair of headlights appeared south of the first.

"Faster, Jimmy."

Hood picked up his pace, and Jimmy grunted with every other step, trying to find a rhythm. He stumbled and fell and Hood helped him stand. Hood looked at the headlights approaching. The two sets had become three.

"Come on, Jimmy. It's now or never for us." But Jimmy ceded even more of his weight to Hood, and Hood looked ahead to the United States and the glint of mirror glass, then looked at the vehicles coming from Mexico, and he reckoned that he and Jimmy wouldn't make it at this speed. "Jimmy, you've got to climb on."

Hood balanced Jimmy upright, then knelt on hands and knees on the sharp ground, and Holdstock lay over his back with a huff. Hood stood and got Jimmy's legs under each arm and started down the path much faster now, but the man's weight was cumbersome and substantial and his big arms were firm around Hood's neck. Hood's legs and back were strong and he took long strides down the path and when the path vanished, he accelerated between the clumps of creosote and the rocks and the infernal cholla, and again judged his distance from the vehicle on the U.S. side against the three-vehicle war party now streaming from the south toward him. He could see the faint contrails of dust in their wakes and he guessed from their speed and violent rocking that they were military all-terrain vehicles of some kind and that they needed no trail to traverse the desert floor.

He broke into a trot. The rise and fall of Holdstock's weight was prodigious, but Hood found a breathing rhythm as he watched the ground in front of him, then looked up to fix his course toward the wall. Suddenly the headlights of the stateside vehicle came on. Then another set of headlights from beside it, but these were much closer together, a quad all-terrain vehicle, thought Hood, maybe even a sand buggy. Both sets started toward him. He was sucking deep for wind now and trying to control the exhale, imposing his will. Holdstock's forearms were hard around his neck because of his useless fingers. "*Jimmy, not so tight. On my neck. Easy.*" From his right advanced the three vehicles from Mexico. He heard footsteps behind him but he couldn't turn without stopping and he couldn't stop. Duarte huffed into his view on one side, short-legged, stomach swaying, an M16 in his hands. On Hood's other side emerged both officers and they also had their assault guns, and these younger men were light in the boots and they moved ahead of Hood a few paces and remained abreast, and the five of them crunched on toward the wall. He could hear the Zetas' vehicles behind him. Ahead of him the two American vessels broke into the lighted security area, a Hummer and a quad runner, trundling back into darkness and coming across the rough desert straight for him. Hood's legs were burning and he could feel the imminent collapse of them and he slowed so as not to fall, and both the young officers and Duarte closed ranks around him. He heard the clatter of small-arms fire and he saw the muzzle flash from all of the vehicles except the quad, which came buzzing at them like a mad badger. Duarte and the officers fell back and fired from the darkness. Hood trudged onward. He labored up a rise, lungs heaving and legs wavering and it felt like a miracle just to clear it but he did, gasping for air as the quad whined at him through the darkness, and Sean Ozburn laid it into a slide that brought its rear end around and to a stop. Hood dumped Jimmy onto the cargo carrier on the back and climbed on top of him. Ozburn drew an M16 from the handlebar scabbard and handed it back to Hood. Then Ozburn turned off the lights and gunned the quad, steering back toward the wall and the light.

The four-cycle engine was game but overburdened. Ozburn's memory of the terrain was good, and in the darkness he was able to keep the quad on its own track most of the time. Hood looked a quarter mile ahead to the pool of security light and the end of the wall. He saw the other American vehicle now, an ATFE Humvee crawling toward them through a sandy plain. The Mexican vehicles closed fast but they were still half a mile out. Hood held to the roll bar with one hand and lowered the assault gun at the oncoming enemy, but in his logic, gunfire wasn't worth betraying their position in the darkness. Ozburn found a hard-packed gulley and the quad groaned along. Hood watched the Humvee, a hundred yards to their left and a hundred yards behind them, make a wide U-turn and pull up slow so Duarte and his men could climb in. The driver kept the rpms high and the speed even, and the heavy machine began across the sand again, back toward the wall.

Ozburn steered them onto American soil. He veered around the floodlit construction area, then brought the smoking ATV to a stop on a rise a few hundred yards from the unwalled border. The engine smoked, and smelled of overheated metal. Hood saw the Humvee lumbering toward them, rhinoceros-like and unfazed. He watched as the three Zeta vehicles stopped forward progress a quarter mile away and began circling like meat bees, their dust-filled headlight beams crisscrossing the night, then finally turning and speeding off into the darkness. He realized he'd never even seen what kind of vehicles they were.

The Humvee rolled to a stop, and Janet Bly got out of the driver's side and headed straight for Jimmy. Soriana exited the front, then the three Chihuahua state policemen, then Mars.

Holdstock stood in the moonlight beside the smoking quad with his bandaged hands at his sides while the Blowdown team welcomed him back and lightly clapped his shoulders and messed his hair and told him how good it was to see him. Bly hugged him, crying, and Ozburn hugged him, swearing they still had plenty of beer to drink and Zetas to kill. Then they stepped away just a little to give Jimmy some breathing room, to hear his piece, to reestablish his place within their pack, and Jimmy looked at each of them in turn before turning his tearful gaze to the desert floor and saying nothing.

Ozburn introduced himself and the others to Duarte and his officers. "We'll give you a ride back to your truck if the Zetas don't blow it up," he said.

Before ten minutes had gone by, an orange ball of flame puffed to life a mile south, roiling and growing and fighting to stay upright against the westerly breeze.

34

Two evenings later, Hood watched Jimmy's taped statement on *World News Tonight*. Jimmy was made up, Hood saw, and his hair was freshly cut and styled. The set was designed to look like a home, but Hood knew that the segment had been taped at the ATFE field division HQ up in Glendale.

Jimmy sat in an armchair, the room bathed in warm lamplight, and there was an end table beside him with a Bible and a vase of yellow roses on it. Jimmy's eyes were glassy, but he had a small smile on his lips, just an upturn, just a hint. The bulbous bandages on his hands were gone, replaced by streamlined wraps of flesh-colored dressings.

"I'm James Holdstock of ATF and I'm back home in the United States now," he said. His voice was soft. "I want to thank my friends for getting me back home, and the Mexican government for helping all of us. I wouldn't be here without them. I know that my abduction has become a controversy, but now it's over. I'm safe and healthy and I'll return to work soon. I'm proud to be an American and an agent of the ATF and I'm proud to call Mexico my friend."

Hood took his beer outside and sat on the flagstone patio. Bly had told him that it had taken nine tries for Jimmy to get the speech right. In spite of the teleprompter, he kept losing focus, slurring words, tearing up. She also said that Jimmy was living in an ATFE safe house now, out of state and heavily guarded. His family had moved in with relatives in St. Paul.

Through the screen door, Hood could hear the anchor interviewing the expert.

First off, was this a matter of derring-do south of the border, or was Mr. Holdstock's release somehow negotiated?

There is no negotiation with narcoterrorists. I can't go into details, but yes—cooperative derring-do involving two countries.

This is far from usual, or is it?

It is, Charles, and I think it's the face of things to come. If we want to win this war against the drug cartels, we must have more cooperation. Much more. And by we I mean the United States and Mexico.

Hood looked out to the sprinkling of lights that was Buenavista, and the tent city of the National Guard sprawling to the west. A convoy was now departing the base, heading through the desert on a just-bladed road, a chain of headlights snaking into the dark. He thought of the steep descent to Batopilas, his own headlights faint in that hostile world, the immense spires of rock engulfing them finally and the sky disappearing. He thought of the bodies and the heads, and of Jimmy sitting defeated upon his horse beside Vascano, and he heard Luna say that his wife was beautiful even in old clothes and that his daughters would marry warriors like themselves, and he saw Luna's great bull's body shiver as the bullet passed through. He heard the twang of that bullet ricocheting off the rock behind him. Hood put his head in his hands.

A few minutes later he brought his stationery and a good pen outside and he set the paper on the old rough table with a *Road & Track* magazine to pad it.

Dear Mom & Dad,

I

But this was all he could muster.

35

Hood parked his Camaro in the improvised lot near the pond on Bradley Jones's ranch. There were scores of cars and a charter bus and a place for taxis and limos to drop off and pick up. A passenger helicopter lowered to a pad cut in the woodland beside the pond. Beth Petty waited for him to get her door and they walked toward the barnyard in the late afternoon.

Hood held a blue box with a white ribbon under one arm and Beth held his other. He wore a new navy suit and a white shirt and a tie and new shoes that had cost him dearly. Beth wore a beige knit dress with cut mother-of-pearl worked into the fabric, and their surfaces shimmered in the sun. Her hair was up and she had sapphires in her ears and around her neck. When Hood had picked her up and first seen her lovely face and chocolate eyes and the joyous blue jewelry, he was speechless. Suddenly he felt alive, when all he'd felt since Mexico was numb. He had smiled for the first time since Batopilas.

Now, as the ranch came into view, Suzanne Jones surrounded him, the memory of her or the ghost of her, but Hood saw no reason to resist it and he didn't try to. She barged right in. He remembered the light in her eyes and the volume of her body and the taste of her and he had a strong feeling that there was something special she wanted to tell him on this, the wedding day of her oldest son.

In the barnyard an oval ring had been made of pipe rail, complete with heavy wooden walls and bleachers all around. It looked like a rodeo ring. White bunting hung from the rails and the grandstand and the rain gutters of the barn and from the ranch house itself and from the arms of the floodlights surrounding the arena and from the generators that would power them. The tremendous old oak tree was hung with hundreds of tiny lights that even in the midday sun twinkled like fireflies.

They walked into the shade of a huge white tent and onto the gleaming wood of a great dance floor. The stage was big and raised, and Hood recognized two of the Inmates, the bass player and the lead guitarist, arguing over monitor placement. There was a long table already heaped with gifts, and Hood added his. It was a heavy lead crystal vase etched near the base with the date and the words *Bradley & Erin, Long May You Run*. He had ventured into Tiffany's in all innocence, and the vase had chosen him.

Beyond the gift table was the bar. The bar itself was forty feet long and backed by a wall of mirrored shelves six feet high and filled with booze, and the barstools were cowhide, many of them taken. Four very beautiful barkeeps were tending and talking with the drinkers. They were done up like saloon dancers. There was a huge punch bowl on a table near the bar, and the pale pink liquid poured from a pitcher held by a glass maiden and spilled down tiers of scalloped ponds to the final basin.

"I think I'll start with the punch and work up to the bar," said Beth.

"Good call."

Hood dipped gold-trimmed goblets into the stream and handed Beth the glass and touched it with the rim of his. "It's good to be here with you," he said.

They drank and she studied him. "You look better than you did a week ago, Charlie. There's a little something coming back into your eyes."

"Mexico took it out of me."

"Maybe this day will put something back."

"I'd like that."

Another large tent was set up near the ranch house. At seven o'clock, with the sun lowering and the heat of the day broken by a distant onshore breeze, Erin came up the aisle through the neck-craning crowd, in a dazzling white satin dress with sequins and lace and a veil through which Hood saw her half-smiling face framed in the red ringlets of her hair and her eyes bright and composed and aware. Her maids were lovely.

Bradley wore a black notch-lapelled tuxedo with a black tie and cummerbund and he bore it as only a slender but well-proportioned man can do, making it casual and unimportant. He glanced at selected faces including Hood's, his expression amused and alert. Hood studied Bradley's retinue: little brother Jordan, Clayton the forger, Stone the thief, and Los Angeles County Sheriff's sergeant Frank Cleary.

The service was Catholic due to the McKennas. The priest was round and big-toothed and smiled greatly. Hood found the ceremony overlong but moving. In his heart was happiness for Erin and sadness and some anger, too, because he believed that Bradley had already come to no good and that his foolishness would eventually harm her.

Before he knew it, Bradley and Erin Jones were striding back down the aisle and the crowd was hollering with reckless abandon.

The warm-up band was Los Straitjackets, who played surf music and wore Mexican wrestling costumes. Hood was a guitar lover and he had played unpromisingly as a boy and always liked the reverb-drenched, double-lead twang of the Ventures and the Surfaris. When Los Straitjackets found a groove, Hood felt a giant metallic wave had broken over him, and notes of music were shearing off the walls to splash him.

He saw Bradley's half brother, Kenny, just three years old now, race onto the dance floor and begin flailing about. His father, Ernest, watched him from the crowd, his big Hawaiian face stoic as an Easter Island statue's. Hood had met them right here at this ranch two years ago. He could see that day. It had been his first assignment as an LASD homicide team trainee. He had driven way down here from L.A. to interview Suzanne Jones, whom he suspected of having witnessed a crime, and by the time he drove off forty minutes later, the path of his life had changed.

The dance floor filled, and Hood and Beth worked their way to the bar, where the dance hall girls were making drinks. The drinkers were two thick the length of the bar. Hood watched one of the bartenders take an ornate faceted goblet and pour an ounce of pale green liquid into it. Then she balanced a flat perforated spoon across the opening and set a sugar cube on it. Next she moved the drink to a small but elaborate stainless steel fountain. It looked something like a hookah. There were six of these bright contraptions set up down the bar. But instead of drawing smoke through the tube, the bartender set the drink under it and began dispensing drops of clear liquid over the sugar cube and into the green fluid.

"What's the green stuff?" asked Beth.

"Absinthe. It was banned a few years ago. Now they're selling it again."

"Why the ban?"

"It was supposed to make you hallucinate, then go crazy."

"Permanently?"

"Temporarily."

"What's in the dispenser?"

"Ice water," said the bartender. She was blond and bustiered and pretty. "The sugar melts slowly and makes the absinthe taste better. It was a popular drink with European artists and writers."

"What's it taste like?" asked Beth.

"Licorice. From the anise."

"I love licorice."

Hood watched Beth talk to the bartender and wondered if she was perhaps fascinated by the science behind the ritual. Beth was curious about the way things worked. She loved learning new facts. Maybe this took her back to med school. Hood watched as the dripping ice water slowly turned the pale green drink a milky white.

"This is called the louche effect," said the bartender. "It's the precipitation of herbal essential oils used in distillation. This is what gives absinthe its color. *There.*"

"What proof is it?" asked Beth.

"This is one forty-eight, or seventy-four percent."

"I could prep a kid for a tetanus shot with it."

"The unique ingredient in absinthe isn't alcohol but a toxin called thujone. This is derived from the bitter wormwood the liquor is made from. Oscar Wilde said of absinthe: 'After the first glass, you see things as you wish they were. After the second, you see things as they are not. Finally, you see things as they really are, and that is the most horrible thing in the world.'"

"Can we have one?" asked Beth.

Hood held up two fingers, and the woman looked at Beth and smiled wickedly as she pushed forward the first drink. "Slowly. Let the thujone do its magic before the alcohol charges in."

Beth turned to Hood and sipped it and smiled. "Licorice, Charlie."

While Hood waited for his drink, he saw Bonnie Raitt and Lucinda Williams and Jakob Dylan and James McMurtry among the revelers and he realized that Erin and the Inmates were getting their music to some important ears. The bartender handed him his drink with a wink and he tipped her well. It tasted like licorice and racing fuel, extrapolating from the smell of dragsters he watched run at Pomona.

Hood and Beth danced two songs. The thujone made him feel as if his feet weren't quite touching the floor, that he was light and swift. Sound was rearranged without spatial logic: The laugh of a woman across the room became a shriek in his ear while Beth right next to him was hard to hear and the music broke apart into shards of sound and rained down. But memories jumped him like muggers from the darkness and he saw Luna in the river and he pushed this memory away and he saw the soldiers piled on the dirt road to Batopilas and these he pushed away also and he saw Jimmy's blank stare and Jenny's tears as she begged for his life on TV and he tried to vanquish these, too, but they were strong and wouldn't go away.

Then the Inmates walked onstage, followed by Erin in her wedding dress. The guests roared. The players took their stations, and Erin announced a song she'd written for Bradley. It was sweet and up-tempo and hopeful. The crowd quieted and Hood closed his eyes, and for three minutes, he believed what Erin believed, that the best was yet to come, that there would be love and hope in the world. For three minutes the bad memories couldn't get in. They hit against Erin's voice like raindrops against a window and ran off dispersed and unnamed.

"Just beautiful," said Beth.

Hood opened his eyes to see Owens Finnegan gliding through across the dance floor alone, on her way toward the bar. At first he wondered if it was the absinthe. Owens wore a silver gray dress the same color of her eyes and she gave Hood a glance as she disappeared into the drinkers.

"Who is she?"

"Mike Finnegan's daughter," he said.

"Do you know her?"

"We've met."

"What is Mike's daughter doing here?"

"Mike knows the groom."

"Mike knows everyone, doesn't he?"

"Apparently, yes."

"Let's have another drink, Charlie."

She smiled at him and held up her empty absinthe goblet. Hood bored through the revelers to get two more drinks and when he got back to Beth, Owens was with her. They were laughing. Hood gave Beth her drink and offered his to Owens, who accepted. He introduced the women.

"Nice to see you, Owens."

"What a surprise," she said. "Do you know the groom or the—"

"I know them both," said Hood. "Beth is Mike's doctor at Imperial Mercy."

"One of them," Beth said.

Owens looked at Beth with her nickel eyes. "Thank you for taking such good care of him. I just left his room a couple of hours ago and he looked, well . . . bandaged. Anyway, I'm going to come and visit again next week. If I survive this drink. *Wow.*"

"Yeah, *wow* is right," said Beth.

Hood went to fetch a drink for himself and when he came back, Owens was gone and Beth had a strange look on her face.

"What did that poor woman do to herself?"

"Mike said she lost all reason to live."

Beth shook her head and sipped her drink, looking over the rim of the absinthe goblet at Hood.

They walked across the barnyard toward the ranch house. Revelers pounded down the dock of the pond and splashed into the black water. Two tractors with livestock trailers came up the dirt road toward the rodeo arena, and Hood saw the moonlit dust rise, then settle in its wake. Up near the ranch house, they walked among the hard-walled tents set up in the grass. Each had an unlit electric lantern waiting outside the door. There were already party guests inside some of them, their lantern light glowing through the thick fabric and spilling out from the mesh vents at the rooflines, and their laughter bouncing out into the night. Hood let go of Beth's hand and clicked on the lantern and held open the tent door. Inside were two cots made up and a stand with folded towels and a wash basin and a soap dish and a water pitcher and cut flowers in a cobalt blue vase.

"Hubba hubba," said Beth, leaning into him. "I guess they weren't fooling about a three-day party. I think it might take me three days to get this second drink out of my blood."

Later they dined on barbecued meat and fowl and fish, all grilled in halved fifty-five-gallon drums in which beds of mesquite and oak smoked fragrantly. Bottles of wine were carried in and placed amidst the platters, all open, with the white wine in damp clay canisters to keep it cool. The wineglasses stood in decorative inverted pyramids, but one of these was suddenly demolished by a man who fell over backward into it, his absinthe glass still half full and held out so as not to spill one precious drop.

The wedding party sat on a dais above the celebrants. Photographers shot pictures, and Bradley threw bones to the dogs, then at the photogs. Two of the Inmate roadies were dancing on the old wooden bar top and kicking unattended goblets into the air, glass slivers shooting through the lights like tiny comets. Hood ate ravenously. Beth spoke in fluent French, stood and told a joke in Italian, then sat back down embarrassed. After dinner and toasts, James McMurtry and the Heartless Bastards took up arms onstage and their first portentous notes issued forth from the amplifiers like the disturbance in advance of a hurricane.

Hood bought a dance with Erin with a crisp Ben and they did a swing to a song about a guy with an Airstream trailer and a Holstein cow. Erin told him they were honeymooning in Moorea but that wouldn't be for a couple of weeks because of some L.A. gigs that the label had added late, and Bradley had some things to do. After the dance, Erin kissed his cheek and put her hands on his shoulders and looked directly into Hood's eyes.

"You're important to him and to me, too," she said. "Watch over him, Charlie. He needs you more than you know."

Bradley came up behind her. "I need *you* more than I know," he said, taking one of Erin's hands off Hood's shoulder and kissing it gallantly.

"Thanks for coming, Charlie," said Bradley. "It means something to me. It would have meant something to my mother, too. Our futures go together, whether she's with us or not."

"Congratulations to both of you," said Hood. And for a moment his hope for them was stronger than his dread.

* * *

Near midnight the crowd surged outside where the rodeo arena was now bathed in the floodlights. The bulls shuffled and snorted in the pen adjacent. There was a black bull in the chute and it stomped and snorted and threw its haunches against the rails, and Hood could hear the crack of wood. When the stands were full, a cowboy climbed onto the animal. The crowd was yelling loud when the black bull exploded into the arena and the kid rode its fury up and down, casually enmeshed in the circling chaos of the animal until he was suddenly flung from it and he landed and rolled and made the wall. There were five more bulls and five more riders. Hood watched them through an absinthe glow, transfixed and grinning.

Then Bradley sprung down from his seat and walked toward the chute. Erin turned and ran from the arena. Bradley stripped off his tuxedo jacket and flung it to his little brother, Jordan, who ran to keep up with him and appeared to be instructing him. Bradley climbed atop the chute, and the crowd roared into the night, and he lowered himself onto the dappled gray-and-white beast. Hood could see the shine of Bradley's patent leather shoes against the great flank of the bull and he watched Bradley take the rope as a cowboy instructed, and the cowboy spoke fast to Bradley, and little Jordan was speaking, too, and Bradley listened with lessening patience, then he shrugged and nodded to the gateman. A gray-white bolt shot to the middle of the arena and went into midair without seeming to have jumped. It landed and Bradley, with his one hand high and his other locked to the rope, crashed hard to the bull's back. The animal twisted and launched itself into the air again and this time Bradley was thrown high. The crowd went silent as Bradley sailed. Hood watched the bull watch him. Bradley gauged his speed and his height correctly and he landed on his feet and pitched forward and bowed. The crowd burst into cheers. He bowed again, then heard the thunder behind him and scrambled over the wall inches ahead of the slashing black horns. The audience mobbed him, and two men began bashing each other with chairs out in the bar area, and another ran for the pond with a bottle of vodka upturned in his mouth, and a Great Dane on its hind legs lapped the pink punch from the glass maiden's bowl, and two of the saloon girls danced burlesque on the bar top, waving their bras overhead like pennants.

"One more teensy little absinthe?" asked Beth.

"I don't see why not."

Beth threw herself into the bar crowd, and Hood found the coffee station and got a triple shot of espresso. Erin and McMurtry were onstage with the Inmates and the Heartless Bastards and two of Los Straitjackets, singing a not quite synchronized duet that advanced like an armored column.

Hood and Beth danced a song that became two more, then a slow one that Erin had written. They leaned into each other, bodies warm and hearts flush. Beth guided Hood off the floor and collected her goblet and aimed him around the rodeo arena and up the sloping barnyard to the tent city. There she delivered him to a unit up near the brushy hillside, set apart and unoccupied and welcoming. He turned on the lantern and held open the door for her. She stepped past him into the tent, clicking the lantern off on her way by.

36

Two days later, Hood sat in his replacement Yukon behind the Pace building and watched through the dark windows. There was a tall container of coffee on the console, and on the seat beside him were a bag of tacos and a package of cookies. He looked out at the rear of the building—warehouse, freight dock, loading ramp. There were pallets stacked along one wall and a motor home along another, the yard lights dull against the filthy windshield. A few minutes later he drove around the block and parked on the street out front, fifty yards away from the entrance.

Again the shift began at five o'clock. He watched the men park their old vehicles in the employee lot out front and wait to be let into the manufacturing floor. They carried plastic bags and beverage containers like his own, and some smoked. They looked relaxed and they talked and laughed quietly. The old ones reminded him of his father before his mind had betrayed him, back when he was easy and content with who he was and what he had made of his life and the working was never bad but never quite so good as being finished for the day.

He watched and thought about Beth Petty and the wedding and

after. They'd made it halfway through the second day of dancing, eating and drinking before running out of energy. Someone had gotten the bulls drunk and let them loose and they had terrorized the dance and bar tents briefly, then wobbled off to lie in the shade of the hillside oaks or graze the barnyard or stand knee-deep in the pond, drinking and peeing. Bradley and several other drunken young men had gotten ATVs from the barn and attempted a roundup. It failed, with minor injuries to two men and one ATV that ran off the dock and sank out of sight in the pond. The bulls were unharmed and barely noticed the men. Hood had driven home with Beth conked out against the window, asleep and snoring at times, her hair dangling wildly, her knit dress somewhat stretched and lightly smudged, sapphires intact and atwinkle in the afternoon light, a wedding-gift absinthe goblet wrapped in wedding napkins peeking from the top of her purse. Hood smiled. She had part of his heart now and that was good.

Deeper into the night, Hood stole across the street and hunkered among the begonias and rhododendrons around the perimeter of the building. He moved slowly and found the place where he could see in. He watched for a few minutes, getting a good look at the handguns being finished inside. They were nice-looking weapons. Hood guessed .32 caliber by the bore, but at this distance they could be .22s or even .38s. He also saw something that wasn't there the last time he'd surveilled Pace Arms: wooden shipping crates. Open and ready. The tops and packing material were stacked separately. The crates were roughly eighteen inches square. There were ten stacks of ten. At ten guns each, a thousand total. All crates awaiting their precious cargo. Soon, Hood thought. Soon.

He stood and was about to cut back across the street to his vehicle when he saw the Porsche Cayenne Turbo tear into the parking structure. The driver waited, then snatched the ticket from the dispenser. A moment later, newlywed Bradley Jones, trim in his Explorer uniform, strode to the Pace Arms entrance and pushed the speaker button on the wall. Then Bradley pulled open the lobby door and let the door swing shut behind him.

Hood's heart raced and fell at the same time. He closed his eyes and opened them. He was surprised but not. Sad but not. Hugely pissed off at Bradley is what he mostly was, and at himself for believing in Bradley. How many times could he look at this boy but fail to see him? Suddenly the stolen fifty thousand rounds of .32-caliber ammunition made simple and terrible sense. And the Tiffany vase became nothing more than a symbol for his own sentimentality and daft hopes.

Bradley and Pace.

Pace and Bradley.

He knelt back down in the darkness again and watched the men make guns and felt the hard thump of his heart down in his chest. A few minutes later, Pace and Bradley appeared amidst the workstations, Pace convivial with the workers and Bradley silent. Bradley walked along the tables, looking down at the emerging weapons, his uniform crisp, his expression speculative, lost in thought.

37

"Mike," said Gabe Reyes. "Meet Father Quang from St. Cecilia's."

"How do you do, Father?"

"Fine, thank you," said Quang. "How are you feeling?"

"Peaks and valleys."

"Gabe tells me you are strong as a horse."

"We all know that isn't true."

"They tell me it's a miracle you're alive."

"I believe in miracles, Father."

"So do I. May I touch your hand?"

"Of course."

Bleary from surveillance and the two-hour-plus drive, bruised by disappointment and self-recrimination, Hood sat in the corner of Mike's room and watched Quang place his hand upon Mike's. The IV line had been removed, and Hood noted that the needle bruises were gone. The books beside the bed were all different from the ones he'd seen last time. On top of the stack was *The End of History and the Last Man*. A cell phone and a charger sat on top of it. Hood had wanted to be here for the meeting between the priest and Finnegan, but he wasn't sure what he hoped to learn.

Hood watched the monitor and saw Mike's blood pressure rise when the priest touched him. His pulse went from sixty-eight to eighty-eight, but Mike's voice was warm and calm. Neither Reyes nor Quang were paying any attention to the screen.

"What brings you here, Father?" Mike asked. "A little early for last rites, I hope."

Quang removed his hand and stood back and laughed heartily. He was short and trim, and his hair was black and shiny with a blaze of gray. "Nothing like that, Mr. Finnegan."

"Then what?"

Quang glanced at Reyes, then at Hood, then turned his gaze back to Finnegan's swathed face, partially visible but mostly not.

"I am waiting," said Finnegan.

"I wondered if you might need a confessor. I thought that a man with a good Irish name like Finnegan might be a Catholic. Are you?"

"Very lapsed, I'm afraid."

"Then you have said confession before?"

"Centuries ago."

"See?" said Reyes. "Centuries. He's always talking about people and things from years ago. I figured he'd have to be hundreds of years old to have done what he says he's done. And that bullet they took from his head, that was made in 1850-something. At first I thought he was hallucinating. Brain swelling from his injuries and all that. Now I think he's either insane or he's possessed. That's what I think."

"*Centuries* was a figure of speech, Gabe," said Finnegan. "The gun was a collectible antique."

"All you do is lie."

"Wait," said Quang, holding up his Bible. "Gentlemen, don't argue. Mike, would you like me to hear your confession?"

Finnegan was silent for a long moment. Hood watched his numbers settle. "Sure," he said.

"Wonderful!" Quang turned to Reyes and Hood. "Gentlemen, we would like some priv—"

"Let them stay, Father. I have nothing to hide. I am as God made me, aren't I?"

"In His image were you made."

"Then I'm ready to begin."

Quang shot a concerned glance at Reyes, and Reyes shrugged. "Mike, how long has it been since your last confession?"

"I truly don't remember."

"Then tell me how you have sinned."

Finnegan said nothing for a moment. "You tell me how I have sinned."

"I don't understand."

"I will explain what I do and do not do, and you can tell me what the sin is. That's *your* job, isn't it?"

"It is God's."

"Come on, Quang. You made it to America. Take the bull by the horns."

"Tell me how you have sinned."

Finnegan said nothing for a long while. Hood's mind wandered. He pictured Bradley in his Explorer uniform, walking along the workstations inside the Pace Arms building, his expression speculative, almost dreamy. Not Bradley's usual look. Was he haunted by the guns that would be used to kill people? Hood remembered his own surprise and anger at that moment. On what basis had he kept alive such high hopes for Bradley? Was it all a sentimental homage to his mother? He saw that Finnegan was watching him.

"I have one God and no other," Finnegan said quietly. "I've never bowed down to an image or likeness of anything in heaven or earth.

I do not take the name of God in vain. I remember the Sabbath unfailingly, though I don't often get to church. Though I am lapsed, I have kept up a lively dialogue with my maker. I honor my parents, but to be honest, I don't remember them well. I do not kill or commit adultery or steal or lie. I am not covetous. I do not entertain impure thoughts."

Hood watched the blood pressure and pulse readouts: no change. The room was silent except for hospital sounds.

Quang stood with his hands in front of him, the good book shielding his privates. "Really, Mike?"

"Yes. Really."

"Do you know that lies offend God?"

"I'm sure they do. But what lies do you mean?"

"Your lie of personal perfection in a fallen world."

"Father, I make no claim to perfection or even exception among the men of the earth. Perhaps I was born without the proper passions to commit sin. Perhaps my capacity for it has been smothered within the vast and terrifying fear that I feel at times for humankind. Perhaps sin bores me. However, I do have one very strong belief that may be a sin to some people and some gods. I believe that all people are free to choose the course of their lives and their deaths, and that the sacred and the profane are ours to name, and that our law is ours to write. Your God judged me thousands of years ago, and by that judgment I stand unblinkingly. But within his commandments, I am blameless."

"You are not what we see," said Reyes.

Finnegan sighed. His vitals had not changed.

"Does this mean anything to you?" asked Reyes. He brought a crucifix from his coat pocket and held it up for Mike to see.

"An exorcism," said Finnegan. "I'm tickled."

"This is no joke," said Reyes.

"What it means to me is aisle eight of the Mercado Toro in Boyle Heights, right beside the candles of the saints, three dollars and ninety-nine cents, made in China."

"Maybe then you would like to see it closer." Reyes leaned across the bed and held the crucifix before Finnegan's steady blue eyes.

"I like the ones made of straw in Mexico. No blood. No thorns. No woeful eyes. More mystery and a hint of the transcendent."

"Maybe you'd like to touch it."

"Now you sound like that uncle we've all had."

Reyes set the crucifix in Finnegan's upturned right hand. Hood watched his pulse and blood pressure rise, then race. The digital readouts raced higher, then higher. The numbers were still scrolling up when the monitor buzzed loud and a nurse flew in from the station outside.

"*What's going on here?*"

"We're not sure, Kathy," said Finnegan. "Something with the sensors again, I'd guess."

His voice was calm, but his numbers had exhausted themselves and an ERROR/RESET message now pulsed across the monitor screen. The warning buzzer continued. Hood watched Finnegan reach the crucifix back to Father Quang.

"Thank you so much for the visit, Father. I've always enjoyed the presence of the faithful."

"*Mike, how do you feel?*"

"Splendid."

"*You may be going into cardiac arrest.*"

"Don't be silly."

Two more nurses squeezed into the room. One took Mike's wrist for a pulse, and the other pulled the monitor module from its stand and commenced pushing buttons. Hood watched as Kathy slid her slender hand inside the body cast below the cranial brace, feeling for the pulmonary sensor down on Finnegan's neck. Suddenly the alarm stopped. The monitor nurse frowned down at the thing and waited a moment, then held it up for Kathy to see. From his stool, Hood read the numbers: pulse 72, blood pressure 118/66. Kathy withdrew her hand from inside the cast.

The other nurse continued to hold Mike's wrist for another few seconds. "Pulse is normal," she said.

"I still suspect a sensor," said Mike.

"The sensor was drenched in sweat," said Kathy. "But they're made to withstand that. It happens. I don't get it."

"I sure love the attention," said Mike.

Hood saw Finnegan work up a lip-only smile, his jaws still wired firm and his head still immobilized by the cranial clamps. His pupils were pinpoints, and his face was bright red and running with sweat.

"Father Quang, I'd be happy to continue this discussion at any time," said Finnegan. His voice was calm and warm. "I might be able to come up with a sin or two I forgot about today. But next time, why don't you confess to me? Gabe and Charlie, you two would be welcome to sit in on that session."

Kathy herded the men into the hallway outside of the ICU, then shut the locking door behind her. Two Guardsmen patrolled past, weapons slung over their shoulders.

"He's proud and intelligent and he's playing with us," said Quang. "He wants attention. He wants control."

"He knows too much," said Reyes.

"He's obviously very clever," said Quang.

"He's more than that," said Reyes. "He is not us. You can't understand the world by believing that it is merely like yourself. There is more and there has always been more and not all of it is good. I can't believe you don't see it." Reyes turned and limped away. Hood watched him turn right for the elevator. When he turned to Quang, the padre was looking up at him with a searching expression.

"Since the death of his granddaughter, Gabriel has not been the same," said Quang. "She was murdered and left in the desert. Unsolved. Now Gabriel expects evil, so this is what he finds. Finding it confirms his hopes. He is still looking for someone to blame. He sits in the fifth row of St. Cecilia's every Saturday night for mass, and his eyes burn up at me until the service ends."

Hood watched the priest walk away, following the same route as the snakebit police chief. He reached into his pocket and took out the cell phone he'd swiped from the book stack on his way out of Finnegan's room. The charge and bars were both full. He searched contacts, new messages, inbox, sent, drafts, and voice mail and found one message, left just an hour ago. He recognized the number as belonging to Owens.

A few minutes later, he was back in Finnegan's room. Kathy was hanging the monitor back onto its holder. "It must have just been that sensor," she said.

"No harm done, Kathy," said Finnegan.

Hood watched her bustle out and turn into the adjacent room.

"That was interesting," said Hood.

"A quaint little assault by a Mexican cop and a Vietnamese priest. I love America."

"Why didn't you tell them what you told me that night we drank the wine?"

"What I told you that night was nonsense, Charlie. I blathered to you under the influence of wine and some sudden impulse that I attribute to another round of swelling in my brain."

"I watched your vitals race when Quang touched you. And I watched them run off the chart when Reyes set the cross in your hand."

"I do have strong reactions to certain people. It always helped me in sales."

"It wasn't the sensor."

"I'll let you experts decide what it was," said Finnegan.

Hood set the cell phone back on top of the book stack.

"Strictly for emergencies," said Finnegan. "And, you know, family matters."

Hood sat on the wheeled stool and watched Finnegan's vitals on the monitor.

"How was the wedding, Charlie?"

"Terrific. They're happy."

"Youth isn't always wasted on the young. Did you take Beth?"

Hood nodded. "I saw Owens. She said she'd been here to see you."

"Oh, my. What a girl. She looks better than I've ever seen her. Thank you so much for helping me with her."

"You're welcome. But there wasn't really much of a problem between you two, was there?"

"She likes you."

"Well."

"Well? Just *well*? Our lovely Dr. Petty must be a factor here. She's had a satisfied look about her the last two days."

"That may be, Mike."

"I love single-minded, dumb-as-a-dog loyalty in a man."

Hood looked up at the vitals monitor and saw Finnegan's usual numbers.

"Charlie, congratulations on the rescue of Jimmy. I saw him on TV. He looks ghastly and lobotomized, but I guess that's to be expected. Tell me what happened to Raydel Luna."

"He brokered the deal with Calderón's government."

"Was he shot down by Vascano?"

Hood said nothing while the Bakersfield tiger glanced back at him and he again felt no basis for understanding this man before him at this time and in this place.

You can't know these things, thought Hood.

Finnegan worked up a slow small smile. "I'm surprised they didn't get to Raydel earlier," he said. "A principled man is always a valuable target. May I tell you something?"

"You may."

"It's never been my wish to exhaust your goodwill."

"It is exhausted. You know things and people you're not supposed to know. You're not affiliated with any law enforcement or intelligence agencies that I can find. You invent histories and stories to obscure your own past, but the histories and stories involve real people and true events and you know details like you were really there."

"There are unlimited stories and multiple truths. Not many people can let themselves believe this concept. But you can and that's why I've talked with you. Opened up. Offered friendship. Charlie, I value your goodwill. I would like to encourage it. I feel the weight that is on you. There's something on your mind, isn't there?"

Neither man spoke for a long while. Hood remembered Finnegan telling him he could hear a man's thoughts at eight feet or less. Maybe that would account for all he seemed to know. Hood waited.

"Weapons, Charlie? Weapons going south? I'll bet I'm getting warm."

"What else would be on my mind, Mike? Guns are my job with Blowdown."

"Something new? Something value-priced and made locally in, say, *Orange County*?"

Hood stared at the little man, thinking: *If he knows I'm surveilling Pace Arms, then my cover is blown or soon could be. But how*

*can he know? By reading my mind a few minutes ago? We're less
than eight feet apart. Fucking ridiculous.*

But Hood tried to keep his mind open and blank. "Why locally?
Why Orange County?"

"Speculation only, Deputy."

"Help me, Mike. Like I helped you with Owens."

"You already know the big picture, Charlie. You know that the
other cartels all need firepower against Armenta and his Zetas. And
against Vascano, who's a bigger threat than Armenta because he
recruits. Vascano's band is growing. They're over two thousand
well-armed men. They'll kill the cartel leaders and consolidate trade.
They'll make a nice profit off American appetites and they'll try to
win the hearts and bellies of Mexico's poor. They may succeed. Finally they'll have to do battle with Calderón's troops. Vascano is
already plucking the best poor soldiers from the Mexican Army and
the Guatemalan Kaibiles. The rate of defection increases weekly.
Everyone needs guns in Mexico. Everyone."

"Where are they leaving from, these new, locally made products?
When?"

Finnegan again went silent. Hood glanced at the vitals, then at
the stack of books, then at the flecks on the linoleum floor.

"I'll see what I can do."

"You owe me, Mike."

"Yes, I do."

Hood stood and plucked the phone off the book and tossed it
onto the crook of Mike's good right arm and walked out.

38

I sit in the penthouse and listen to the sounds of the last eighty Love 32s coming to life down in manufacturing. Three more nights should complete the job, and this night is already half over. One thousand units, nine hundred thousand dollars and the promise of more. I am not prone to contentment, but I smile slightly and circle the cold martini glass in my hand. Through the picture window, I look out across South Coast Plaza and the Trinity Broadcasting Center and beyond them I see the bank of pale coastal fog inching in from the night.

Sharon has gone for take-out sashimi and ice cream. I watch the fog drift in, but suddenly the window glass holds another great pale shape that is not fog. Uncle Chester stands before the open penthouse door, left unlocked of course for Sharon. He comes into the room with small steps, his immense bald head catching the light, his unstructured linen suit adding to his enormity. He carries a leather briefcase. He stands in the middle of the room, looking at either the back of my head or the reflection of my front side in the window.

"And where is Sharon?" he says softly.

"Out."

"That's too bad. Ron, I have the documents."

"What documents?"

"The creation of our new company. You were right about going legitimate again. Utterly right. I was a fool to think we could make a living illegally. What kind of living is that, really? I've paid for a battery of lawyers on this one. Expensive lawyers. But they have found ways to re-create what we once had. They can protect us from the past and open up our future. You will be most pleased, I promise—as head of research and development. And Sharon—straight to marketing. Where is the best place for us to sign these?"

"I'm not signing anything."

"You will change your mind when you see what I have."

"I doubt it, Chester." I stand. I do not want to see or hear Uncle Chester.

I lead him to the beveled glass dining room table under the twinkling glass chandelier. Chester is deferential and insists that I sit at the head. He sets the briefcase on the glass and moves his thumbs across the combination locks. The latches spring open.

Sharon bursts through the door with two handfuls of dangling plastic bags. I've never been happier to see her, which is saying something. She looks at Chester and her face goes pale, then she glowers at me.

"Sharon, you are beautiful," he says.

In fact she is. Her summer dress is a weird shade of green that looks ravishing on her, her espadrilles have good heels, her body is tanned beautifully from all the swimming and sunbathing we did down in Laguna this last weekend.

"*Help, Ron?*"

But Chester is up and there before I am, sweeping the bags from Sharon's grip and small-stepping across the hardwood floor to the granite countertop, where he gingerly lands the bags and smiles at her. Still smiling and oddly formal, he moves toward the dining room.

Sharon sets her purse on the counter beside the shopping bags and gives me an even darker look than the one she gave me when we were seventeen and I declared my love for her. "*Get him out of here*," she whispers. "*Fast.*"

But Chet has gone back to his briefcase on the table and brought out a bottle of wine. From my occasional splurges at the locked premium rack of the wine store, I recognize it as a two-hundred-dollar bottle of Anderson Valley cabernet sauvignon. Then he's back in the kitchen again between Sharon and me, twisting the lead cork sealer off the bottle with one little white hand and then pushing the corkscrew in and turning, all the while chattering away about possible names for the new company—Chetronsha Arms being his favorite, a neat compounding of all our names, equal billing with allowances for seniority and . . .

"You've got five minutes of my time, Chester," says Sharon. "Starting right now."

We sit at the dining room table, and Chester passes the documents to us. The cover sheets bear the name of a prominent Newport Beach business law firm. In a soft voice, Chester summarizes the contents and intentions of each thick clipped packet. He makes them sound logical and simple. There are scores upon scores of thin rubber arrows stuck to the edges of the sheets to mark the places for signature and dating—blue for me, pink for Sharon, and black for Chet. Among the docs are a draft general description of the new Chetronsha Arms, a DBA form, a business plan, a tax plan, an asset sheet describing the real property and furnishings here at the *former* Pace Arms address, and several shorter agreements, addenda, letters of intent, an applicable compendium of State of California corporate laws, and finally a draft proposal of Chetronsha Arms corporate bylaws.

Sharon has gone silent as she reads. I do, too. I can hear the faint tap-tap-tapping of the gunsmiths downstairs and their music, which I know is loud down there but barely audible up here. When Chester looks at me, his expression tries to confirm my joy and pride in these sounds. I'm not much of a businessman, so I just scan the pages, looking for God knows what. Sharon, on the other hand, is a very attentive and discriminating reader of business documents. She used to drive Contracts crazy with her eye for minutiae when she was tasked with proofing their drafts.

Five minutes comes and goes. I've drunk half the wine. I look out the window and see nothing now, just a pale infinity of fog through which come no shape and no light and no color.

Sharon reads on for another five. During the last two minutes, she's not really reading, just flipping pages with increasing speed and loudness. When she turns the last page, she is shaking her head.

"Thanks for all your hard work, Chester," she says. "I see you spent a lot of money on good counsel. They've been thorough and thoughtful. Ron and I have talked long and hard about this company. We have dreamed about it. We have worked hard to put ourselves into the position of making it a reality. We have a vision for it, and this vision does not include you as the president and CFO. It does not include you at all. With due respect, Chet, I now ask you to take these documents with you and leave this building forever. Ron?"

"She's right, Chester. I'm sorry. That's just what it is."

The great whiteness of Chester's face has changed to pink, and his small blue eyes blink quickly as if in defense. He sets a hand upon a stack of documents. "I have given you everything you wanted. I've provided for your dreams. Surely there can be a place in them for me."

"I'm sorry, Chester," I say.

"I'm not," says Sharon.

"For your father, Ron? My brother? For old times?"

"We're starting up a company, Chet, not putting a contract out on you."

"Man to man, blood on blood?"

"No."

A long pause while Chester stares into space. "I'm very, very disappointed."

Chester stacks the documents neatly and sets them in the still-open briefcase. He squares them, closes the lid, snaps down the latches, and spins the small steel combination numbers. He stands and sets the briefcase upright before him, both hands on the leather handle. He looks at Sharon, then at me. He bows his head formally. Then he turns and sweeps the briefcase from the table, and when his back is to me, he pivots around once like a discus thrower and slams the corner of it into my head. I get my hand between my skull and the briefcase but not much of it. Then I'm on my back on the floor, looking up at the chandelier. However, the chandelier is not bright and white but the color of my eyelids. I try to open them as in a nightmare, but they will not open. I hear grunts and whimpers and the gagging of strangulation. I hear the tearing of fabric. I hear gasps. Then these sounds lose volume, and I fear that I am losing consciousness. I stand. I fall. I stand again and my eyes open. The penthouse whirls around me. I stagger toward the sounds in the bedroom. I stand in the doorway looking in. Chester has his enormous back to me and he has planted his bulk upon Sharon on the bed, her legs splayed and her heels raining helplessly down against his huge haunches. He's got her hands pinned over her head to the mattress with one of his own, and with the other he's trying to get off his belt. They're both growling.

Without thinking, I throw myself onto him. It takes him a moment to acknowledge me. I smell baby powder. Then he rises up smoothly like a breaching whale and wrenches himself off the bed. I land on the floor. He towers over me. He looks down and his expression is the same as it always is. He pulls me up by my shirt collar, tosses me into the air just a little, and catches my head between the meaty vises of his hands. He holds me up to face him, eye to eye, and I'm struggling and kicking and hanging on to his forearms with both hands to try to keep my skull from buckling. He squeezes. *"There are no new ideas. Only old imperatives,"* he whispers. I feel my skull plates grinding. My vision constricts, then fractures. All I can see for certain is the bed below me, the blessedly empty bed.

Then I hear three sharp cracks. Through Chester's palms I register three small tremors. His hands shiver and his eyes widen and he growls again, then grimaces, his small even teeth not a foot away from my face. He drops me to the floor. I roll toward the door and there is Sharon, standing just inside the doorway, her dress ripped and dangling and a Pace Arms Hawk .22 up in both hands, aimed at Chester. He lumbers toward us. I stay down on my knees to give her a clear sight line. If he gets close, I'll spring onto him to keep him from her. She shoots him three more times and Chester stops. I can see two small bloody circles on his shirtfront and a bright red gash high up on his skull where the bullet has bounced off. He grunts and twists one arm behind his back as if trying to scratch an itch, and I realize this is where the first three shots hit. Sharon has eight shells left if the magazine was full, nine if there was also one cartridge in the chamber. Chester steps forward and Sharon shoots him three more times, pretty much dead center at this close range. He rocks and staggers backward. He sways, then steadies himself. "Nobody does that to me," Sharon says dreamily. She fires and misses and misses again. The bullets smack the wall. Then she cracks a shot between his small blue eyes. His head shakes and settles and he looks at us. He sits on the foot of the bed and places his hands on his thighs, as if he were about to say something. There's blood running down his mouth and off his chin. He extrudes a small pointed tongue and tastes it. His torso is drenched in the red blood of his lungs and the black blood of his heart. He collapses then, like a building imploded, his lower body slumping to the floor first and his head whipping down last with a sharp centrifugal splat. The back of his cream linen coat is a bloody thing, too. Sharon hands the gun down to me and walks unevenly away, one shoulder and half her back showing above the flap of her torn green dress, one foot bare and the other still shod.

I find her in the kitchen, wiping out two martini glasses. Her eyes are wide and her hands tremble and she doesn't look at me. I come up behind her to put my hands on her shoulders.

"Do not approach me."

"Okay. I won't. Sharon, he didn't—"

"No, he did not."

"I'm thankful for that, Sharon. I'm going downstairs to talk to Marcos while you make those drinks. We'll need to make some adjustments."

"The ice cream is melting."

"I'll get it."

"What if he's not dead."

"He is dead."

"But what if he's not."

I read the old inscription on the Hawk, then set it on the counter.

For Sharon, safe forever in the arms of Pace.

"I didn't know you kept this."

"It's been in my purse since the day you gave it to me."

"If he's not dead, shoot him again."

She looks up toward me, but I don't think she sees me. She smiles vacantly. "Terrific, Ron. Don't be long."

I look in on Chester to make sure no miracle cures have occurred. He's still as a boulder, and the hardwood floor around him is a dark slick. I feel regret that he's dead and an odd sense of loss, but very small amounts of each. I never understood how he could have been the brother of my reasonably sized, generous, sensitive, good-natured father. I still don't. The wood floor is a modern laminate and will clean up well.

As I walk toward the front door, I see Sharon in the kitchen, scooping ice into the martini shaker. Her hair washes over her face, and tears run down her cheeks, but her hands are steadier now. She has tucked the torn shoulder of her green dress up under her bra strap. I am so proud of her, and that she chooses to spend her time with me. She looks back at me with an expression that says: *Don't say one word.*

I don't dare.

I ride the elevator down into manufacturing. I'm trying to figure out how to tell Marcos what I now need from him, but my phone rings and I see that it's Bradley.

"Bra—"

"Don't talk," he says. "Only listen."

I listen and do not talk. Bradley tells me that ATFE knows what I'm making, that the Pace building is probably under surveillance right now. I can't understand *how* they would know. Chester? At Bradley's orders I write down an address and a time, and I make a list of the things he wants me to buy and in what quantities. Some of these things make sense to me and others do not. I see that what I'm going to need from Marcos is small potatoes compared to what Bradley needs from me.

"You got it, Bradley. Done."

I punch off and stab the phone back into the belt holder. I take a deep breath and straighten my back.

Rounding the corner into the intensified smells of solvents and lubricants and blued steel and loud Mexican music, I raise my hand and hail Marcos. It's just dawning on me how to pull this all together.

39

Hood watched the Pace Arms entrance through slitted eyes, his head back on the rest, radio turned to a music station. It was nine P.M. At ten thirty, Sharon came down and drove her Z-car from the parking structure. At eleven o'clock he saw Chester Pace's black Town Car roll into the same structure and a moment later the big man lumber from the darkness to the building. Just as Chester reached the entryway, the door opened and one of the gunmakers looked up at Chester and nodded and held open the door for him.

A minute later, Hood saw a slight change of light in the penthouse, then movement behind the blinds. Fifteen minutes later, Sharon parked and walked out of the structure with plastic bags in both hands. She was dressed in a green dress and looked tanned and casually lovely.

Hood turned down the radio and watched. A few minutes later, the fog settled over the building tops and descended over the streetlights, muting the world. Hood rolled the windows up against the chill. The next time he checked his watch, it was after one A.M. No Chester. No nothing. Four hours to go to end of their shift.

Just after seven o'clock, the men emerged from the building into the foggy morning light. They shuffled to their cars wordlessly and began to drive away. Hood watched them go and counted them. Twelve had gone in. Only ten had left. He felt addled from lack of sleep, and he was sore from the sitting. He felt like he had worked the shift alongside them.

His phone vibrated and he saw a new text message waiting:

> my journeyman skills are exhausted
> you are on your own maybe this
> is how it should be i wish i could
> have tempted you with bigger things
> what you did for me and owens i
> will not forget even to the close
> of the age
> mike

Hood called Beth Petty and asked her to have the ICU nurses concoct a reason to wheel Mike out of his room for a few minutes around eight A.M. When she asked why, he said it had to do with guns, cash, and human life. She agreed to do it. Then he called Gabe Reyes and told him to be at Imperial Mercy ICU at eight o'clock to retrieve Mike Finnegan's cell phone and check it for calls or messages left or sent.

Forty minutes later, Hood was stuck in traffic in Corona. He slowed to a crawl and cursed and answered a call. Reyes gave him both of the numbers he had found on Finnegan's phone, both outgoing and both made within the last nine hours. One went to a number that Hood recognized as belonging to Owens, placed not long after Hood had left the ICU at Imperial Mercy. The most recent was a text message to Hood.

40

Late the next night a small army surrounded Pace Arms under the cover of fog and darkness. The air was cool and still and it misted the windshield of Hood's Yukon, but this was not a time for wipers.

Behind the building, Hood watched from his Yukon as a big raised Dodge Ram pickup truck backed up through the bright shipping yard lights. It finally came to rest against the Pace loading dock, beside a battered white Ford F-250. Hood had figured two vehicles for two thousand pounds of iron, plus the weight of the crates. Two vehicles wouldn't betray the weight, and would either cut the risk in half or double it, depending on how you looked at it. The big motor home sat parked against a far wall, its awning now extended for shade over two white plastic chairs. It was as dirty as it had been before, all its windows opaque with dust except for the big black windshield. Hood wondered if someone lived there, a watchman perhaps. There was a clean black panel van parked across from it.

Ron Pace came trotting down the loading ramp. Bradley and Clayton got out of the truck and shook hands with the gunmaker. Bradley wore white shorts and red canvas sneakers and a Bush-Cheney

T-shirt, with his holster and sidearm bobbing unashamedly on his right hip. Clayton wore a light blue seersucker suit and what looked like white Hush Puppies. Pace was dressed for safari in cargo shorts, suede work boots, and a shirt plastered with pockets and epaulets.

Hood looked into his rearview at Janet Bly. He could barely make her out behind the wheel of her SUV with a San Diego office ATFE agent beside her.

"Charlie, Janet here—look at those dorks," she said over the radio. The headsets were made for hands-free contact between the teams, and the sound was excellent. "I can't believe this Jones kid. You *know* him?"

"Long story."

"I can't wait to see his cute little face when we cuff him and shove him in a car. His buddies, too."

"All units," Hood said. "We've got Bradley Jones and Clayton Farrar on scene. Pace is here, too."

Hood knew that Ozburn was parked around front of Pace Arms with an agent on loan from Glendale. There were four other vehicles involved: an undercover sedan parked down the street from Hood with two more agents inside, another two-agent sedan near the Pace Arms entrance, two more ATFE agents in an unmarked SUV watching the on-ramp to the 405 freeway, and one roving unit. All drivers were radio-wired, all agents armed with .40-caliber autoloaders, one shotgun and one tear gas launcher per vehicle. The ATFE Bell would track high and loose until the ground agents made their move.

Bradley and Clayton and Pace laid out tie ropes in the bed of the Ram, then walked up the ramp and into the warehouse. A few minutes later they emerged one-two-three with hand trucks, and the hand trucks each held four wooden gun crates. In turn each man went down the ramp, arms extended, leaning back against the weight. Pace and Clayton lifted the boxes into the truck bed, and Bradley hopped into the bed and arranged them.

The crates seemed lighter in Bradley's hands, and Hood wondered at the strength of his body and the audacity of his mind. He had to hand it to Bradley for sheer boldness. In this young descendent of Joaquin Murrieta, Hood saw outlaws dead and outlaws not yet born, and he also saw Suzanne, and he even glimpsed something dark and tempting that he had long ago banished from himself. In its place he had installed the straight and the narrow, the pledge of allegiance, the call of duty, to protect and serve. All of this he had done willingly and with his eyes open. He could have chosen differently. But a man could not be both things, both the law and outside the law, no matter how valiantly Bradley Jones was trying to be. And if Bradley succeeded at being both, then Hood and his choices were superfluous.

He watched the young men push the hand trucks back up the ramp and bring down another load. They finally stopped when the Dodge held five rows of ten crates. Then Bradley spread a large blue tarp over them and brought the ropes up and tied it all down with a flourish of exotic knots. Another fifty cases went into the worn Ford. The words ALL SAINTS CHARITY and an El Monte address appeared in fading paint on the door.

Hood yearned to make the pinch here and now, but without the money it wasn't a sale, and without a sale, arrests would net little. The money was everything—the money and who supplied it and where it came from.

"Charlie, this is Sean. Whazzup back there?"

"They're ready to leave. The black Ram and the All Saints Ford."

"Let Bly take the lead. They've never seen her."

"Fine."

"You cool with that?"

"I said fine."

"Something wrong, Charlie?"

"I don't like the look of the gun crates or the motor home. And there are three more men inside that building, not counting Ron and his girl."

"Talk to me, Hood."

"The crates are heavy to Pace and Clayton and lighter to Bradley. The motor home is dirty and the awning is out and there are chairs set up outside it, but the windshield is clean. Yesterday it was filthy. I'm talking the whole windshield, not just where the wiper blades would go—clean like somebody's going to drive it soon. Ron's uncle is still inside, and two of the workers. It's just not adding up."

"Okay, what, then?"

"I want to hang back and see, Sean. You guys take Bradley and Clayton."

"You want Unit Four to back you up?"

"I'll take Unit Four, you bet."

"Unit Four, Frankie, you there?"

Hood watched Bradley guide the Ram onto the street. The charity Ford followed, driven by Clayton, his left hand out the window with a cigarette, tapping against the door in a fast rhythm.

The vehicles rolled slowly down the street and made right turns toward the boulevard. When they had gotten out of sight, Hood heard Bly's engine start up and he watched in the rearview as her black Suburban pulled from the curb. Light from the streetlamp played along the flank of the big machine, then vanished. The Unit Four GMC lurked half a block down, unmoving.

"Frank," said Hood.

"Charlie, I'm here. We're not missing the fun, are we?"

"You can go if you want."

"I'll keep that in mind. I hope you have a good view of that thing, because I can only see the top of it."

"I'm locked. When something happens, you'll be the first to know."

Half an hour later, Hood saw two of the gunmakers walk from the warehouse into the yard lights and continue down the ramp. They moved self-consciously, as if they knew they were being watched. The short one wore a Dodgers cap, and the taller one a rugby shirt and a Windbreaker.

They moved across the shipping yard, past the Sun King motor home to the black Econoline. The short one keyed open the driver's door and hit the UNLOCK button and climbed inside. The engine came to life.

"Frank, we've got the two workers in the van. They're taking off."

Hood watched the van pass through the yard lights to the gate, and the gate slide open on its runners. It was heavy on its back wheels. It bounced dramatically as it crossed the gate runner. The driver signaled his turn onto the empty street.

"They're riding heavy," said Hood. "They're yours, Frank."

"What, you heading for Denny's?"

"Just a hunch."

"The Grand Slam breakfast is still the best."

In his rearview, Hood saw Frank's Unit Four SUV start up. Ahead of him he saw the black van signaling its next turn.

Hood sat and waited. An hour later, Ron Pace reappeared on the loading dock with Sharon. They held hands and each pulled a small rolling suitcase. Pace dropped her hand to answer his phone. No

Chester. The sun was rising. Ron looked around as if expecting someone or something. He nodded and put the phone back on his hip. Sharon wore khaki slacks and a light sweater and carried a blue-and-white purse that matched her athletic shoes.

Hood watched Ron check his watch, then say something to Sharon, and they walked down the ramp and across to the Sun King. Ron set his suitcase by the motor home. Then he stacked the plastic chairs and set them aside and removed the legs from the awning. He went inside and a moment later, the awning retracted onto its roller. Sharon followed him into the motor home, collapsing the handle of her rolling bag and heaving it up the steps to Pace. A moment later he came back and got his own suitcase and carried it in and shut the door behind him.

The Sun King started up with a rumble and a cough of smoke that rose into the beams of the yard lights. Then the motor home lurched toward the exit gate, slowed, and made the cumbersome turn onto the street. Its headlights came on, and Hood watched it turn out of sight toward the boulevard before starting his engine.

He followed well back. The Sun King was large and easy to see in the growing light and there was already generous traffic heading down the surface streets for the freeways.

Hood clicked his other headset when his cell phone rang.

"Ozburn, checking in."

"Two of the gunmakers rolled in the Econoline," said Hood. "Frank's on them. Pace and Sharon just pulled out in the Sun King. They're dressed up nice and they've got overnight luggage."

"Roger. We're about seventy miles from Tecate. These guys are oblivious. Dumb as sticks."

Hood followed the Sun King south on Bristol Street, headed for the freeways. The fog was thinning and the traffic was thickening and Hood had the unhappy thought that Ron and Sharon were getting away for a couple of days, maybe to celebrate the big sale. But Pace didn't get onto the San Diego Freeway and he didn't get onto the 73 and he didn't get onto the 55.

Hood eased up to let more cars between them. Pace made a left onto Red Hill, then a quick right on Lear, and Hood realized they were taking the back way into John Wayne Airport.

He remembered that this south end of the airport was for private and charter aircraft, and smaller cargo planes. He watched the Sun King turn onto Airway and roll up to a small commercial hangar. Hood pulled off the road and watched from three hundred yards away. The motor home approached the hangar, but it didn't stop. Instead it accelerated across the tarmac like a runaway horse. Hood traced its path but saw nothing. Then he took up his binoculars and saw a Red Cross CH-47 cargo helicopter idling far out on the vaporous edge of the runway, its cargo bay open and waiting like the maw of some great beast. The Sun King charged into view, aimed straight for it.

He gunned the Yukon back onto Red Hill. He ran the stop signs at Lear and Airway and skidded a left turn toward the hangar. At fifty miles an hour he veered off road across the infield straight toward the runway and the Sun King. It was less than half a mile out. He saw the motor home slow to a stop, then crawl a few yards forward onto the lift, a man directing with hand signals. Hood stood on the gas. He was only a quarter mile away by then, but as he watched, the cargo lift rose and the transport helo swallowed the motor home whole. The director scrambled up into the cockpit. Hood hit a hundred, throwing infield dirt that rose into the rearview. He felt the tires riding the shocks high up into the wheel wells as he flattened reflectors and runway lights and a row of red plastic pylons dividing the tarmac. Then he was suddenly upon the huge helicopter, and Hood had to veer right to miss it and as he did, the CH-47 lifted off into the sky with a thundering rebuke of dust and sound.

The Yukon shuddered into a skidless horseshoe turn and Hood stomped on the gas again. Through the windshield the helo was so close he could see the new welds on the underbelly and the bright new red cross on its clean white background. Then the steel monster was suddenly high above him and climbing hard west toward the Pacific. He pursued across the tarmac. But the distance between the helo and his earthbound vehicle lengthened by the second, great acres of sky multiplying between them, and the hope drained from Hood's young heart as his foot moved to the brakes.

He sat watching the aircraft diminish to the west as he called Ozburn to dispatch the ATFE chopper, then called the Orange County Sheriff's, the Coast Guard, the Miramar Navy Base, and Camp Pendleton to report the fugitive Red Cross impostor.

For the entire drive south to Tecate he waited to hear something back and he even listened to the news and he called Soriana in the San Diego ATFE office four times, but he heard not one word from anyone about an intercepted helicopter.

By the time he made Tecate, the Blowdown team was going through the last ten crates. They were just outside of town, and the Imperial County Sheriff's and CHP and even some Guardsmen were there. There were network uplink vans parked on the wide dirt shoulder, and stand-up news crews cordoned off by the ICSD deputies, but the cameramen were shooting video regardless. Two news helicopters circled noisily and low. The traffic was routed down to one lane, a highway patrolman directing, and the city-bound cars were backed up for half a mile, the passengers hanging from windows to better see the action.

The opened crates were strewn about the roadside, scores of them, all apparently filled with new jeans, all folded neatly, the manufacturer's labels still stapled to the back pockets, some with their sizes on clear plastic strips taped to the thighs. Hood saw that many of them were children's. There were pink ones and black ones and yellow ones and a hundred shades of blue.

Hood stood and watched Bly use a pry bar to open another gun crate. More denim. A man in a passing car asked if they had a pair of thirty-six/thirty-fours. Hood told him to move his fat ass along. Bly looked up at Hood with dampened fury in her eyes, then shoved away the case, toppling its contents into the shoulder dirt. She cursed and used the crook end of the pry bar to yank the next crate toward her.

Hood gazed down at the bounty of new pants. Bradley and Clayton and Ron had faked the weight of the boxes, Hood thought. They had known they were being watched. They had acted their parts. And he had watched them do it but not understood what he was seeing.

Hood found Ozburn in his SUV, tapping on his laptop. Ozburn was getting ready for an undercover assignment and trying to make his face scarce. He rolled down the darkened window. "The Econoline had a blowout in Temecula, so Frank made his move. It was loaded with bags of ready-mix concrete. Ninety pounders and lots of them. Charlie, these dolts had some help. They could never have pulled this off on their own. Pace just drove that motor home right into a transport helo?"

"It had a cargo lift."

"Then a thousand guns just crossed the border by air while we got a hundred crates of jeans. Who are these guys?"

"Bradley is Allison Murrieta's son."

"The teacher? The armed robber?"

Hood nodded. "Clayton is a forger."

"They say they're volunteers with All Saints. They say they've been doing this for two years and they've got priests and social workers and towns full of poor people who will tell us so."

"They probably do."

Bradley sat handcuffed in the back of one government SUV and Clayton in another, each watched by an ATFE agent. Bradley shook his head as Hood walked up and swung open the front door and looked in.

"Charlie. Tell these guys who I am."

A videographer had escaped the media area and came crunching along the shoulder toward Hood and Bradley, camera up, shooting as he walked. "Gentlemen—let's have a shot of the Good Samaritan here."

Hood wrenched away the recorder and popped the video card out before tossing the camera back at the stunned man. "Get back where you belong or I'll arrest you, too."

Hood was watching the man retreat when his phone rang. It was Beth Petty. "Charlie, something's happened to Mike."

"*What?*"

"He, um . . . he walked out."

41

The nurses trailed along wordlessly as Hood and the doctor hurried through the ICU. Beth opened Mike's room door and pulled back the privacy curtain. Hood looked at the chunks of plaster, some on the bed and some on the floor, some in the wastebasket, some pieces separate and some still attached by gauze. The girdle stood whole on the floor where Mike had apparently stepped out of it. Hood saw the dressing gauze ripped and wadded and strewn about the room. The collar and blood-smeared cranial rods were set in a corner. There were a few drops of blood on the floor. The catheter tube was tied around the bedrail uphill of the bag so it wouldn't leak. The room smelled bad.

"Who was with him?"

"No one. He tore out of his cast and walked out alone."

"Wearing what, a hospital gown?"

"Owens came yesterday. She brought him some new clothes, though I told her he was far from ready for discharge. She said she knew that, but maybe the clothes would inspire him. I thought that was fine. She had a Hawaiian shirt, a navy Windbreaker, a pair of chinos, a pair of Vans slip-ons, underwear and socks, and a Padres hat. She put them all in the closet there. She used hangers for the shirt and jacket and pants. Later in the day, Mike asked me to show them to him and he said he hoped they weren't too big, that Owens always bought a size too big. I thought it was endearing, a guy in a full-body cast worrying about the fit of clothes he wouldn't be able to even put on for weeks."

Hood looked at the closet, empty except for four metal hangers, the shoulder of one uplifted and caught on the shoulder of another as if a garment had been yanked off in a hurry.

"He walked out of the room to the nurses' station," said Beth. "It took them a moment to realize who he was. They ordered him back into his bed, but he politely refused. He thanked them graciously for all they had done, especially all the good books, and as soon as he left ICU, they called security. Security caught up with him in the lobby and he explained that his account was paid in full and that he was feeling very good. He did a little dance that left him with the toe of one shoe pointed up and his hands spread out. He smiled. Security said the smile looked weird. It was probably because his jaw is still wired shut. Outside he got into a black Mercedes convertible possibly driven by his daughter. I have the plate number."

"You're telling me he ripped out of that cast on his own?"

"Yes. Nobody could have helped. Nobody can get past the station without being seen."

"Why the blood?"

"From the cranial rods. The flesh heals over them, but when they're removed there's bleeding. You see, there isn't much blood here. About right. The hat would hide those wounds."

Hood squatted and picked up a piece of plaster cast. It was slightly concave and roughly the size of a paperback book and ragged on all four sides. White mesh dressing clung to the inside and extended past the torn edges of the plaster. It smelled of unwashed cotton and an unwashed human being. Hood turned it over and saw the sweat-stained gauze and the four crushed indentations where Mike had torn away this section of solid plaster as if it were a piece of bread.

"I wouldn't believe a single word of what I just said except I saw half of it," said Beth. "The other half I believe because I know these nurses."

"It was the strangest thing I ever saw in my life, Deputy," said one.

"When he came through that door all dressed and I realized who he was, this giant cold shudder went through me," said another.

"He really did manage to smile," said another.

Hood stood and tossed the piece of plaster onto the bed. "Nurses, doctors, security, cops, deputies, marshals, and two thousand Guardsmen, and he walks right out."

"We can't keep him," said the first nurse. "We can't hold anyone against his will. That's what you do."

Hood parked across from Owens Finnegan's El Centro home just after three o'clock. The desert lay darkening beneath the stacked thunderheads, and a heavy wind had picked up. Her garage door was open, but the black Mercedes convertible was gone.

He knocked at the front door and waited but she didn't answer, as he knew she wouldn't. The door was unlocked. Hood walked in and closed it behind him and stood for a moment in the empty living room, then walked through the empty kitchen and down the hall to the once beautiful bedroom into which he had been invited, and this was vacant now, too. The bathroom was cleaned out, but on the counter was a wedding absinthe goblet, and beneath the goblet were two sheets of paper. Hood moved the goblet and looked down at a drawing. It was done in charcoal, masterfully rendered, sharp true lines and deep smudges of shadow pierced by light. It depicted Bradley Jones inside the Pace Arms manufacturing bay, dressed in his smart Explorer uniform, examining the newly born firearms as he walked along the workstations, his face locked in the exact speculative, lost-in-thought expression that Hood had seen that night through the window.

Exactly as I saw it, thought Hood. Every detail, every mood.

In the bottom right corner, the name Mike was written in a neat, forward-slanting draftsman's hand.

I can hear what they think and see what they see. Sometimes very clearly. It's like hearing a radio or looking at a video.

Hood slid the drawing to the side to see the paper under it. It was a note written in the same neat hand:

> *Charlie:*
>
> *I took from you. Next time, and there will be a next time, I will give back. Something you desire, something you need.*
>
> *MF*

That evening when Hood finally got to Mike Finnegan's apartment across from LAX, he pulled up, saw the FOR RENT sign in the window, and kept on going all the way to Bakersfield.

He sat with his mother in his boyhood home and they talked

until late and he slept in the same bed he had slept in as a high schooler. He woke up early and left a note for his mother and father, then drove home as the darkness evaporated. As it often had been in his life, the passing of time and miles was a comfort to Hood, a man navigating an iron river, adrift with blunt instruments and crude charts.

42

You haven't lived until you've sat next to Sharon Rose Novak in a Sun King motor home carrying one thousand machine pistols and one iced, four-hundred-pound corpse, being swept away from ATFE agents in the belly of a relic Red Cross Chinook helicopter.

The helo briefly landed way out in the Southern California desert and I backed the motor home down the cargo lift and onto a decent dirt road that Bradley had said would lead us to a Joshua tree with a white ribbon tied to one cluster of spines. No sooner had I driven the motor home outside the rotor diameter than the CH-47 lifted off again. Bradley believed that a Sun King driven by a well-groomed young man and his lovely companion would draw less attention than a Red Cross helicopter thundering through U.S. airspace over Norton, Pendleton and Miramar military bases, etc., on its way south. Especially if no one was looking for the motor home to begin with. One of Herredia's helo crewmen had put on new Arizona plates while Sharon and I sat thousands of feet in the sky, experiencing the hypnotic, otherworldly, and slightly nauseating feeling of being inside a motor home inside a transport chopper doing a hundred fifty knots over God knows where.

Sharon spotted the white ribbon a few minutes later, and I backed the Sun King to it and with some difficulty we managed to push/drag/drop Uncle Chester's tarped and dry-iced remains into the waiting hole. Bradley's men had left one shovel that Sharon and I used to cover Chet. I offered to do the spadework myself, but Sharon insisted on doing half of it, and I watched her during her turns from the meager shade of the Joshua tree. She was grim and silent and determined about it. I could tell that every shovelful of sand she put between herself and Chet was something she needed to do to keep him away from her, literally and symbolically, too. I closed with the Lord's Prayer though I kind of hurried through it. I thought of my mother.

The Love 32s were more or less loose in the Sun King, since the wooden gun crates had been used for the new jeans for charity. The ruse was Bradley's idea, though how he learned that ATFE agents were surveilling Pace Arms I'll probably never know. Sharon had found late-summer bargain beach blankets on sale at a supermarket for three ninety-nine each, and in these forty blankets we wrapped and folded and duct-taped our thousand guns. We had guns under the motor home beds, guns in the overhead sleeper, guns in the cupboards and closets, guns in the bathroom and shower, guns in the bench seat storage chests, guns under the dining table and upon it and piled on the padded seating around it, guns in the walkway from cab to bath. The silencers and extra-capacity magazines, being smaller and more conveniently shaped, fit nicely inside the new but inexpensive pillowcases that Sharon found at Big Lots, and these we stashed anyplace that wasn't already filled with guns.

We crossed into Mexico at Nogales, were stopped briefly for the usual questions by the U.S. ICE agents, and were simply waved through by their Mexican counterparts. Shortly we were intercepted by a small flotilla of Suburbans that escorted us into the middle of

Baja California. The flotilla personnel were either Mexican Federal Judicial Police or *narcos* dressed in the uniforms of the MFJP. Bradley had told me that both were in the employ of Carlos Herredia.

After two hours of driving, we were suddenly run onto the very narrow shoulder of the road by several of the Suburbans. We were boarded, and at gunpoint we were herded back into the vehicle, where the policemen blindfolded us. I held hands with Sharon as they did this, wondering if we were about to be shot. I honestly couldn't figure what we had done to deserve that. But we were then politely helped out of the Sun King and into one of the Suburbans, and a short hour later we were unblindfolded within Herredia's compound, known as El Dorado.

I got out of the Suburban and helped Sharon down, then I looked out at the beautiful hacienda and the adobe outbuildings and the casitas and the glimmering pool beneath the *palapas,* and beyond that the airstrip with its sock luffing in the breeze, and all of this surrounded by green ranchland dabbed with cattle, and I wondered how a country with such a rich pastoral soul could have descended into such brutality. You don't have to be a student of history to realize that it has more than a little to do with people like me.

Late that first night when Sharon and I went back to our casita with the six hundred thousand dollars, I sat for a long while looking at the four rolling suitcases that contained it and I felt briefly discontent. I love the Love 32. I know it will become a part of history. I loved designing it. I loved procuring its elements and recruiting its builders. I loved *making* it. I loved shooting it. I even loved smuggling it down here. I know that lives will be taken with my creations—the lives of the bad and the good. The destruction is only just beginning. It will grow. But I am an American and I believe we choose our actions and I believe that the business of America is business. We are free. I've made my fortune and I've made myself and for this I will not apologize. We all need a break in these tough economic times.

Right now I'm sitting by the El Dorado swimming pool. It's late morning and warm but not hot. Herredia is doing laps. He doesn't really swim, he pounds. He's terrifically strong and he's been at this for forty minutes.

Bradley left last night to reunite with Erin in Valley Center. He was particularly moony and distracted yesterday, a newlywed pining for his bride. And he was richer.

Sharon is in our casita, soon to arrive. She slept late, as usual, and it will take her a while to get ready to face the world. Her ruined wedding and Chester weigh heavily on her.

When she gets here, I'm going to ask her to take a short walk with me, just down the road a bit. I'm going to tell her what it was like the first time I saw her sitting there at her new workstation at Pace Arms, a seventeen-year-old girl who said she was eighteen because she needed the money. I'm going to tell her how it felt when we hardly talked for a year after I told her I loved her. I'm going to tell her what it was like seeing her sitting there at her *old* workstation at defunct Pace Arms, a twenty-one-year-old woman who had just had her heart broken. I've got the ring, a carat and a half, near colorless, SI1, brilliant cut, set in platinum, in a box in the pocket of my cargo shorts. I'm no genius, but I'm not going to make the same mistake that idiot Daryl made.

43

Bradley came home to Valley Center late at night after a ten-hour patrol shift in L.A. County. He parked his Porsche out front of the ranch house and stood for a moment on the deck. Erin would be home soon from her own L.A. gig.

He looked out at the three-quarter moon and heard the breeze hissing across the hills. The rodeo arena was still up from the wedding, and the bunting still dangled in places from the buildings, and the tiny lights still twinkled in the big oak tree in the barnyard. It was Bradley's job to get the place back to normal, but he liked the wedding stuff, wanted it around for a while. What a great three days those had been.

Tonight he'd been assigned to a humorless old veteran named Spencer, and the first thing Spencer had said to him was *Boy Scouts don't touch my radio unless I tell them to.* Boy Scouts being his name for Explorer cadets. Over the hours, Spencer had lectured Bradley on the dangers of female deputies, use of intimidation during citizen interviews, and the use of force in detaining suspects. *I'm still quite fond of the old baton,* he rhymed with an asinine grin.

Spencer coached third base in the department slow-pitch league and took offense when he invited Bradley to try out and Bradley told him he had better things to do with his time. After shift, the big deputy wordlessly left Bradley with the car and gear check, then shuffled into the substation, headed for the shower. Bradley had stood in the parking area for a long moment, considered the substation and the deputies coming and going, the fleet of aging patrol cars, felt the cotton-poly blend of his uniform shirt on his skin and thought: *I'm lucky to have more than this*. He'd seen Caroline Vega in the lunchroom before shift again, always a good thing, and they had continued their ongoing dialogue about the bad guys having all the fun but being too dumb to enjoy it. Just kidding. Of course. He'd use her someday. He had the feeling their lives would cross, and he was almost never wrong when he felt this way. Draper had taught him that the power of one was one, but the power of two was many times greater, and the power of three many times greater than that. And so on.

He showered and changed, then went into the barn and cleared the Ping-Pong table and found the switch. The table rose and revealed the stairs. He walked down into the vault and hit the wall switch, and the floor/ceiling replaced itself over him, Ping-Pong table and all.

He opened one of the safes to look again at his ninety-thousand-dollar transport payment from Herredia. You bet it looked good, and Bradley felt that low-down grinning happiness of cash on hand. He uncovered Joaquin and poured himself a bourbon and sat down at the workbench. Beside the bottled head now rested the chain mail vest, Joaquin's own, a gift from Mike Finnegan, delivered by Owens, on Bradley's wedding day. Bradley knew the story of the vest, how Joaquin had commissioned it from an arrogant French armorer, and how Joaquin had not trusted the armorer, so before he would make payment on the allegedly bulletproof vest, Joaquin had made the Frenchman put it on himself, then drawn his revolver and shot him in the heart. The speechless Frenchman collected his payment, and Joaquin rode the rest of his brief life protected by this armorer's art. Bradley loved the story, but he loved even more the mystery of how Mike Finnegan had gotten the vest. Owens wouldn't say. He could see that she knew, but she protected her knowledge with armor of her own—her pewter eyes and her damaged beauty. Bradley believed he would see those most strange people again. He all but knew it. He'd have a crack at the little guy, maybe trade him something precious for the story of how he had gotten the vest, maybe just hold him up by his throat until he was ready to croak out the truth.

Bradley had been working on a poem down here for weeks now, but there wasn't much on the page.

He looked up from his yellow notepad and down the bench to see what was left of his ancestor. He sipped bourbon and read what he had written:

If you were a map and I had drawn you
In my blood, who would know where
Your border became my border or where
Your . . .

What? Where your what became my what? And who was he talking to, anyway, Erin or Joaquin or himself or the whole world or maybe no one at all? Why were emotions a flood but words to convey them a dry little creek? He wished he could think and write like Erin, wished he could write something as beautiful for her as the songs she wrote for him.

He looked up at Joaquin. "Thanks for your protection on a dangerous job, El Famoso. There were some moments you would have appreciated. The look on Hood's face. Priceless."

He turned back and reread his fragment. Bradley wondered if his problem as a poet was his age. At nineteen he felt huge tidal emotions about many things, not just Erin: the tawny hills around him, the great machinery of the stars at night, the way a river changed every moment, the goofy nod of the poppies in the spring, his mother. He was once brought to tears by a baby horned lizard, a miniature thorn-crowned dinosaur enjoying the warmth of his palm. And not just nature, either: He experienced strong feelings when he saw good paintings and read good poems or saw something physically beautiful like a black Stratocaster with a maple fretboard or a staunch Craftsman cottage in Pasadena or a red Sears Craftsman toolbox or an M5. The trouble with being nineteen wasn't the feelings, it was the words. He hadn't lived long enough to get familiar with them. They weren't his friends yet. They were still formal, standoffish. He sipped the bourbon and wondered if there was a way to hurry things along without getting old. He'd seen old and it looked like hell. What was old if not finally having the words but no passions left to describe?

He looked up again. "They'll catch me someday like they caught you. I don't think they'll get my head. I'll have lawyers and appeals. You only made it to twenty-three. I'm hoping for ninety-three, Gramps. So, any advice, you just pipe up anytime you want."

Bradley reread his three lines and one word. Maybe the whole map deal was the problem. Nobody drew maps now. You got them on a cell phone screen. Technology is the end of poetry, he thought. What bullshit.

He thought for a long while with the pencil in his hand and the notepad before him. He opened a workbench drawer and pulled out the shred of cover torn from his LASD Explorer class syllabus on which Caroline Vega had written her phone number. He considered it, then he put the paper back.

Then he covered Joaquin and hit the switch, and the ceiling rose, and he climbed the stairs from the vault toward the few acres of earth that belonged to him.

44

Hood served the dinner outside on his patio after the sun went down. Beth sat in the high-backed rattan chair, her skin moist from the heat and her eyes reflecting the candlelight. Her dog sat beside her, viewing Hood with doubt. Minnie was a Labrador/golden mix, black and gentle.

"That was a bad scene today in the ER with the sergeant."

Hood nodded and forked the asparagus onto Beth's plate. He had noticed over the years that cops and medical professionals often made unusual dinner conversation. Maybe that boded well. As a cop's daughter, Beth liked to talk crime.

"Did you know him?" she asked.

"No. But I heard he assigned the guards for the hospital that night those two men came for Jimmy. Well, *didn't* assign them is more like it."

"This is cop talk, right—not public knowledge?"

"It's going to get public."

"This guy made sure the real guards weren't on duty, so the fake ones could kill Jimmy? That means he was doing a favor for the Gulf Cartel."

"Yes."

"Has there ever been an American cop on the take from a Mexican drug cartel?"

"Not that I know."

"That's going to be a huge scandal."

"It will fit right in with everything else that's happening."

"Five cops murdered in Tamaulipas just today, Charlie. Heads in coolers left in a park. Notes on top."

Today's body count, thought Hood. Heads. Coolers.

The Imperial County Sheriff's sergeant had shot himself this morning with his service gun. Hood heard that ICSD's internal affairs team had been investigating him. Hood had learned that law enforcement rumors were almost always true. It was said that the sergeant had made the overtime deputy assignments for Imperial Mercy that shift, when Jimmy Holdstock's room had gone unprotected. Investigation ongoing. Beth had seen the sergeant as they wheeled him into ER just moments before he expired.

"I treated a man once who lived through a wound like that," she said. "But he was never the same. Not even close to the same. Imagine."

Hood poured the wine. "We have a lighthearted pinot noir for your enjoyment."

"No absinthe?"

"I'll make you one later."

"No. Please no."

After dinner they sat with their backs to the house and the candles flickering and looked out at the new Buenavista. There was still the border town with its odd clash of old and new—its zocalo and Jack in the Box, the Rite Aid and St. Cecilia's—and its wall right through the middle dividing Mexico from the United States, but a low wall, where people gathered and talked and exchanged news and sometimes gifts—grapefruit from El Centro, beer from Tecate. Now there was the National Guard headquarters to the west and the sprawl of tents and the mobile command center and field hospital and the new roads scratched through the desert for the convoys and the tanks and the half-tracks and the little machine-gun jeeps that bounced along the roads with an almost recreational joy. And to the north was the new airstrip that was dozed out of the desert by the big Cats in just a few days' time, wide and long and flat. And at this hour the town and the camp were alive with lights, headlights and searchlights and house lights and yard lights and landing strip lights and the lights of helos and the lights of jeeps skidding along the new dirt paths, coming and going like ants, thought Hood, hard to say what they were really doing out there.

"Where do you think he is—Mike."

"Somewhere in California," said Hood. "They'll ditch the stolen plates on the convertible and get others. Or maybe just sell off the car and get a fresh one."

Of course Hood had gotten LASD to issue an all-units watch for Mike and Owens Finnegan, and a BOLO for Mercedes plates, but he knew these would come up empty.

Unless the little devil gets another flat and a lady runs him down and breaks practically every bone in his body, Hood thought. *Yeah, if that happens again, we've got him.*

"Why California?"

"He seems to like it here."

Owens had called him earlier in the day.

What are you to him?

An associate. I do what he tells me to do.

How much money does he pay you?

It doesn't matter.

Where is he?

You don't know anything.

Since he had seen the drawing that Mike had done, not one waking hour had passed without Hood thinking of him. He propped the drawing up beside the coffeemaker in his kitchen each morning and rested it against the lamp on his bed stand at night. If Mike was a man, then he was certainly the most cunning and intuitive and physically prodigious human being that Hood had ever met. If Mike was a journeyman devil, then almost everything Hood knew and believed was null and void, and he was little more than a blind man trying to read a map. More than once, Hood's nerves had buzzed with the idea of good and evil walking the earth all around us since the beginning of time, doing their jobs. As the son of only faintly Christian parents, this concept exhilarated him. God and Satan? Angels and devils? Really? Hood felt that he should do something. Talk to a wise man. Read a truthful book. Skydive.

The one thing he had come up with was that whoever and whatever Mike was, he had wanted Hood for something. Something more than having his brain picked and fouling a bust and letting a thousand guns get through, that is.

A partnership? Mike had joked about that. But maybe it wasn't a joke.

Hood and Beth took their wine and sat side by side on a wooden bench that had been there when Hood moved in. He heard the snapping of brush off to the south and Minnie growled. Beth shushed the dog and together the three of them listened to the slow sporadic advance of something bulky and large through the brush in the darkness before them. It was followed by a swishing sound, as if made by a tail.

A moment later in the moonlight, Hood saw them moving down in the arroyo, a man in the lead and a woman behind him. The man carried a handful of plastic shopping bags with one hand, their necks stretched and thinned by the weight of their cargo. In his free arm he snuggled an infant up close to his chest. A few steps behind her husband, the woman walked backward with a handled plastic water jug cut down to its shoulders, broadcasting sand to cover their tracks, bending to refill the jug and toeing the dirt to cover the marks made by the bottle, then hurriedly backing to catch up to her family and continuing to spread the sand in their wake.

Hood and Beth and the dog watched them traverse the dry gully south to north and when the couple was directly below Hood's home, they stopped. Briefly they looked up at the candlelight. The woman slowly straightened and placed her hand against the small of her back. Then they continued. Hood listened to the sowing of the sand in the vast desert, and the warrior engines thrumming at the border and the thump of the helos and the thump of his heart, and to him these were one sound, the sound of human beings scratching along the pathways of their own free will.

Not long after the family had vanished into the northern darkness, a sudden wind came up and blew out the candles. It was a southern wind, monsoonal and sweet. Beth put her hand in his and they watched the lights.

ACKNOWLEDGMENTS

A thousand thanks to John Torres and the Los Angeles field division of the ATF.

A thousand more to those who have written about this before me and often better, among them:

W. Dirk Raat and George R. Janecek, *Mexico's Sierra Tarahumara*
Richard Grant, *God's Middle Finger: Into the Lawless Heart of the Sierra Madre*
Luis Alberto Urrea, *The Devil's Highway*
William Langewiesche, *Cutting for Sign*
Charles Bowden, *Down by the River*
Frank Latta, *Joaquin Murrieta and His Horse Gangs*

The terrific reporting team behind the *Los Angeles Times* series "Mexico Under Siege"—Josh Meyer, Tony Perry, Ken Ellington, Tracy Wilkinson, Scott Craft, Richard Marosi, Sam Quinones, Christopher Reynolds, Andrew Becker, Patrick J. McDonnell, Evelyn Larrubia, Denise Dresser, Frank James, Paul Pringle, Raoul Ranoa, Richard Serrano, Don Bartletti, Deborah Bonello, Lorena Iñiguez Elebee, Cecilia Sanchez, Miguel Bustillo, and Marla Dickerson.

Norman Mailer, who gave the devils their due in *The Castle in the Forest*.

Another thousand to Dave Bridgman and Sherry Merryman for answering my endless questions.

Photo by Rebecca Lawson

T. Jefferson Parker is the author of sixteen previous novels, including the Charlie Hood thrillers *L.A. Outlaws* and *The Renegades*, and the Edgar Award winners *Silent Joe* and *California Girl*. In 2009 Parker won his third Edgar, his first in the short story category. He lives with his family in Southern California.

Read on for an excerpt from
T. Jefferson Parker's novel

THE BORDER LORDS

Available in hardcover from Dutton.

Prologue

"Charlie, Gravas here. Reporting live from the Wild West."

"Good to hear from you, friend."

"My machine gun peddlers got a whiff of something. Me waiting there with my cash and meth like a dude with flowers and chocolates. They stood me up. How's my Seliah?"

"She sounded great like she always sounds."

"She doesn't tell you how hard this is for her."

"Neither do you."

"I feel strong, and clear in the eye. I want someone bigger than those machine gun punks anyway. I want someone with heft. I'm making some contacts out here. I'll get within spitting distance of Carlos Herredia if it kills me. Maybe I shouldn't put it that way."

"You're where you need to be. And when it's done you're out and rolling home."

"If Seliah needs something, she's going to call you."

"As always."

"I keep coming back to her, don't I?"

"You're supposed to come back to her."

"Gotta go now. Bad actors, incoming."

"*Vaya con Dios.*"

"Yeah. I always go with God when I waddle around in hell."

I

Just before sunset the first bat fluttered from the cave and came toward him, wobbling and breeze-blown, like a black snowflake ahead of a storm. It rose and navigated between the trunks of the banana trees, then climbed into the magenta sky. Another flew, and then another.

The priest stood facing them, his feet together and his back straight and his hands folded before him. The reeking cave mouth yawned and the bats spilled out. He watched them come at him, then veer abruptly.

From the first few, he heard faint chirps but soon there were too many and all he could hear was their muffled flight. Then the air was heavy with them, a great dark blanket of membranous wings and small faces and tiny feet. One of them brushed his cheek and another glanced off his hair and another screeched at him in fear. Some of them dropped guano that tapped against his Windbreaker but the priest stood motionless and let the flood of hair and skin rush past. *My music*, he thought. He considered the centuries and still the flood rushed.

When it was over he stepped inside. The smell was stronger. He lit a candle with a plastic lighter. Before he spoke he cleared his throat as he would before the homily.

"Yoo-hoo, little creatures of the night. Father Joe, here to see you."

His candle revealed the holdouts still hanging from the walls by their feet, wrapped like football fans, not in blankets but in their wings. Some of them squinted into the insult of the light; some shifted irritably like insomniacs, all snouts and elbows.

"Not quite feeling up to it tonight? The halt and the lame and the old and the sick. Feeling just a little off, are we?"

The priest strolled deeper into the darkness and the stench. A bat ran across his path, upright, wings raised overhead like a tiny man with an umbrella, looking back and up at him.

The priest stopped and held up the candle. A bat peered down from the wall and the man saw the glitter in its purblind eyes, the quivering, inquisitive expression on its face. The man cocked his head. The bat bared its teeth and screeched. The mouth was large for the face and the incisors were large for the mouth, and needlelike. The leafed nostrils were flared and its ears were enormous. The little animal began breathing faster, and it extended its wings and resettled them back around its body.

"Cold, my little friend?" The man saw the froth of saliva gathered at the chin, and when the bat sneezed the foam flew off.

The priest extended his free hand toward the animal. Again the bat bared its teeth and screeched but the priest didn't move, and a moment later the animal crawled down the wall a few feet closer to him. It was a cumbersome movement, with the thumb hooks grappling for purchase on the rock, and the minute toes spread for traction, and the sheer wings clumsy and useless. "Come closer, little *fliedermaus*. I'm not going to climb up there to get you!" The bat clambered closer and the priest stood on his toes and offered his finger and the bat climbed on.

The priest relaxed and lowered both arms and studied the animal in the light. Its eyes were bright in spite of their weakness. The man blew a puff of breath onto the animal, rippling its thin fur and revealing the almost-human shape of the rib cage. The bat cringed and screeched and bared its teeth again, and in this the priest saw humankind's embodiment of evil distilled into a single horrific face.

"Thank you," said the priest.

He dropped the candle to the cave floor, where the guano devoured the flame and left him in darkness supreme. He gently cupped the bat between thumb and forefinger, then put it in his Windbreaker pocket, zipping it halfway for security and oxygen. Then he carefully picked his way back out of the cave.

2

Charlie Hood sat in the ATF field station in Buenavista and watched the live-feed monitors. Hood was thirty-two, tall and loose, with an earnest face and calm eyes. He had been watching the screens for eight hours, doing his job for the ATF Blowdown task force. It was not pure excitement. He was on loan from the L.A. Sheriff's Department but by now he had spent fifteen months in this often infernal, often violent, often beautiful desert. He liked this place and he feared it. He palmed another handful of popcorn from its paper container without taking his eyes from the screen.

Buenavista was a California border town with a population of thirty thousand and an elevation of twelve feet. The monitors displayed live feeds from a "safe house" in one of Buenavista's nicer neighborhoods, three miles away. The Blowdown team called the house *the Den*. ATF had bought it on the cheap as a foreclosure, then wired it for sound and video. Hood's friend Sean Ozburn, an ATF agent operating deep undercover as a meth and gun dealer, had arranged to have it rented as a home for four young gunmen of the North Baja Cartel.

The assassins ranged in age from seventeen to twenty-two, and

ATF figured them good for thirty murders between them. Some in Mexico. Some stateside. Almost all business related, the business being recreational drugs. Sales of those drugs brought Mexico some fifty billion dollars a year—by far the single largest contributor to its economy.

Hood watched one of the pistoleros, Angel, standing in his kitchen while a pot of *carnitas* warmed on the stovetop. Hood knew it was *carnitas* because two nights ago he'd watched Angel prepare the pork for boiling. Now the pot was on the stove again and a tortilla was warming on one of the electric burners and there was a skillet of eggs going.

It was unusual for any of the young killers to be up this early but Angel was here in the kitchen and Johnnie and Ray were in the living room. Angel was the only one who ever cooked anything. He was a skinny little guy with a wisp of a mustache and an overbite. He stood still a moment and watched his own monitor, a little kitchen-size DVD player on which he watched nothing but American gangster movies. This morning it was *Scarface* again, in Spanish, Angel at times mumbling along with Pacino, mimicking his expressions. A machine pistol with a noise suppressor and an extended magazine lay on the counter by the DVD player.

These guns had first come to Blowdown's attention in Mexican crime scene photographs late last year. Nobody at Blowdown had ever actually seen one except possibly Hood, two summers ago, though he wasn't totally sure at the time *what* he was seeing. He knew for certain that brand-new semiautomatic handguns were being packed for shipment at a Southern California gun factory. This he had confirmed with his own eyes. Then these illegally made guns had slipped away from Blowdown, right under their collective noses—one thousand gleaming new handguns, gone. Hood suspected they were headed south to Mexico.

Now he wondered again if one of those apparently humble handguns could somehow be converted into a curve-clipped, silenced beauty like the one lying on Angel's kitchen counter. Hood would bet on it. If he was right, he knew for certain who had built the one thousand silenced machine pistols—a talented young gunmaker named Ron Pace. And if that was true, Hood also had very strong ideas about who had delivered them into the hands of Carlos Herredia's North Baja Cartel gunmen—a fellow LASD deputy named Bradley Jones. Hood was hot to get his hands on one of those guns. All of ATF was hot to get one. And Hood wanted to send Pace and Jones to the slammer where they belonged.

He ate and watched and opened another soda. Graveyard was hard on sleep and diet. He wondered if the assassins were up early because they had a job to do. Usually they slept until noon. His mind wandered back to Sean Ozburn again, and Hood wondered why Ozburn had gone silent. Almost fifteen months undercover, and once a day Sean would call one of the Blowdown team—usually Hood—even when he had nothing substantial to report. He called it *touching his life raft*. Fifteen months UC was a long run in anyone's book. Too long, according to many with experience. The calls had been Sean's established pattern and it had worked for him, and now he had broken it. Six days and no call.

So maybe Sean had been made, Hood thought. He wasn't sold on the whole idea of the bugged safe house, because of that possibility. One whiff of suspicion or one person who recognized Ozburn, and boom—he was dead, or worse. The Den was supposed to be an ATF jewel but they all knew its potential cost to their man undercover.

And the bugged safe house wasn't only a risk; it was frustrating, too. Hood understood that they didn't have enough evidence to arrest any of the four assassins. Most of their murders were committed across the border where ATF was essentially helpless. And the murders they were suspected of committing in the States were quiet and neat: no willing witnesses, no weapons left behind, no written warnings or mutilations or beheadings, just plenty of shots to the head and heart and that was that. Always .32 Automatic Colt Pistol rounds. Nobody heard. Nobody saw. Nobody knew anything. *All this manpower and technology, and not an arrest made*, thought Hood.

But the truth, and he knew it, was that ATF didn't want to roll up the Den and go to court just yet, because although the four young *sicarios* were only small-time killers, they were gold mines of information. Since this "safe house" had been activated four weeks ago, their conversations and phone calls had provided ATF hundreds of hours of talk and video, giving the Blowdown team a street-level view of the North Baja Cartel's blood-soaked battle for Southern California.

Behind Hood, three large, rolling whiteboards were backed against the far wall. Two of them were jammed with writing and one was beginning to fill—names, crimes, suspects, straw buyers, timelines, organizational charts, routes, possible tunnel locations, turf, family relations, feuds, debts—many grouped in circles and linked by solid lines or broken lines or some by strings of small question marks. Certainties were written in black. Suspicions were rendered in red, speculations in blue. It looked like graffiti. And all of it was gathered by ATF eavesdropping on the four baby-faced hit men. Blowdown wasn't after the likes of these boys. They were after the lieutenants and up, to the top of the food chain—the men who bought the guns and called the shots.

So, Hood thought, *the whiteboards are full of intel but the killers are free to roam about the cabin.*

He looked at monitor two and watched Johnnie and Ray playing Halo on the living room fifty-four-inch TV. Hood lifted an audio headset to his ear and winced: As usual the boys had the volume up loud. The hidden mikes were so good they could pick up both ends of a phone call, and this video combat game blaring through the home theater system sounded like Armageddon itself.

Johnnie and Ray were the two Americans, poor kids recruited from the rough Buenavista streets, kids with voracious desires and stunted notions of self-control. Hood knew their plan for happiness: Get a gun, get a job using it, get some decent clothes, get a better gun, get a car, get a big-screen television, get a truck, get a girl. Then, if you were still alive, get a house, somewhere to put your girl and your stuff. They always bought the house last. It was the same for all the young pistoleros along the border. The cartels didn't care if they were American or Mexican. *Global economy*, thought Hood. Johnnie was the seventeen-year-old and he had earned a new Dodge Ram 1500 two weeks ago as a bonus for a hit in Tijuana. *Chunks flying out the back of his head*, as he'd bragged to Ray one evening, over and over. Johnnie had washed the gleaming black truck four-teen consecutive nights, up late, inside the garage of the Agate Street safe house so the neighbors wouldn't see him. He talked to the truck as he polished its coat.

Only Oscar was unaccounted for now. He claimed to have a girlfriend in Buenavista, but no matter how much the other assassins teased him, Oscar had so far refused to bring her to his lair.

Hood heard two sharp knocks on the front door of the office, then the buzz from the ID reader. He glanced up at the security cam-era, then looked at the first light of the October morning just now touching the drawn blinds.

Dyman Morris came into the room with a tall cup of coffee and his war bag, and he set both on the desk, then sat two chairs down from Hood. He looked up at the screens. There were six of them.

Dyman smelled of soap and his dark skull was cleanly shaved. "Look at this. The baby killers are stirring."

"Maybe they've got something coming up."

"Still nothing from Sean?"

Hood shook his head and watched Angel flip his tortilla. "I left him another message. That's three in six days."

In the silence that followed, Hood thought of their comrade Jimmy Holdstock, kidnapped last year on U.S. soil and taken to Mexico. Hood knew that Dyman was thinking of Jimmy, too. Jimmy hadn't even been working UC like Sean. Jimmy wasn't setting up bugged safe houses for the North Baja Cartel like Sean. Jimmy was just a former divinity student, part of the Blowdown team checking ATF Firearm Transaction forms, keeping an eye on the licensed dealers, trying to stem the flow of the iron river—the guns heading south.

"What I don't get," said Hood, "is who tells these boys they can do this."

"Do what, Charlie."

"Kill people for money."

"The cartel recruiters tell them that."

"But what about the consequences?"

"You've seen the consequences, man—a new truck for a bonus, and free prostitutes, like last week. Remember when Ray got that ten grand for a job well done?"

"What I mean is, who tells them it's okay?"

"Who do they have to tell them different? Their parents either don't care or don't know what to do. These boys don't go to school. Probably haven't been inside a church their whole life. So who are they gonna listen to except each other, and the actors in the movies they watch, and the cartel dudes with all the cash?"

Hood thought about that. "Still seems like something's missing. Some kinda horse sense or something."

"You had advantages you didn't know you had. I had them, too. Bakersfield is like Beverly Hills compared to these border towns."

Hood, a Bakersfield boy, nodded. Morris of the South Bronx sipped his coffee.

By six thirty A.M. agents Janet Bly and Robert Velasquez had arrived. This was the transitional hour, when the graveyard watcher went off duty and the three-agent day team took over for another shift of interviewing firearms dealers, recruiting informants, shadowing suspected buyers and sellers, posing as straw men and illicit buyers, answering the phones and watching the young killers on live feed— all in a day's work for Blowdown.

"Well, look who's up bright and early today," said Bly. "Is that Angel with his *carnitas*?"

Hood nodded, looking at Angel's machine pistol again.

"Sean call in?" asked Janet.

Hood shook his head, saw the hardness in her face.

"Then maybe he called Mars or Soriana."

"He'd call us first if he was in trouble," said Hood, confident that his good friend Sean Ozburn would call Blowdown well before he'd call the ATF field station in San Diego. Ozburn was a soldier, loyal and focused.

But six days and no calls. So the ghost of Jimmy Holdstock— retired now with long-term disability from injuries suffered in the line of duty; in his case, torture—hovered there in the war room once again.

Then, as if that ghost had cast its long, dark shadow over the room, one of the monitors went white, then black, and the audio died.

Hood's attention had been drawn to it just a split second before it went blank.

"The hell," said Bly.

"Don't worry," said Velasquez, their techie. "It'll come back. I'm not sure what's . . ."

Thirty seconds later the other monitors suddenly all turned bright white, then black. And the audio feeds died with them.

Blowdown was on its feet now. Velasquez looked down at the main control panel, head cocked. The others stared at the dead screens. They had lost camera transmissions before but never all of them at once.

"This is what my son does when the satellite goes out during SpongeBob," said Morris. "He just stares at the TV like he can make it come back on."

"It'll come back," said Velasquez.

Hood dialed Buenavista police chief Gabe Reyes and asked for an unmarked unit to drive by the Agate Street safe house, and Reyes said the shift was changing right now but consider it done. *Ten long minutes*, thought Hood, ringing off.

"Cops are changing shifts," he said. "Ten minutes."

"We can't lose all six feeds," said Velasquez. "Even in a power outage, even if someone cuts the line. Those cameras have two hours of battery backup. You have to shut them down from here, or in the control panel on the side of the safe house. But I built that control panel, and I disguised it as a breaker box, and it's got a lock, and the only people who have keys are us. So what the—"

"I saw something on screen six," said Hood. "Just before it went out."

"I was watching Angel make his breakfast," said Bly.

"I was seeing if Johnnie's gravity hammer can kill brutes," said Morris.

"I saw something, too," said Velasquez. "Then it was gone."

"The Den is only three miles away," said Hood.

"Wait," said Bly, the senior agent.

Velasquez pushed various control buttons but nothing happened. "It's gotta be at our end. I'm going outside to check the cable."

"I'm with you," said Hood.

They emerged through the back door into the young light of morning, Hood first, his hand on the sidearm holstered on his hip. They walked quickly, looking up at the black coaxial cable fastened along the fascia board above the eaves. It entered the field station through a hole low on the eastern wall, and Hood could see the cable and the hole and the nest of gray steel wool crammed in to keep the rats and snakes out. Velasquez knelt down and tugged at the cable, then shrugged and stood.

They checked the circuit breaker panel and the relay boxes and the splitters and the transformers for the coax and the telephone landlines, and all of these Velasquez said were fine.

"The problem is at the Den," he said. "Unless some fine citizen plowed a car through a phone company switch box between here and there."

"What did you see on monitor six?"

"I don't know, Charlie. It happened too fast."

"It'll be on the tape."

"Monitor six is the side yard," said Velasquez.

"Where the control box is," said Hood.

They exchanged looks and went back inside.

The screens were still dead. Hood could tell by the forced calm of her voice that Bly was talking to Soriana out in San Diego. Bly was impulsive and Soriana was deliberate, and this tried her patience sorely.

She rang off and lowered her cell phone. "Soriana says give it five."

"I'd go right now," said Hood.

"I would, too," said Bly. She was a stout woman whose sweet

round face the years with ATF had started to harden. "He's afraid the *narcos* will make us if we drive by looking like tourists. But we'll give it five, all right? Because he's the boss. Yes. Five *seconds*, that is. You guys ready?"

Dyman Morris, once a point guard for NYU, made it to the door first, swinging an armored vest off the coatrack like a kid going out to play in the cold.

A few minutes later Hood was guiding his Durango down Agate Street, looking at the little crowd of people standing outside the Den in the dawn's early light.